DREAMING OF THE BONES

Five years after the death of talented Lydia
Brooke, Dr Victoria McClellan is writing the
biography of the tortured poet. Finding it
increasingly difficult to accept that Lydia
committed suicide, Victoria calls on her ex-
husband, Superintendent Duncan Kincaid of
Scotland Yard, to ask for his help in proving
Lydia was murdered. At first Duncan suspects
that Victoria simply does not want to believe
that Lydia would take her own life, but then
he receives some terrible news that will change
his life for ever ...

DREAMING OF THE BONES

DREAMING OF THE BONES

by
Deborah Crombie

Magna Large Print Books
Long Preston, North Yorkshire,
England.

British Library Cataloguing in Publication Data.

Crombie, Deborah
   Dreaming of the bones.

A catalogue record for this book is
available from the British Library

ISBN 0-7505-1315-2

First published in Great Britain by Macmillan, an imprint of
Macmillan Publishers Ltd., 1998

Published in Large Print 1998 by arrangement with Macmillan
Publishers Ltd.

Magna Large Print is an imprint of
Library Magna Books Ltd.
Printed and bound in Great Britain by
T.J. International Ltd., Cornwall, PL28 8RW.

This book is for Terry,
with gratitude for her voice,
among many other things.

Acknowledgements

Thanks are due: Dr Mary Archer, for her gracious hospitality in inviting me to visit her home, The Old Vicarage, Grantchester, and for allowing me to see her Rupert Brooke archives (complete with ghost stories); to Jane Williams, personal assistant to Dr Archer, and to Mary Ann Marks, for their kindness in showing me around The Old Vicarage; to Dr Karen Ross, M.D., of the Dallas County Medical Examiner's Office, for her help with poisons and toxicology; to Betty Petkovsek, R.Ph, for her pharmaceutical advice; to Diane Sullivan, RN, BSN, for her help with other medical matters; to Paul Styles, retired Chief Inspector, Cambridgeshire Constabulary, for help with police procedures; to Terry Mayeux, Barbara Shapiro and Carol Chase for their reading of the manuscript; to the members of the EOTNWG for the same; and to my husband, Rick Wilson, for his patient and continuing technical support.

Part One

There are four ways to write a woman's life: the woman herself may tell it, in what she chooses to call an autobiography; she may tell it in what she chooses to call fiction; a biographer, woman or man, may write the woman's life in what is called a biography; or the woman may write her own life, in advance of living it, unconsciously, and without recognizing or naming the process.

Carolyn Heilbrun, from
Writing a Woman's Life

Chapter One

Where Beauty and Beauty meet
All naked, fair to fair,
The earth is crying-sweet,
And scattering bright the air,
Eddying, dizzying, closing round,
With soft and drunken laughter;
Veiling all that may befall
After—after
Rupert Brooke, from
Beauty and Beauty

The post slid through the letter box, cascading onto the tile floor of the entry hall with a sound like the wind rustling through bamboo. Lydia Brooke heard the sound from the breakfast room, where she sat with her hands wrapped round her teacup. With her morning tea long gone cold, she lingered, unable to choose between the small actions which would decide the direction of her day.

Through the French doors at the far end of the room, she could see chaffinches pecking at the ground beneath the yellow blaze of forsythia, and in her mind she tried to put the picture into words. It was habit, almost as automatic as breathing, this search for pattern, metre, cadence, but today it eluded her. Closing her eyes, she tilted her face up towards the weak

11

March sun slanting through the windows set high in the vaulted room.

She and Morgan had used his small inheritance to add this combination kitchen/dining area to the Victorian terraced house. It jutted into the back garden, all glass and clean lines and pale wood, a monument to failed hopes. The plans they'd had to modernize the rest of the house had somehow never materialized. The plumbing still leaked, the rose-patterned wallpaper peeled delicately from the walls in the entry hall, the cracks in the plasterwork spread like ageing veins, the radiator hissed and rumbled like some subterranean beast. Lydia had grown used to the defects, had come to find an almost perverse sort of comfort in them. It meant she was coping, getting on with things, and that was, after all, what was expected of one, even when the day stretching ahead seemed an eternity.

She pushed away her cold cup and rose, tightening the belt of her dressing gown round her slight body as she padded barefoot towards the front of the house. The tile felt gritty beneath her feet and she curled her toes as she knelt to gather the post. One envelope outweighed the rest, and the serviceable brown paper bore her solicitor's return address. She dropped the other letters in the basket on the hall table and ran her thumb carefully under the envelope's seal as she walked towards the back of the house.

Freed from its wrapping, the thick sheaf of papers unfolded in her hands and the words leapt out at her. *In the matter of the marriage of Lydia Lovelace Brooke Ashby and Morgan Gabriel Ashby* ... She reached the bottom of the stairs and stopped as her brain picked out words from amongst the legalese. *Final decree* ... *petition of divorce granted this day* ... The pages slipped from her numb fingers, and it seemed to her that they drifted downwards, cradled on the air like feathers.

She had known it would come, had even thought herself prepared. Now she saw her hollow bravado with a sudden sickening clarity—her shell of acceptance had been fragile as the skin of algae on a pond.

After a long moment she began to climb the stairs slowly, her calves and thighs aching with the burden of each step. When she reached the first floor, she held on to the wall like an unsteady drunk as she made her way to the bathroom.

Shivering, shallow-breathed, she closed and locked the door. The motions required a deliberate concentration; her hands still felt oddly disconnected from her body. The bath taps next, she adjusted the temperature with the same care. Tepid—she'd read somewhere that the water should be tepid—and salts, yes, of course, she added the bath salts, now the water would be warm and saline, satin as blood.

Satisfied, she stood, and the deep blue silk of the dressing gown puddled at her feet. She stepped in and sank into the water, Aphrodite returning from whence she came, razor in hand.

13

Victoria McClellan lifted her hands from the keyboard, took a breath and shook herself. What in hell had just happened to her? She was a biographer, for Christ's sake, not a novelist, and she'd never experienced anything like this, certainly never written anything like this. She had felt the water slide against her skin, had known the seductive terror of the razor.

She shivered. It was all absolute rubbish, of course. The whole passage would have to go. It was full of supposition, conjecture, and the loss of objectivity which was fatal to a good biography. Swiftly, she blocked the text, then hesitated with her finger poised over the delete key. And yet ... maybe the more rational light of morning would reveal something salvageable. Rubbing her stinging eyes, she tried to focus on the clock above her desk. Almost midnight. The central heating in her draughty Cambridgeshire cottage had shut off almost an hour ago and she suddenly realized she was achingly cold. She flexed her stiff fingers and looked about her, seeking reassurance in familiarity.

The small room overflowed with the flotsam of Lydia Brooke's life, and Vic, tidy by nature, sometimes felt powerless before the onslaught of paper—letters, journals, photographs, manuscript pages and her own index cards—all of which defied organization. But biography was an unavoidably messy job, and Brooke had seemed a biographer's dream, tailor-made to advance Vic's position in the English Faculty. A poet whose brilliance was surpassed only by the havoc of a personal life strewn with difficult relationships and frequent suicide attempts, Brooke survived the late-Sixties episode in the bath for more than twenty years. Then, having completed her finest work, she died quietly from an overdose of heart medication.

The fact that Brooke had died just five years before allowed Vic access to Lydia's friends and colleagues as well as her papers. And while Vic had expected to be fascinated, she hadn't been prepared for Lydia to come alive. She'd seen Lydia's house—left to Morgan Ashby, the former husband, who'd leased it to a doctor with four small children. Littered with Legos and hobby horses, it had seemed to Vic to retain some indefinable imprint of Lydia's personality—yet even that odd phenomenon provided no explanation for what had begun to seem perilously close to possession.

Lydia Lovelace Brooke Ashby ... Vic repeated the names in her mind, then added her own with an ironic smile. Victoria Potts Kincaid McClellan. Not as lyrical as Lydia's, but if you left off the Potts it had a bit of elegance. She hadn't thought much about her own divorce in the last few years—but perhaps her recent marital difficulties had caused her to identify so strongly with Lydia's pain. Recent marital difficulties, bloody hell, she thought with a sudden flash of anger. Couldn't she be honest even with herself? She'd been left, abandoned, just as Lydia had been left by Morgan Ashby, but at least Lydia had known where Morgan was—and Lydia hadn't a child to consider,

15

she added as she heard the creak of Kit's bedroom door.

'Mum?' he called softly from the top of the stairs. Since Ian's disappearance, Kit had begun checking on her, as if afraid she might vanish, too. And he'd been having nightmares. She'd heard him whimper in his sleep, but when she questioned him about it he'd merely shaken his head in stoic pride.

'Be up in a tic. Go back to sleep, love.' The old house groaned, responding to his footsteps, then seemed to settle itself to sleep again. With a sigh Vic turned back to the computer and pulled her hair from her face. If she didn't stop she wouldn't be able to get up for her early tutorial, but she couldn't seem to let go of that last image of Lydia. Something was nagging at her, something that didn't quite fit, and then with a feeling of quiet surprise she realized what it was, and what she must do about it.

Now. Tonight. Before she lost her nerve.

Pulling a London telephone book from the shelf above her desk, she looked up the number and wrote it down, deliberately, conscious of breathing in and out through her nose, conscious of her heart beating. She picked up the phone and dialled.

Gemma James put down the pen and wiggled her fingers, then raised her hand to her mouth to cover a yawn. She'd never thought to get her report finished, and now the tension flowed from her muscles. It had been a hard day, at the end of a difficult case, yet she felt a surprising surge

16

of contentment. She sat curled at one end of Duncan Kincaid's sofa while he occupied the other. He'd shed his jacket, unbuttoned his collar and pulled down the knot on his tie, and he wrote with his legs stretched out, feet rather precariously balanced on the coffee table between the empty containers from the Chinese take-away.

Sid took up all the intervening sofa space, stretched on his back, eyes half-slitted, an advert for feline contentment. Gemma reached out to scratch the cat's exposed stomach, and at her movement Kincaid looked up and smiled. 'Finished, love?' he asked, and when she nodded he added, 'You'd think I'd learn not to nitpick. You always beat me.'

She grinned. 'It's calculated. Can't let you get the upper hand too often.' Yawning again, she glanced at her watch. 'Oh, lord, is that the time? I must go.' She swung her feet to the floor and slid them into her shoes.

Kincaid put his papers on the coffee table, gently deposited Sid on the floor, and slid over next to Gemma. 'Don't be daft. Hazel's not expecting you, and you'll not get any good mum awards for waking Toby just to carry him home in the middle of the night.' With his right hand he began kneading Gemma's back, just below the shoulderblades. 'You've got knots again.'

'Ouch. Mmmm. That's not fair.' Gemma gave a half-hearted protest as she turned slightly away from him, allowing him better access to the tender spot.

'Of course it is.' He scooted a bit closer and

17

moved his hand to the back of her neck. 'You can go first thing in the morning, give Toby his breakfast. And in the meantime—' The telephone rang and Kincaid froze, fingers resting lightly on Gemma's shoulder. 'Bloody hell.'

Gemma groaned. 'Oh, no. Not another one, not tonight. Surely someone else can take it.' But she reached for her handbag and made sure her beeper was switched on.

'Might as well know the worst, I suppose.' With a sigh Kincaid pushed himself up from the sofa and went to the kitchen. Gemma heard him say, 'Kincaid,' brusquely after he lifted the cordless phone from its cradle, then with puzzled intonation, 'Yes? Hello?'

Wrong number, thought Gemma, sinking back into the cushions. But Kincaid came into the sitting room, phone still held to his ear, his brow creased in a frown.

'Yes,' he said, then, 'no, that's quite all right. I was just surprised. It has been a long time,' he added, a touch of irony in his voice. He walked to the balcony door and pulled aside the curtain, looking into the night as he listened. Gemma could see the tension in the line of his back. 'Yes, I'm well, thanks. But I don't see how I can possibly help you. If it's a police matter, you should call your local—' He listened once more, the pause longer this time. Gemma sat forward, a tingle of apprehension running through her body.

'All right,' he said finally, giving in to some entreaty. 'Right. Hang on.' Coming back to the coffee table, he picked up his notepad and scribbled something Gemma couldn't decipher upside down. 'Right. On Sunday, then. Goodbye.' He pressed the disconnect button and stood looking at Gemma, phone in hand as if he didn't know what to do with it.

Gemma could contain herself no longer. 'Who was it?'

Kincaid raised his eyebrow and gave her a lop-sided smile. 'My ex-wife.'

Chapter Two

I only know that you may lie
Day-long and watch the Cambridge sky,
And, flower-lulled in sleepy grass,
Hear the cool lapse of hours pass,
Until the centuries blend and blur
In Grantchester, in Grantchester ...

Rupert Brooke, from
The Old Vicarage

Following Vic's directions, Kincaid left the M11 at Junction 12, just before Cambridge and took the Grantchester road from the roundabout. The Cambridgeshire sky spread wide before him in a clear light, for the April day had dawned exceptionally mild. He'd tried to persuade Gemma to change her mind and come with him, but she'd been adamant, saying she'd not give up her Sunday with Toby. They'd had their Sunday breakfast and tidied up, and she'd kissed

19

him when he'd left her Islington flat, but he felt some discomfort between them. Well, he'd see what Vic wanted—it seemed the least he could do for courtesy's sake, if nothing else—then that would be that.

He slowed as the first straggling houses appeared, then soon the road became a neatly tended village street. At the T-junction he turned right, into the High Street as Vic had told him, watching carefully for the house on his left. 'You can't miss it,' she'd said, a smile in her voice. 'You'll see.' And almost immediately he did, for it was a higgledy-piggledy tile-roofed house washed in bright Suffolk pink, surrounded by the new growth of roses.

Kincaid pulled into the gravelled area in front of the detached garage, stopped the car and got out, and it was only then that he realized he had absolutely no idea what he was going to say to her. He'd spent the journey remembering Vic as she'd been when he'd first known her. Her reserve had intrigued him—he'd taken it for shyness—and he'd found the seriousness with which she approached her studies endearing, even amusing. 'Bloody arrogant, condescending idiot,' he said aloud, his mouth twisting with disgust. He'd assumed knowledge of her that he hadn't earned, and had paid the consequences when she left him without a word. And now, more than ever, they were two strangers, made more so by the awkward history between them.

How had she changed, he wondered? Would he even recognize her?

Then the side door of the house opened

and set his fears to rest, for her face was as familiar as his own. She came out to him, her plimsoled feet crunching on the gravel, and took his hand as easily as if they had parted on good terms only yesterday. 'Duncan. Thanks so much for coming.' She tilted her head to one side, considering him as she kept hold of his hand. 'I'd swear you haven't changed a bit.'

Finding his tongue with an effort, Kincaid said, 'Nor have you, Vic. You look wonderful.' She looked tired, he thought, and too thin, perhaps even a little unwell. A network of tiny lines had begun forming round her eyes, and the creases between her nose and the outer corners of her mouth stood out sharply. But her hair, though it fell now to her shoulders rather than the small of her back, was still flax-fair, and if she wore more sombre colours than the pastels he remembered, they gave her a dignity which suited her.

'It has been a long time,' she said, smiling, and he realized he'd been staring.

'Sorry. It's just ... I don't quite know what to say and I think I'm making an utter fool of myself. Is there an etiquette manual for this sort of situation?' In the moment's silence following his words, bird song swelled from tree and thicket, a raucous chorus, and a coal tit whizzed past his head, scolding.

Vic laughed. 'We could always invent one. Why don't I start by inviting you in. Your car should be all right with the top down, at least for a bit.'

Kincaid remembered suddenly that his acquisition of the Midget had caused one of their final conflicts, but Vic had glanced at the car without any sign of recognition. He'd opened his mouth to offer to park it elsewhere when he saw a black-and-white flash and felt the hair stir on the top of his head as the coal tit flew another kamikaze run.

'Come on,' Vic said, turning towards the house. 'You'd better dive for cover while you can.' Over her shoulder she added, 'It's such a lovely day I've set lunch out in the garden. I hope you don't mind.'

He followed her into the house and through a sitting room, where he had a fleeting impression of pale gold walls and faded chintzes, and of a grouping of silver-framed portraits on a side table, then she led him out through French doors on to a stone-flagged terrace. The garden sloped away from the house, and beyond the low wall at its end he could see a meadow, then a curving line of trees which looked as though it marked the course of a river.

'Grantchester gets its name from Granta, the old name for the Cam,' Vic said, pointing toward the river.

'The garden's lovely.' Dandelions and wild onions sprang up in the shaggy lawn, but there were recent signs of prep work in the beds, and against the low wall stood the garden's crowning glory—an immense old crab-apple tree, covered with bright pink blossom.

Vic gave him the sideways glance he remembered as she gestured towards one of the chairs she'd pulled up to an ironwork table. 'Here, sit down. That's a bit generous of you. My friend Nathan says the garden's a disgrace, but I'm not a real gardener. I just like to come out and dig in the dirt on nice days—it's my alternative to tranquillizers.'

'I seem to remember that you couldn't keep alive a potted plant. Or cook,' he added as he examined the lunch she'd laid out on the table—cheese, cold salads, olives, wholemeal bread, and a bottle of white wine.

Vic shrugged. 'People change. And I still can't cook,' she said with a flash of a smile, 'Even if I had the time. But I can shop, and I've learned to make the most of that.' She filled their glasses, then raised hers in salute. 'Here's to progress. And old friends.'

Friends? Kincaid thought. They had been lovers, adversaries, flatmates—but never that. Perhaps it was not too late. He lifted his glass and drank. When he had filled his plate and tasted the potato salad, he ventured, 'You haven't told me anything about yourself, about your life. The photos ...' He nodded towards the sitting-room doors. The man had been thin and bearded, the boy fair and sturdy. He stole a glance at Vic's left hand, saw the faint pale mark circling her fourth finger.

She looked away as she drank some of her wine, then concentrated on a piece of bread as she buttered it. 'I'm Victoria McClellan now. Doctor McClellan. I'm a fellow at All Saints', and I'm a Faculty teaching officer, specializing in twentieth-century poets. That gives me more

23

time to pursue my own work.'

'Faculty?' Kincaid said a bit vaguely. 'Poets?'

'The University English Faculty. You do remember my Ph.D. thesis on the effect of the Great War on English Poetry?' Vic said with the first hint of sharpness he'd heard. 'The one I was struggling with when we were married?'

Kincaid made an effort to redeem himself. 'That's what you wanted, then. I'm glad for you.' Seeing that Vic still looked annoyed, he blundered on. 'But I'd have thought two jobs would have meant more work, not less. You're saying you work for the University and for your college, right? Wouldn't you be better off to do one or the other?'

Vic gave him a pitying look. 'That's not the way it works. Being a college fellow is a bit like indentured servitude. They pay your salary and they call the shots—they can stick you with a back-breaking load of supervisions and you have no recourse. But if you're hired by a University Faculty, well, that gives you some clout—at a certain point you can tell your college to go stuff itself. Politely, of course,' she added with a gleam of returning good humour.

'And that's what you've done?' Kincaid asked. 'Politely, of course.'

Vic took a sip of her wine and settled back in her chair, looking suddenly tired. 'It's not quite that simple. But yes, I suppose you could say that.'

When she didn't pursue the topic further, Kincaid ventured, 'And your husband? Is he

24

a lecturer as well?' He kept his voice lightly even, a friendly enquiry one might make to an acquaintance.

'Ian's at Trinity. Political science. But he's away on sabbatical just now, writing a book about the division of the Georgian states.' Vic put down her bread and met Kincaid's eyes. 'I don't know why I'm beating about the bush. The thing is, he's writing this book about Russia from the south of France, and he just happened to take one of his graduate students with him. Female. In the note he left me he said he thought he must be having his mid-life crisis.' She gave him a tight smile. 'He asked me to be patient.'

At least, Kincaid thought, he left you a note. He said, 'I'm sorry. It must be difficult for you.'

Vic drank again and picked at a bit of salad. 'It's Kit, really. Most days he's furious with Ian, occasionally he's angry with me, as if it were my fault Ian left. Maybe it is—I don't know.'

'Is that why you called me? You need help finding Ian?'

She gave a startled laugh. 'That would be bloody cheek! Is that what you thought?'

When he didn't answer, she said, 'I'm sorry, Duncan. I never meant to give you that impression. What I wanted to talk to you about has nothing to do with Ian at all.'

'It's that damned McClellan woman again,' said Darcy Eliot as he unfolded the damask napkin and laid it carefully across his lap. 'As if it weren't enough to have to put up with her at College and in the Faculty, she came round to my rooms yesterday to pester me with her tedious questions. Gave me the most frightful headache, I can tell you.' He paused while pouring himself a glass of wine, then sipped and rolled it around his mouth with satisfaction. His mother's Mersault was excellent, almost as good, in fact, as the store All Saints' set aside for its Senior Fellows. 'If I'd had my way, she'd never have been given a Faculty position, but Iris absolutely dotes on her. What can you do with all these bloody—' With his tongue loosened by several glasses of his mother's equally excellent sherry before their ritual Sunday lunch, he'd been about to say, 'With all these bloody women about the place,' but a look at his mother's raised eyebrow brought him to a full stop. 'Never mind,' he amended hastily, burying his nose in his wine again.

'Darcy, darling,' said Dame Margery Lester as she ladled out the soup Grace had left in a tureen on the table, 'I've met Victoria McClellan on several occasions and I thought her quite enchanting.' Margery Lester's voice was as silvery as the hair she swept back in a classic chignon, and although she was well into her seventies, it sometimes seemed to her son that she had condensed rather than aged. The qualities that made Margery uniquely herself—her keen intelligence, her self-assurance, her dedication to her craft—all these seemed to have become more solid as her body inevitably diminished.

Today she looked even more elemental than usual. The pearls she wore against her pale grey cashmere twin-set seemed to give a shimmery lustre to her skin, and it occurred to Darcy to wonder if one would find quicksilver in her veins rather than blood.

'Just what is it exactly that you find objectionable about her?' Margery asked as she served Darcy his soup, adding, 'Grace made cream of artichoke in your honour.'

Darcy took his time tasting the soup, then eased a surreptitious finger into his collar. Perhaps he had been imbibing a bit more than he should lately. His vanity had for many years provided a useful counterbalance to his appetites, but it might be that the flesh was gaining ground. 'You know how I feel about the earnest politically correct,' he said as he lifted his spoon to his lips again. 'They give me the pip. And there's nothing I abhor more than the feminist biographer. They take some trivial piece of work and inflate it with Freudian psycho-babble and grandiose feminist theory until you wouldn't recognize it if it bit you.'

Margery's left eyebrow arched itself more pronouncedly, and Darcy knew that this time he had indeed gone too far. 'Surely you're not suggesting that Lydia's work was trivial?' she asked. 'And you make Victoria McClellan sound like some sort of unwashed blue-stocking. She struck me as being quite sensible and well-grounded, certainly not the sort I'd expect to lose track of the work in the process of theorizing about it.'

Darcy snorted. 'Oh, no. Doctor McClellan is anything but unwashed. Quite the opposite—she could model for an American shampoo advert on the telly, she's so well washed and groomed. She's an example of the perfect nineties' woman—brilliant academic career, model mother and wife—only she wasn't good enough at the wife part to keep her husband from shagging a succession of graduate students.' The image made him smile. Ian McClellan's only failure had been his lack of discretion.

'Darcy!' Margery pushed away her empty soup bowl. 'That was unkind as well as common.'

'Oh, Mother, really. What it is is common knowledge. Everyone in the English Faculty knows all the libidinous details. They just take care to whisper them when the fair Victoria is out of earshot. And I don't see what is so unkind about the bald truth.'

Margery pressed her lips together, darting a still disapproving glance at him as she uncovered the main course and began serving their plates. Point to me, thought Darcy with satisfaction. Margery was no prude, as the increasingly graphic sexuality of her later novels revealed, and Darcy thought she merely enjoyed playing the shocked matron.

He breathed a sigh of contentment as Margery set his plate before him. Cold poached salmon with dill sauce; hot buttered new potatoes; fresh young asparagus, crisply cooked before chilling— he would rue the day if he ever lost his ability to charm Grace. 'And don't tell me'—he put a hand to his breast as if overcome—'a lemon tart for afters?'

Still unrelenting, his mother attacked her fish in silence. Darcy concentrated on his food, content to wait her out. He took small bites to prolong the pleasure, and gazed out into the garden as he chewed. He'd brought Lydia here once, years ago, to his family's Jacobean house on the outskirts of the village of Madingley. His father had been alive then, tweedy and self-effacing, his mother sleek in her success. It had been a spring day much like this one, and Margery and Lydia had walked together arm-in-arm in the garden, admiring the daffodils and laughing. He'd felt an oaf, a lout, excluded by their delicacy and by their aura of feminine conspiracy. That night he'd lain awake wondering what secrets they'd confided.

He remembered Lydia's profile in the car on the way from Cambridge, pinched with nervousness at the thought of meeting Margery Lester, remembered her too-prim dress and neatly combed hair—for once the rebellious young poet had become every inch the small-town schoolteacher's daughter. It had made him laugh, but he supposed in the end the joke had been—

'Darcy. You haven't heard a word I've said.'

He smiled at his mother. He'd known her pique would pale against the appalling social prospect of a silent meal. 'Sorry, Mummy. I was meandering among the daffodils.'

'I said, "What did Doctor McClellan want to know about Lydia today?" ' Margery's voice still held a trace of exasperation.

'Oh, the usual tiresome things. "Did Lydia show any signs of depression in the weeks before her death? Had she communicated any particular concerns, become involved in any new relationships? Etc, etc, etc ..." Of course I said I had no idea, nor would I have told her if I had, as none of that nonsense has any relevance to Lydia's work.' Darcy wiped his mouth with his napkin and finished the wine in his glass. 'Perhaps this time I made myself quite clear.' A shadow fell across the garden as a cloud obscured the sun. 'Look, the rain's coming on, after all. Why do the bloody weather boffins always have to be right?'

'You know, darling,' Margery said reflectively, 'I've always thought your position on biography a bit extreme for someone who loves a good gossip as much as any old woman I know. Whatever will you do if a publisher offers you an obscene amount of money to write mine?'

Nathan Winter wiped his perspiring brow and looked up at the clouds scudding across the sky from the northwest. He'd hoped to finish setting out the plants he'd bought that morning at Audley End's garden centre before the weather turned, but he'd got rather a late start. It had been well worth the drive down to Suffolk, though, for the nursery at the Jacobean manor house stocked some old-fashioned medicinal herbs he'd not found elsewhere. And once there, of course, he'd been unable to resist the temptation to wander in the grounds and gardens, had even had a cup of tea and a sandwich in the restaurant.

Jean had loved Audley End, and they'd spent many a Sunday tramping up and down the staircases, admiring Lord Braybrooke's specimen collection, even giggling as they fantasized about making love on the round divan in what Jean always called 'the posh library'. He'd brought her one last time, in a wheelchair on a fine summer day, but the house had been impossible for her and they'd had to content themselves with a slow perambulation round the herb gardens.

Now that he thought about it, he supposed Audley End must have first given him the idea of planting a traditional medicinal garden, but they'd lived in Cambridge then, in a house with a postage-stamp-sized back garden, and Jean had wanted every inch given over to flowers.

Nathan sat back on his heels and surveyed his handiwork. This was his first major project for the cottage garden, and he'd spent the winter months studying Victorian herbalists and garden design, adapting them, then meticulously drawing his own plans. Mullein, tansy, St John's wort, juniper, mugwort, myrtle, lovage—he stopped at that one, grinning. People always thought it sounded so romantic, and he supposed it did make an excellent cordial for a cold winter's night, but it was also a powerful diuretic.

A gust of wind lifted his empty plastic

containers and rattled them along the ground. Nathan took another look at the dark shelf of cloud building to the north and set hurriedly to planting the last of his seedlings. He tamped the soil carefully round them, collected his tools and his rubbish, then pushed himself up from the damp ground. His knees protested, as they often did these days when the weather changed, and he remembered ruefully the days when he'd been able to spend hours kneeling without feeling the least bit stiff. Maybe he'd better have a good long soak in a lavender and arnica bath before dinner—*dinner!* How could he possibly have forgotten that he'd invited Adam Lamb for drinks and an early supper? And the man was a devout vegetarian, which meant Nathan would have to come up with something suitable or risk offending him. He made a mental inventory of the contents of the fridge. Eggs, a few mushrooms—he could whip up omelettes ... a green salad ... there was half a loaf of granary bread from the bakery in Cambridge ... a meagre supper, but it would have to do. And for pudding he could use the trifle he'd bought at Tesco's, though he'd hoped to save it for more festive circumstances.

What on earth had possessed him to ask Adam round? Guilt, more than likely, he admitted with a grimace of disgust as he started for the house. He'd always felt a bit sorry for Adam, for reasons he found hard to articulate. Maybe it was that Adam seemed to try too hard at life, but his dedication to any number of good causes never produced much visible result. And the ironic thing, Nathan thought as he held on to the doorjamb and struggled out of his wellies, was that yesterday when Adam had rung him, he'd had the distinct impression that Adam was feeling sorry for him.

Adam Lamb nursed his old Mini out the Grantchester Road, past the Rugby Grounds, coasting downhill when he could to save petrol. Although he didn't believe in owning automobiles, his parish work rendered some form of transport a necessity, so he salved his conscience by driving a car that only passed its MOT each year by the grace of God. His rationing of petrol had an economic as well as a moral impetus—a few carefully consolidated trips a week were all his meagre budget would allow.

A gust of wind rattled the car and Adam looked back at the overtaking bank of clouds. He should have walked tonight—it was less than two miles, after all, along the river path, and they'd done it without thinking when they were students—but the threat of rain had combined with a nagging cold to dampen his enthusiasm. He felt old, suddenly, and tired.

Adam slowed almost to a walking pace as he came into the outskirts of Grantchester. As near as it was to Cambridge, he hadn't been here in years. He'd certainly never expected Nathan to come back, at least not alone. When he'd heard through mutual friends that Nathan had inherited his parents' house and meant to live in it, he'd felt a little frisson of unease.

The Grantchester Road became Broadway, and as Adam inched round the last curve before the High Street junction, he blinked in surprise. Surely this couldn't be it? The cottage of his memories had been shabby, with crumbling stucco, brambles in the garden and sparrows nesting in the thatch. But a look at the houses either side assured him that he had indeed found the house, for they fitted his dim recollection of the neighbours. He stopped the car against the left-hand kerb and got out just as the first fine drops of rain began to fall, forgetting the parking brake in his bemusement. He stood, gaping at the cottage's new bricked drive and circular walkway, putting-green lawn and immaculate perennial borders, pristine whitewash and thatch—someone had worked a miracle.

The front door opened and Nathan came out, grinning. 'Leaves you speechless, doesn't it?' he said as he met Adam and shook his hand. 'Good to see you.' He gestured back at the house. 'I know it's embarrassingly quaint, but I have to admit I'm enjoying it. Come in.'

Nathan looked surprisingly well. His hair had gone completely white since Jean's death, but it suited him, setting off his dark eyes and naturally rosy complexion. Adam remembered how they'd teased Nathan when he started to grey in his twenties, but Nathan had met Jean by then and hadn't cared a fig for what any of them thought, not even Lydia.

Shying away from the thought of her, Adam made an effort to collect himself. 'But how did you ... I mean, it must have ... surely your parents didn't ...' A big drop of rain splattered on his spectacles, momentarily blinding him.

Nathan put a hand on his shoulder and propelled him towards the door. 'I'll fix you a drink and tell you all about it, if you like.' Once inside, he shut the door against the rain and took Adam's anorak, hanging it neatly from a pegged rack. 'Whisky suit you?'

'Um, yes. Fine.' Adam followed him into a sitting room as transformed as the exterior. Gone was the dark antimacassared furniture, the Victorian and Edwardian nick-nacks that Nathan's mother had loved. Now the accommodating-looking upholstered pieces sported a cheery red and blue William Morris print, a thick rug covered the floorboards, and the wood fire burning in the hearth winked from the leaded glass windows. All in all it was a delightful room, seductive in its comfort, and Adam thought of his Cambridge rectory with a shiver of regret. He went to the fire and warmed his hands as he watched Nathan pour their drinks from a bottle of The Macallan on the sideboard. 'A great improvement over the old electric fire,' he said as Nathan handed him his glass. 'Cheers.'

Nathan laughed as he settled himself into one of the chairs near the fire. 'I'm surprised you remember that. It was a bit feeble, wasn't it?' Stretching his legs out towards the warmth, he sipped his drink. 'My parents had the central heating put in, of course, but it was only allowed on for an hour in the morning and an hour in the evening. I suppose it did make bathing and getting in and out of bed bearable, but the rest of the time we huddled in here in front of that silly electric bar. The chimney always worked, you know, but once they'd made up their minds that the electric fire was less costly to run, there was no going back.' He shook his head. 'I don't think they ever recovered from the war, or stopped fearing that the hard times would come again. When I cleared out the larder I found tins of food as old as I am—my mother hoarded them.'

'I never felt deprived here,' said Adam, leaving the fire and taking a seat in the other armchair. 'Your mother was kind to us, and fed us all without complaint, ungrateful louts that we were.'

Nathan smiled. 'I'm sure she never thought that.'

'I was sorry to hear about your parents.' Adam reached automatically to adjust his dog collar, then remembered he'd worn mufti instead. He always worried that his clerical garb made people uncomfortable in a social situation—even those, like Nathan, who had known him long before he became a priest. 'It must have been difficult for you, so soon after Jean.'

Staring into the fire, Nathan turned his glass round in his fingers and said slowly, 'I don't know. I was numb at that point, and it seemed as though I just went through the motions. I'm still not sure I've really taken it in.' He looked up at Adam and smiled. 'But I was going to tell you about the cottage. That's what made

36

up my mind for me, about what I should do. I didn't think I could bear staying in the Cambridge house without Jean, and I'd been toying with the idea of taking rooms in College, but I couldn't quite make up my mind to do that either. Then when Mother and Dad passed away within weeks of each other and left me this ...' Nathan stood and went to the window, shutting the curtains against the rain now driving against them. 'It was paid for, of course, but in quite horrendous condition,' he continued. 'I felt utterly at sea. It took a friend to pound the reality of the situation through my thick skull. Jean and I had lived in the Cambridge house for almost twenty-five years; the mortgage was near to being paid off, and the property values had shot up.'

'So you sold the house and used the proceeds here?' Adam gestured more largely than he intended, the whisky having rather gone to his head. He'd fasted before communion this morning, then discovered the bit of vegetable flan he'd been saving for his lunch had gone mouldy.

Nathan retrieved his drink and stood cradling it, his back to the fire. 'It's actually been quite liberating, funnily enough. Jean and I put off so many things over the years, thinking we'd wait until we could afford them, but somehow it never came to pass.' Grinning, he added, 'Having two daughters probably had something to do with it. Those two delicate little things could go through pound notes like starving dogs in a sausage factory.'

37

Adam remembered Nathan's daughters not as the young women, dark-clothed and red-faced with weeping, that he'd seen briefly at Jean's funeral, but as two little girls in white frilly dresses and pink hair ribbons. 'Are they both married, then?'

'Jennifer, yes, but Alison's too busy making her mark on the world to have time for men right now, other than as a temporary convenience,' Nathan said, affection evident in his tone.

'She was always Lydia's favourite, wasn't she, your Alison?'

'From the time they were babies, Lydia said Jenny was born with a conventional soul, but that Alison was destined for greater things. Lydia was Alison's god-mother, as a matter of fact. I'm surprised you remembered.' Falling silent, Nathan swirled the dregs of his drink, then finished it in one swallow. 'Come through to the back, and I'll fix us something to eat.'

Pushing himself up from the depths of his chair, Adam followed Nathan into the entry again. Now he saw that in the room to the left, which had been a seldom-used formal parlour in Nathan's parents' day, a baby grand piano stood alone on the bare polished floorboards. Adam remembered the old upright that had stood in Nathan and Jean's sitting room, the recipient of much abuse by Nathan as he pounded out the old music hall tunes he'd learned from his mother. Before he could comment, Nathan beckoned him through the centre door.

The back of the house, which had originally

been divided into kitchen, scullery and dining room, had been opened into one large room. A kitchen-dining area filled one end, a comfortable den the other, and windows had been added along the back of the house from which Adam imagined one could see the river on better days.

Nathan gestured towards the table, already laid with placemats and stoneware, as he went through to the kitchen. 'Sit down while I organize things a bit. I found some carrot and lentil soup in the freezer, then I thought we'd have omelettes and a green salad, if that suits.' He checked a pot on the stove, gave it a stir, then went to the fridge and pulled out a bottle of Australian Chardonnay. 'It's all down to Ikea,' he said with a glance at Adam as he started a corkscrew into the wine. 'From the furniture to the cutlery. I'd never have managed otherwise.'

'It's brilliant, Nathan, really brilliant.' Adam took the glass Nathan poured him. 'Here's to your new life,' he said, raising his glass, then choked as the wine bit unexpectedly at his throat. 'Sorry.' He spluttered and coughed, then took another, more careful, sip. 'You and Jean always entertained well, and you seem to have gone right on with things. I admire that.'

Nathan stopped with a soup ladle poised over a bowl. 'The first couple of years I ate frozen dinners in front of the telly. When I ate. And I dare say I didn't do too well at the housekeeping and laundry, either.' He shrugged and went back to distributing the soup between two green bowls. 'But after a while I began to think about how exasperated Jean would have been with me. She followed me around the house, nagging. *Nathan, you should be ashamed of yourself, letting things go this way.* So I cleaned up my act, and I've found I actually enjoy it.'

'Do you think you'll marry again?' asked Adam as Nathan brought soup and a basket of hot bread to the table, then slid into the chair opposite. 'It's been my experience that those who've been most happily married often do.'

For the first time, Nathan took his time answering. He buttered a piece of bread, tasted his wine, then said, 'I don't know. A year ago I'd have said absolutely not—even six months ago, the same. But now ...' Shaking his head, he grinned at Adam. 'Never mind. I'm a foolish middle-aged man who shouldn't allow himself to indulge his fantasies. I suppose I'm suffering from a case of delayed adolescence, and that it will pass.'

'And if it doesn't?' asked Adam, his curiosity aroused.

Nathan picked up his spoon, dipped it into his soup. 'Then the Lord help me.'

Chapter Three

So light we were, so right we were, so fair faith
*   shone,*
And the way was laid so certainly, that, when
*   I'd gone,*
What dumb thing looked up at you? Was it
*   something heard,*
Or a sudden cry, that meekly and without a
*   word*
You broke the faith, and strangely, weakly,
*   slipped apart?*

Rupert Brooke, from
Desertion

A particularly vicious gust of wind snatched Vic's paper napkin from her lap and whirled it away across the lawn. Kincaid watched her start up out of her chair, then sink back, admitting defeat as the napkin disappeared over the wall. The clouds had been building in the western sky as they'd idled over their garden lunch, and now Vic looked up and frowned. 'I think the weather gods have abandoned us, don't you? It might be prudent to move inside,' she added, beginning to gather their dishes. 'I'll just get a tray.'

Watching her slip from her chair and walk away from him across the patio, Kincaid thought how odd it was to be with her again—and yet how familiar. He was acutely aware of the angle

41

of her shoulder blades beneath the thin fabric of her dress, the length of her fingers, the particular shape of her eyebrows, all things he hadn't thought of in years. He remembered her quiet way of listening, as if what one said were terribly important—but he also noticed that she still hadn't told him why she'd called him, and that too struck a familiar chord. When they separated he realized how seldom Vic had told him how she felt or what she thought. She'd expected him to know, and now he wondered if he'd once again missed his cue.

Returning with a tray, she said, 'I've lit the fire in the sitting room.' She'd slipped on a long chenille cardigan the colour of oatmeal, and she hugged it to her body for a moment before she began loading up the lunch things. 'So much for our picnic. But I suppose it was nice while it lasted.'

Stacking plates, Kincaid quipped, 'One could say that about a lot of things,' then swore at himself as he saw her wince at the direct barb. 'Sorry, Vic. I—' He broke off, unsure what to say. How could he apologize without opening the very can of worms he'd meant to avoid?

Vic took the dishes without comment, then paused with the laden tray in her arms and looked at him steadily for a moment before she spoke. 'Sometimes it takes experience to know just how good things are. Or to recognize someone's worth. I was a fool, but it took me a long time to figure it out.' She smiled and added as Kincaid stood gaping, 'Come on, give me a hand getting these things into the kitchen, then I'll make us some tea. Unless you'd rather have something stronger?'

Taking refuge in the commonplace, Kincaid said, 'No, no, that's all right. Tea's lovely. I've got the drive back to London and the wine will have put me close to the limit.'

He took the tray from her, and as she held the door he manoeuvred it into her small kitchen and set it on the worktop. Retreating to the doorway, he watched her as she filled the kettle. Her apology went against all his expectations and he had no idea how to respond.

Gathering cups and a teapot, Vic said matter of factly, without looking at him, 'You have someone waiting for you.'

'Is that a specific or a general statement?' he asked, grinning. He thought of Gemma, of the precarious balance they'd striven for these last few months, and wondered if her refusal to come with him today reflected more than her desire to spend time with her son. She'd invited him back to her flat tonight, but that didn't ensure the quality of his reception.

Vic glanced at him, then shut off the kettle as it came to the boil. When she'd filled the pot and set it on the tea tray, she motioned Kincaid to follow her to the sitting room. Over her shoulder, she asked, 'Does she appreciate you?'

'I'll tell her you said nice things about me. A sort of past-user guarantee.'

'Oh, right out of the tabloids, that is. *Ex-Wife Gives Endorsement.* Very effective, I'm sure.'

They settled in the squashy armchairs before the fire, and when Vic had tucked her feet up

43

under the folds of her dress and sipped her tea, she said, 'Seriously, Duncan, I'm glad for you. But I haven't asked you here to pry into your private life, though I have to admit I'm curious.' She smiled at him over the rim of her china cup.

The familiarity of the floral pattern had been nagging at him, and its juxtaposition against her face clicked the memory into place—Vic opening a gift box, lifting out a cup and holding it aloft for him to inspect. The china had been a wedding present from her parents, a proper set, her mother had called it, as if afraid his own family might offer something unsuitable.

'Curiosity always got Alice into trouble,' he teased. Alice had been his pet name for her, and it had suited her in more than physical resemblance.

'I know,' she said a bit ruefully. 'And I'm afraid things haven't changed all that much. What I wanted to see you about has to do with my work, and it's a bit difficult. But first I thought I'd get to know you again, see if you'd think I was just some hysterical, bloody female.'

'Oh, come on, Vic. You—hysterical? That's the last adjective that would have come to mind. You were always the epitome of cool detachment.' As he spoke he thought of the one place she had abandoned reserve, and he flushed uncomfortably.

'Some of the people in my department might use a bit less flattering terms.' She grimaced. 'And my choice of subject matter for my book

44

has made me decidedly unpopular in certain quarters.'

'Book?' Kincaid dragged his attention from the photo of Vic's errant husband. What had she seen in him? McClellan looked tweedy and bearded, handsome in a studiously academic way, and Kincaid could easily imagine him chatting up his students. He supposed he ought to be glad that life had seen fit to make Vic the butt of one of its little retribution jokes—the biter bit—but instead he felt a surge of anger on her behalf.

He had not been blameless in the break-up of their marriage, and they'd both been young, just beginning to discover what they wanted out of life. But he could imagine no excuse for Ian McClellan's behaviour—and what sort of man, he wondered, would go off without a word to his son?

'My biography,' Vic answered. 'That's what I've been working on this last year. A biography of Lydia Brooke.' She reached up and switched on the reading lamp beside her chair, casting her face into shadow and illuminating her hands as they clasped the teacup in her lap. 'Ian said he'd been displaced, and I suppose in a way it's true. Men—I don't like men very much these days. They want you to be brilliant and successful, just as long as it doesn't take any of your attention away from them and their needs. And as long as your accomplishments don't outshine theirs, of course.' She looked up at him and smiled.

'I sound an awful bitch, don't I? I'm

45

generalizing, and I know there are men capable of more, but I'm beginning to think they're the exception. Ian didn't start on the graduate students until my salary equalled his.' Her mouth twisted in disgust and she shook her head. 'Never mind. What do you know about Lydia Brooke?'

Frowning, he searched his memory, turning up a vague recollection of slim volumes on the shelf in his parents' bookshop. 'A Cambridge poet, a sort of symbol of the sixties ... She died quite recently, I think. Wasn't she related to Rupert Brooke?'

'She was obsessed with Rupert Brooke when she came up to Cambridge. Whether or not she was related to him is another matter entirely.' Vic shifted in her seat so that the light fell across her face again. 'And you're right, Lydia did burst upon the scene in the mid-sixties. Her poems were full of an aching disenchantment, and I suppose they touched something particular in that generation. After a disastrous marriage, she tried suicide, but recovered. She attempted suicide again in her early thirties, then finally, five years ago, she succeeded. She was forty-seven.'

'Did you know her?'

'I saw her once at a College function, not long after I came here. Unfortunately I didn't know anyone well enough to ask for an introduction, and I never had another chance.' Shrugging, Vic added, 'I know it sounds odd, but I felt a connection with her even then ... the old across a crowded room thing.' She smiled, mocking

46

herself, then sobered. 'It's not necessarily sexual, that sort of recognition, and it's only happened to me a few times. And then when I heard she had died, I felt devastated, as though I'd lost someone very close.'

Kincaid raised an eyebrow and waited.

'I know that look.' Vic grimaced. 'Now you're beginning to wonder if I am completely bonkers. But I think that sense of kinship with Lydia has contributed to the uneasy feeling I have about the manner of her death.'

'But surely there was no question that it was suicide?'

'Not legally, no.' Vic gazed out the window at the sky, heavy now with darkening cloud, and seemed to gather her thoughts. After a moment, she said, 'Let me see if I can explain. Lydia was thought to have killed herself in the midst of one of the periodic bouts of depression she'd suffered all her adult life, but I don't believe her death fits that pattern.'

Kincaid couldn't help remembering the hours he'd spent on similar theorizing when he and Vic had first been married, and how utterly uninterested she'd been in his cases. It had been understandable, he supposed, as he'd been new to homicide then, and fascinated with it to the point of boring even the most patient listener. 'Why not?' he asked mildly.

Vic slid her feet to the floor and sat forward. 'Both early suicide attempts coincided with long periods where she seemed unable to work. I think Lydia was truly happy only when she was writing, and writing well. If her personal problems coincided with a dry spell, she had difficulty coping, and I believe that's what happened after the breakup of her marriage. But as she grew older she seemed more and more content alone. If she had a serious relationship in the last ten years of her life, I've not been able to discover it.'

'And was she suffering writer's block before she died?' Kincaid asked, finding himself intrigued.

'No.' Vic put her cup on the side table and rubbed her palms together as if her hands were cold. 'That's it, you see. When she died she was in the process of editing the manuscript of a new book, the best thing she had ever done. The poems have such depth and richness—it's as if she suddenly discovered another dimension to herself.'

'Maybe that was it,' Kincaid suggested. 'There was nowhere left for her to go.'

Vic shook her head. 'At first I considered that a possibility, but the better I know her, the less likely it seems. I think she'd found her stride, at last. She could have done so much more, given so much—'

'Vic.' Kincaid leaned forward and touched her hand. 'You can never be sure what's in another person's heart. You know that. Sometimes people just wake up one day and decide they're tired of life, and they don't leave behind any explanation at all. Maybe that's what happened to Lydia.'

She shook her head, more vehemently this time. 'That's not all. Lydia died from an overdose of her own heart medication. Don't suicides usually keep to the same pattern, escalating the violence if they're not successful?'

'Sometimes, yes. But that doesn't necessarily mean it's always the case.'

'The first time she slit her wrists in the bath—it was only a friend coming in unexpectedly that saved her. The second time she drove her car into a tree and managed to give herself serious concussion. Later she said her foot slipped from the accelerator just at the crucial moment. Do you see?'

'The third attempt should have been more violent still?' Kincaid shrugged. 'I suppose it's possible. So what are you suggesting?'

Vic looked away for a moment, then said slowly, 'I'm not sure. It sounds so daft in the light of day ...'

'Come on, out with it.'

'What if Lydia didn't kill herself? I know with her history it was a logical assumption, but just think how easy that would have made it for someone else.' Vic stopped the rush of words and took a breath, adding more slowly, 'What I'm saying is ... I think Lydia might have been murdered.'

In the silence that followed, Kincaid counted to ten in his head. *Tread carefully,* he cautioned himself. *Don't tell her she's too close, that she's lost her perspective. Don't tell her how far people go to deny the suicides of loved ones—*and he had no doubt that Vic felt closer to Lydia Brooke than many did to their flesh and blood—*and for God's sake don't tell her she's hysterical.* 'All

49

right,' he said finally. 'Three questions. Why, how, and who?'

Voice rising, Vic said, 'I don't know. I've interviewed everyone I could contact, and I can't even find anyone who had a minor quarrel with her. But it still doesn't feel right.'

Kincaid drank the dregs of his tea while he considered how to answer. Ten years ago, twelve years ago, he'd been a by-the-book copper, and he probably would have laughed at her suspicions. But he'd learned not to discount intuition, even as unlikely as it sometimes seemed. 'Okay,' he said, 'let's assume for a moment that you're right, that there is something fishy about Lydia's death. What is it that you want *me* to do?'

Vic smiled, and he saw to his astonishment that her eyes had filled with tears. 'I wanted you to tell me I'm not crazy. You can't imagine what a relief it is just to talk about it.' She hesitated, touching her fingers to her throat. 'And then I thought maybe you could look into it a bit ...'

Trying to contain his exasperation, he said, 'Vic, the case is five years old, and it's not in my jurisdiction. What could I possibly do? Why don't you talk to someone on the force here—'

She was already shaking her head. 'You've got to be kidding. You know perfectly well they'd send me away with a condescending pat on the back and never open the file. They've too much to do with gangs and drugs these days to spend time on something like this. Surely there's something you could do, someone you could talk to, at least open a door for me?'

Kincaid thought of his own caseload, of the scramble for time to spend with Gemma, of his credibility—he'd be an idiot to take this on. Then out of the corner of his eye he saw the photograph, silver-framed on the side table—Vic and her son, and Ian McClellan, smiling into the lens—and he knew he couldn't refuse her.

Under his breath he muttered, 'Oh, bloody hell.' He knew someone on the Cambridgeshire force, a colleague who'd transferred there, hoping for a less stressful life. Just how far could he impose on past acquaintance? 'All right, Vic. I'll try to get a look at the case file. Just don't expect miracles, okay? More than likely everything in that file is so clean and above board you could eat off it.'

She gave him a quick smile. 'Thanks.'

A crack of thunder made them both jump, and as he looked up, rain began pelting against the window. He glanced at his watch, aware suddenly of the lateness of the hour, and wondered if Gemma would be back from her parents and waiting for him. 'I'm sorry, Vic,' he began, standing and depositing his cup on the side table with a clink, 'I've got to—Oh Christ'—he swore as the thought struck him—'I've left the bloody top down.'

'You'll get soaked,' Vic said, jumping up. 'I'll get a brolly, and a towel.'

Before he could say, 'There's no time,' she'd slipped out of the room ahead of him, and when he reached the door she had a towel and an old umbrella waiting. He grabbed them and

51

sprinted across the gravel, trying to work the catch on the umbrella as the rain stung his skin. As he reached the car the brolly sprang open with a pop, pinching his finger, and he struggled to hold it with one hand while he wrestled the top up with the other. When the latches clicked into place he looked down at the towel, now sodden, that he'd dropped on the bonnet, and laughed. He carried it ruefully back to Vic, and after trying unsuccessfully to wring it out single-handedly, said, 'Sorry.'

'I can't believe you still have that car,' she said, so close to him now that he could see the faint dark flecks in the irises of her eyes. 'You know I always hated it.'

'I know. Here's your umbrella,' he said, hand on the catch.

'You'll let me know, won't you, what you find?' She touched his arm. 'And Duncan, that's not the only reason I called. I owed you something. It's been eating at me for a long time.'

'It's okay.' He smiled. 'They say time heals all wounds—well, sometimes it even brings a little wisdom. We both had a lot of growing up to do.' He touched his cheek to hers, an instant's brushing of damp skin, then turned away.

As he eased the car out of the drive he looked back, saw her still standing motionless behind the curtain of rain, watching him.

'You agreed to do what?' Gemma turned and lifted a soapy finger to push a stray wisp of hair from her face. Kincaid had shown up just as she

52

and Toby were sitting down to their tea. Taking Toby on his lap, he'd zoomed carrot sticks into the child's open mouth with appropriate aeroplane commentary, but he'd hardly touched anything himself, not even the warm meat pies her mother had sent from the bakery. Nor had he said anything about his day until she asked him, and then his account of his meeting with Vic had been cursory at best.

'I only said I'd get in touch with an old mate of mine on the Cambridge force, see if I could have a look at the file,' he said now, and it seemed to her that his tone was deliberately casual.

Gemma unstoppered the sink in her cupboard-sized kitchen and dried her hands on a tea towel before she turned. From where she stood she could see Toby in the boxroom that served as his bedroom, rooting in a basket for a favourite picture book Kincaid had promised to read to him. 'Why?' she said, trying to pitch her voice low enough so that Toby wouldn't hear. 'Why would you volunteer to do anything for her? This woman walked out on you without a word, without a note, marries another bloke as soon as the ink on the divorce papers is dry, and twelve years later she reappears and wants you to do her a favour? What are you thinking of?'

Kincaid had been sitting on the floor, playing at blocks with Toby. Now he pushed himself to his feet and looked down at her. 'It's not like that—it wasn't like that at all. You don't know her. Vic's a decent person and she's having a rough time just now, as you certainly should know. What would you have had me do?'

The direct jab stung, but she knew from his tone that she'd ventured into forbidden territory, so she smiled, trying to make light of it. 'Oh, tell her to sod off, I suppose. To wherever it is ex-wives are supposed to go and never be heard from again.'

'Don't be silly, Gemma,' he said, not sounding the least bit amused. 'Look, I'll ring Alec Byrne in Cambridge tomorrow, see if he'll let me have an unofficial look at Lydia Brooke's file. Then I'll put Vic's mind to rest, and that will be that. Let's not quarrel about this, all right?'

'Me found it, Mummy,' shrieked Toby as he came trotting into the sitting room bearing aloft a book in a tattered dust jacket. *'Alfie's Boots.'* He tugged on Duncan's trouser leg. 'Read me it, Duncan. You promised. Read me *Alfie's Boots.'*

'It's *Alfie's Feet,* lovey,' corrected Gemma. Toby had developed a strong sense of identification with the little blond boy in Shirley Hughes's books and demanded the stories so often that Gemma knew them by heart. Kneeling, she took the book from him. 'I'll tell you what, darling. Why don't you go back in your room and find *Dogger,* too. Then *I'll* read them both to you before bed.' She gave him an encouraging pat on the bottom as she stood and faced Duncan again. 'I'm not quarrelling,' she said. 'You're being patronizing.'

'You're making a fuss over nothing, Gemma,' he said, leaning back and propping his hip against the black half-moon table that served

54

as both dining area and worktop in her tiny flat. 'You wouldn't be so upset if I'd agreed to do this for someone else.'

'That's just too bloody condescending,' she hissed at him. 'You wouldn't have done it for someone else!'

A shadow passed across the uncurtained garden windows, then a moment later came a tap at the door. Gemma took a breath and rubbed at her already flushed cheeks.

'Expecting someone?' Kincaid asked. Arms folded, he looked maddeningly unperturbed.

'It must be Hazel.'

Gemma gave him one last furious look, crossed the room and slid back the bolt. When Gemma had given up the house she'd shared with her ex-husband and moved into the garage flat in Islington, she'd acquired an unexpected friend in her landlady, Hazel Cavendish, and Toby, an ally in her daughter, Holly.

'Hello, love.' Hazel greeted Gemma with a hug, then brandished a video in one hand while waving at Kincaid with the other. 'Hello, Duncan. We've rented *The Lion King*—again— and I thought maybe Toby could watch it with us before bed. And if the kids should happen to fall asleep on the sofa in front of the telly, we'll just tuck them up and let them snooze.' She gave Gemma and Duncan a conspiratorial grin.

'You're too good, Hazel,' said Gemma in an effort to recover a little composure.

'I'm not. You've had him out all day and Holly's pining for him. I can't bear listening

to her whine another second. Humour me.'
Hazel crossed the room to Kincaid and gave
him a peck on the cheek. 'Mmmm, you smell
lovely. Nice shirt, too,' she added, rubbing a
bit of the sleeve fabric between her thumb and
forefinger.

'Thanks, Hazel. I'm sure that's the nicest
thing anyone's said to me all day.'

It was Gemma's favourite shirt, a fine-textured
dark-blue denim that made his grey-blue eyes
look uncompromisingly blue. The realization
that he'd worn it to visit Vic made her
temperature start rising again.

'Auntie Hazel.' Toby darted into the room
and clung to Hazel's leg like a limpet. 'Are
we going to watch *The Lion King?*' He made
growling noises and pranced around them, king
of the jungle.

'I suppose you are,' said Gemma, giving in
gracefully. 'We'll get no peace otherwise now.'
She tousled his fair hair.

'You too, Mummy,' he demanded. 'You
watch, too.'

'No, sweetheart, I—'

'Do, Gemma,' Kincaid broke in. 'I've got to
go, anyway. It's been a long day, and we've
an early start in the morning.' He retrieved his
jacket from the back of the chair, gave Gemma
a quick kiss that just missed the corner of her
mouth, then knelt and held out a palm for Toby
to slap, saying, 'See ya, sport.' At the door he
turned back. 'Bye, Hazel. Gemma, see you at
the Yard first thing, all right?' He smiled at
them and slipped out.

Gemma and Hazel stared at each other as the echo of the door closing died away, then they heard the distant sputter of the Midget's engine.

'Gemma, love, did I do something wrong?' asked Hazel, frowning. 'Put my foot in it somehow?'

Gemma shook her head wordlessly, then managed a strangled, 'Of all the bloody cheek—'

Assessing the situation, Hazel said, 'I think it's time for a bit of female bonding. I vote we move the party. What do you say, Gemma?' Seeming to take Gemma's nod for acquiescence, she shepherded them out the door.

The garage flat stood at right angles to the Cavendish's Victorian house, below and behind its garden. Gemma locked the flat's yellow door, then they climbed the steps which led up from the garage forecourt. Squeezing through the iron gate, they picked their way along the flagged garden path in the dark, Toby leading as comfortably as a cat. The flat's windows were now at a level with Gemma's knees, and glancing down, she could see through the half-open slanted blinds. Empty, the flat looked serene in its simplicity, yet lived in, and with a jab of awareness Gemma realized how much she loved it. To her it represented escape from the conventional semi-detached life she'd been expected to embrace—and independence, for she could afford it without help and without strain.

Toby reached Hazel's back door first and let himself in, as at home here as he was in his own flat. Gemma, trailing, entered the kitchen to find Hazel's husband, Tim, stirring something on the cooker, and the children chanting, 'Chocolate, chocolate,' like little demons. Hazel referred to them as Night and Day, for blue-eyed Toby's barley-fair hair was straight, and Holly had inherited her mother's curls along with her father's dark hair and eyes.

A clinical psychologist, Hazel had taken leave from her practice to care for her small daughter, and had soon insisted on taking Toby as well—on the grounds that two were much easier to entertain than one. She charged Gemma the going rate for child-minding—though Gemma suspected this had more to do with salving her pride than Hazel's financial gain—and never seemed fazed by the demands of the boisterous three-year-olds.

'Fancy a milky drink while we watch the video, Gemma?' Tim flashed her a welcoming smile, just visible through his dark beard.

Giving her husband an affectionate pat as she passed, Hazel said, 'I think Gemma and I will join you in a bit, love. We've a weekend's worth of gossip to catch up on.' She moved efficiently about the kitchen, fetching mugs, spoons and the Cadbury's tin.

After removing a broken crayon and a naked baby doll, Gemma sank into her usual chair at the kitchen table. It seemed impossible not to relax in this room—Gemma had often told Hazel that its essence should be bottled and sold as a sedative. She looked about her, noting the details, deliberately letting their familiarity calm her. Colourful cookery books vied with Hazel's knitting wool for space on the worktops, a basket filled with toys and picture books stood next to the Aga, the braided rug on the floor invited games of make-believe beneath the table. Even the sponged peach walls and dusty-green cabinets added comforting warmth.

'I was going to offer you coffee and fresh strudel,' Hazel said to Gemma when she'd dispatched Tim into the sitting room with a tray, children in tow. 'But let's open that bottle of Riesling I've been saving for you instead. You look as though you could do with a medicinal drink.'

'No, coffee's fine. It would be a shame to waste the wine on me tonight. I don't feel very festive.' Then, afraid she'd sounded ungrateful, Gemma made an effort to smile and added, 'And I'd hate to miss your strudel.'

Hazel gave her a considering look, her round face grave, but said only, 'The carbohydrate will make you feel better.' In a few moments she'd settled opposite Gemma with the filter pot and a warm pan of apple strudel. She poured coffee and served generous portions of pastry onto two plates, pushing Gemma's across the well-scrubbed pine table. 'Thank God for frozen puff pastry,' she said as she took a test nibble, then, satisfied, she fixed all her attention on Gemma. 'All right, tell.'

Gemma shrugged, shook her head, picked at her strudel, then put her fork down. 'He went to see his ex-wife today. Doctor Victoria

Kincaid McClellan, he said her name is now. After twelve years of absolutely eff-all she rings him up and he shot off to her like a bloody homing pigeon, can you believe it?

'She has some case she wants him to look into, and he agreed to that, too. Apparently her husband has run off with a graduate student, and instead of saying *serves her right*, he feels sorry for her.' Pausing, she sipped at her coffee and winced as it scalded her mouth.

'Do I take it he told you about this beforehand?' asked Hazel, brows lifting. 'That he intended seeing her?'

'Well, he couldn't very well help it, could he? I was there when she rang.' Reluctantly, Gemma added, 'Although ... I suppose he did ask me to go with him.'

'You suppose?' Hazel asked, amused. 'And I suppose you climbed on your high horse and refused?'

'I'd promised Toby we'd visit Mum and Dad today. You know how they look forward to our coming.' It sounded a weak excuse to Gemma even as she said it—she could have easily postponed the visit a week.

Hazel didn't offer any encouragement. 'So who are you really angry with, him or her?'

'Her, of course,' said Gemma, incensed. 'Of all the nerve, after the way she treated him.' She raised her cup to her lips again, more gingerly this time, then stopped as she saw Hazel's expression. 'Oh, all right. I'm bloody furious with him, if you want to know. He was such a *pig* about it. He said I didn't know anything, and he more or less told me to mind my own business.'

Hazel took a bite of strudel and chewed it. 'Well, what do you know about their marriage?'

Gemma shrugged and went back to flaking off bits of strudel with her fork. 'Just that she left him without a word.'

'Has he said why?'

'He *said* it was because he worked too much and didn't pay her enough attention,' Gemma admitted grudgingly.

'So if he's not blaming her—what's her name? Victoria?—then why are you? Surely you don't wish she hadn't left him?' Hazel grinned impishly. 'Then you might have some real competition.'

'No, of course I don't wish that.' Gemma pushed her coffee cup away. 'Can we open that wine after all?' She watched as Hazel went to the fridge and retrieved the bottle.

'What's so complicated about it?' Hazel asked as she brought the bottle and two glasses to the table. 'Why do you feel threatened by his relationship with Victoria?'

'Vic. He always calls her Vic.'

'Vic, then.'

'I don't feel threatened,' Gemma protested. 'And I'm not jealous. I don't go about thinking he's going to chat up every woman he meets.' She accepted the glass Hazel filled and handed to her. 'It's just that ... I don't know where he stands with her.'

'Why don't you ask him how he feels? Tell him that the situation makes you uncomfortable.'

'How can I?' Gemma choked on the wine she'd been sipping and coughed until her eyes teared. When she could speak again, she added, 'I'm the one who insisted we not set those kinds of limits on each other, because I didn't want to feel suffocated. And how could I possibly say anything after he was so bloody about it?'

'Has it occurred to you that he might have been reticent about his visit because he was worried about *your* reaction?' asked Hazel. 'And I gather you certainly lived up to expectations.'

'I did, didn't I?' Gemma said disgustedly. 'I'd been stewing all weekend, and tonight I waded into it at the first opportunity. Sometimes I think I should have been born with my foot in my mouth.' She shook her head. 'So what do I do now?'

'Grovel?' suggested Hazel kindly. 'Look, love.' She leaned towards Gemma, elbows on the table. 'Just for once, forget your dreadful ex-husband, ignore all those little red flags that pop up at the mere suggestion of setting parameters. One of the reasons you and Duncan work so well together is that you communicate.' She jabbed her finger at Gemma for emphasis. 'Why not extend the same honesty to your personal life? You've been tiptoeing around this *we don't make demands on our relationship* crap for how long now—since November? That was all very well in the beginning, but relationships are about demands, and obligation, and commitment. If this one is to continue, one of you is going to have to step up to the net.'

The storm had passed through, leaving the air cool and cleansed. Vic tightened the belt on her dressing gown, and stepped from the terrace into the dark garden so that she had an unobstructed view of the stars. She'd never managed to learn the constellations, and as she looked up she felt a sudden longing to put names to the clusters, to match them to the stick-like drawings she'd seen as a child. Perhaps she'd buy Kit one of those glow-in-the-dark sets she'd seen at the bookshop in Cambridge, and they could learn them together.

Poor Kit, she thought with a sigh. Since Ian's disappearance, her parents had taken it upon themselves to fill the gap in Kit's life, and had succeeded in giving his hostility a new target. The more he resisted, the harder they pushed, and Vic was finding the contest more and more difficult to referee. Today they'd met him off the King's Cross train, determined to take him to an exhibition at the British Museum, while Kit had been equally determined to cajole them into visiting the Piccadilly Circus video arcades.

He'd come home sullen and disappointed, of course. Vic had known his wishes wouldn't stand a chance against her mother's agenda, but she'd made him go because she hadn't been ready for him to meet Duncan. Not yet, not until she was sure about him, sure he hadn't changed in the things that counted.

Turning, she looked to the north, where Nathan's cottage stood out of sight just round the bend in the road. She'd meant to ring him, perhaps even to slip away for a glass of wine and a half-hour's visit before the fire in his sitting room. But Kit had needed her attention, and her guilt had dictated she spend the evening with him in front of the telly, watching some awful action film he'd begged to see.

Now it was too late to ring anyone, but she felt restless, unable to settle. She ought to be in bed, but she knew she'd only lie awake, wide-eyed, replaying the afternoon's conversation with Duncan in her head. Did she say too much? Did she say enough? Did he take her seriously, or was he merely humouring her?

She closed her eyes for a moment, letting herself drift in the dark, then turned and let herself quietly back into the house. There must be something she'd missed, something conclusive that she could show him. Making her way by touch down the dim corridor, she slipped into her office and stood staring at the clutter of papers illuminated by her desk lamp. She would simply start again, from the beginning.

7 October 1961
Newnham

Dearest Mother,
Oh, how I wish you were here. It's everything we dreamed of, yet in some ways nothing like we imagined. Newnham isn't the least bit cold and forbidding; its red brick and white trim are charming, and I've been given the loveliest set of rooms, on the corner, overlooking the gardens. You'll have to think of me here,

once I've hung my prints and put my bits and pieces about, curled in my chair in front of the gas fire, reading, reading, reading ... I met my Director of Studies today, Dr Barrett, and I think we'll get on famously. The trouble is going to be in choosing which lectures to attend and which papers I'll do this term. I feel like the proverbial child in the candy store, overwhelmed by bounty.

So far the other girls seem nice enough, if a bit standoffish. Daphne, the tall redhead across the hall, seems the best prospect for striking up a real friendship, as she's from some village in Kent the size of your thumb. That gives us at least one thing in common.

Last night I went to Evensong at King's for the first time. Oh, Mummy, it was incredible. The voices soared, and for a little while I soared with them, imagining myself floating above Cambridge in the clear night, held only by a silver tether of sound. I sat next to a Trinity boy, very serious, who invited me to a poetry reading on Thursday in his rooms. So you see, I already have a social engagement, and you needn't have worried about me.

If the weather's fine on Sunday I mean to walk to Grantchester along the river path. I'll pretend I'm Virginia Woolf going to visit Rupert Brooke. We'll have tea in the garden at the Old Vicarage and discuss important things; poetry and philosophy and life.

Darling Mother, I'm sure I haven't thanked you properly. You made me work when I felt tired or cranky; you encouraged me when I couldn't see past some trivial setback; you built me up when I lost faith in myself. If it weren't for your vision and determination I'd probably be standing behind the chemist's counter today, dispensing cough syrup and Milk of Magnesia, instead of here, in this most glorious of places. I'll write in a day or two and give you my schedule. I want to share this with you.

Your loving ... Lydia

Chapter Four

My restless blood now lies a-quiver,
Knowing that always, exquisitely,
This April twilight on the river
Stirs anguish in the heart of me.

Rupert Brooke, from
Blue Evening

Kincaid had kept his word to Vic, ringing his friend, Chief Inspector Alec Byrne, first thing Monday morning, but it wasn't until midday Wednesday that he found the time to go to Cambridge. Having decided he'd put enough wear and tear on the Midget for one week, he took the train, stretching his legs out in the empty compartment and dozing between stations. A little more than an hour after leaving King's Cross, he paid off a taxi in front of the cinder block building on Parkside Road which housed the Cambridge Police Station.

66

A blonde constable with traffic-stopping legs escorted him to Byrne's office, ushering him in with a smile and the merest suggestion of a wink.

'Watch out for our Mandy,' Byrne said with a grin as the door closed. He stood and came around his desk. 'She's been through every man in the department once, and now she's starting on the second round.'

'I'll exercise proper caution,' Kincaid assured him. 'It's good to see you, Alec. They seem to be treating you well, if the accommodations are anything to go by.' He raised an eyebrow at the furniture and carpeting, a definite step up from Scotland Yard standard issue.

'I can't complain. Executive loo and three squares a day.'

Something nagged at Kincaid, and after a moment he realized what it was. Alec Byrne had quit smoking. His desk no longer held ashtrays, and the hand he'd held out for Kincaid to shake was scrubbed pink, only the nails of thumb and forefinger still showing faint yellow stains. When they'd been fledgling detective constables together, his friend had seldom been seen without a cigarette adhering to his lip or dangling from his fingers. Kincaid had always found it odd, as Byrne was a most fastidious man in other ways.

'I see you've given it up,' he said as he settled into the visitor's chair.

'Had to, I'm afraid. Developed a bit of a spot on my lung.' Byrne shrugged a bony shoulder beneath an exquisitely tailored suit jacket. 'Decided it wasn't worth dying for.'

'You look well.' Kincaid meant it sincerely. A tall man, still as thin as he'd been when Kincaid had first known him, Byrne looked whippet-fit. His reddish-fair hair had receded above the temples, leaving him a pronounced and rather distinguished widow's peak.

'I'm not too stubborn to admit that I feel better.' Byrne smiled. 'I knew becoming a fanatic was the only way I could do it, so I changed my diet and I started exercising—I'm rowing again, can you believe it? Joined a club.'

Byrne had been nonchalant concerning his Cambridge blue, but he'd also made sure it got about among his fellow rookies and his athletic prowess had done much to alleviate their distrust of his upper class background. The suspicion Byrne's Cambridge degree had aroused seemed odd now, in this new era of educated policing, but it seemed to Kincaid that the man had always had an instinct for being ahead of his time.

'Thanks for seeing me, Alec. I know how busy you must be.'

'You know all too well, I'd imagine—and of course that makes me wonder what you're doing here, but I'll try to keep my curiosity in check. I've had the file you asked for brought up from the dungeon. I'd suggest you take it to the canteen and look at it while you have a cuppa.' Byrne handed a folder across his desk to Kincaid. 'But you owe me, old chap.'

'I'm sure you'll find some suitable revenge.'

Kincaid accepted the fat file and realigned the errant papers.

'You can buy me a pint when you've finished. I'm sure they'll never miss me.'

'Privilege of rank?' Kincaid suggested.

Byrne answered in his most sardonic drawl. 'Hardly worth it, otherwise, I dare say.'

'I see you didn't handle Lydia Brooke's case,' Kincaid said as he set two foaming pints of bitter on the table at the Free Press. The pub was tucked away in a residential street behind the station, and was, Byrne had informed him zealously, the only non-smoking pub in Britain, at least as far as he knew.

'No, the Brooke case was Bill Fitzgerald's, one of his last before he took his peptic ulcer and his pension off to a bungalow in Spain. He sends us a postcard occasionally.' Byrne raised his pint to Kincaid. 'Cheers. May we someday do the same.'

'I'll drink to that.' For the first time in years, Kincaid had a brief vision of his honeymoon with Vic in Majorca. Sun and rocks and scarlet bougainvillaea climbing on stuccoed walls ... He shook himself back to reality. 'About Lydia Brooke—did you know her when you were at Cambridge?'

Byrne shook his head. 'No, she left a few years before I came up, but I heard the occasional odd thing about her. I remember the case well enough, though. Just about this time of year, wasn't it, five years ago? She died from an overdose of the medication she took for her heart arrhythmia, leaving everything to her ex-husband. It seemed a fairly obvious suicide, and it at least got her a mention on the local news. You know—*tragic death of award-winning Cambridge poet*—that sort of thing.'

Kincaid pulled his notebook from his breast pocket and flipped it open, then drank off a bit of his pint. He'd taken the bench, putting the wall at his back, and from where he sat he could see the day's specials carefully lettered on the chalkboard over the bar. *Mushroom Stroganoff* it read, and *courgette flan*. It followed, he supposed, that a smoke-free pub would also be vegetarian. Glancing at the notebook, he said, 'I understand that Brooke had a history of more violent suicide attempts.'

'She had a reputation as a bit of an hysteric, if I remember correctly. All part of the artistic persona.'

'What crap,' Kincaid said. 'In my experience, artists are more likely to be driven like furies, and are a hell of a lot more disciplined than your average accountant.' He sat back and lifted his pint once more. 'Do you remember the details of the previous attempts?'

Byrne shook his head. 'Not really, except that they seem to have been rather elaborately staged, as was this one.'

'Yes ... except there were one or two things about this one that seemed a bit odd to me. Her clothes, for instance.'

'Clothes? I don't remember that there was anything unusual about them.'

'That's the point. Lydia Brooke seems to have

70

had a heightened sense of the dramatic, I will give you that ...' Kincaid smiled at Byrne, then glanced again at his notes. 'According to her file, there was music repeating on the stereo when her body was discovered, Elgar's "Cello Concerto", to be exact. I don't know if you're familiar with the piece at all, but I'd say it's probably the most wrenchingly sad music I've ever heard.'

'I know the piece,' Byrne said. He closed his eyes for a moment, then hummed a few bars, keeping time with his finger. 'And I'd be inclined to agree with you. It's quite powerful stuff.'

'So picture this,' Kincaid continued. 'She lay on the sofa in her study, arms crossed on her breast, a candle burning on the table beside her. In her typewriter there was a fragment of a poem about death, and the music playing.' He pushed his pint aside and leaned forward. 'But she was wearing khaki trousers and a T-shirt with the slogan Eat Organic Food. She had dirt under her fingernails. For Christ's sake, Alec, she'd been gardening. Are we to surmise that Lydia Brooke had a particularly difficult encounter with her herbaceous border and decided to end it all?'

Byrne tapped his long fingers on the tabletop. 'I take your point. After she went to so much trouble to set the scene, you'd think she'd have worn something more suitable to the occasion. But I think you're stretching it a bit—suicides aren't always so logical.'

Kincaid shrugged. 'Perhaps. It just struck me,

that's all. I don't suppose anyone checked to see if she'd left her gardening tools out?'

'Haven't the foggiest. I wouldn't be willing to wager on it.'

'Do you remember the statement of the man who found the body?'

'No,' Byrne answered, beginning to sound a bit exasperated. 'I can't say that I ever actually read the file. I only know what was circulating in the department at the time.'

Consulting his notes again, Kincaid said, 'His name was Nathan Winter. He was a friend, apparently, as well as her literary executor. Brooke had rung him and asked him to come round, but when he arrived later that evening he found the porch dark. She didn't answer when he rang the bell, so he tried the door and found it unlocked. Do you know if anyone ever found out why the light was out?'

Frowning, Byrne studied Kincaid. 'I suspect where you're going with this, and I think I've contained my curiosity long enough. Why this interest in a straightforward case that's been closed for almost five years? Do you think we're not capable of doing a job properly?'

'Oh, bollocks, Alec. You know perfectly well that's not true, so don't come the injured provincial with me. Besides, it wasn't your case. You were the new boy on the block then, remember? And isn't it just possible that old Bill was more interested in looking at travel brochures than in doing much digging on a case that came all wrapped up in a pink ribbon?'

For a moment Byrne seemed to be concentrating on placing his tankard in the exact centre of his beer mat, then he looked up at Kincaid. 'Even supposing you're right—and I'm not sure I'm willing to go that far, mind you—why are you sticking your nose in?'

It was Kincaid's turn to fiddle. He drew rings in the moisture on the tabletop, wishing he'd started as he meant to go on. Finally, he said, 'It's personal.' When Byrne merely raised his brows expectantly, Kincaid went on. 'My ex-wife—her name is Victoria McClellan—is working on a biography of Brooke. She's at All Saints'—a fellow—and she lectures at the University as well,' he added quickly, as if Byrne had questioned her credentials.

'I see,' Byrne drawled. 'She asked you to ferret out the details so she could use them in her book. And you agreed?'

Kincaid bridled at the mildly amused censure. 'Not at all. I'd not have agreed to it, for one thing, and for another, I think scandal value is the last thing on Vic's mind. Look, Alec, I know how it sounds, but Vic isn't given to flights of fancy. I dare say she knows Lydia Brooke down to the colour of her knickers, and she doesn't believe Brooke committed suicide.'

'Murder?' Byrne laughed. 'Tell that to the AC, with bells on. Just let me be there to see his face turn that lovely apoplectic purple.' His mirth subsiding, he looked pityingly at Kincaid. 'Duncan, I can tell you now, you don't stand a hope of getting the AC to reopen this case unless you come up with some new, absolutely

73

incontrovertible physical evidence—or you get a confession.' He shook his head and eyed his friend ruefully. 'And I'd say your chances of doing either are about on a par with the proverbial snowball's.'

Kincaid stood outside the police station, watching squirrels chase one another across the green expanse of Parker's Piece. Two young men played a desultory game of Frisbee with a mongrel dog, and a woman pushing a pram crossed the space slowly on the diagonal.

Reluctantly, Kincaid pulled his phone from his breast pocket and punched in Vic's number. He supposed he might as well get it over with, see her while he was in Cambridge and tell her he'd done what he could. Alec Byrne was right, of course; a few unanswered questions were not going to arouse the local lads' interest in an old case more conveniently let lie.

As he listened to the distant ringing, a cloud skittered across the sun, momentarily erasing the long afternoon shadows. He heard a click, then Vic's voice, and so immediate and natural did she sound that it took him a moment to realize he'd reached her answering machine. At the beep he hesitated, then hung up without leaving a message. He glanced at his watch before again consulting his notebook. There might still be time to catch her at her office, but he realized she hadn't given him the number. Glancing up, he saw a taxi rounding the corner. If he hurried, he might just make it in person.

A black cab delivered him swiftly to a Victorian house across the river. He stood a moment after paying off the driver, regarding the sign near the gate which informed him that this was the University of Cambridge Faculty of English, No Unauthorized Parking Allowed. A heavy screen of evergreens partially concealed a gravelled car park, but in a sheltered spot near the house he could see a battered Renault and an N registration Volvo. It looked as though he might find someone lingering past the stroke of five.

The grey-brick, peaked-roof house had seen grander days. Overgrown shrubbery and a swathe of dead creeper across the façade gave it a desolate air, alleviated only by clean white trim round the windows and a glossy navy-blue door. Kincaid knocked lightly, then turned the knob and stepped inside. He found himself in a small reception area which originally must have functioned as the entrance hall, and as he stood for a moment wondering which door he should try, the one on the left opened and a woman looked round the edge at him.

'Thought I heard someone come in, and I didn't recognize the tread.' She smiled and came through into the hall, and he saw that she was plump and pleasant-looking, with wavy brown hair and glasses that slid down the bridge of her nose. 'Can I help you?' she asked.

'Um, I was hoping I might catch Doctor McClellan before she left for the day,' said Kincaid, wondering a bit late about the advisability of intruding unannounced into Vic's life.

'Oh, too bad. You've just missed her by a few minutes. Kit had a soccer match this afternoon and she does like to be there if she can.' The woman held her hand out. 'I'm Laura Miller, by the way, the department secretary. Can I give her a message?'

'Duncan Kincaid,' he said, shaking her hand. 'Just tell her I dropped by, if you wouldn't—' He paused as a door slammed above, then came the sound of quick, heavy footsteps on the stairs.

'Damn it, Laura, I can't find that bloody fax anywhere. Are you sure it's not gone out with the rubbish?' A man—large, leonine and flushed with the high colour that derives from quick temper—followed the voice round the last landing of the stairs. 'You know what liberties Iris takes with other people's papers, it's a wonder one ever finds any—' He stopped in mid-tirade as he reached the bottom of the stairs and saw Kincaid. 'Oh, hello. Sorry, sorry, didn't know anyone else was about. You'd think we had pixies, the way things disappear in this place.' A lock of the thick grey-brown hair flopped over his brow as he gave Kincaid an apologetic grin. 'And poor Laura bears the brunt of our frustration, I'm afraid.'

The secretary gave him a sharp look, but answered easily. 'For once it is on Doctor Winslow's desk, Doctor Eliot. But since it concerned the entire department—' She glanced at Kincaid, then amended whatever she'd been about to say. 'I'll just get it for you. I'm sure she won't mind you taking care of it.'

With a smile for Kincaid, she slipped back

into the office on the left and returned a moment later with a flimsy sheet of fax paper. 'Iris Winslow is our Head of Department,' she explained. 'We've been in a bit of a bother over a change in some of the University exam procedures. Doctor Eliot—' she nodded at the large man by way of introduction—'teaches the history of literary criticism, among other things. Doctor Eliot, this is Mr Kincaid. He was asking after Vic.'

Kincaid felt the level of interest rise in the room as Eliot eyed him speculatively.

'You don't say. Is it anything we can help with?' The urgent fax apparently forgotten, Eliot slipped a hand inside his jacket, resting it against his plum-coloured knitted waistcoat in a vaguely Napoleonic gesture.

The waistcoat, Kincaid thought at second glance, looked to be cashmere, and the jacket Harris tweed. Eliot and the secretary watched him expectantly, smiles hovering, eyes bright, and he had the sudden feeling he'd wandered into a tank of barracuda. 'No, thanks. Please don't trouble yourselves over it. I'll just give her a ring.' He nodded and went out.

He walked slowly down West Road until he reached Queens' Road again. The crossing light was red and he looked about him as he waited, hands in pockets. The way to the train station lay to his right, across the river. The carriages would be jam-packed this time of day, stuffy with the remnants of the afternoon's warmth, and he found the prospect of fighting the crowds

77

unappealing. He cursed himself doubly for not bringing the car—as well as avoiding rush-hour on British Rail, it would have allowed him to drive to Grantchester and wait for Vic at her cottage.

But even though he couldn't fulfill his main objective, he thought, shrugging, why should he hurry back to London? Since Sunday, Gemma had treated him with studied politeness at work and had been conveniently busy afterwards, and he had no reason to suppose this evening would be any different.

The light flashed yellow and he crossed with the flow of pedestrian traffic, then paused on the opposite pavement. With sudden decisiveness he turned left, taking the path that meandered along the Backs. He could see King's College Chapel across the river, and as he walked, the clouds parted and the last of the sun's rays gilded the tips of the spires. Did one take such sights for granted, he wondered, if one saw them every day?

Had Lydia Brooke grown accustomed to them as she went about Cambridge on her business, her head full of lectures and love? And most likely in reverse order, he added to himself, smiling, then he sobered as he thought of the report he'd read that afternoon. He understood Alec Byrne's defensiveness, but the case had an unfinished feel, and he thought if it had been his he would not have been satisfied with such a pat solution. Had anyone tried to discover what she'd been doing that day? Or whom she'd seen, and what she might have said to them? And if she'd been gardening, as seemed obvious, had there been anything unusual about that day's tasks? Had she done what looked to be a final planting, for instance, or some sort of grand tidying up, as if she were taking her leave of the garden?

The business about the porch light nagged at him as well. Had anyone checked to see if it had been out for some time, or had it just coincidentally expired on the night of Lydia's death?

Kincaid stopped and consulted his pocket map of Cambridge. To his right a lane led to an arched bridge over the river, and Vic's college lay just the other side. He took the turning, and when he reached the summit of the bridge he paused for a moment and leaned on the railing, gazing downstream at the willows whose drooping fronds reached out to touch their own reflections. The tightly furled pale yellow buds dotting the branches might have been painted there by Seurat, and the tethered punts provided contrast, solid blocks of green and umber, gently rocking.

Across the river a sturdy red-brick building stood guard over a walled garden. It would be All Saints' Fellows' Garden, he supposed, thinking it unlikely that the dons would allow mere students the best view.

As he turned to continue on his way, a bicycle whizzed soundlessly by him, nearly clipping his shoulder. He went on more warily after that, staying close to the railing and checking behind him for oncoming cyclists. The lane narrowed the other side of the bridge, with the walls of All Saints' rising on the right and those of Trinity College on the left. At the first All Saints' gate he stopped and peered into the manicured quad curiously. Didn't Lydia's file mention that the Nathan Winter who discovered her body was a don at All Saints'? And hadn't Vic mentioned a friend called Nathan? Cambridge was indeed a small world, he thought, if the two were the same, and he wondered if Vic had met him in the course of her college duties, or as a result of her research on Lydia Brooke. Winter was a botanist, according to the file, and he vaguely remembered Vic referring to Nathan when they'd talked about her garden. It seemed a bit odd, now that he thought of it, that Lydia had named a botanist as her literary executor.

He shrugged and walked on, rounding the corner into Trinity Lane. And yet there was something odder still, he thought as he went over his conversation with Vic. He could only recall her mentioning one marriage, and that quite early in Lydia's life. Why would Lydia have left everything to a man from whom she'd been divorced for almost twenty years?

He hugged the wall as another cluster of cyclists shot by, then he stumbled into a bicycle left standing outside a shop. Bloody bikes, he thought. You could hardly move for them in this town.

16 November 1961
Newnham

Darling Mother,
Your birthday gift was much appreciated, and was just enough to purchase a good second-hand bike. It has a few dents in the fenders and scrapes in the paint, but those just add character in my opinion. You'd be proud of me—I've got quite good already, and cycle my way round almost as easily as if I were navigating the lanes at home on Auntie Nan's old clunker. I was sure you wouldn't mind my spending the money before my actual birthday, as the bike was so sorely needed.

I can't imagine Cambridge without bicycles. They fly by, the student's black gowns flapping like crow's wings, or stand riderless, clumped together in mute and inebriated herds. Even if undergraduates were allowed cars, there would be no place to park them, so I suppose the system works rather well.

Thanks to the bike I venture a bit farther afield each day, so that I am beginning to feel I own this place, with its narrow twisty streets and forests of chimney pots. I seem to find a fascinating little shop round every new corner. I gaze at knitting wools, and jumpers, and cookware, but I spend my pocket money in the second-hand book shops. I love the dry, musty smell of the volumes, the tissue-thin feel of the paper. Even the typefaces speak of vanished elegance. Already the books are accumulating in my room, and nothing, I think, makes a place more like home. In the evenings I curl up in my window seat and look out over the rooftops as the light fades. Sometimes I read, sometimes I just hold a book, and I feel the strongest sense of contented elation.

If it sounds as though I've been leading a solitary life, I assure you that's not the case. Cambridge has societies representing everything from doily-making to penguin equality—well, maybe they're not quite that outrageous, but some of them are certainly bizarre— and they are all enthusiastically recruiting. The major inducement at these functions is free drink, so one has to be rather carefully abstemious, and not carry one's cheque book just in case one is too easily persuaded. The only thing that does *not* seem to be well represented is writing, but I'm fast making like-minded friends and perhaps we can create our own sort of society. In the meantime I am seriously considering joining the University paper. That should at least give me a creative outlet until I can schedule time for my own writing.

I've been invited out and about so much that I've decided it's time I should reciprocate, so therefore I'm hosting my first sherry party in my room on Thursday. I've invited Adam, the boy I told you about meeting at King's. He's a Trinity man, reading Philosophy, and he seems to see poetry primarily as a vehicle for expressing social views. On this matter we have already had some wonderfully heated discussions.

Adam took me to a Labour Club dance last Saturday, where I met a delightful boy called

Nathan whom I've invited as well. He's sturdily built, with fair skin, dark hair and the merriest brown eyes I've ever seen. A Natural Sciences student, he means to be a poet as well as a botanist, in the manner of Loren Eisley.

Daphne from across the hall will make up a fourth, and I intend to serve them decent sherry and biscuits, and feel, oh, so sophisticated.

And in case you think from this account that I've done nothing but swan about, I assure you, Mummy, dear, that I have been a model student. I've chosen the three exams I will read for, and have begun the lectures Miss Barrett and I decided would be most helpful in preparing me. My lecture schedule is about eleven hours during the week and includes such luminaries as F.R. Leavis on criticism, and I must admit I feel quite intimidated, being lectured to by men whose books are filling my shelves. Most of my lectures are in the morning, and there are surprisingly few women. I usually cycle back to Newnham for lunch in Hall, then most afternoons are divided between supervisions and reading either in the library or in my room. Such order makes me feel as though I might possibly grasp all this, if only I am disciplined and dedicated enough.

I've chosen to celebrate my birthday this evening alone in my room. This is not because I'm feeling sorry for myself, mind you, but because this is the way I feel closest to home, and you. It's a lovely crisp evening with the hint of wood smoke in the air, and I picture you and Nan sitting by the fire after tea, reading, talking now and again, perhaps deciding whether or not to make cocoa and listen to a programme on the wireless. I know your thoughts are reaching out to me as mine are reaching out to you, and I think if I close my eyes and concentrate hard enough I could almost ... be there.

Love,
Lydia

Vic pulled her old cardigan from the hook and slipped out the back door as soundlessly as possible, reminding herself to lubricate the hinges. She'd tucked Kit into bed at ten, amidst the nightly routine of his protests. He thought eleven much too grown up to have a set bedtime, in spite of the fact that if she let him stay up much past ten o'clock he'd sleep straight through his alarm the next morning.

Shrugging into her cardigan, Vic stood on the terrace a moment, looking up at the sky. The clear day had become a crisp night, but the stars looked blurred round the edges from moisture in the air, and to the north they faded against the pink glow that was Cambridge. She doubted tomorrow would be as fine.

When her eyes had adjusted, she stepped from the terrace on to the lawn, crossed it swiftly and let herself out the gate at the bottom of the garden. There was no moon, but she knew the path to the river almost by instinct. A shadow moved beneath the chestnuts at the water's edge. As she drew closer the shape coalesced into a man, stocky, starlight gleaming faintly from the surface of his oiled jacket and his silver hair.

'Nathan.'

'I thought you might come. Kit giving you fits again?'

So rich was his voice in the dark that it seemed to her it might stand alone, disembodied, a condensation of personality.

'It's these dreams,' she said, huddling a bit more tightly into her sweater as she felt the chill rising from the river. 'It's odd—he never had nightmares when he was small.' She sighed. 'I suppose it has to do with Ian, although if he misses Ian he never says so. And he won't tell me what the dreams are about.'

'Children's capacity for forming little hedgehog balls around their suffering never ceases to amaze me. Our adult propensity for exposing all our traumas to the world must be a learned behaviour,' he said, chuckling, but she heard the sympathy in it.

'It's silly of me, but sometimes I forget you've been through all this. I just see you as Nathan, complete in yourself, without all these family appendages that most of us carry around.' Then, as she realized what she'd said, she gasped and put a hand to her mouth. 'Oh, Nathan, I'm so sorry. That was incredibly thoughtless of me.'

This time he laughed outright. 'On the contrary, I take it as a compliment. Have you any idea how hard I've worked these last few years to achieve that sort of self-sufficient independence? At first it was merely a defence against the well-meaning—I couldn't bear being fussed over—and then it became something I needed to do for myself. I'd had twenty years of operating as one half of a whole, and there were times when the task seemed insurmountable.' He paused, as if aware of the weariness that had crept into his voice, then added more heartily, 'And as for my girls, you just haven't met them yet. You'll have no doubt that I'm fully parentally qualified, though I have to admit I sometimes find it difficult to believe they're my biological off-spring. Perhaps all parents feel that way.'

How little she knew him, thought Vic, and how odd that she felt so comfortable with him as she had never been one to form easy alliances. She must have come to All Saints' shortly after his wife died, and she remembered having a vague awareness of him as an attractive, if somewhat abstracted, man with whom she exchanged occasional pleasantries over sherry in the SCR. But their paths rarely crossed outside college functions, and it was not until she began her preliminary research on Lydia Brooke that she'd learned Nathan was Brooke's literary executor.

When approached, he'd been helpful enough in supplying Lydia's materials, but he had not offered any reminiscences. It was only when she'd mentioned living in Grantchester by chance one day that he'd responded in a more personal way, and since Ian's disappearance they had spent more and more time together.

'Listen.' Nathan put a finger to his lips. 'Do you hear that?'

Vic held her breath, listening. She heard the blood in her ears, then on the threshold of sound, a shriek. 'What is it?' she whispered.

'A barn owl. It takes some perseverance to hear them these days, they're becoming quite rare. Reminds me of my childhood, that and the sound of the tree frogs. I loved the river then. Sometimes I would imagine it moving in my blood.'

'Kit feels that, too, I think. I envy you both a bit. I appreciate this—' she gestured around her—'but it's in an objective way. What you and Kit have seems to be almost organic. He can stay down here for hours at a time, watching bugs in the grass.' She smiled.

'A naturalist in the making,' Nathan said thoughtfully. 'I'd like to know him better. Does he read? He doesn't look bookish, and I suppose I'd thought of him as a rugger and football sort of boy.'

'Oh, he's capable enough at games, and he does what's necessary to fit in at school, but his heart's not really in it. And it's odd, because he's always been ferociously competitive about his schoolwork—even more so since Ian left. The other day I found him crying over an exam score, and then he was furious with me for catching him at it. He didn't speak to me for two days.' Vic hadn't told anyone this, and now she didn't know if she felt relieved, or guilty for betraying Kit's confidence. These were the sort of things meant to be shared by parents, she thought, but she wouldn't have told Ian even had he been around to tell. He'd have gone all pompous and preachy about it, and he'd somehow always manage to miss the point.

'Poor kid,' Nathan said, his jacket rustling as he moved in the dark. 'Perhaps you could encourage him to love the acquisition of knowledge for its own sake, separate from the carrot system of education.'

Vic heard a soft plop from the direction of the river. A frog? Or a fish jumping? Did fish sleep? she wondered. She thought of asking Nathan, then dismissed it as being too humiliatingly ridiculous. How ignorant she was of anything outside her own little area of expertise. Tonight the river seemed merely a dark void in the landscape—she had never thought of it being full of life as complicated and messy as her own.

Now she found that if she stared long enough at the water she could see light and movement, the reflection of starlight filtering through the chestnut branches. 'So how do I go about it, teaching Kit to love knowledge for itself?'

'Look at yourself,' said Nathan softly. 'Have you forgotten why you do what you do? That's a start. And I've some books he might like. Why don't you come up to the cottage with me?' he added, cupping a hand round her elbow. 'I've something for you, as well.'

Vic found that her odd new awareness had spread from the perception of outward phenomena to her body. She felt the heat from Nathan's hand through the bulky sleeve of her cardigan and the sensation left her suddenly ripe, aching, weak-kneed with desire. Oh, lord, she had forgotten this, the strength of it, and she was not prepared. She thought of Nathan's hand on her breast and stumbled, gasping.

'Are you all right?' He tightened his grip on her arm.

'Fine,' she said, a bit breathlessly, fighting laughter, trying hard to stamp down the singing joy rising in her. 'Just fine.'

'Fancy a drink?' Nathan asked. 'Wine or—'

'Whisky,' Vic interrupted decisively. She stood before the fire in his kitchen-sitting room as if she were cold, but her cheeks were stained with pink.

Watching her while he filled two tumblers from the bottle he kept in the kitchen cabinet, Nathan wondered if she might be coming down with something. Come to think of it, she'd been behaving very oddly these last few minutes. She'd not often touched him, yet tonight when he'd let go of her arm on reaching the level path, fearing he'd overstepped his bounds, she'd walked so close beside him that their shoulders bumped.

Nathan delivered her glass and raised his. 'Cheers.'

Vic took what on anyone less delicate-looking he would have labelled a swig, then coughed and sputtered. When he patted her solicitously on the back, she shivered.

'Honestly, Vic, I think you're not well. Let me—'

'No, I'm fine, Nathan, really,' she said, her eyes still watering. 'I just got a bit carried away with this stuff.' She took a much smaller sip. 'See? I'm quite all right. Now tell me about those books for Kit.'

He went to one of the bookcases that lined the wall opposite the garden windows, and she came to stand beside him. 'Gerald Durrell,' he said, running his finger along the shelves as he scanned, then stopping on some slender spines. 'Has he read these? They're marvellous, all about his childhood on Corfu with every kind of insect and animal imaginable. And what about Laurens Van der Post? He made me want to see Africa, follow in the tracks of the bushmen. Or Konrad Lorenz, the grandfather of animal behaviour?' *Stop it,* he told himself, pulling books from the shelves. *You're chattering like a bloody adolescent on a first date.* And to make it worse, he was probably imagining that her nearness was deliberate.

When Vic took the proffered books and retreated to the chair beside the fire, he excused himself. 'Idiot,' he said aloud as he stepped into the darkness of the hall, then he took a deep breath before going up to his study. When he returned he found her leafing idly through a book, but her gaze was focused on the fire, and he suspected she hadn't the least idea which volume she held.

'I found this the other day,' he said, sitting opposite her. 'There were still a few boxes from the Cambridge house in the loft. I thought you might like to have it.' She blinked and smiled a bit vaguely as she took the book from his hand, then her breath caught as she took in what it was.

She touched the cover. 'Oh, Nathan, it's lovely.' Opening it, she lifted the tissue paper flyleaf with care, then smiled as she looked down into Rupert Brooke's eyes. 'And what a wonderful photograph. I've never seen this one.' She went back to the cover, then looked at the back of the title page. 'It's a first printing of Edward Marsh's Memoirs of Rupert Brooke,' she said unnecessarily, as if Nathan didn't know perfectly well what it was. 'Nineteen-nineteen. Where ever did you get it?'

'It was Lydia's.'

She looked up. 'But ... are you sure you should ... are you sure you want to—'

'I can do whatever I please with Lydia's things, and I think it only fitting that you should have it.'

'Surely it must be valuable.'

'It doesn't matter.'

Vic laid the book in her lap and spread her long, slender fingers over the cover, and he took it as acquiescence. 'Nathan, there's something I've been wanting to ask you.' She paused and took another sip of her almost empty drink. 'Lately I've wondered if this biography was jinxed from the start. When I began, I'd never have imagined that two of the people who could help me the most were the two I'd feel the least comfortable asking. Does that make sense?' she added, tilting her head to one side and frowning. 'Anyway, you can imagine how difficult it is to talk to Darcy—' She rolled her eyes and Nathan laughed. 'He's insufferable enough without further instigation.'

'Are you saying you've found *me* difficult to

talk to?' asked Nathan, refusing to be diverted.

'It just seemed such an imposition. I was afraid it might upset you to talk about Lydia, and I didn't want to do anything that might damage our ... friendship. And the others—' Grimacing, she tossed back the last of her whisky. 'Of course her ex-husband, Morgan Ashby, refused to see me at all.' She coloured as if she found the memory unpleasant and hurried on. 'Daphne Morris was perfectly cordial and as bland as unbuttered toast. You'd have thought she barely knew Lydia, from the way she talked. And Adam Lamb—' Vic looked away from Nathan, into the fire. 'Adam Lamb wouldn't even talk to me on the telephone.'

'Vic, what is it exactly that you want me to do?'

She placed the book on the side table, then rose abruptly and stood before the fire, her back to him. 'I hate asking favours. That's all I seem to be doing lately, asking favours and apologizing to people. And now I sound churlish when you've been so kind.'

'Vic—' He got up from his armchair and stood beside her, so that she had to turn and face him. She held her arms crossed tightly across her chest.

'Would you talk to Adam Lamb for me?' she said in a rush. 'Ask him if he'd see me for just a few minutes?'

Nathan laughed. 'Good God, is that all? I thought you were going to ask me for something I couldn't do. Of course, I can't guarantee I'll have any influence with Adam—sometimes the

92

Lord moves him in mysterious ways—but I'll give it a try.'

Vic smiled and seemed to relax a little. 'And you don't mind talking about Lydia?'

'It's not that I *mind*, exactly, it's just that it was all so very long ago. You've been immersed in Lydia's life in a way I never was, and you must understand that it's much more immediate for you than it is for me. But you can ask me anything you want, and I'll try.' He resisted the impulse to touch her cheek. Surely he had said nothing to deserve the intentness of her expression?

'Nathan.' Vic took a breath and dropped her arms to her sides. 'Take me to bed.'

'What?'

'You heard me. This has nothing to do with Lydia, or Ian, or anything in the past. It's just between us. Do you not want to?'

So she had drunk the whisky for the Dutch courage to seduce him, and all the while he'd been bumbling around like an idiot, trying not to presume too much. 'Of course I want to. But I didn't think ... and I'm old enough—'

'Don't you dare tell me you're old enough to be my father. That's absurd, unless you were a very precocious adolescent, and anyway what would it matter?'

'But it's been—' he found his tongue hung on the words *since Jean died.* He swallowed and substituted, 'such a long time—' but Vic was laughing now and he couldn't go on.

'It's just like riding a bloody bike, Nathan, for heaven's sake,' she managed to sputter. 'You

93

won't have forgotten how.'

Her laughter died as suddenly as it had begun. He reached out and touched her cheek, and when she turned her face into his hand he felt her trembling.

'No,' he said, tracing the curve of her jaw with his fingers, then the corner of her mouth. 'I think it will all come back to me very, very quickly.'

Chapter Five

Is it the hour? We leave this resting place
Made fair by one another for a while.
Now, for a god-speed, one last mad embrace;
The long road then, unfit by your faint
smile.
Ah! The long road! and you so far away!
Oh, I'll remember! but ... each crawling day
Will pale a little your scarlet lips, each
mile
Dull the dear pain of your remembered face.

Rupert Brooke, from
The Wayfarers

Morgan Ashby pulled his battered Volvo into the drive of the house on Grange Road. There was just enough light left for him to see that the hedges needed trimming, yet the lamps in the houses next door and opposite had come on, defence against the evening. No light shone through the stained-glass transom above the door of Number Fifty-three.

The door of the Volvo creaked as he swung it open, and he felt an answering ache in his knees as he stood. *Rheumatism? The afflictions of age so soon in what he staunchly maintained was the prime of his life? Perhaps,* he thought, but he knew the truth. It was dread.

The bequest of this house had been Lydia's last malicious joke, perpetrated from beyond the grave, and he had cooperated, God rot both their souls. Taking the key from his pocket, he fumbled at the front door's lock in the dusk of the porch. He should have sold the house. He'd known then that he should sell it as soon as the ink on the probate papers dried. Francesca had pleaded with him to sell it, to sever the last link, and yet some perversity in him had made him hold on. Had he thought some positive thing would come of the nagging discomfort, some pearl of good character form under his hide? He snorted derisively in the darkness and the tumblers clicked over.

In the end he'd leased it to a doctor and his wife, and their tribe of screaming children. They had stayed for five years, troubling him little but for the occasional request for a plumber or repairs to the roof, and had just last week decamped on the improvement in their financial fortunes.

He felt for the switch inside the door, then blinked as light flooded the entry. Leaves had crept over the sill and littered the black-and-white tile floor, their twisted brown shapes looking for a moment like small dead birds.

The rose-patterned wallpaper that lined the entry and climbed up the stairs looked even more dilapidated than he remembered. The seams curled, and in a few places near the ceiling it had come away entirely—Lydia would probably have said the drooping swags looked like stained petticoats, he thought with a grimace. At thigh level the children had scrawled across it with crayons.

It would mean keeping the tenants' bloody deposit back, he supposed, but he was not sure he could be bothered. Moving towards the back of the house, Morgan steeled himself to assess the rest of the damage. First the sitting room, cold and empty, the carpet threadbare and spotted, the cushion on the window seat ripped with the stuffing spilling out. Lydia had liked to read here on fine mornings when the sun flooded through the bay window, warming the room. He remembered her choosing this wallpaper, with its intricate pattern in rose and green and dull gold. It had been years before the resurgence in popularity of William Morris, but Lydia had been determined to find something with the feel of the Arts and Crafts movement.

They'd had a furious row over it, because even her innocent decorating enthusiasms had reeked to him of her involvement with her pretentious literary friends, and he had despised them.

He moved on, down the hall, bypassing the door to Lydia's study. Whatever havoc the little

96

monsters had wreaked in there would have to go unremarked, because he could not bring himself to enter the room where Lydia died.

The kitchen was best, he thought as he opened the door at the end of the hall. First the little reception area with the space for the telephone, and the bookshelves for the cookery books. Then round the corner into the kitchen proper, and beyond that the dining area with its vaulted ceiling and windows overlooking the garden. This they had planned and built together, using part of his small inheritance, and it had been clean and untainted. His reflection stared back at him from the black mirror of the uncurtained garden window—a tall, thin shape, shoulders hunched, dark curling hair, a white blur of a face. He framed the shot in his mind, blinked.

They had shared thinking in images, he and Lydia. He had understood her need to write poetry, for he had gone about photography with the same dedication. It was the other things he hadn't understood; her need for drama and atmosphere, her desire to exist within a group, her obsession with the past.

He looked upwards, towards the first-floor bedroom. For a long while they had patched over their arguments with love-making so fierce it left them sobbing and exhausted. Destructive, yes, but he had never since known anything so intense, or so addictive. In his blackest moments he wished he had killed her then, and himself, put them both out of their misery.

The sound of a door closing came from

the front of the house. Morgan stopped his prowling about the empty room to listen. Some neighbour come to investigate lights in a vacant house, perhaps? God forbid he should have to be sociable, especially here, and now.

'Morgan, darling?'

Oh, Lord, it was Francesca. The last thing he'd meant to do was upset her. How in hell had she found him?

'In here,' he called out, and hurried to meet her in the more neutral territory of the hall. She stood beside the cold radiator at the bottom of the stairs, huddled in the old brown coat she kept for taking out the dogs.

He grasped her shoulders and looked down into her anxious face. 'Fran, what are you doing here?'

'I came into town with Monica to get some knitting wool. I ran out of the indigo. And then when we drove by I saw the car.'

'The wool shop is nowhere near Grange Road,' he said gently. 'Nor do you go to town in that old rag of a coat.' He put a finger under her chin and tilted her face up so that she had to look into his eyes. 'How did you know?'

'I knew you'd have to come. And I knew you wouldn't tell me.'

'Only because I didn't want to worry you.'

Francesca reached up and pushed a stray lock of hair from his brow. 'When will you ever get it through your thick head that the not knowing, the not talking about it only makes it worse? You've been moping about the house for days, working yourself up to this. I could feel it.'

'You'd think I'd have learned, by this time, that I can't keep anything from you,' he said, forcing himself to smile. 'But the house had to be attended to, and I didn't see why you should be upset by it.'

'Then let it go this time, Morgan. Let her go. You've been picking at this scab for more than twenty years and it will never heal unless you stop. Call an estate agent tomorrow and you need never set foot in this place again. We have a good life together. Let us get on with it. Please.'

Morgan gathered his wife into his arms, her cheek pressed against his chest. He stroked the top of her head, then the thick plait of brown hair, now finely threaded with grey. Francesca had rescued him from the disaster of his first marriage, and he had loved her because she was everything Lydia was not. She had less pretension about her than anyone he had ever met, and though intelligent, she lacked any intellectual conceit. Steadfast, she had supported him in his battle with depression, buffered others from his moods and his temper, and she'd borne with grace and courage their failure to conceive the children she had wanted so badly.

They *had* made a good life. Francesca's reputation as a textile artist had grown over the years, as had his as a photographer, and together they'd turned their renovated farmhouse studio in the countryside west of Cambridge into an artistic retreat. What more, he asked himself, could any man want?

And how could he possibly tell Francesca that he could not let Lydia go?

Afternoon tea at last, Daphne Morris thought with a sigh of relief as she heard the knock at her office door. She looked up from the history essays she'd been marking and called, 'Come in,' as she pulled off her glasses and massaged the bridge of her nose.

'Sorry it's a bit late,' Jeanette said as she manoeuvred the tea tray through the heavy door. 'What with one thing and another.'

Daphne smiled beneath her tented fingers. Jeanette was always 'a bit' late, what with one thing or another. But she was so invaluable to the running of the school that Daphne had learned to adapt. After all, what did a few minutes matter?

'It's that Muriel again,' Jeanette informed her as she set the tray on the desk and poured tea into Daphne's favourite mug. 'She's been bothering Cook, telling her the girls have all decided to eat "lower down the food chain", or some such nonsense, and so apparently they've decided to boycott beef. Can you imagine?' She sank into the chair on the other side of Daphne's desk and sighed. 'I had to chase her out of the kitchen, then it took me a good half hour just to smooth Cook's feathers.'

'I'm afraid I can imagine all too well.' Daphne rolled her eyes in exasperation. 'Are you not having yours?' she added, nodding at the teapot as she sat back with her mug and nibbled on a Rich Tea biscuit.

'Had my tea with Cook. Seemed the best way to mend the bridges.'

Daphne smiled and made a mental note to add that to her collection of Jeanette's mixed metaphors. 'You'd better send Muriel on to me and I'll sort her out,' she said without relish. 'I'm sure this was all her idea, but still I suppose I'd better speak to the Assembly about it. I wouldn't mind if I thought this business was motivated by any genuine concern for the environment, but I smell the unpleasant odour of lemming-like political correctness.'

'I heard her instructing some of the more feeble-minded girls, in a huddle under the staircase. Jarvis, and the new girl, what's-her-name with the horn-rimmed spectacles and beetle brows.'

Daphne laughed. 'Oh, Jeanette, you're too awful. You know perfectly well her name is Quinta. You're just being stubborn because you think it's affected. And anyway, it's not the poor girl's fault her parents gave her a dreadful name, and she's really not that bad, just easily influenced.' The thought sobered Daphne, and brought her back to the matter under discussion. 'The girls can certainly leave meat off their plates if they are so inclined, but I won't have Muriel browbeating them into submission.'

Thank heavens this was Muriel Baines's last year at St Winifred's, for the Head Girl had sorely tried Daphne's policy of impartiality. Some of the teachers whose heads had been turned by Muriel's flattery had coaxed Daphne

101

into appointing her Head Girl, against her better judgement. She had never liked Muriel, with her bossy manner and jutting bosom, and closer acquaintance had done nothing to improve her opinion.

As difficult as it was not to show her dislike of Muriel and a few other girls, it was more difficult to disguise her affection for those she did like. But that, Daphne had learned early on, was something a good headmistress must never do. Girls were too vulnerable to crushes, and the slightest remark could be misinterpreted under the influence of adolescent longing, the simplest gesture mistaken for a declaration.

'Well, I'd best be getting back to the fray,' said Jeanette, pushing herself to the edge of the chair. 'Rested my pins for long enough.'

Startled out of her reverie, Daphne said, 'Oh, Jeanette, I'm sorry. Was I daydreaming? It's been that sort of day, I'm afraid.'

'Never mind. It gave me a space to collect myself.' Jeanette smiled, and Daphne thought, as she often did, what a good, kind face her assistant had. She might never by any stretch of the imagination be called beautiful, with her pockmarked skin and the limp, fair hair which she wore chopped off at the chin and pulled back from her face with a hair slide, but when she smiled she looked beatific.

Jeanette was more than an assistant. In fact, in the years since Lydia's death she had become a friend—someone to confide in, if not to love in the way Daphne had loved Lydia.

Turning back from the door, Jeanette said,

'Don't forget I'm going to ferret out that Muriel and send her to you. You'd best be prepared.'

As she watched her go, Daphne noticed that the cardigan she wore over her navy polyester dress sagged in the back, and a sleeve had started to fray. Jeanette had a birthday coming up—perhaps she should buy her a new one. Of course, Jeanette might interpret the gesture as criticism, and Daphne would never wish to hurt her feelings. Maybe she should just leave it alone.

Rising, Daphne went to the window. Her office was on the second floor, overlooking the circular drive and the parkland running down to the road. Even in the early evening dimness she could still see the splash of the daffodils in the grass under the spreading trees. They had been late this spring, hesitant to show their faces after a particularly harsh winter.

For a moment she allowed herself the indulgence of imagining that nothing had changed, that she could spend this April evening as she had spent so many others. She would slip away after dinner in Hall and take out the little Volkswagen she kept parked behind the outbuildings. Down the drive, and within a few minutes she would be turning into Grange Road. Then a precious hour or two with Lydia, curled up on the sofa in the study, drinking sherry, listening to music, talking about their respective days.

She would tell Lydia the latest Muriel anecdote—Lydia would laugh and they would spend a delicious few minutes inventing mythical

103

punishments for the poor girl. Daphne smiled at the thought of Muriel chained to a windy crag, awaiting the arrival of a fire-breathing dragon. A lot of good her busty bossiness would do her then.

Lydia would read Daphne the poem she'd been working on that day and they would discuss it, tweaking it here and there until Lydia pronounced herself satisfied. Although Daphne's field was history, she had a good ear, and Lydia often said that the mere act of reading a poem aloud let her see what it needed.

Their companionship had been easy, un-demanding, yet more satisfying than any Daphne had ever known.

She turned away from the window and straightened her skirt. Enough was enough. Too much nostalgia quickly became a maudlin wallow, and she had business to attend to. A small framed mirror on her bookcase allowed her to pat her hair into place and adjust the collar of the white silk blouse she wore with her suit. She supposed she had better put on the tailored navy coat, the better to intimidate Baines.

How could she possibly have imagined, in those long ago Cambridge days when they had defied anything and everything just for the sake of it, that she would become the very thing railed against?

Frowning, Kincaid sidestepped the group of giggling teenagers who had nearly cannoned into him. Hampstead High Street seemed exceptionally busy for a Thursday evening, and as he walked downhill from the Underground station, he negotiated the crowded pavement with less than his usual good humour.

He'd stalled at the office, finishing paperwork that could have been put off till tomorrow, hoping for a word with Gemma, only to discover she'd left for the day without telling him.

Now, as he made his way home in the twilight, he felt both exasperated and unsettled. Accustomed as he was to making professional decisions with ease, he found himself at a loss when it came to dealing with the polite distance Gemma had put between them. Was she waiting for an apology? he wondered as he turned into Carlingford Road. But why should he apologize, when he'd done nothing deserving of censure?

Entering his building, he climbed the stairs without bothering to switch on the lights, relying on the faint illumination from the window in the upstairs landing. In the dim silence of the stairwell he heard the pounding of his heart, and the small voice asking him if he were sure Gemma had no cause to be upset. What did he feel about Vic, seeing her again after all these years?

The question hung unanswered as he let himself into his flat. At the sound of the door opening, Sid looked up from his position on the sofa, stretched, blinked, and promptly went back to sleep.

'So you're not thrilled to see me, either,' Kincaid said, giving the inert cat a scratch

105

behind the ears. He went on through the sitting room and out the French doors to the balcony. The garden lay in deep evening shadow, and the kitchen lights came on in the house opposite as he watched. He felt isolated, and suddenly the prospect of an evening alone in the flat with only the cat for company seemed very uninviting.

He remembered when he'd welcomed such evenings as a much-needed buffer from the demands of work, had even resented all but the occasional social obligation. But it seemed he had changed without realizing it. He missed Gemma, damn it, and to his surprise he found he missed Toby and the usual confusion of their evening routine.

A shadowy movement in the garden below caught his eye, and the shape coalesced into his downstairs neighbour, Major Keith, rising from a kneeling position. Although he and the major had become friends upon the death of their neighbour, Jasmine Dent, and the major often looked after Sid for him, Kincaid had seen little of him in the past few months. 'Major! Come up for a drink,' he called on impulse. That omission, at least, was something he could rectify.

The major waved at him in acknowledgement, and a few minutes later appeared at Kincaid's door, looking freshly scrubbed and brushed. A short, stocky man, his skin had never lost the tropical sunburn acquired during his years in India, and his thinning, iron-grey hair still bristled with military correctness. Kincaid had found, however, that the man's gruff and

106

reticent manner concealed a kind heart and a keen perception, and he had come to both like and trust him.

When the major had settled into Kincaid's armchair with a generous whisky, he cleared his throat and drew his brows together. 'So, Mr Kincaid, I haven't seen your young lady about much recently.'

It was as close to a direct question as Kincaid had ever heard the major ask, and deserved an honest answer. 'Um, she's a bit put out with me, actually. My ex-wife rang me up out of the blue, asking a favour, and the whole business seems to have made Gemma cross.'

'Did you grant the favour, then?' asked the major.

'As much as I could, yes. It was a professional matter, and I haven't quite wrapped it up.'

The major looked at him thoughtfully, and after a moment said, 'Could it be that you're not eager to wrap things up, as it were?'

Kincaid looked away from the major's direct gaze. Was he delaying things unnecessarily? In the beginning he'd been motivated only by curiosity and courtesy, but now a simple phone call telling Vic what he'd learned would have discharged his obligation—had he really needed to arrange to see her again?

He had to admit he was intrigued by the contrast between the woman he'd known and the woman she'd become, and yet at the same time he was drawn by the familiarity of her. 'I don't know,' he said finally.

The major appeared to give this inadequate

answer due consideration while he sipped his drink, then said slowly, 'Tempting as it may be, I've found it unwise to try to recapture the past.'

21 April 1962
Newnham

Dearest Mummy,
I'm a bit late with my letter this week, but I'll write until I can't keep my eyes open a moment longer.

The day began grey and drippy, a good day for working, so I settled in early at my desk, surrounded by an enormous pile of books, and started the outline for my paper on the English Moralists. This is my opportunity to synthesize all the reading I've done the last two terms, as well as to express my own opinions, and I must say I feel enthusiastic about it, daunting as it is.

By noon the wind had scoured the sky of clouds and I was bursting to get outside and stretch and breathe in the glorious day, so I knocked up Daphne and told her to get dressed for a walk. Poor girl, she was still yawning and knuckling her eyes in her nightdress after an all night swot, and with that mass of auburn hair and oval face she looked a bit like the risen Venus. But she's a good sport and soon had herself tidied up and kitted out, so off we went.

It was a cold, clean day, and our feet seemed to take the way to Grantchester without volition.

We swung briskly along on the river path with the north wind pushing at our backs, and before we knew it we'd reached the meadows. There is a certain spot that I love, perhaps a bit more than halfway, and I always feel I deserve to stop and rest for a minute and survey my domain. To the north the spires of Cambridge float, disembodied, above the plain. Revolve, and to the south lie Grantchester's huddle of rooftops, and above them spires of wood smoke rising to dissipate in the flat blue bowl of the Cambridgeshire sky.

The sky here is like nowhere else I've ever seen, so wide and limitless, and yet I have the oddest feeling of belonging, of having been here before. Daphne has been studying Comparative Religion, and we've talked about different philosophies. I've found myself wondering lately if there isn't something to the idea of reincarnation—if that doesn't shock your good old C of E sensibilities, Mummy, darling—but it at least provides some explanation of what I feel. And this is not only a matter of space, but of time as well. I quite often feel displaced in the present.

Of course, Cambridge itself is bound to give one a sense of continuity, of timelessness, but I seem to have a particular affinity for the years before the Great War. When I read about Rupert Brooke and his friends, it's as if I can almost see them. I know what it felt like to be there, having tea in the garden at the Orchard, reading poetry aloud to one another before the fire in Rupert's study at the Old

Vicarage, swimming in the Mill Race.

We did just that, Daphne and—had tea at the Orchard, I mean—sitting in the lawn chairs under the apple trees with our faces turned up to the sun. We had pots of tea and huge slabs of cake to warm ourselves, then when the light began to fade we went inside and had more tea before the roaring fire.

Afterwards we went and peered through the fence at the Old Vicarage next door, watching the lights come on in the dusk. The place looks a bit rundown, and the garden overgrown, but I think Rupert Brooke preferred it that way.

As I watched, I imagined them moving on the dim paths of the garden, arm in arm, the women in long, white, high-collared dresses, the men in tennis whites or striped blazers. Their voices came faintly, fading in and out on the wind, but I thought I recognized their faces. Dudley Ward, and Justin Brooke, Ka Cox, the Darwins, James Strachey, Jacques Raverat, and is that little Noel Olivier, perhaps, on Rupert's arm, her dark head tilted up as she listens to him? They are talking of politics, socialism, art, and I dare say there's much silliness and teasing as well.

I feel a kinship with Rupert that goes beyond our common name. I share his passion for words and dedication to his craft—and I hope I have his discipline. How little things change. In 1907, Brooke and some of his friends at King's formed a society called the Carbonari just for the purpose of thinking and talking, a way of sorting out what they thought of the world. One night Brooke said, 'There are only three things in the world. One is to read poetry, another is to write poetry, and the best of all is to live poetry.' According to Edward Marsh (from whose biography I just quoted), Brooke said that at rare moments he had glimpses of what poetry really meant, how it solved all problems of conduct and settled all questions of values.

So inspired have I been by these words that I've given up all ideas of working for the paper, etc., in short of doing anything other than practising my craft. Putting it off until I could schedule big blocks of time for my own work was the worst sort of procrastination, like waiting to live until one's life is perfect—the day never comes. So I'm writing whenever I can, in between lectures and papers and required reading, and I find everything is fuel for my fires. You can't separate poetry from life—life insists on bleeding over, in all its myriad and messy ways.

I've finished a long poem I think is quite good, called 'Solstice,' and I'm enclosing a copy for you. Tell me what you think, Mummy, darling, and be honest (but gentle if you think it's awful). I've sent it off to some of the magazines as well, and wait for the inevitable rejections.

Daphne and I plunged home in the almost-dark, arm in arm, heads down against the buffet of the wind. Then hot baths to thaw us, and late suppers in our respective rooms, as we'd missed dinner in Hall. But well worth it, such a lovely day, to be taken out and remembered when the crush of study seems too overwhelming.

We'll anticipate summer evenings and picnics on the river. Nathan's family actually live in Grantchester, did I tell you that? He's promised to invite us home for a weekend when the weather is fine, and perhaps we'll even try a midnight swim in Byron's Pool, just downstream from Grantchester, past the Mill. Rupert Brooke is reported to have convinced Virginia Woolf to swim naked there one summer night.

Much love to you, and Nan,
from your sleepy—Lydia

He *had* said half-past six, Vic thought as she glanced at her watch and gave another frustrated push on the bell. She'd written the time down carefully in her calendar, and the place, although she knew the grey stone church in Trinity Street well. In fact, when Adam Lamb had first refused to see her, she'd thought of coming here to a Sunday service just so that she could see him from a distance.

Would Nathan be pleased that his intervention had saved her from a spot of spying? she wondered, smiling. It was tempting to think of Nathan, even standing in the chill of the vicarage porch, but much too distracting. Instead she made an effort to prepare herself by picturing Adam Lamb as he'd looked in one of Lydia's old photographs, a thin-faced boy with tight, dark curls, unsmiling—and now, a hostile man who had agreed to her presence only at the request of an old friend.

112

Vic licked her lips and rang the bell once more.

The door opened when she'd half turned away. She hadn't heard footsteps, or the lock turning, and she took a sharp surprised breath.

'Hello, I'm—'

'So sorry, so sorry,' said Adam Lamb breathlessly. 'A distraught parishioner on the telephone. It's always something, isn't it? And one can never get off when one needs to, not until they're satisfied they've told you every detail three times over. Let me take your coat,' he added, and smiled at her.

The vicarage hall was even colder than the porch, and Vic shivered as she felt a current of frigid air against her bare calves. She'd worn a very tailored Laura Ashley suit in navy, a long double-breasted jacket over a short pleated skirt, in hopes both that she looked reassuringly business-like and that Adam Lamb appreciated legs. Now it seemed that neither option was to do her much good. 'No, thank you,' she said regretfully. 'I think I'd better keep it.'

'Quite wise of you. If you think this old place is draughty now, you should feel it in midwinter. But I've got the gas fire lit in the sitting room, and I thought we could have some sherry, or Madeira if you prefer.'

'Sherry would be lovely,' Vic said as she hurried after his retreating back, trying to collect herself. He was taller than the photographs had shown, and still thin. The dark curling hair had gone mostly grey but was still abundant. The thin face was heavily lined, as if he'd not lived

113

an easy life, and he wore a heavy grey cardigan over his clerical garb. All this she could fit over the image in her mind as one would lay a transparency over a diagram—even the gold-rimmed thick spectacles which gave his blue eyes an owlish look—but nothing had prepared her for the grave sweetness of his smile.

She registered faded lino beneath her feet and dark mustard colour on the walls, then he opened a door at the end of the passage and ushered her through. It was warm, amazingly enough, and she sat gratefully in the armchair he indicated.

'If you'll just excuse me for a moment,' he said, 'I forgot to turn the answer phone on, and I'd better do it else we'll be interrupted.'

His absence gave Vic a chance to examine the room, and she saw that this was where he had made his mark on the shabby anonymity of the vicarage. A colourful rag rug covered most of the fitted mustard and brown patterned carpet, and deep red velvet curtains covered windows which she thought must overlook the narrow lane beside the church. A fine set of cut-crystal glasses stood on the low table before her chair, and the jewel-like reds, greens and blues winked at her in the light of the gas fire.

Books lined every available bit of wall space, and that, at least, didn't surprise her.

She had just slipped out of her coat and stretched her feet towards the fire when Adam Lamb returned. He poured her a sherry from the crystal decanter, and when she sipped it

114

she found it fine and very dry, just the way she liked it.

He folded his long body onto the red Victorian love seat opposite her, and raised his glass. 'Here's to warmth,' he said with feeling. 'I spent five years out in Africa, and I don't think my blood ever regained its good British fortitude. Sometimes I dream of the sun, and of nights under the mosquito netting. But you don't want to hear about that.' He gave his disarming smile again and sipped from his glass. 'You came to talk about Lydia.'

'You've been very kind,' Vic said hesitantly, 'and I don't mean to seem rude, but I had the impression when I rang you before that you didn't want to talk about Lydia.'

'It wasn't that I didn't want to talk about Lydia,' Adam explained. 'But, you see, I didn't know you.'

'Me?'

Adam sat forward, hands on his knees, his expression earnest. 'I didn't know if you were *sympathetic* to Lydia. You might even have been—if you'll excuse the expression—a muckraker. And I couldn't participate in a book that focused on the more scandalous personal episodes in Lydia's life rather than her work. *The poet as neurotic,* you know the sort of thing.'

'You talked to Darcy, didn't you.' It came out as a statement rather than a question. 'To check me out.'

'You said you were on the English Faculty when you wrote.' Adam seemed suddenly much preoccupied with examining his fingernails. 'So

115

he seemed the obvious person to ask for a reference. I didn't know you knew Nathan. Personally, I mean, rather than merely as Lydia's executor.'

'And Darcy told you that I wasn't academically sound, didn't he? That I intended writing some hysterical feminist tract.' Vic could feel the hot patches of colour burning in her cheeks. She told herself she wouldn't undo Darcy's damage by getting angry at Adam, and took a calming breath.

'He didn't actually *say* that ...' There was an amused twist to Adam's long mouth, and much to her surprise, Vic found herself smiling.

'He merely implied it.'

'Something like that.' Adam had the grace to look sheepish. 'I think I owe you an apology, Doctor McClellan. I've lived in Cambridge long enough to know what intra-departmental rivalries are like, and I should have taken it for just that.'

It was best to let it pass, she thought, and give Darcy a piece of her mind at the first opportunity. 'You can start by calling me Vic,' she said. 'My friends do.'

'And Adam,' he responded. 'Call me Adam. My motley flock calls me Father Adam, but there's no need for you to do so.'

Now that they were so cosily established on a first-name basis, Vic thought she'd better make sure they had no further misunderstandings. 'Look ... Adam,' she said, and found that the use of his name made solid the link in her mind between the boy in Lydia's letters and the man

116

sitting across from her. 'I think it's important I make my position clear to you. I don't intend to focus on the emotional difficulties in Lydia's life, but I can't gloss over them, either. There's not much point in my writing this book if I don't attempt to portray Lydia as a whole person. Either you take Darcy's deconstructionist view and hold that no artist's life is relevant to his work because no one's life is relevant, period, but is merely a feeble construction by the ego to camouflage our inadequacies.'

Vic took a sip of sherry to wet her lips and continued, 'Or you decide that art, or in this case poetry, springs from life and experience and is only truly meaningful in that context. It's not that I don't appreciate the power of language—that's what draws us to poetry in the first place—but I believe that if you see it only as an exercise in style and imagery, you create a moral vacuum.' She found she'd sat so far forward that she was in danger of sliding off her chair, and that she'd clenched her fingers around the stem of her sherry glass. Setting the glass carefully on the butler's table, she sat back and said, 'I'm sorry. That's my soapbox, I'm afraid, and I do tend to get a bit carried away.'

'That's quite all right.' Adam reached out and refilled her glass without asking. 'For a moment I thought I was at college again. We used to have the most marvellous talks. Sometimes we'd walk all night in the courts and along the river, and we debated things with such passion. We thought that we were revolutionaries, that

117

we would change the world.' He said this without cynicism or bitterness, and just for an instant Vic saw him as he must have been, an innocent beneath the sophisticated trappings of a university undergraduate. Was that what had drawn Lydia to him?

'You came from a village, too, didn't you? Like Lydia.'

Adam smiled. 'Only mine was in Hampshire, and had no literary distinction. I remember Lydia telling me the night I met her that she came from a place quite near Virginia and Leonard Woolf's house. She was quite fascinated by Virginia Woolf.'

'Do you suppose that was the beginning of her interest in Rupert Brooke?'

'It could have sparked it, certainly. She'd read everything she could get her hands on about Bloomsbury, and would have come across a multitude of references to him, even though he was never officially a member of that group.'

A gust of wind rattled the casements behind the red velvet curtains and Vic took another warming sip of sherry. 'Bloomsbury, the Neo-Pagans ... Why do you suppose Lydia was so drawn to the idea of an intellectually compatible group?'

Adam shifted and recrossed his long legs, and Vic saw that his black lace-up shoes were scuffed and worn down at the heel. 'Her background provides the obvious explanation. A fatherless only child growing up in a small village ... If she had any real friends, she never spoke of them, so I suppose from the time she learned to read

118

she longed for that sort of companionship.'

'And her mother? Was Lydia really as dutiful a daughter as she sounds in her letters?'

'They had an odd relationship—' Adam held up a hand as if to stop an expected response. 'And I don't mean in the sense that it was unhealthy, although nowadays any parent-child relationship seems to be suspect. They were more like sisters, or friends, and if Lydia felt she'd been pressured to live out her mother's dreams, she never showed any obvious resentment.'

'She was a schoolteacher, wasn't she?' Vic prompted, although she knew all the recorded details of Mary Brooke's life.

'A very bright girl, apparently, who'd earned a place at Oxford before the War,' said Adam. 'But she didn't take it up. She stayed at home and married her childhood sweetheart, afraid he wouldn't come back from France—'

'And he didn't,' Vic finished for him, and sighed. 'I wonder if she ever regretted her choice.'

'She'd not have had Lydia,' Adam said reasonably, as if that alternative were unthinkable. 'What else would you like to know?' He cast a surreptitious glance at his watch, and Vic suspected he had another appointment but was too tactful to say so.

'The impossible.' Smiling at Adam's startled expression, Vic said softly, 'You see, I want to know what she was like. I want to see her through your eyes, hear her through your ears ...'

Adam looked past her, and after a moment he

119

said, 'That was the first thing one noticed about her—her voice. She was small and quick, with a dancer's litheness and that wonderful dark, wavy hair cut in a twenties bob—but when she spoke you forgot everything else.' He smiled at an image Vic couldn't see. 'She sounded as though she'd sung in every smokey bar from Casablanca to Soho. It made her seem exotic, and yet beneath the huskiness you could hear the Sussex village.'

'Still endearingly English?'

Adam laughed. 'Exactly. But that's not what you want to know, is it? How she looked, I mean.' Pausing, he refilled his glass and took a small sip. 'How can I possibly condense Lydia?'

'Pick an adjective,' suggested Vic. 'Just off the top of your head, without thinking about it.'

'Parlour games?' Adam sounded dubious.

'You think that doesn't sound suitably academic? Think of it as a poet's game,' Vic challenged him. 'After all, you were a poet, too.'

Adam made a rueful grimace. 'But not a very good one, I'm afraid. All right, I'll give it a try.' He frowned and thought for a moment. 'Intense. Moody, funny, bright, but most of all, intense. Intense about loves and hates—and especially intense about work.'

Nodding, Vic gathered her courage to venture into painful territory. 'You kept up with one another, didn't you, after her separation from Morgan? I know,' she added carefully, 'that it was you who found her, and saved her, that

120

first time. What I don't know is whether you had any idea what she meant to do.'

'She certainly didn't threaten suicide, if that's what you mean. Didn't even hint at it. But ...'

Vic felt her heartbeat quicken. 'But her behaviour wasn't normal, was it? How was she different?'

'Calm.' said Adam. 'Much too calm, in a dazed sort of way, but I didn't realize then. She'd forget what she was saying in the midst of a sentence, and then she'd smile.' He shook his head. 'I should have known—'

'How could you?' Vic protested. 'Unless you'd had some experience dealing with depression.'

Adam shook his head. 'Oh, I see it so often now that I recognize the earliest symptoms. But common sense should have been enough, even then.' His hands moved restlessly over his knees. 'If I had been thinking of Lydia, rather than myself ...'

'What do you mean?' Vic asked, puzzled.

'I had another agenda, you see,' he said, not meeting Vic's eyes.

'I don't understand.'

'It all sounds ludicrous ... too ridiculous. But what harm can it do now, other than make me look as big a fool as I did then?' He pinched his lips together in a self-deprecating grimace. 'I was *glad* when Morgan left her. I thought she would get over him soon enough, and then perhaps we could go back to the way things were in the beginning.'

'In the beginning? You and Lydia?' Vic heard

the surprise in her voice and silently cursed herself. She couldn't afford to alienate him now. 'Of course,' she added quickly, 'what could have been more natural? And when she didn't seem to be terribly unhappy, you thought ...'

'Well, it was all a long time ago, and hopefully I've grown less foolish in my dotage.' He set his empty sherry glass down on the butler's table in a deliberate way that suggested he'd had enough of talking as well.

He was the same age as Nathan, Vic thought, and yet she had the sudden impression that he felt life had defeated him.

'Adam,' she said, before he could politely terminate their interview, 'what about the second time Lydia tried to kill herself? Did she have the same symptoms of depression, or disassociation? Surely there must have been some indication—'

'I wouldn't know,' he interrupted her. Then, as if afraid he'd been too sharp, added, 'I was gone by that time. Kenya. Teaching in a mission school.' Standing up, he went to the bookcase behind the love seat and took something from the shelf. 'One of my students made this for me,' he held out a small pottery vase for her inspection. It was clear-glazed, the colour of sunburnt skin, and black-etched antelope ran endlessly around its circumference.

'It's lovely.' Taking it from him, Vic closed her eyes and ran her fingers over the surface as if she were reading braille. 'It reminds me of a poem of Lydia's, the one called Grass. I always wondered where the images came from. Did you write to her?'

Adam shrugged. 'Occasionally. The evenings could be very long. I suppose she didn't save the letters?'

'If she did, I've not seen them among her papers,' Vic said, not sure whether that would please or hurt him, but she felt a spark of hope on her own behalf. 'Did she write to you, by any chance?'

'Yes, but we had a fire in the mission not long before I came back to England. I lost most of my personal belongings, such as they were, and Lydia's letters were among them. I'm sorry,' he added, and Vic knew her disappointment must have shown.

'Never mind,' she said, forcing a smile. 'I'm sure it was a much greater loss for you than it is for me. But I wonder ...' She hesitated to push him, but on the other hand she'd best make the most of her opportunity. 'Do you remember anything odd about her letters before—'

'She ran her car into a tree?' For the first time, Adam sounded angry. 'What a bloody stupid thing to do. I heard afterwards that she said she just lost control, but I never believed it for a minute. She was a good driver, very focused, as she was on most things she undertook to do well.'

'But the letters—'

'I wasn't privy to anything but the most innocuous gossip,' Adam said, and stood up abruptly. 'If you want to know about her state of mind, you had better ask Daphne.'

Chapter Six

In the silence of death; then may I see dimly,
*   and know, a space,*
Bending over me, last light in the dark, once,
*   as of old, your face.*

Rupert Brooke from,
Choriambics—I

20 June 1962
Newnham

Darling Mummy,
There's so much to tell you that I don't know
where to begin. I haven't been to bed since night
before last, but I'm still too wound up for sleep
and so thought I'd try to describe May Week to
you before the lovely details fade.

As soon as I finished my exams (in a haze of
exhaustion) the parties began, and a good thing,
too, otherwise I think I would have felt quite
ill while waiting for the results to be posted.
It's all a bit hysterical, as everyone is feeling
the same sort of relief and trepidation, and
most are muddle-headed as well from end-of-
term all-night swotting. Daphne and I trooped
bravely from college to college and staircase to
staircase, determined not to miss out on a single
invitation. Some of the do's were quite elegant,
while others were last-minute affairs dependent

upon potato crisps and bottled beer, and often those were the jolliest.

Even the posh parties were very relaxed and informal, with lots of drinking and talking and dancing and people wandering about. If anything marred our fun, it's that I seem to have acquired a persistent suitor, through no fault of my own. He's a dark, brooding, Welsh boy named Morgan Ashby, an arts student who has a knack for turning up wherever I make an appearance. He then looks soulfully at me from across the room, which is quite off-putting. Finally he mustered the courage to ask me to his May Ball, but I have no desire to play Cathy to his Heathcliff, and refused. Besides, I'd accepted Adam's invitation months ago and wouldn't have stood up dear, sweet Adam for the world.

We made a foursome, Adam and I, Nathan and Daphne, and the heavens conspired to make it perfect for us—the end of our first year at Cambridge, and our first May Ball. Moon full, stars shining, an almost tropical night (truly a gift of the gods, it was so warm we could wear our gowns outside the marquee without wraps). In the garden they'd strung fairy lights in the trees, making it look quite enchanted, and we danced on the lawn. Daphne and I both wore gossamer white, and pretended we were naiads (or is it dryads?) floating diaphanously about.

We can now count ourselves among the Survivors. We stayed up through the wee hours, and at dawn we punted to Grantchester for breakfast, a bit bedraggled but still game. There we met up with Adam's friend Darcy Eliot and his date, an insipid blonde girl from Girton who hadn't a sensible word to say about anything. It was too bad, really, because I think Darcy is destined to be one of us. Not only is he smashingly good-looking and charming and a promising poet, but his mother is Margery Lester, the novelist. Talk about icing on the cake! You know how much I love her books—you're the one who introduced me to them. I daren't allow myself to hope that I might meet her one day, and if I did I'm sure I wouldn't be able to think of a thing to say.

Picture me, curled up in my window niche in my nightdress, scribbling away to you. The morning light has gone all soft and shadowless, and if I close my eyes I think I can smell the faintest hint of rain through the open window. My ball gown lies discarded across the chair, a bit tawdry, perhaps, in daylight, and for a moment I feel bereft, Cinderella the morning after. This time won't come again, and I wonder if I can bear to let it go.

Needs must, though, as Nan would say, and my eyelids feel heavy as the best parlour curtains, thick and velvety, with the scratch of old dust. One more thing to tell you, though, the best last. When we finally straggled back to Cambridge, my exam results had been posted on the boards outside the Senate House. It was a good thing I had Adam to hold me up. My knees went all jelly and I had to close my eyes while he read them to me, because I couldn't bear to look myself. But it was all right. I did

126

better than I expected, in fact, I really did quite shockingly well.

But nicest of all, darling Mother, is that we'll have all the Long Vacation to be together. I'll have to study, of course, for they don't expect me to be idle, and it will take me another week or so here to organize all the books and things I'll need over the summer. Then the counties will click by outside the train windows, and you'll be waiting at the station with the old Morris. And maybe Nan will come, too, and you'll bring Shelley, who will pant and tail-wag in doggy anticipation, and then I will be home.

Lydia

Gemma regretted her decision more with every passing mile. After their disagreement last Sunday over his visit to his ex-wife (*You started a row*, she reminded herself), she and Duncan had spent the work-week avoiding one another. It wasn't that they made a habit of spending every minute together, but he usually came round to her flat several evenings during the week, and when circumstances permitted she went to his. By Friday, having found herself missing him dreadfully, she faced up to the fact that she was going to have to apologize.

She'd caught him in his office just as he was slipping into his jacket. 'Um, could we have a word?' she asked a bit hesitantly. 'I thought maybe we could go round the pub for a drink, that is if you're not too busy.'

Kincaid had stopped shuffling papers into

his briefcase. 'Business or personal?' he asked, looking up at her, still pleasantly neutral.

'Personal.'

He raised an eyebrow. 'Are you buying?'

She smiled. His teasing was a good sign that he wasn't still too miffed with her. 'You're tight as a miser's bum, but I suppose I can stand you a drink.'

'That's settled then,' he said, and ushered her out the door.

Without discussion they walked towards the pub on Wilfred Street, not too far from the Yard, where they'd gone for after-work drinks since they first became partners. A surprisingly bitter wind had sprung up during the course of the day, and by the time they reached the pub they felt grateful for the warmth of the closely packed room. Gemma watched for a table to open up while Kincaid braved the crush at the bar. 'I'll let you off the hook tonight,' he said over his shoulder as he disappeared into the haze of smoke. 'But next time, it's on you.'

They had a favourite table, in the corner near the gas fire, and Gemma thought it a good omen when the couple occupying it stood up just as Kincaid appeared bearing their drinks. She dived for it like a rugby forward, and beamed up at him when he reached her.

'Good job,' he said as he waited for her to wipe up the drink rings and crisp crumbs with a tissue she'd found in her handbag, then he set the drinks down and slid in beside her. He raised his glass to her. 'It's been a long week.'

He'd given her an opening, Gemma thought,

and she'd kick herself if she didn't take it. She took a sip of her shandy to wet her lips, and plunged ahead. 'I'm sorry about last Sunday. About what I said. I was way over the mark, and it was none of my business.' She'd been studying her beer mat intently—now she raised her eyes to his. 'It's just that ... I know it sounds stupid ... but the idea of your seeing her makes me feel ... uncomfortable.' She looked away again.

He was silent for a long moment, and she wondered just how big a fool she had made of herself. Then he said, 'I know. I should have realized from the first.' Startled, she looked up and started to speak, but he continued, 'But you haven't any need to feel uncomfortable. Or threatened.'

She made a small gesture, halfway between a shrug and a nod of assent, but didn't trust herself to speak.

Moving his glass a fraction of an inch on the beer mat, he added, 'I have to admit that it threw me a bit, seeing Vic again. We'd left a lot of things unfinished.'

'Did you ...' Gemma stopped and swallowed. 'I mean, have you resolved them?' she finished carefully.

'I've been thinking about it all week. And I've found, rather to my surprise, that I like her very much. But I'm not still in love with her.' He met her eyes. 'Vic said she knew, somehow, that I had someone waiting, and I said I thought I did.'

Gemma felt herself flush with shame at the thought of the reception she'd given him. 'And this thing she asked you to look into—what did your friend in Cambridge say about it?' she asked, hoping to change the subject.

'It wasn't his case, but he let me see the files.' Kincaid shrugged. 'And I think there are some very odd things about it, but I don't see what I can do.'

'Have you told her yet?' Gemma asked, not having reached the point where she felt comfortable saying Vic.

Shaking his head, he said, 'Thought I'd better do it in person. And I wanted to go over the notes I made from the files with her, in case she found any of it helpful. I've rung her and said I'd come again on Sunday.' He paused, looking at Gemma, then smiled his most winning smile. 'Would you go with me this time? I could use some moral support.'

She managed to nod *yes,* and before she could backtrack, he took her hand in his and said, 'Are you busy tonight? I've missed you.'

Gemma was suddenly very aware of the shape of his fingers covering hers, the day's end shadow along the line of his jaw, and his knee touching hers under the table. She cleared her throat. 'I told Hazel I might be a bit late tonight, end of the week and all ...'

He grinned. 'Clever girl. Come to the flat. We'll collect a take-away for dinner—unless you'd rather go out somewhere posh?' Her expression must have been answer enough, because he pulled her up, leaving their unfinished drinks on the table. 'Let's get out of here.'

And so they had made up very satisfactorily, and on Saturday they had spent the day together, taking Toby to Regent's Park Zoo.

Now it was inevitably Sunday and they were speeding down the motorway towards Cambridge. 'When are you going to buy a new car?' Gemma asked, grousing to cover her increasing nervousness. 'I swear these springs have poked holes in my bum.' She shifted in the passenger seat of Kincaid's Midget, trying to find a more comfortable position. 'And this window's starting to drip at the join again.' It was drizzling, just enough to coat the windscreen with the slimy muck thrown up by the other cars' tyres, but not enough to wash it clean.

She glanced over at him. 'I know what you're going to say, so don't bother. "It's a classic," ' she mimicked, rolling her eyes. 'Now an old Bentley is what I'd call a classic. Or a Roller. Something with style and lots of chrome. This is not a classic.'

'That'll give you and Vic something to talk about,' he said with a wicked smile, then he sighed and added, 'But I suppose you're right. It is getting a bit doddery. And it makes it difficult taking Toby anywhere.'

Gemma absorbed this unexpected remark in silence. She'd no idea such concerns had even occurred to him, and the thought implied an intended permanence to their relationship that both pleased and terrified her.

'That's true enough,' she finally replied, as

offhandedly as she could manage. 'For outings and things.'

'We could go to the seaside in the summer, the three of us. Toby would like that, don't you think?' He flicked on his indicator. 'Here's our turn-off.'

'Mmmm,' Gemma answered distractedly. If only she'd said no when he'd invited her to come with him today, she thought. Surely she could have come up with some brilliantly clever, spur of the moment excuse. A tactful and gracious refusal—a sick aunt in Gloucestershire would have done nicely. She unclasped her hands and swallowed against the tight feeling in her throat. The mild curiosity she'd felt about Vic, and even the barely admitted desire to do a bit of possessive crowing over Kincaid, seemed to have evaporated entirely and she wished herself anywhere else.

But a few short moments later Gemma glimpsed a straggle of cottages facing the road, then a few semi-detached villas, and she knew they were coming into Grantchester. Kincaid slowed, turned right into the High Street, then almost immediately left into the drive of a slate-roofed cottage washed in Suffolk pink. Even in the rain the colour looked warm and welcoming, and Gemma told herself that perhaps the woman who'd chosen a pink house might not be as bad as she'd imagined. In any case, there was nothing for it now but to carry on as if she met her lover's ex-wives every day.

She waved away Kincaid's offer of an umbrella. Opening and shutting it would be more trouble than it was worth in the soft drizzle, and she needn't worry about her clothes since she'd refused to dress up for the occasion. A natural wool jumper over a printed cotton skirt, lace-up boots, her hair pulled loosely back in a clip at the nape of her neck—all good enough for her usual weekends, and so would have to do for this. Gemma climbed out of the car bare-headed. She walked slowly to the porch, enjoying the feel of the cool moisture beading on her face and hair after the over-heated interior of the car. By the time he rang the bell she felt more collected, and readied her face for a polite smile.

Then the door flew back with a crash, and Gemma found herself staring down into the inquisitive blue eyes of a boy with a shock of straw-coloured hair flopping on his forehead and a faint dusting of freckles across his nose. He wore a faded rugby shirt several sizes too large, jeans, and the dirtiest white socks she'd ever seen. In his right hand he held a slice of bread spread with Marmite.

'Um, you must be Kit,' said Kincaid. 'I'm Duncan and this is Gemma. We're here to see your mum.'

'Oh, yeah. Hello.' The boy smiled, a toothy grin that won Gemma instantly, then took an enormous bite of his bread and said through it, 'You'd better come in.' He turned away and started down the hall without waiting to see if they followed.

They wiped their feet on the mat, then hurried to catch up with him as he disappeared round a turn in the passage. As they came up behind him, he shouted 'Mum!' at ear-splitting volume and entered a room on the right.

Gemma had a vague impression of a small room, crowded with books and papers, but her gaze was held by the woman who sat at the computer. The heels of her long, slender hands rested on the keyboard, but as Kit came in she swung round and turned a startled face to them.

'Duncan. I didn't hear the door. The bell's not working properly.'

'It just makes a little pinging sound, but *I* can hear it,' volunteered Kit as he propped himself on a small clear space at the end of his mother's desk.

'Anyway, it doesn't matter. I'm glad you're here,' said Vic, smiling. She took off the pair of tortoise-shell glasses she'd been wearing and stood up. A bit shorter than Gemma, she was slender in a fine-boned way, with straight fair hair falling to her shoulders, and a delicate face bare of make-up. She wore a long aubergine-coloured tunic over black leggings, and would, thought Gemma, have looked elegant in a flour sack.

'You must be Gemma,' said Vic, holding out a hand to her. So he'd rung ahead and warned her, thought Gemma as she touched Vic's cool, soft fingers with her own. She glanced at Kincaid and was not surprised to see a self-satisfied smirk on his face. He was enjoying this, the bastard. Suddenly she wished she'd at least brushed her hair and checked her lipstick.

134

'Come through into the sitting room,' said Vic. 'Kit and I have made a proper tea. All that's lacking is to boil the kettle, and that won't take but a minute.'

'You shouldn't have gone to such trouble,' protested Gemma as she stepped back to let Vic pass.

'Actually it's a treat—and an excuse to make Kit the goodies he likes. We don't have guests very often.' Vic led them back the way they'd come and through a door at the opposite end of the passage.

Following her, Gemma saw a comfortable, lived-in sort of room, with a squashy sofa and armchairs, fringed lamps, and the Sunday papers neatly stacked on an end table beside silver-framed photos. At the far end, French doors led into the rain-damp garden.

'Make yourselves comfortable, and Kit will light the fire. Won't you, sweetie?'

Kit made a disgusted face at his mother as he knelt by the hearth. 'I told you not to call me that.'

'Ooops. Sorry.' Vic grinned unrepentantly, and suddenly looked about ten years old herself.

'Can I help?' asked Gemma, feeling she ought to offer.

'No, we've got it all under control. Kit's promised to be my dogsbody today—it's my reward for making scones and cake.' Vic put a hand on Kit's back as he returned to her, and pushed him gently out of the room.

When the door had closed behind them, Gemma joined Kincaid, who stood with his

135

back to the fire, warming his hands.

After a moment Gemma broke the silence. 'She's nice.'

Kincaid glanced down at her. 'What did you expect?' he asked, sounding definitely amused. 'Horns and tail?'

'Of course not. It's just ...' Deciding she'd better not dig herself into an inescapable hole, Gemma changed the subject. 'Did you meet Kit when you came before?'

'He was away that day, visiting his grandparents, I think.'

Slowly, Gemma said, 'He seems so familiar ... Maybe it's just that I imagine Toby will look like that in a few years.' Toby's hair would darken to just that barley colour and he would move with the same coltish grace. Already Toby was fast losing his baby softness. Soon he'd grow into Kit's sort of stretched leanness, as if every calorie spared from upward growth was shunted directly into the production of kinetic energy.

The hallway door creaked open and Kit shouldered his way through the gap, bearing a heavily laden tea tray. Hastily clearing the table for him, Gemma said, 'I can see why you like an excuse for your mum to make a proper tea. And I think it's a good thing we didn't have any lunch.'

'She'll do scones or cake sometimes if it's just the two of us, but not both,' Kit said, glancing up at Gemma as he knelt with the tray. He transferred plates and dishes from tray to tabletop then arranged them with meticulous care. A platter of scones, a dish

136

of strawberry jam, a dish of cream, a plate of thin sandwiches on brown bread, another with thick slices of raisin-studded cake—all apparently had to occupy a certain position, and Gemma knew better than to offer help.

Sitting back on his heels as he surveyed his handiwork with a satisfied expression, Kit said, 'Mum's bringing the tea.'

'I thought your mum couldn't cook,' Kincaid said from his stance before the fire.

'She can't, really,' Kit admitted. 'She only learned these special things for me. And anybody can make sandwiches.' Reaching towards a slice of cake, he glanced furtively up, then smoothly returned the offending hand to his knee when he saw them watching. 'I can cook,' he offered as a distraction. 'I can do scrambled eggs on toast, and sausages, and spaghetti.'

'Sounds a perfectly good repertoire to me,' Kincaid said, then he nodded towards the platter. 'Go on, have some cake.'

Kit shook his head. 'She'll kill me if I forget my manners. I'm not to touch anything until the tea's served.'

'Then I'd not take the risk,' Kincaid said, grinning. 'It's hardly worth the consequences.'

Pushing himself up from the floor, Kit straddled the arm of the sofa and studied Kincaid curiously. 'You're a cop, aren't you?' he said after a moment. 'Mum told me. Why aren't you wearing a uniform?'

'Well, it's my day off, for one thing. And I'm an investigator, and investigators don't usually wear uniforms.'

Kit thought about this for a moment. 'Does that mean you can ask people things and they don't know you're a copper? Cool.'

'Whenever we question anyone we have to show them our identification,' Kincaid said a bit apologetically. 'Otherwise it wouldn't be fair.' When he saw Kit's disappointed expression, he nodded towards Gemma and added, 'Gemma's a police officer, too.'

Kit's eyes widened. 'No way. I thought that was just on the telly. The only copper I know is Harry. He's the bobby here in the village, and he's thick as two planks, you know—'

'Kit!' Vic had come in quietly, carrying a second tray. 'What a horrid thing to say.'

'You know it's true.' Kit sounded more injured than abashed. 'You said so yourself.'

'I said no such thing. Harry's very nice.' Vic looked daggers at her son.

'*Nice* is the first requirement for village bobbies,' Kincaid put in diplomatically. 'Except we call it *community policing.*'

Gemma controlled a snicker and went to help Vic. 'Here, let me take the cups.'

When the tea had been poured and handed round, Kincaid said, 'Kit's shown great restraint over the cake, I think.'

Vic laughed. 'Oh, all right, go ahead. Just save some for the rest of us.'

Kit fell upon the cake with a whoop and slid the two largest slices on to his plate.

'I swear I don't know where he puts it,' sighed Vic. 'It just disappears. And the cake won't stop him stuffing himself with sandwiches

138

and scones.' She took a sandwich and bit into it. 'I hope you both like cucumber.'

Gemma took a sandwich for herself and sat back, nibbling and letting the talk eddy round her. Listening to the easy banter between mother and son, she had to keep reminding herself that this slender woman with the pleasant smile was the cold and formidable ex-wife who had callously walked out on Kincaid. For the first time she wondered if she might have distorted the few comments he'd made about Vic to suit her own ends. What had he actually said?

Suddenly she wished she knew how Vic had seen things. *Why did you leave him?* she thought. *And why did you leave him that way, without a word?* But of course she couldn't ask. Watching them, she tried to imagine them together, but she couldn't separate Kincaid from her own experience of him.

Vic had taken the armchair opposite, with Kit perched on its arm like a tawny-crested bird, while Kincaid sat beside Gemma on the sofa, tea plate balanced on his knee. She was as aware of the warm solidity of his presence as if he'd been touching her, and she wondered what had been more important to Vic than that.

'Another scone, Gemma?' asked Vic.

Startled, Gemma thought she had better make an effort to pay attention. 'Oh, I couldn't manage another bite, but thanks. It was all lovely.'

They'd all reached the wiping up the crumb stage, Kit having polished off the last piece of cake. Gemma saw Vic glance at Kincaid and sensed the unspoken communication that passed between them before Vic said, 'Kit, if you've finished—'

'I know, you want to be rid of me,' he said, vaulting from the sofa arm and landing with a thump. He didn't sound the least bit unhappy. 'Since you're not using the computer, can I play Dark Legions? Please, please, Mummy?' he wheedled, grinning, already sure of getting his way.

'Oh, all right.' Vic gave in gracefully. 'Just be sure to save my document.'

Kit leaned down and gave her an unselfconscious kiss on the cheek. 'Brilliant cake, Mum,' he said, then bounded from the room before she could change her mind.

When the door had slammed behind him, Vic said, 'I don't know why I nag him. He knows more about the computer than I do. He's the one who helps me when I get stuck.'

'Illusion of power,' said Kincaid, teasing.

'You're lucky. He's a nice kid,' said Gemma, knowing even as she did so how inadequate the word sounded, but Vic gave her a pleased smile.

'I know. He doesn't deserve what he's been through this last year.' Vic glanced at Kincaid, then back at Gemma. 'He's told you about Ian?'

Gemma nodded. 'I'm sorry.'

'Don't be. At least not for my sake, and I'm beginning to think it may not have been such a bad thing for Kit either. Ian was so critical ... Kit must have felt he could never please

140

him.' For a moment Vic gazed consideringly into her teacup, then looked up at Gemma and said softly, 'And you know what's odd? After so many years together, I've never missed him. Not for a day, not for a minute. You'd think that just the familiarity would be enough to make you miss a person a little, no matter what they'd done. Oh, well.' She set her cup on the table and smiled at them. 'You didn't come to talk about that.'

Kincaid shifted beside Gemma as he reached into the inside breast pocket of the sports jacket he'd worn over his jeans. 'I've brought you the notes I made from Lydia Brooke's case file. I thought you might like to see them yourself.' He handed over a folded sheaf of papers which Gemma recognized as torn from his spiral notebook. 'You understand that I couldn't take the file away with me.'

Vic took them as though they were fragile, then moved across to the other chair so that she could unfold them in the cone of light from the lamp. She read slowly, frowning in concentration, and they waited in silence. Gemma was suddenly aware of the fire hissing, and of the almost imperceptible sound of the light rain against the window panes.

Finally, Vic settled the pages back in their original order, and looked up at them. '*Nathan* found her?' she said, as if she couldn't quite believe her own words. 'Nathan never told me he found her.'

The strong lamplight lit her face and Gemma saw for the first time the tiny creases round her

141

eyes and the lines running from her nose to the corners of her mouth.

'Should he have done?' asked Kincaid.

Vic coloured and looked away. 'It's just that ... I thought ... we were friends.'

'Maybe he didn't want to distress you,' suggested Gemma, wishing now that she'd read the notes herself and not been satisfied with Kincaid's quick summary. 'Or he found it too difficult to talk about.'

'Surely there was some other record,' said Kincaid.

'Such as? There were two brief mentions in the local paper, the first stating that Lydia Brooke had been found dead in her Cambridge home; the second that she had died from an overdose of her own heart medication, and that her death had been ruled a suicide by the coroner's office. Full stop.'

'What about academic gossip?'

'For once the gossip mill proved strangely unproductive,' Vic said disgustedly. 'You'd think that a door had slammed shut when Lydia died—after that, no speculation, no reminiscences, nothing.' Then, as if she could contain her frustration no longer, she stood and began pacing before the hearth. 'I wasn't prepared for this. And it's not as if I see myself as Quentin Bell writing about Virginia Woolf, either. Lydia wasn't a major literary figure. Nor was she particularly well-connected in literary circles, so I knew I couldn't hope for scads of revealing letters turning up among other people's correspondence. But I never expected

142

this ... this ... *possessiveness* about her, as if no one who knew her can stand to let anything go. Her ex-husband was actually abusive when I tried to talk to him.

'And this—' she waved the sheaf of papers she still held—'This is all wrong.'

'What do you mean, wrong?' Kincaid asked, and in spite of his casual tone Gemma sensed his interest.

Coming back to sit on the edge of the armchair, Vic leaned towards them. 'Nathan, for one thing. Why did Lydia call Nathan and tell him she wanted to see him?'

'I imagine they assumed she wanted him to find her, rather than the cleaning lady or some unfortunate neighbour,' Kincaid offered.

'She would never have done that, don't you see? Not to Nathan. They were very old friends, and he'd just lost his wife a few months before after a long battle with cancer. She wouldn't have deliberately subjected him to such distress.'

'Sometimes when people are depressed they do un—'

Vic was shaking her head adamantly. 'And what about her clothes? Lydia had style, dammit—you can't possibly think she'd have set such an elaborate scene, then killed herself in old grubby things?'

'I have to admit it seemed a bit queer to me,' Kincaid said cautiously. 'But sometimes—'

'And the business about the poem is absurd,' Vic went on, unheeding. She started rifling through the pages. 'Let me just—'

143

'Why?' The sharpness in his voice made Vic look up, hands stilled for a moment on the pages. 'Why is it absurd?' he repeated.

'Because she didn't write it,' Vic said flatly. 'It's an excerpt from a Rupert Brooke poem called "Choriambics".'

'Could I see it?' asked Gemma. She took the page from Vic's outstretched hand, and when she found they were both watching her, she began to read aloud slowly.

In the silence of death; then may I see dimly, and know, a space,
Bending over me, last light in the dark, once, as of old, your face.

Gemma looked up. 'It does seem fitting, especially if she'd lost a great love.'

'And if she was obsessed with Rupert Brooke, what could have been more appropriate than to use one of his poems as her final message?' said Kincaid.

'Rather than her own voice?' Vic shook her head and took a breath, a calming effort. 'Lydia was a poet first. That's what made her who she was. That's why I wanted to write about her. Women need those kinds of models—we need to hear the stories of women who have lived out their dreams, regardless of the cost. That way maybe we can get there, too, and without so much suffering along the way.'

'Then why would she have had an excerpt from a Brooke poem in her typewriter, if it wasn't meant for a suicide note?' Kincaid asked,

144

raising a sceptical brow.

'I haven't a clue. All I can tell you is that she would never have used someone else's words.' Vic rubbed at her face, then said through splayed fingers, 'Oh, how can I make you understand? Words were everything to her—her joy, her sorrow, her comfort. She would not have abandoned them in the final extreme. It would have been a betrayal beyond measure.'

The fire popped, and in the silence that followed, Gemma said, 'I do. Understand, I mean. I think I understand what you're saying.'

'You don't think I'm daft?'

'No. Even if I don't know much about poetry, I understand about not giving up who you are.'

Vic turned to Kincaid. 'And have I convinced you?'

After a long moment he said a bit grudgingly, 'Yes, I suppose so. But I still don't see how—'

'There's more,' Vic said. 'Since I saw you last. Last week Nathan gave me a book he found among Lydia's things, Edward Marsh's *Rupert Brooke: A Memoir*. It was published in 1919, and included the first posthumous collection of Brooke's poems. It was one of Lydia's treasures—she found it in a second-hand bookshop her first year at Cambridge.

'I put it in the stack on my bedside table'—She flashed a smile at Kincaid, and Gemma wondered if Vic's habit of taking books to bed had been a point of contention between them—'but it wasn't until last night that I settled down to have a good look at it. You

145

can't *imagine* how I felt when I leafed through it and the manuscript pages fell out.' Vic smiled as if even the memory were delicious.

'What manuscript?' asked Kincaid, sounding thoroughly confused. 'What did you say the author's name was?'

'Edward Marsh,' Gemma said helpfully, but Vic was shaking her head.

'No, no, it was poems, drafts of *Lydia's* poems. Let me show you.' She went quickly from the room, returning a moment later with some folded papers and wearing her tortoise-shell glasses. Sitting across from them again, she held the pages up for their inspection. 'Lydia still used a typewriter rather than a computer. She was stubborn about it—she said she needed to feel some sort of physical connection between herself and the words and the paper. Sometimes she wrote first drafts in longhand, but when she typed she always made carbons.'

Gemma could see that the paper was tissue-thin copy paper, and the typescript had the smudgy look of carbon ink.

'Some of these poems were published in her last book,' Vic said, folding the pages in half again and smoothing them across her knees. 'But there are others I've never even seen drafts of before.'

'Student poems she didn't think worth saving?' suggested Kincaid. 'If she'd had the book since she was at college.'

'No. These are better than her best— polished and mature. And they explore the same themes as many of the poems in her last book.' Vic paused as if weighing her words, then she said deliberately, patting the sheets on her knee. 'These were meant to be read with the ones in the book, I'm sure of it.'

Kincaid glanced at Gemma before he said, 'Maybe she was dissatisfied with them.'

'No. Lydia was unfailingly honest with herself about her writing. She recognized crap, and she knew when she'd done good work.'

'So what are you suggesting?'

Palms up in a helpless gesture, Vic shrugged. 'I don't know.'

'Could she have decided not to publish them for some other reason?' Gemma asked.

'I don't know what it could have been,' Vic said, then added thoughtfully, 'One of the things I admired most about Lydia was her utter disregard for whether or not she offended people.'

Kincaid reached for the teapot and poured a little cold tea into his cup. 'Would these'—he nodded at the sheets in Vic's lap—'have offended anyone?'

'Some men. In a series of metaphors, she equates sex with death. It's couched in symbolic terms, but there are men who are incapable of dealing with ideas about gender roles except in a personal way.'

'God forbid I should be one of them,' Kincaid said in mock horror.

Vic rolled her eyes at Gemma. 'Is he as liberated as he thinks he is?'

'Not half.' Gemma smiled at her and a spark of understanding passed between them.

147

'If you ladies have finished amusing yourselves at my expense ... Perhaps we could get on with things.' Kincaid sipped at his cold tea and grimaced. 'Vic—'

'Let me make another pot,' Vic said, reaching for the teapot, but he glanced at his watch and shook his head.

'We'd better be getting back. Toby will have worn out his welcome at Gemma's parents', I'm afraid.'

Vic sat back in her chair and folded her hands in her lap, like a child awaiting bad news.

Kincaid cleared his throat. 'Vic, I'll agree with you that there are things about Lydia Brooke's death that seem odd, but I simply don't know what we can do about it at this point. It's all supposition, and the police won't even consider reopening the case without some sort of hard evidence.'

When she didn't respond, he said, 'One of the things I've learned over the years in police work is that sometimes we just can't know all the answers—life doesn't always tidy itself into neat little compartments. It's frustrating and infuriating, but if you don't learn when to let go, you can't stay in the job.'

'Is that what you're saying I should do? Let it go?'

He nodded. 'Write a good book about Lydia and about her work. It's the story that counts, not how it ends.' Shrugging apologetically, he added, 'I'm sorry. I don't want to disappoint you, but I don't know what else to suggest.'

Vic sat quite still, her face blank with disbelief.

After a moment she seemed to collect herself. 'I don't know what I expected,' she said, and gave him a brittle smile. 'It was kind of you to listen to me, and to take as much trouble as you have.'

'Vic—'

'Don't worry, Duncan. I know you mean well. You've been a great help, really. Not to mention the fact that your visit to the Faculty will fuel the office gossip for months. I'm sure they've all paid up their outstanding parking tickets, just in case you come back.'

'I'm sorry,' he said, sounding a bit injured. 'I didn't mean to make things difficult for you.'

'I should be used to difficult by now. I can't imagine the days when I thought academia would provide a peaceful life. Do you mind if I keep your notes?'

'Not at all.'

She scooped the pages from his notebook off the lamp table and added them to the neat stack in her lap. 'Will you get in trouble with your mates if I use this information in the book?'

'I'm not going to worry about it.' Kincaid's smile held a hint of acid. 'Besides, you know policemen don't read.'

'Too right,' Vic said, making a visible effort to parry the thrust lightly. 'Well, if you must go, I'll see you out.'

In the hall she stopped and called out to Kit.

'Just a sec,' he yelled back, and a moment later appeared from the office. 'I had to pause it,' he explained. 'I made it all the way to the seventh level.'

149

'What does that mean?' asked Gemma.

'It means I'm lean and mean and one cool dude.' Kit swaggered. 'And I toasted a whole platoon of aliens.'

'Kit!' Vic tousled his hair. 'You sound like some character in a bad American film. I think we'll have to cut back on the videos.'

Ignoring this for the empty threat it undoubtedly was, Kit caught up to Kincaid at the door. 'Can I look at your car? Mum says it's awful, so it must be pretty cool.'

'Sure. You can even start it.' They went out and walked across the gravelled drive to the Midget.

Gemma and Vic stood on the porch, watching them. The rain had stopped, and a few gaps in the western clouds hinted at a glorious sunset. 'Is Toby your son?' asked Vic.

'He's three. And he already loves cars. Must be genetic.'

'I know. And to think I used to believe all that stuff about raising your children free of gender stereotypes.' She laid light fingers on Gemma's arm. 'I'm glad you came.'

The Midget's engine sputtered to life. Kit jumped out of the driver's seat and ran across to them. 'It's really neat, Mum. Can we get one like it? Our car is so boring.'

Vic laughed. 'I like boring.'

Kincaid had followed Kit, and now shook his hand. 'I'll sell it to you when you're sixteen.' He pecked Vic on the cheek, then took Gemma by the elbow. 'Bye, thanks for the tea.'

There was something in Vic's stance, thought

150

Gemma, looking back as they pulled away, that could be read as easily as words on a page—an invisible angle of determination. Liking the pattern the words made in her mind, she repeated them to herself, and she felt an odd quickening inside her, as if something stirred in its sleep.

By the time they reached the motorway the fissures in the clouds had widened, revealing the sunset in full hue. Kincaid always thought of sunsets as feminine, and this one was particularly voluptuous, with rosy-gold billows of cloud forming shapes reminiscent of reclining Rubenesque nudes. He smiled at his metaphor and glanced at Gemma, wondering if she'd accuse him of sexism if he shared it with her.

She sat silently beside him, watching the sky, not even complaining, for once, about his car. He thought about asking her what she was thinking, but just then a passing lorry spattered sludge on the windscreen and fighting its back draft while momentarily blinded required all his attention. When he could see again, he put a piano cassette in the tape player and concentrated on his driving.

They found the lights switched on in Gemma's flat and a vase of daffodils on the table. Beside it lay a note from Hazel, a pot of beans, and a loaf of homemade bread. 'Have a good feed,' the note read. 'Gourmet beans on toast.'

'I see your fairy godmother's been,' said Kincaid, dipping a finger into the still warm beans for a taste. 'If she weren't already taken I'd snatch her in a minute.'

'She wouldn't have you,' Gemma said equably. 'Just count yourself lucky to get some of the fringe benefits.'

When Toby had been fed and put to bed, and they'd finished up the last of their toast and tea, Kincaid rolled up his shirt sleeves. 'I'll do the washing up,' he offered, 'if I can have a glass of wine. I could swim in the tea I've drunk today.'

'Red or white?' Gemma stood on tiptoe as she reached for the glasses in the cupboard.

He admired the elongated line of her body as she stretched, and the curves hinted at beneath the bulk of her jumper. Stepping up behind her, he laid his hands lightly on her waist. 'Mmmm, red, I think.'

Gemma slipped out of his grasp with an abstracted smile. When she'd poured them both a glass of burgundy, she cleared the dishes from the half-moon table while he ran hot water and squirted soap in the basin.

'Sit,' he ordered her as he began the soaping and rinsing. 'There's not room for us both in here—or there is, but it's quite distracting.' When this mildly flirtatious comment received no response, he looked round as much as his dripping hands would allow. She sat in one of the slatted chairs at the table, booted feet stretched out before her, staring into the wine glass cradled in her lap. He started to speak, then thought better of it, slotting the last of the plates into the drying rack before he wiped his hands and turned to her.

'Gemma, what is it?' he asked, taking the other chair so that he could look directly into her face. 'You've hardly said a word since we left Cambridge.'

'Oh.' She looked at him as if surprised to find him there. 'I'm sorry. I was just thinking.'

'So I gathered. Care to elaborate?'

She frowned. 'I'm not sure. I mean I'm not quite sure I've worked out how to put it into words.'

With some trepidation, he asked, 'Is this about Vic?' He'd thought taking Gemma with him the best way to allay her fears, but perhaps it had been a mistake.

To his surprise, the corners of Gemma's mouth turned up in a smile. 'I didn't expect to like her, you know, but I did. Even though there's still a connection between the two of you, I found I didn't mind. I don't know why I was so frightened of it, or why I expected to be so intimidated by her.'

'Intimidated by Vic? Why?'

Hesitating, Gemma looked away from him, then said slowly, 'You know I did my A levels, but then I decided on the Academy rather than University. I thought I wouldn't be able to talk to her—that we wouldn't have a thing in common. Or worse, that she'd talk down to me, be all smug about her education and her career.'

'Why on earth should she—'

'No, wait, let me finish.' Gemma gave him a quelling look, her brows drawn together again.

153

'It didn't turn out that way at all. The things she said made sense to me, and the funny thing is, I think I understood something you didn't.'

'What are you talking about?' he asked, thoroughly puzzled now.

'You told her that the end of her book about Lydia didn't matter. You didn't see that it's the end that gives the book its truth.' He must have looked blank, because she shook her head in frustration. 'Look at it this way. Vic's right about women needing stories about other women's accomplishments. Do you know how much it would have meant to me when I started out in the Met if I'd had another woman's experience to guide me?

'There were less than a handful of female DCI's then, and they were playing by men's rules. But I wanted something different. I thought that I could be a good police officer—maybe even a *better* police officer, *because* I'm a woman, not in spite of it, and there were times, especially in the beginning, that I almost gave up. There was nobody to reassure me that I had something special to offer, that I wasn't crazy, that it could be done.'

'I'm sorry,' he said, taken aback by her intensity. 'I didn't know that's how you felt. You've never said.'

'Those aren't things that are considered appropriate to say.' Her smile held little humour. 'And that makes other women's stories even more important, including Lydia's. But if Lydia killed herself it changes her story. I'm not saying that it makes it invalid, but it

154

does make it a *different* story.'

'I don't understand. Surely she would still have accomplished the same things?'

'But they wouldn't matter in the same way. Suicide is an admission of defeat. It tells us that she couldn't put all the pieces of her dream together, and if she couldn't, maybe we can't, either.'

'Are you saying I shouldn't have told Vic to leave it alone?'

Gemma took a belated sip of her wine. 'Not exactly. I'm saying that it doesn't matter what you said, because Vic needs Lydia not to have committed suicide, and she *can't* let it go. And you didn't see that.'

'What else could I have done?' he said defensively, feeling as though he'd been tried and found wanting. 'You were the one who thought I shouldn't bother with it at all.'

Shrugging, Gemma said, 'I'm allowed to change my mind, aren't I?'

30 January 1963
Newnham

Dearest Mummy,
Sometimes I think this poetry is a curse, not a gift. The words haunt me when I should be sleeping, haunt me when I should be working, and they're black, cold beasts I can't tame into acceptable shapes. Six rejections just this week, without even a hint of encouragement. Why can't I give it up, concentrate on my studies?

Last term's workload was difficult— this

155

term's may be insurmountable. If I had been better prepared I might not be floundering so now, trying to make up for the lack of depth and breadth in my reading. And what shall I do with this degree, if I somehow manage to earn one of any distinction? Teach sixth-form girls in some dreary comprehensive, in the hopes that one of them will possess the gift I lacked?

Do you know how many women manage to publish poetry? And of the few that do, most have their work reviled by the critics for being too pretty, too feminine, but if they write anything else it's said to be unsuitable. If I'd had any sense I'd have taken that clerk's job in the Brighton Woolworth's. I'd be taking the bus home in the rain, warm and dry on the upper deck, not cycling everywhere through slush and sludge, rain cape and boots perpetually soaked. I'd have met some nice fellow and I'd go to the cinema with him on Fridays, and if he were persistent enough I might bring him home for tea. Marriage and babies would lurk in the offing, and these spiky thoughts would not jostle so in my head.

Oh, poor Mummy, forgive me this outpouring of misery. I feel small and mean, burdening you with it, but I simply couldn't go on without the hope of comfort. Tell me these feelings will pass, that the rain will stop, that my dreadful cold will go away, that someone, somewhere, will publish one of my poems.

Your,
Lydia

Chapter Seven

Tenderly, day that I have loved, I close your eyes,
And smooth your quiet brow, and fold your thin dead hands.

Rupert Brooke, from
Day That I Have Loved

Vic often thought that this was her favourite time, Kit asleep, the house still and quiet except for the occasional creak as it breathed. She sat at the kitchen table with a cup of milk hot from the microwave, for once neither reading nor writing, but simply thinking about her day. This was a habit begun in the last years with Ian as a way of avoiding bed until she knew he was asleep, and now enjoyed for its own sake.

They'd never had the money to do the kitchen up properly, so she'd got creative with paint and jumble sale finds, discovering an unexpected sense of pleasure in the process. Blue on the cabinets, sunflower yellow on the rough plaster walls, junk shop jugs and pitchers on the counter tops and window sill. The Welsh dresser with its blue-and-yellow Italian pottery she'd found for a song at an estate sale, along with the small, oak, drop-leaf table and her Tiffany lamp. At least she always thought of it as her Tiffany lamp—it was probably a cheap imitation, but she meant

157

to have it valued some day, just in case.

Her mother, whenever she came to visit, threw up her hands in despair at the sight of Vic's kitchen. A proponent of hygienic synthetic surfaces, with a fetish for appliances (her latest acquisition was a rubbish compactor), Eugenia Potts had no patience with her daughter's contentment. It was a good thing, thought Vic, that she didn't really want a dishwasher, or a refrigerator the size of a cave, because without Ian's salary the possibility of refitting had receded farther than ever.

For a moment, she allowed herself the luxury of wondering what her life would have been like if she'd stayed with Duncan. Would they live in the flat he'd described in Hampstead, with its sunset view over the rooftops? Would she be teaching at London University, in a department less difficult? Would she and Duncan have ironed out their differences, she growing less jealous of his work as she became more absorbed in her own?

The one thing she felt quite certain of was that she wouldn't have begun a biography of Lydia Brooke, and she was beginning to think that might have been a blessing. Even after so many years apart, it had felt quite odd today to see him with another woman. She hadn't felt jealous—she had in fact found herself unexpectedly drawn to Gemma—but she had experienced a sense of displacement.

Just how honest had she been with herself about her reasons for contacting him? Oh, she'd had legitimate need, and he had been helpful, but now that he'd done as much as he felt he could in the matter of Lydia, she found herself wanting very much to maintain the friendship, for Kit's sake as well as her own. Kit had few enough male role models, and it was especially important now that Ian—

The phone rang. She lunged for it instinctively, hoping it hadn't wakened Kit. Even as she lifted the handset from the cradle, she knew who it was.

'Vic? I hope it's not too late, but I managed to get away from the conference a day early.'

'No, it's all right. I'm still up,' she said, her breathing quickening at the sound of Nathan's voice.

'It was a bloody weekend, I can tell you,' he said, and she could imagine him smiling. He'd gone unenthusiastically on Friday to a botanists' meeting in Manchester, mumbling that they could hardly have picked anywhere less appropriate.

She hadn't often talked to him on the telephone, and she thought how much she liked his voice, deep, with laughter resonating under the surface. She'd always been a sucker for voices, Duncan's too, with its hint of Cheshire drawl, blunted now by so many years in London.

'Come round and I'll tell you about it,' Nathan urged.

Hesitating, Vic felt the anxious knot of dread forming in her stomach. Did she want to confront him tonight? No point putting it off, she thought, and took a deep breath.

159

'Yes, all right. I suppose I can come over for a bit.'

'Come the front way. The garden's a bog.' He added, teasing, 'I don't think the neighbours will see you this time of night.' The phone clicked, then the dial tone buzzed in her ear.

He still wore his jacket and tie, though he'd undone his collar button and pulled the knot of his tie down to a rakish angle. 'I've got the fire going,' he said, ushering her into the hall. 'Let me get you a drink.'

She shook her head. 'Not just now.' The door to the music room stood open and the lamp on the piano was lit. 'You've been playing,' she said, wandering in and touching the sheet music open on the stand. It was handwritten, and she recognized Nathan's strong, black script.

'Just doodling while I waited for you.' He stood in the doorway, looking perplexed.

Vic slid on to the piano bench and stared at the keyboard. After a moment she began to pick out a hesitant, childish version of Chopsticks, all she remembered from the brief lessons forced on her by her mother. Her rebellion had taken the form of stoic silence coupled with an adherence to the exact number of minutes she was required to practice. After a few months her mother had given up in defeat. Vic was not musically gifted.

Ballet had been next. She should have stuck with piano.

'Didn't you tell me that you were writing music based on DNA sequences?' she asked. 'Is that what this is?'

160

'In part. It's an idea mentioned briefly in a lecture by Leonard Bernstein, and I've always been fascinated by it. An innate universal musical language.' He left his position by the door frame and came towards her. 'Vic, I happen to know that your interest in the mechanics of music lies somewhere on a par with your interest in particle physics. And you haven't once looked at me since you came in. What is the matter? Has something happened?'

She turned towards him. 'Nathan, why didn't you tell me that you found Lydia?'

He stared at her. 'It never occurred to me. I suppose if I'd thought about it, I'd have assumed you knew.'

'No. I'd no idea until I saw a copy of the police report today.'

'Does it matter?' he asked, sounding baffled. 'Did you think I was deliberately keeping something from you?'

'No, not really,' she said, not willing to admit what she had thought in the face of his matter-of-factness. 'It's just that everything surrounding Lydia's death seems so elusive.' She shivered with a sudden chill.

'It's cold in here. Come in by the fire,' Nathan said with instant concern, and this time she followed him obediently.

'Why didn't you ask me?' he said when he'd settled her in the armchair nearest the heat. 'I'd have told you anything you wanted to know.'

'I didn't know to ask. And even now I feel uncomfortable, because I'm afraid talking about it might distress you.'

161

'Ah.' Nathan sat across from her and took a sip of a drink he'd apparently made while waiting. 'It was very distressing, actually, at the time,' he said slowly. 'And I didn't speak about it to anyone except the police, but I'd always assumed it had got about somehow, as everyone seemed to avoid the subject so assiduously. But it's been a long time, and I don't mind talking about it now, if you like.'

A simple explanation after all, thought Vic, and she had worked herself into a lather over it. Was she becoming paranoid, imagining conspiracies, and suspecting Nathan of all people? Collecting herself, she said, 'The police seemed to think that Lydia asked you to come that evening because she wanted you to find her.'

Nathan shrugged. 'I suppose that's the logical explanation. Or perhaps at some level she was hoping to be rescued.'

'As Adam rescued her the first time?'

'Poor Adam. At least I didn't find her floating in her own blood. Sorry, love,' he added with a grimace. 'Not a nice picture.'

'She wrote about it—*Life blood/Salt and iron/cradle gentle as a/mother's kiss ...*' Vic recited softly. She stood up and went to the old gramophone cabinet Nathan used to store drinks in the sitting room. Pouring herself a generous sherry, she said, 'What did she say when she called you that day, Nathan? How did she sound?'

He thought for a long moment. 'Tense ... excited ... almost combative. I suppose all of

162

those would be natural if she were working herself up to suicide.'

'But what exactly did she say? Can you remember the particular words or phrases?' Vic came back to her chair and curled up with her feet beneath her.

Nathan closed his eyes, then said slowly, 'She said, "Nathan, I simply must see you. Can you come round this evening?" And then she said, "We need to talk." Or was it, "There's something I need to talk to you about?" ' He shook his head. 'I'm sorry, I can't remember.'

'And then what did she say? When she rang off?'

'Oh, Lord.' Nathan rubbed his chin. 'Let me think. She said, "Come for drinks around sevenish?" A question, rather than a statement, but she didn't wait for me to answer. And then, "See you then. Cheerio," and she hung up.'

'And you thought that sounded like someone intending suicide?' Vic's voice rose to an incredulous squeak.

'Well, I have to admit it sounds a bit absurd, now,' said Nathan, exasperated. 'But I had indisputable evidence, damn it. She was dead.'

'What did you think about the poem in the typewriter?' asked Vic, ploughing on.

'The Rupert Brooke? I supposed she had never quite got over Morgan, and that was her way of saying goodbye to him. It did seem a bit sentimental for Lydia, but when I heard she'd left him everything it seemed a fair assumption.'

163

'The police thought Lydia wrote it.'

'Did they?' Nathan's brows lifted in surprise. 'Well, they never asked me. I'd have set them straight. But what difference does it make?'

Not yet, she thought. She wasn't ready to lay her cards out quite yet. And there was still the matter of the poems. 'Nathan, did you know about the poems in the book you gave me?'

'The Rupert Brooke? Of course it had poems in it,' he said, looking at her as if not quite sure of her sanity. 'It was the first collection of his poems, along with Marsh's rather sexually biased memoirs, if I remem—'

'No, no, I don't mean those poems,' Vic protested, laughing. 'I meant Lydia's poems.'

Nathan just looked at her blankly. 'What are you talking about, Vic?'

'Did you look in the book before you gave it to me?'

'Just the copyright page, and that marvellous photo on the flyleaf. No wonder Marsh—'

'That's all right, then,' Vic said on a breath of relief. 'No wonder you didn't see them.' She proceeded to explain about finding the manuscript drafts of Lydia's poems in the book, and that she thought them among the last of Lydia's work.

When she'd finished, Nathan said thoughtfully, 'Well, no one would know better than you. But how odd. I suppose the logical step would be to ask Ralph if he knows anything about them.'

'Ralph Peregrine? Her publisher?' she asked,

while silently blessing Nathan for not questioning her competence.

'A nice chap, and he seems to have had a good working relationship with Lydia. Have you met him?'

Vic nodded. 'Briefly. He was very accommodating. He told me as much as he knew about Lydia's methods of working, and made me copies of his correspondence with her.'

'And there was nothing about these poems?'

'No. She wrote him a series of friendly, chatty letters from abroad over the years, but they seem to have conducted most of their business in person or over the telephone.'

'I suppose that makes sense, in view of the fact that they were both in Cambridge.' Nathan fell silent for a moment, then smiled brightly at her. 'You could ask Daphne.'

'That's exactly what Adam said, only about something else. What—'

'How did your visit go with Adam?' Nathan interrupted, sounding avuncularly pleased with himself.

'He wasn't at all what I expected,' Vic said, smiling. 'He was quite charming, and he gave me very good sherry. It seemed all I needed was your seal of approval.'

'Adam always did have a taste for expensive sherry—it's probably the one little luxury he allows himself, poor chap. It was he who began the sherry party tradition at college, you know.' As if reminded of his empty glass, Nathan got up and poured himself a bit more whisky. Returning to his chair, he said, 'In

165

fact, that must be where I met Lydia for the first time, at one of Adam's little parties. I'd forgotten that.'

'Why refer to him as a *poor chap?*' Vic asked, intrigued. 'I'll admit the rectory is a bit shabby—well, I suppose I'd have to admit that Adam's a bit shabby himself—but he seemed quite comfortable with his circumstances.'

Nathan grimaced. 'You're quite right. That was bloody condescending of me. That's what comes of projecting your own ambitions onto someone else.' Frowning, he sipped at his drink. 'But you see, all of us—Adam and Darcy and I—came from the same sort of comfortable middle-class background. Well, mine was a bit less comfortable than Adam or Darcy's, but the point is, we started with the same aspirations, and Darcy and I made a moderate success of it. Adam, though ...'

'What?' said Vic, her curiosity further aroused by his hesitation. He looked up at her and for once she found his dark eyes opaque, unreadable.

'All of a sudden, one day Adam decided that wasn't good enough for him. He wanted to *contribute* something, save his own little corner of the world. And I can't say he's made a great success of it—a failed mission, then a decaying church that's in danger of closure, full of ageing and decrepit parishioners.'

'Nathan,' said Vic, taken aback, 'you actually sound as if you're jealous! I'd never have thought it.'

He looked at her for a long moment, then

166

said, 'It's more guilt than jealousy, I'm afraid. At least he made an effort to do something for someone, poor bastard, while the rest of us just grew fat and content and more blind by the day. I used to tell myself that do-gooding was just as self-serving, but I'm not sure I can swallow that any more.'

'I wouldn't have thought you'd make a very good cynic.'

'Thanks.' He smiled at her. 'Perhaps your good opinion means I have some hope of redemption.'

'What about Daphne? Did she get a case of middle-aged tunnel vision, as well?'

'Daphne?' Nathan tilted his head to one side as he thought. 'I'm afraid I couldn't say, really. I never had much contact with Daphne after college. She's certainly been outwardly successful, though.'

'But you said—'

'It was Lydia and Daphne who stayed close. And I must say I wondered even then if Daphne only put up with the rest of us for Lydia's sake. It was Daphne who was most privy to Lydia's work, especially in the later years.'

'But I interviewed her.' Vic slid her feet to the floor with an outraged thump. 'From the way she talked you'd have thought they'd hardly seen one another since college, nodding acquaintances in the street sort of thing. And there's no record in Lydia's papers, except for the occasional mention in her letters to her mother—'

'Daphne's a very private person, as was Lydia.

When Lydia died, Daphne asked me to return all the letters she'd written to her over the years. I saw no reason not to.'

After a moment Vic realized she was gaping and snapped her mouth shut. 'But couldn't you have ... But what about—'

'Literary posterity?' Nathan supplied helpfully. 'I rather thought that the wishes of the living people involved came first.'

Vic stared at him for a moment, then gave a deflated sigh and rubbed her cheekbones with the tips of her fingers. 'You're right, of course. You couldn't in good conscience have done anything else.' She shook her head. 'What's happened to me? Am I turning into some sort of dreadful vulture?'

Nathan grinned at her. 'Next thing you know you'll be applying for a job on the *Sun.*'

'God forbid I should come to that,' Vic said, smiling back in spite of herself. 'But, oh, Nathan, I was so ignorant when I took this on. I actually thought that biography was an academic and critical pursuit—can you imagine that? But it's as much fiction as any novel. How else can you create a whole person out of the bits and pieces we leave behind? And where do you draw a morally defensible line as far as privacy is concerned, for both the living and the dead?'

'I don't know, my dear,' said Nathan, all trace of levity vanishing. 'But I trust your judgement. And I think if you are going to be happy with yourself, you're going to have to trust *your* judgement, too. And don't be afraid to follow your instincts, else you might end up fat and self-satisfied. What was it that Rupert Brooke advocated to his friends? That they should all live together in licentious freedom on an island, then kill themselves when they reached middle-age?'

'You're not fat or self-satisfied.'

'Vic—'

She interrupted him, intent on following her train of thought. 'All right, then, what am I missing about Daphne? In Adam I caught the occasional glimpse of what Lydia must have seen, but I couldn't imagine Daphne had ever been anything but a middle-aged and very proper headmistress.'

'For starters, Daphne was anything but proper,' said Nathan with a glint of amusement. 'And she was gorgeous. They both were, but in different ways. Daphne could have posed for any number of mythical or biblical paintings—you know, The Rape of Lucretia sort of thing. She had that timeless, feminine corn-goddess quality, all heavy breasts and flowing copper hair.' He paused, then said more slowly, 'While Lydia—there was something more androgynous about Lydia, with her slender body and her triangular, almost feline, little face—but she was no less appealing for that. And she certainly made up for any sexual aggressiveness that Daphne lacked,' he added, as if it were an afterthought.

Frowning, Vic said, 'But I thought ... that it was always you and Daphne. And Adam and Lydia. I mean ...'

'Are you trying to be tactful, Vic?' Nathan

asked, the veiled amusement evolving into a wicked grin. 'I'd never have thought it of you.'

She felt herself blushing and said defiantly, 'All right, then. Are you telling me that you slept with them both?'

'You must remember that this was, after all, the early sixties, and that we thought we had invented it all.' His tone was still teasing, but the laughter had gone from his eyes. 'It all seemed so daring and liberated, and we were so smug with it.'

'You don't sound as if you enjoyed it much.'

'I was ... what? Nineteen? Twenty? I'm not sure *enjoyment* is the operative word with males at that age. It's a bit more basic than that.'

Vic tried to imagine Nathan as he had been then, but his presence now was too real, too strong. She found the thought of him making love to Daphne and Lydia surprisingly arousing, and found also that it gave her an odd sense of connection to the two women. She would have to see Daphne again. And she would certainly have to revise her picture of Lydia's university days, which up until now had been gleaned mostly from Lydia's early poems and the oh-so-innocent letters to her mother. 'Nathan,' she said as she slid from her chair and positioned herself at his feet, her chin resting on his knee, 'tell me what it was really like.'

He stroked her hair. 'Maybe when you're older.'

'No, seriously.' She looked up at him. 'I need to know.'

'Seriously,' he countered, 'I will. But not

tonight. It's getting late and I'm afraid you're going to turn into a pumpkin.'

'Not until you've taken off my glass slippers,' Vic said, and smiled.

29 April 1963
Dear Mummy,

Oh, glorious, glorious red letter day. Now I truly understand the expression for the first time.

Flying back from afternoon lectures with the sun shining and the east wind nipping my face, there was the post in my box in the JCR. Sorting the letters as I climbed my staircase, I saw the familiar envelope at the bottom of the stack.

There is a necessary ritual for these things. The sanctuary of my room, and the putting away of books, and the making of a cup of tea, and then the paper knife. I saved the magazine's envelope till last—I always save them till last—and opened it with only half my attention. I was thinking of the paper I'm writing on some obscure eighteenth-century poets, and doing a fairly good job of ignoring the knot that always forms in my stomach, more dread than hope. But finally, I slit the envelope with razor neatness, unfolded the very ordinary letter and carefully smoothed out the creases, and had no further excuse for delay.

'What an odd rejection,' I thought as I read, then had to read it over twice more before the words penetrated.

I've sold not just one poem, but three! And to Granta, no less. 'The Huntsman', and 'The

Last Supper', and 'Solstice'. And they like the English myth series ('Huntsman', 'Solstice') so much that they want to see the rest.

How is it possible to feel numb and ecstatic at the same time? Haven't told anyone yet, not even Daphne, as I wanted you to be the first to know.

I realize you've been concerned for me these last few months, but I seem to have got over the sticky patch, and the sale of the poems confirms to me that I have been going in the right direction all along. I have to admit I had doubts this last winter, wondering whether I had the courage and the stamina to succeed as a poet, and the truly awful thing about it was not being able to imagine doing anything else.

But it seems that I have made a beginning, and now it is up to me to live up to it.

Your loving,
Lydia

The front door creaked and Vic looked up from her desk, listening. She glanced at the clock. It must have been the wind, she thought—she had half an hour yet before Kit should be home from school.

When the second supervision of her Monday afternoon schedule had been cancelled due to flu, she'd taken advantage of the opportunity to come home early and put in an extra hour's work. She'd cleared a space on her desk and laid Lydia's manuscript pages out like pieces in a jigsaw puzzle, shuffling and reshuffling the order of the poems.

That they were good she had no doubt—brilliant, even—a final step in the evolution of Lydia's work. The poems reached back, integrating elements from her early mythically-themed poetry with the later confessional style, and in doing so achieved a new balance. And when these missing poems were added to the ones published in her last volume, the book gained a wholeness, a sort of unity Vic had not seen in her work before.

She would see that the book was published as it should have been, a testament to Lydia's talent.

But there was something more, she thought as she swapped two of the poems again, a feeling that there was a sequence, a pattern to them that kept shifting just out of her mind's reach. Perhaps if she read them once more, in a slightly different order—

The door slammed, Kit's signature, and a moment later she heard the thud of his backpack hitting the floor outside her study. 'Hi, sweetheart,' she said, not looking up. 'How was school?'

No answer. She turned and saw Kit standing in the doorway, face set in a sullen scowl. Although he suffered from the occasional pre-adolescent mood, he was normally a good-natured child, and particularly boisterous when let out of school for the day. 'What's the matter, love?' Vic asked, concerned. 'Are you all right?'

He shrugged and didn't speak.

All right, thought Vic, *try another tactic.* She

took off her glasses and stretched. 'Bad day?' she asked mildly.

Another shrug. He wouldn't meet her eyes.

'Me, too,' she said as if he'd answered. 'Maybe we'd both feel better if we took a walk. What do you say?'

This time she thought the shrug looked a bit more positive.

'Want a snack first?' she asked, and received a sharp, negative head shake. A bad sign—he was usually ravenous after school. 'Then let me get my coat.'

She heard him stomp through the kitchen as she stopped in the loo, then the back door slammed. Oh, Lord, she thought, leaning against the sink for a moment. One was never prepared for these things, and she *had* had a particularly bad day already. Lost lecture notes this morning, then an hysterical student, and to top it off, a furious row with Darcy after lunch.

The argument had started, of all the silly things, over whose turn it was to use the photocopier.

Vic had taken a stack of books into the photocopier room, intending to make handouts of some selected poems for her lecture on the Romantics, then had to run back to her office to retrieve a volume left on her desk.

When she'd returned to the photocopier a few moments later, she'd found her books moved and Darcy firmly in position over the humming machine.

'Oh, so sorry. Were those yours?' he'd said.

'One should really be more careful about leaving one's property untended. So much petty theft these days, even the hallowed halls of the English Faculty might not be sacrosanct.'

'You knew perfectly well that they were mine,' she said, exasperated. 'And no one in their right mind would steal second-hand copies of Keats and Shelley.' She eyed the stack of papers in the machine's In tray with dismay. 'Couldn't you let me run these few things, Darcy? I need them for tomorrow morning's lecture, and I've got a supervision in ten minutes. After all, I was here first.'

His presence seemed suffocatingly large in the small room, and she could smell the beer on his breath, no doubt the result of a rather liquid pub lunch. He still wore his gown, and as he leaned against the copier with his arms folded, he looked like a dissipated King Lear. Or Olivier playing Lear might be more like it, she thought. There was always something a bit overly theatrical about Darcy.

Smiling, he said, 'Perhaps if one were better prepared one wouldn't be in such a panic.'

The fury that seared through her caught her completely by surprise, and she found herself suddenly shouting at him, 'Don't you dare criticize me, Darcy. You've no right. And you had no right to undermine me to Adam Lamb. You knew how important it was to me to see him.'

'My dear Victoria.' Darcy raised his brows and looked down his rather fleshy nose at her. 'I have a perfect right to express my

175

professional opinion to *my* friends, and I am not responsible for the success or failure of your little projects.'

'Don't patronize me,' she hissed back, making a belated effort to keep her voice down. 'Of course you're not responsible for my work, but you've no right to deliberately sabotage it just because it doesn't fit into your archaic *little* definition of academic respectability. Did you say the same sort of things about me to Daphne Morris that you said to Adam?'

'Oooh,' said Darcy with pursed lips, mocking her. 'On a first-name basis with Adam, now, are we? How chummy for you.' Coldly, he added, 'For your information, I haven't seen Daphne since Lydia's funeral, and I have no intention of doing so in the foreseeable future. I quite despise the woman. I'd have thought the two of you would have got on quite well.'

While Vic struggled to think of a suitably stinging retort, Darcy had scooped up his papers from the photocopier's trays and turned towards the door. 'Take all the time you want,' he said sweetly, over his shoulder. 'I shan't need my copies until next week's lectures.'

Just thinking about it made Vic flush painfully. Darcy Eliot could be quite charming—she'd even seen him behave considerately to other staff members on occasion—so why did she let the man reduce her to such childish behaviour? She had meant to talk to him about Adam, meant to do it in a civilized, rational way, in a place and time of her own choosing. But somehow she and Darcy always seemed to get at cross purposes with one another, and their constant infighting did her reputation no good in the department. In future she'd have to make more effort to find some sort of common ground, difficult as it might be.

With a sigh, she splashed some cold water on her face, ran a brush through her hair, and went out to meet Kit in the garden.

She found him at the gate, scuffing his feet in the pile of last year's leaves she'd been meaning to rake up. He still wouldn't meet her eyes, but when she said, 'The river path?' he nodded.

Once through the gate, they automatically turned left, towards Cambridge. Vic put her mind in neutral as they swung along in silence, trusting that the exercise and companionship would eventually loosen Kit's tongue. Now she found herself glad of the excuse to be out, for it was her favourite sort of day—soft, still and damp, the world a comforting and uniform grey. She had no objection to sunshine, in fact she liked it as well as the next person after a long wet spell, but clear days didn't exhilarate her in the same way. *Gloomy,* her mother had disapprovingly called her as a child, but Vic didn't see how she could help something as innate as a love of rainy weather.

The moisture in the air intensified odours, and as she breathed in, the rich, earthy spring scent came to her so strongly that she thought she must actually be smelling things growing. Glancing at Kit, she saw that his scowl had softened, and he was looking about with almost his usual interest. Judging her moment, she said casually, 'Do you want to tell me what happened at school today?'

He glanced at her and shrugged, but after a moment he said grudgingly, 'I heard Miss Pope talking to the new P.E. teacher.'

'Miss Pope? Your English teacher?'

Kit gave her the disdainful glance she deserved for such an asinine comment. She knew Miss Pope perfectly well. Thirtyish and single, Elizabeth Pope had been obviously smitten with Ian, and had requested regular and unnecessary parent-teacher conferences. Whether or not Ian had taken his advantage, Vic had not known, nor had she particularly cared, except for Kit's sake.

'And what did Miss Pope say?'

'They were in the lunch queue, and I went back for a fork,' he began circuitously. 'They didn't see me. I didn't mean to eavesdrop.'

'No, I'm sure you didn't,' Vic said encouragingly, but he hunched his shoulders, turtle-like, and looked down at his trainers. She thought fleetingly and irrelevantly that he had outgrown his shoes again, and wondered when he would begin to catch up to his feet. 'Were they talking about me?' she asked, when he didn't speak.

Nodding, Kit kicked hard at a stone in the path, then spit out the words with the same violence. 'Miss Pope said you worked all the time, and that Dad wouldn't have left if you'd paid more attention to him. She said you weren't a proper wife.'

Bitch, thought Vic, holding her breath and

178

counting to ten. She'd have a few choice words to say to the nosy Miss Pope, but she would not take her anger out on Kit. And where had Elizabeth Pope got her nasty ideas, anyway? Pillow talk?

'Darling,' she said when she thought she could control her voice, 'it was very wrong of Miss Pope to be talking about things that are none of her business. You do know that, don't you?'

Kit made a slight movement with his shoulders, but kept his head down.

Vic sighed. How could she explain to him what she didn't understand herself? 'In the first place, no one can ever really know what goes on between two people except the people themselves. And things are never as simple in a relationship as Miss Pope made it sound.' She couldn't blame Ian—tempting as it was, she knew that trying to enlist Kit on her side could damage him even further. 'Sometimes people just grow in different directions, develop different needs and interests, and one day they wake up and discover there's no reason to be together any more.'

'Except me,' said Kit, taking her generalization personally. 'Wasn't I a good enough reason?'

There it was, thought Vic, the crux of the matter, and she had no excuses to offer for Ian. And the truth, even if it were possible to tell Kit, would still not suffice. Haltingly, she said, 'Sometimes grown-ups decide they're not ready to be grown-ups, and they do things without thinking about other people's feelings. It may not be right, but it happens, and we

179

just have to make the best of it.' She couldn't bring herself to reassure Kit that Ian loved him, for she was not at all sure that he did, and she knew Kit would sense any falsity on her part.

They had walked almost to the outskirts of Cambridge. She could see the goal posts of Pembroke's Sports Grounds in the distance, a thin black vertical frame against the poplars. The daylight was fading by imperceptible degrees, for the heavy cloud cover hid any hint of sunset, and a chill little wind had sprung up in the dusk. Putting her arm lightly round Kit's shoulders, she said, 'Come on, love. Let's turn back. It's getting cold.'

They turned their backs to the wind and started homewards. Glancing at her son's still-averted face, Vic sensed that she hadn't yet reached the heart of his distress. What mattered to him so much that he couldn't say it?

Slowly, she asked, 'Did Miss Pope make you angry because you feel I'm not paying you enough attention?'

Kit jerked his head in a nod. His lips were pinched so tightly together that they'd turned white, an effort, Vic guessed, to keep them from trembling. *Damn Miss Pope,* she thought, *and damn Ian, damn them all.* But she knew she was shifting blame, that Kit's security was her responsibility alone, and she had fallen down on the job.

She'd been a fool to get involved with Nathan. Aware of Kit's vulnerability, she'd still put her own needs first, and now she wasn't sure she could bear the thought of giving Nathan up.

And Lydia? Was her obsession with Lydia Brooke worth hurting Kit more than Ian had hurt him already? Perhaps Duncan had been right, and she should let it go, but she knew that was impossible even as she thought it. But she would have to tread more carefully, making sure it no longer took first place in her life.

'I'm sorry, Kit,' she said, giving his shoulders a squeeze. 'I'll just have to do better, won't I?'

He nodded and gave her a swift upwards glance before his face relaxed into a ghost of a smile.

Vic hugged him again. 'What do you say we start with a fire, and some hot chocolate, and a serious game of Monopoly?'

Chapter Eight

Dear, we know only that we sigh, kiss, smile;
*   Each kiss lasts but the kissing; and grief*
*   goes over;*
Love has no habitation but the heart.
Poor straws! on the dark flood we catch awhile,
Cling, and are borne into the night apart.
The laugh dies with the lips, 'Love' with
*   the lover.*

Rupert Brooke, from
Mutability

The hall clock chimed six as Margery Lester fastened the pearl stud in her ear. Her dress

181

was new and rather successful, she thought, silver with the faintest hint of green, a high collar, and a row of tiny pearl buttons down the back. She'd had to ask Grace to do up the buttons—that was one disadvantage to having outlived one's husbands; they were occasionally useful.

Yes, the dress would do, she thought as she gave it one last survey in her dressing-table mirror. She avoided pinks and blues and lavenders—old lady colours, she called them, although she certainly couldn't deny that she had crossed the threshold of that category. But there were still occasions when she caught a fleeting and unexpected glimpse of herself in a mirror and thought, who is that old woman? Surely not little Margery!

Margery was lithe and brown from tennis in the summer sun, Margery drove open cars a bit too fast, Margery laughed and took lovers ... But the boundaries between life and fiction had blurred with the years, and she wondered now if she had ever been that girl, or if she had constructed her in memory as she would a character in a book.

She heard Grace's heavy footsteps in the hall, then a moment later her face appeared, reflected in the dressing-table mirror.

'Madam, the guests will be arriving any time now and you should be down to greet them,' fretted Grace as she crossed the room to flick imaginary particles of dust from Margery's shoulders. A frown added extra creases to her already furrowed face.

'I'm coming, I'm coming,' sighed Margery. 'You're such a tyrant, Grace,' she added, and gave the hand on her shoulder an affectionate pat. 'I promise I'll be down before the bell rings.' She'd given up years ago trying to stop Grace calling her Madam, for Grace was getting on as well, and seemed more determined with each passing year to turn herself into a parody of an old English family retainer.

Grace met her eyes in the mirror. 'You know these parties are too much, you'll be exhausted tomorrow. Did you remember to take your tablets?'

'Oh, don't fuss so, Grace,' said Margery, splashing a bit of scent on her throat and wrists. 'I'll be perfectly fine.' In truth, it was Grace who would be exhausted tomorrow, even though Margery had insisted she get help with the cooking and serving. But Margery had had a little weak spell recently, and Grace had been hovering like a mother hen ever since. Margery stood and gave herself a final once-over in the three-way glass, then followed Grace obediently down the stairs.

Her dinner parties, and Grace's cooking, were renowned, but although she would never admit it to Grace, she was beginning to find them a bit wearing. Perhaps it was just people in general—it took more and more effort to leave her writing long enough to keep up the most basic of social connections. Fictional characters, after all, *usually* behaved in the ways one intended, though there were no guarantees, even there.

Or perhaps it wasn't people at all, but only that she was growing more jealous of her time—she sensed the grains speeding through the hour-glass, and she had so much still to say.

The doorbell chimed as she reached the bottom of the stairs. 'See, I told you so,' she said to Grace with a smile.

It was Darcy, early as always, so that he could help with the coats and the drinks. 'Mother, dear,' he paused to kiss her, 'you look divine.'

'Flatterer,' she said, laughing, and reached up to touch his cheek. 'You're frozen, darling. Come in by the fire, and pour yourself something before the hordes arrive.'

'A bloody puncture, can you believe it?' he said as he made himself a gin and tonic, then went to stand with his back to the fire. 'And on the Madingley Road, in traffic so heavy you'd have sworn it was Friday rather than Tuesday. I'm damp as an old dog, and will soon fill your sitting room with the aroma of steaming fur. But at least I'll be warm on the inside.' He smiled at her and knocked back half his drink. 'Who's coming, then? Can one have a singular horde?'

'It's a minimal horde tonight, I'm afraid,' said Margery as she poured herself a small sherry. 'Just Ralph and Christine, and Iris. Enid cancelled at the last minute, a bad case of the grippe, Iris said. Oh, and I almost forgot, Adam Lamb.'

Darcy laughed. 'Where on earth did you dig up old Adam?'

184

'In the Food Hall at Marks and Sparks, actually. I bumped into him in the frozen foods, frowning over two dinners as if he might take all day debating their relative merits. He looked as though he hadn't had a decent meal in months, and I took pity on him.'

'I'm sure he grovelled accordingly.'

'Darcy, that's neither fair nor kind, and you know it. He was polite, and he seemed pleased to be asked, and I see nothing wrong with that.'

'You'll forgive him anything just because you were at school with his mother,' said Darcy, teasing. 'Next thing I know, you'll be calling him a "nice boy." '

The bell chimed again, and Margery said as she rose from the sofa, 'I can say anything I like. But you, my dear boy, had better behave yourself.'

Enid's absence had actually suited very nicely, thought Margery as she surveyed the guests assembled round her table. For one thing, it made them an even number, and for another, she always found Enid's fluttering rather tiring.

She'd put Adam beside Iris, as they weren't well acquainted, and Darcy next to Christine, and that left her to make comfortable conversation with Ralph.

Adam had turned himself out quite well. The elbows of his suit jacket might be a bit shiny, but he wore a crisply starched shirt, and he appeared to have got himself freshly barbered for the occasion.

185

Darcy was right, of course, she did have rather a soft spot for Adam because his mother, Helen, had been an old school friend. His parents had held such hopes for him—they'd been sure he would take a distinguished degree in history, then read law, and after that, of course, follow his father into politics. Margery, though, even then, had doubted the wisdom of investing oneself in one's children, and had watched their disappointment helplessly.

It was ironic that she, who had not cared so desperately, had no cause for complaint, for Darcy had done quite well for himself. She supposed that Iris would be forced to retire soon, and that Darcy would succeed her as Head of Department. The position would allow him to exercise both his taste for power and his unfailing charm.

The charm was in evidence now, as he bent close to Christine Peregrine's sleek blonde head, telling some ribald story. It was a good thing that he and Ralph had known each other a long time, and that Ralph was not easily ruffled.

'Darcy's on fine form tonight,' said Ralph as he reached for the decanter and refilled her wine glass.

'Just what I was thinking,' said Margery. 'And that Christine is looking especially lovely.'

Ralph smiled. 'Just what I was thinking. I'm not getting much opportunity to appreciate her from either side of the table these days—she's been on a lecture tour.' An eminent mathematician, Christine Peregrine looked on her husband's passion for books with the same fond incomprehension he felt for her maths.

What an attractive man Ralph was, thought Margery, glancing at him in the candlelight. Thin and dark, with that certain indefinable air of bookishness that she had always found appealing—though she had to admit his dark hair had thinned in the years she'd known him. They'd met at some literary soirée given in her honour, he with a fresh degree in classics and a dream he had no money to implement, and she'd been captivated. She had helped him, although few people even now were aware of it, and today the familiar Peregrine Press logo was synonymous with the leading edge in fiction and poetry.

At the other end of the table, Iris gave a bark of laughter at something Adam said. She'd held the floor long enough for Adam to polish off a large serving of Grace's veal osso bucco, and now he seemed to be proving he could hold his own against Iris's rather domineering conversational style.

Adam's job would have given him considerable experience, thought Margery, in dealing with formidable older women, and she imagined he would listen attentively while suspecting the little weaknesses Iris's manner concealed. Iris, the terror of both staff and students, was madly devoted to her Persian cat, and could not sleep at night without a cup of Horlicks and a hot water bottle.

Margery brought her attention back to Ralph, who had begun telling her about a new talent he'd discovered, and as she listened to his voice interspersed with the soft rhythmic clinks of silver and crystal, she found herself glad of having made tonight's effort.

They'd finished the veal and started on Grace's chocolate mousse when Margery heard the distant ringing of the telephone.

'Dame Margery, this pudding is absolutely heavenly,' said Adam. 'If you'll forgive me the rather inappropriate adjective,' he added with a self-deprecating chuckle.

'Surely your boss would allow you the slight impertinence, given the exquisite nature of Grace's mousse?' said Darcy.

'Or you could substitute ambrosial,' suggested Ralph. 'Which is both inoffensive and true.'

The door to the kitchen opened, and as Grace came in, Darcy said, 'How do you do it, Grace? Do tell us your secret.'

'Yes,' said Christine, 'do tell, please. It's so amazingly light—'

'I'm sorry,' said Grace, interrupting the flow of compliments, 'but there's a phone call for Miss Iris. It's Miss Enid, and she sounds dreadfully upset.'

Iris paled, and her spoon clattered into her dish. 'Oh, God. It's Orlando, something's happened to Orlando.' She rose, knocking the table, and turned to Grace.

'You can take it in the sitting room, Miss Iris,' said Grace, and led her out.

'Who is Orlando?' asked Adam, understandably puzzled.

'Her cat,' explained Margery. 'She dotes

188

on him. He's named after Virginia Woolf's character.'

'Rather suitably, don't you think?' said Darcy. 'Since the poor emasculated beast is neither one thing nor the other.'

This comment brought a few guilty smiles, but the silence round the table grew uneasy as they waited for Iris to return. What on earth would they say to her, thought Margery, if something had indeed happened to the poor cat?

But when Iris came back into the dining room a few moments later, she showed no sign of incipient hysterics. She walked slowly to her chair and stood behind it, grasping its back with her hands. How odd, thought Margery, who prided herself on her powers of observation, that she had not noticed her friend's enlarged knuckles, white now with the strength of her grip on the chair.

'I'm sorry, Margery—all of you—to spoil such a lovely party, but I'm afraid I have some very distressing news. Vic McClellan died this afternoon.'

Part Two

... women have been deprived of the narratives, or the texts, plots, or examples, by which they might assume power over ... their lives.

Carolyn Heilbrun, from
Writing a Woman's Life

Chapter Nine

*... Do you think there's a far border town,
somewhere,
The desert's edge, last of the lands we know,
Some gaunt eventual limit of our light,
In which I'll find you waiting; and we'll go
Together, hand in hand again, out there,
Into the waste we know not, into the night?*
Rupert Brooke, from
The Wayfarers

Kincaid tossed the last of his paperwork in his Out basket, glanced at his watch and yawned. Only half-past six. Mondays were reputed to be the longest day of the week, but this bleak Tuesday had far surpassed its predecessor in tediousness and he would be happy to go home.

Now he had only to wait for Gemma, who was out dredging up the last facts on a case that was over, bar the shouting. At least it had got her out of the bloody office, he thought as he rocked back in his chair and stretched. His phone rang and he picked it up lazily, expecting to hear Gemma's voice. 'Kincaid,' he answered, cradling the phone with his shoulder as he tidied a few things into his drawer.

'Duncan? It's Alec Byrne here.' The reception was poor and Byrne's voice faded tinnily in and

193

out. 'Sorry about the ... it's this bloody mobile phone. There, that's better,' he said, coming in more clearly. 'Listen, Duncan—'

Byrne sounded hesitant, almost diffident. Amused, Kincaid said, 'What's the matter, Alec? Did you change your mind about the Lydia Brooke case?'

'No. Listen, Duncan, I'm sorry, but I'm afraid I have some bad news.'

Kincaid brought the front legs of his chair back to the floor with a thump. 'What are you talking about, Alec?' He couldn't remember Byrne having a penchant for bad jokes.

'I happened to be in Control when the call came through, so I came myself. I recognized the name from our conversation the other day. You said your ex-wife was called Victoria McClellan?'

Kincaid knew the drill too well. His heart jerked in sudden fear. 'What do you mean was, Alec?'

'I'm sorry, Duncan. She's dead. The medics say probable heart attack. There was nothing they could do.'

The room receded oddly and he heard a buzzing in his ears. Byrne's voice came distantly to him, then the words seemed to assemble themselves into something that made sense.

'Duncan, are you all right?'

'There's been a mistake, Alec,' he managed to say against the weight pressing on his chest. 'It must be a different Victoria McClellan—'

'An English lecturer living in Grantchester?' Byrne said with reluctant certainty. 'I'm sorry, mate, but I thought you should know. Can you tell me how to contact her hus—'

It couldn't be. Byrne was wrong, there must be some silly mistake, Kincaid thought, but he heard himself saying, 'I'm on my way.' Byrne's voice still came faintly from the handset as he replaced it in the cradle.

Struggling into his jacket in the corridor, he ran full tilt into Chief Superintendent Childs.

'Been sneaking out to the pub?' said Childs, steadying him with a hand on his shoulder. Then, as he looked into Kincaid's face, 'I say, Duncan, are you all right? You're white as a sheet, man.'

Kincaid shook his head and pulled away from Childs' restraining fingers. 'Have to go.'

'Wait, lad.' Childs reached for him again with a hand the size of a ham, and it was the sheer bulk of him that finally made some impression on Kincaid's dazed mind.

'Tell me what's up,' Childs said. 'You can't just go haring off like that without a word.'

'It's Vic,' Kincaid managed to say. 'My wife ... ex-wife. They say she's dead. I've got to go.'

'Where?' Childs asked, to the point as always.

'Cambridgeshire.'

'Where's Gemma? You don't look fit to drive.'

'I'm all right. I'll be all right,' Kincaid repeated as he slipped from his superior's grasp like a footballer evading a tackle and dodged his way towards the lift.

Even in his shock, he realized his chief was right. He had no business driving the Midget at high speeds in bad weather, so he took the best car available from the pool, a late model Rover with a powerful engine.

All the way to Cambridge he repeated his litany of disbelief to the rhythm of his tyres on the motorway's wet tarmac. *It couldn't be Vic. Vic couldn't die of a heart attack, for God's sake—she was too young. It couldn't be Vic.*

Some small rational voice in his head reminded him that he and Vic both were getting near to forty, they weren't all that young. And a few months ago, the wife of one of his mates, younger even than Vic, had died suddenly of an aneurysm.

All right, it happened. Of course, it happened. But not to him. And not to Vic.

His armour began to weaken as he reached the Grantchester cut-off. He clamped his hands tighter on the wheel to stop them trembling, and tried not to think at all.

He saw the blue flash of the emergency lights as he made the turn into the High Street. Two patrol cars were parked up on the kerb in front of Vic's cottage, but there was no sign of an ambulance. Kincaid pulled the Rover up into the gravelled drive and stopped it where he had parked on Sunday. *On Sunday,* he thought, *Vic had been fine on Sunday.*

Slowly now, he got out of the car and shut the door. His knees felt insubstantial as he stepped deliberately on the gravel, and he took

196

a breath to clear the sudden swimming in his head. Vertigo. *What a solid word for such an unanchored feeling.* The door opened and a dark form appeared, silhouetted against the light. *Vic. No, not Vic. Alec Byrne, crunching across the gravel to meet him.*

Byrne reached him, touched his arm. 'Duncan. There was no need for you to come all this way. We've everything in hand.'

'Where is she?'

'I'm afraid they've taken her to the morgue,' Byrne said gently. 'The medics pronounced her dead on scene.' He searched Kincaid's face. 'Come on. We'd better get you a cup of tea.'

Morgue. No, not yet. He wasn't ready to think of it, not yet.

Kincaid allowed himself to be led into the house, then through to the sitting room, while the detached part of his mind commented on how odd it was to be the one ministered to. Byrne directed him to sit on the sofa, and a constable brought him hot, sweet tea. He drank it obediently, thirstily, and after a few moments his mind began to function again.

'What happened?' he asked Byrne. 'Where was she? You're sure it was—'

'Her son found her in the kitchen when he came home from sports. Unconscious, or perhaps already dead—we can't be sure.'

'Kit?'

'You know the boy?' asked Byrne. 'We've not been able to contact the father, and he ought to have someone with him he knows.'

Kit, dear God. He hadn't even thought of Kit.

197

And Kit had found her. 'Where is he?'

'In the kitchen with Constable Malley. I believe she's made him some tea as well.'

'In the kitchen?' Kincaid repeated, and all the things he'd pushed out of his mind came rushing back. *Lydia Brooke found dead in her study, of apparent heart failure. A suicide note that wasn't. Candles and music and gardening clothes.* He stood up. 'You're not treating it as a crime scene?'

Byrne looked at him warily. 'I really don't see that it's necessary, under the circumstances—'

'You don't know the circumstances!' Kincaid shouted at him, then made an effort to lower his voice. 'Don't let them touch anything until after the post mortem. God knows what damage has been done already.' His anger came as a relief, making a clean burn through the fog in his head.

'Look, Duncan,' Byrne said, standing to face him. 'I realize you're upset, but this is not your jurisdiction, and I'll handle a routine death in the way I see fit—'

Kincaid stabbed a finger at him. 'What if you're wrong, Alec? Can you afford to be wrong?'

They stared at each other, both flushed, then after a moment Byrne relaxed and said, 'All right. I'll humour you. After all, what do I have to lose?'

'I'm going to see Kit,' said Kincaid. 'And you can keep everyone else out of the bloody room.'

Kit sat huddled in the near kitchen chair, his back to Kincaid, while a female constable occupied the other.

'We've notified the grandparents,' Byrne said in Kincaid's ear as they stood in the doorway. 'They're on their way.'

'Vic's parents?'

'Yes. Her mother was quite ... distraught.' Byrne jerked his head at the constable and she rose, coming to join them. 'We'll wait for you in the sitting room,' he said to Kincaid, and they went out, closing the door behind them.

The room looked ordinary, domestic, un-marred by what had happened in it. Kincaid walked round the small table and slid into the chair the constable had vacated.

'Hello, Kit.'

The boy looked up. 'You came,' he said with a sort of distant puzzlement, and so blank was his face with shock that Kincaid wasn't sure he'd have recognized him had he passed him on the street.

'Yes.'

'I couldn't wake her,' Kit said, as if continuing a conversation. 'I thought she was asleep, but I couldn't wake her. I rang 999.' The cup of tea before him was untouched.

'I know.' Kincaid reached out and felt the cup; it was cold. He took it and poured the contents down the sink, then set about making fresh cups for them both. Kit watched him without interest.

When the kettle boiled, Kincaid ladled a generous amount of sugar into Kit's tea and

199

added enough milk to cool it to drinkable temperature. He returned to the table with both cups and pushed Kit's across to him. 'Drink your tea.'

Kit lifted the cup with both hands and drank it without stopping, like a small child. Kincaid watched him, waiting, and after a few moments a little colour returned to his cheeks.

'You had sports after school today?' Kincaid asked, sipping his own tea.

Kit nodded. 'Running. I'm going for the five hundred metre.'

'Do you walk home?'

A negative shake. 'Too far. I ride my bike, most days.'

'What time did you get home today?' The questions came out of habit, a need to lay the details out like a grid, perhaps to build a framework that would support them both.

'Fiveish. The usual.'

'Tell me what happened next.'

Kit moved his feet restively. 'She wasn't in her office, so I looked in the sitting room. We started Monopoly yesterday, and she promised we'd play when I got home.'

Kincaid had seen the game without registering it, pushed to one side of the sitting room table. 'And then what?' *Gently, gently, but he must know.*

No response. The silence stretched so long that Kincaid thought he'd lost his tenuous link with the boy, then Kit said, violently, 'They didn't believe me.'

'Didn't believe what?' Kincaid asked, frowning.

'I saw someone. I came in the kitchen ... looked out the window. Before I saw—' His glance skittered away from Kincaid's.

Kincaid knew what he couldn't say. 'What did you see before that? When you looked out the window?'

'A shape. A dark shape. By the gate at the bottom of the garden. Then I didn't think of it again.'

Kincaid's pulse quickened. 'Man shape or woman shape?'

'I don't know.' For the first time, Kit sounded close to tears. 'It was too quick, just a flash. But I saw it. I know I did. Why won't they listen to me?'

'I believe you,' Kincaid said with growing conviction.

Kit met his eyes. 'You do?'

The door opened and Byrne looked in, motioning for Kincaid to join him.

'I'll be right back,' Kincaid said to Kit, and went out into the corridor.

'There's nothing more we can do here tonight,' said Byrne. 'Would you be willing to wait for the grandparents?'

No, Kincaid thought, dealing with Vic's parents was not an obligation he'd take on willingly, but he couldn't see leaving Kit, either. 'All right,' he said. 'I'll wait. Alec, you didn't tell me Kit said he saw someone in the garden.'

Byrne shrugged. 'He was incoherent, poor kid. Imagining things.'

'He's not incoherent now. And he's a reliable kid, Alec. You had better get the crime scene lads out there at first light.' Seeing Byrne start to bristle, he added, 'Just in case. It always pays to cover your arse, Alec, just in case. And bloody hope it doesn't rain between now and then.'

After a moment, Byrne said grudgingly, 'All right. And I've rung the pathologist, but he says he can't get to the p.m. till tomorrow afternoon. Do you want to attend?'

Kincaid shook his head, said harshly, 'No.' *Not that, not yet. It didn't bear thinking of.*

'Sorry,' said Byrne. 'Tactless of me. Listen, Duncan, I really am sorry, about all of this.' He shrugged his thin shoulders. 'I'll ring you after the p.m.'

Kincaid, finding the words lodged in his throat, nodded his assent.

'We still haven't a clue as to how to contact the husband. Do you think you could get something out of the boy? Or her parents? We'll try his college in the morning.' Byrne grimaced. 'Bloody nuisance.'

They made arrangements about the keys and the closing of the house, then Byrne took himself off with poorly concealed relief. Kincaid watched him drive away, followed by the other officers, then went slowly back into the house.

In the kitchen, Kit sat as if he hadn't moved at all since Kincaid had left him. Without speaking, Kincaid made a quick search of the provisions. He found bread in the bin and cheese in the fridge, and within a few minutes had put together a cheese sandwich with butter and pickle. He'd touched as little as possible, making do with a small paring knife from the drawer and a towel from the kitchen roll under the cabinet. They had already contaminated the scene, but he saw no point in making it worse.

He set the sandwich before Kit and sat down opposite. 'I know you think you can't possibly eat,' he said. 'But it's important that you do. Give it a try.'

For a moment Kit looked as if he might protest, then he raised the sandwich to his mouth and took a listless bite. He chewed mechanically at first, then he seemed to realize he was hungry and wolfed down the rest. 'I hate pickle,' he said when he'd finished the last crumb.

'Sorry.' Kincaid smiled. 'I'll do better next time.'

'Are you staying?' asked Kit, a spark of hope in his eyes.

Shaking his head, Kincaid said, 'Only until your grandparents come for you.'

'I won't go,' Kit said vehemently. 'I hate them. I want to stay here.'

Kincaid closed his eyes and wished desperately for Gemma. She would know what to do. She would say, 'Come on, love, let's get your things together,' in her matter-of-fact way. She might even put her arm around Kit, or tousle his hair, but those were things Kincaid did not dare attempt.

He blinked and said, 'You can't stay here, Kit. And as far as I know your grandparents are your legal guardians until we can contact your father. Have you any idea how to reach him?'

Kit shook his head impatiently. 'No, I already told them. He didn't write to us. Mummy didn't even have an address for him.'

'We'll find him,' Kincaid said with more certainty than he felt. 'He must have left instructions with his college. But in the meantime, you'll have to go to Reading with your grandparents, and I doubt you want your grandmother packing for you.' He gave Kit a conspiratorial smile, and after a moment Kit smiled grudgingly back.

'All right. But I'm not staying more than a day. There's nothing to do, and they won't even let me watch telly.'

Kincaid didn't comment. He remembered the sterile household all too well, and suspected there would be little solace for a grieving child. He led Kit to the bottom of the stairs, and when Kit hesitated, Kincaid said, 'I'll come up in a bit, shall I? See how you're doing.'

He watched Kit disappear up the staircase, all long legs and big feet from that angle. Then he turned and wandered down the hall into Vic's office. Almost, he thought to see her turn from her keyboard and smile, and he knew he still hadn't taken in the undeniable fact of her death. But he could go on pretending, and he could use his eyes to observe and his mind to record, just as he would on any case.

The room looked odd to him, and he studied it for a moment without touching anything. On Sunday her desk had been covered with books and papers, but it had had the look of organized clutter, with everything in its proper place. Had she moved the books? One lay face down on the floor, its pages crumpled. Vic had been almost obsessively neat—surely she would not have left a book like that?

Unless, said the small detached voice in his mind, *she had begun to feel ill, and knocked the book from its place as she got up to go to the kitchen, perhaps for a glass of water.*

A logical explanation, possibly, but he couldn't yet allow himself to think of Vic ill, in pain, frightened, alone. So he ignored the voice, and went on with his examination of her desk. A thick stack of manuscript pages lay beside the computer. He closed his eyes and thought of how it had looked on Sunday—the edges of the pages had been neatly aligned, and now they lay askew. They were also out of sequence, he discovered when he rifled through them. He thought of how much Vic had cared for her book, and he felt the hairs rise on the back of his neck.

He felt suddenly unwilling to leave the manuscript here, untended, and he straightened up, looking for some way to carry it. There, on the floor, an empty leather book satchel—it was, he imagined, what Vic used to carry papers back and forth to work. It would do.

Carefully, he put the pages into the satchel, then, seized by an urge he didn't understand, he started on the milk-crate file beside the desk. It held the original materials for the biography, letters in a strong hand he didn't recognize—Lydia's, of course—notes in Vic's handwriting, photos, even a few postcards. He put them all into the bag, and anything else that seemed relevant that he could glean from her desktop, and then he carried it all outside and locked it in the boot of the Rover.

In her office once more, he had a brief look at the computer, but Vic had apparently saved her work on the hard disk rather than a floppy, and he knew he hadn't time to access the files properly. He'd left Kit alone too long as it was, so he would just have to hope that Vic had been as obsessive about printing hard copy as she had been about everything else.

He was climbing the stairs when he realized he had not seen the notes he'd given Vic, or the copies of the poems she'd found.

Kit sat on the edge of his bed, an open grip at his feet. When Kincaid came in, he looked up and said dully, 'I don't know what to take.'

The room might have been Kincaid's own at that age, cluttered with books, and sports equipment, and barely outgrown toys. One shelf held a collection of bird's nests, another of rocks.

Glancing in the bag, Kincaid saw one jersey and a pair of jeans. 'Um, pyjamas?' he suggested. 'Toothbrush? A dressing gown?'

Kit shrugged. 'I suppose. They're all in the bathroom.'

He'd need things to wear to the funeral, Kincaid realized, but he also needed a few days before he even had to think of it. 'I'll tell you what,' he said. 'Why don't you go and get them, and I'll throw some things in the bag for you?'

'All right,' Kit agreed, and when he'd gone, Kincaid went quickly to the closet. A school blazer, a tie, some dark trousers, a white shirt. They would have to do. He found some black, lace-up shoes and those went in first, in the bottom of the bag. Then the other things, neatly folded, and on top of them the jeans and jersey. Next he added socks and underpants from the bureau drawers, then a Cambridge sweatshirt. Sitting back on his heels to survey the room for last minute necessities, he spied a worn teddy bear on the shelf above Kit's bed, and that he tucked in last.

Kit came in with a bundle of night things, and when Kincaid took them to fold he discovered the purple jersey Vic had worn on Sunday among the folds of the dressing gown. It smelled of her perfume, and very faintly, of her skin.

Their eyes met as they knelt either side of the bag, and after a moment Kincaid folded the jersey and packed it without a word.

Kit's room was on the front of the house, and as they zipped his bag they heard the sound of car tyres on gravel, then the slam of a car door.

'Just in time, eh?' said Kincaid, attempting a casual tone.

'No.' Kit sat back on his heels, almost quivering with distress.

The boy looked like a frightened rabbit ready to bolt, and Kincaid knew he mustn't let him lose control now. 'Come on, mate,' he said, standing and lifting the bag. 'I'm right behind you. We'll do this together.'

'No, wait, I forgot Nathan's books. I can't go without Nathan's books.' Kit swept a pile of books from his bedside table and they stuffed them into the already bulging bag, then Kincaid guided him down the stairs with a hand on his shoulder.

Kincaid had not seen Vic's parents since the Christmas before she left him, and he doubted whether time or circumstance would have altered their mutual dislike. He and Kit met them at the door, and he, at least, had the advantage of foreknowledge.

Eugenia Potts' face, already red and puffy with weeping, went slack with shock at the sight of him. An expression of mild surprise furrowed Bob Potts' bland face, and Kincaid wondered if, even now, the man felt anything at all.

'Hello, Bob. Mrs Potts.' He had never been able to bring himself to call her Eugenia, and Mum had been unthinkable.

'You!' she breathed. 'What are you doing here?'

Her tone was accusing, but he answered as mildly as he could. 'They rang me, I'm afraid. Look, you'd better come in.'

'You! What right have you to invite us into our daughter's house?' Pushing past him as he stepped back, she continued, her voice rising. 'You don't belong here, and I'll thank you to get—' She saw Kit then, for he'd been using

Kincaid's body as a shield. Changing gears in mid-tirade, she shrieked, 'Christopher, oh, my poor darling,' while grabbing him to her and pressing his blond head against the bosom of her tweedy coat.

Kincaid saw Kit stiffen, then struggle to extricate himself. A touch on his arm reminded him that he had, as usual, forgotten Bob Potts.

'Duncan, thank you for coming,' Potts said with quiet courtesy. 'But there's no need now for you to stay. Is there anything ... I mean, should we ...'

Feeling that perhaps he'd misjudged the man, Kincaid said softly, 'No, there's nothing you can do. Not until tomorrow, at least, and I'm sure someone will be ringing you. The police are very anxious to contact Kit's father, however. Have you any idea—'

'That man,' hissed Eugenia, for having finished throttling Kit, she'd caught the tail-end of their conversation. 'I blame him for this. If he hadn't abandoned her, none of this would have happened. My baby would be alive—'

Kit's face lost all colour, then he turned and ran from the room.

Kincaid rounded on Mrs Potts with a shout of anger. 'Enough! Keep your useless speculations to yourself, you silly woman, where they won't do any more damage.' He left her standing open-mouthed, and ran after Kit.

He found him in the sitting room, crouched on the floor over the wreckage of the Monopoly game. 'I kicked it,' Kit said, looking up at

Kincaid. Tears streamed down his face. 'I shouldn't have, but I was so angry. And now I can't ... I can't put it back—'

Kneeling beside him, Kincaid said, 'I'll help you,' and began sorting the paper money into its slots. 'Kit, don't pay any attention to what your grandmother said. She's just upset. You did absolutely the right things this afternoon, and no one could have done better.'

'Why does she have to be so beastly?' Kit said, hiccuping. 'Why did she have to be so beastly to you?'

Kincaid sighed. He felt suddenly too exhausted to think, much less talk, but he made an effort. 'She doesn't mean to be cruel, Kit. She just doesn't think. Some people are like loose cannons—they go off all the time at the nearest target, and it makes them feel better. And I'm afraid the more your grandmother hurts inside, the worse she's going to be, so try to be patient with her.'

'You weren't,' said Kit. 'I heard you shouting.'

'No, I wasn't, was I?' Kincaid admitted, smiling. 'So don't take me as an example.' He'd been half listening to the murmur of voices from the hall, hers rising in protest, her husband's coaxing, then the sound of desolate sobbing. The front door closed softly. 'They've gone to the car, I think,' he said, fitting the board into the top of the box and closing the lid. 'Come on. I'll walk you out.'

When they reached the porch, Potts climbed out of the car and came over to them. 'So sorry about all that,' he said. Light from the porch lamp glinted from his spectacles, so that Kincaid couldn't see his eyes. 'A sedative, and bed, I think, is what she needs.'

And what about Kit? thought Kincaid, but he didn't speak.

'Eugenia thinks ... that is, we feel that the house should be secured, and that we should keep the key ...' Potts said, twisting his hands together. 'That is, if you don't mind ...'

Kincaid fished the key Byrne had given him from his pocket. 'I didn't intend going off with the silver, Bob,' he said dryly as he held the key out.

'No, no, I didn't mean ... what I meant was—' Potts gestured helplessly at the house. 'Would you ... could you possibly, before you go ... I don't think I could possibly go back in the house, just now, you see.'

Kincaid did see, finally, and silently chided himself for an insensitive clod. 'Of course. You wait here with your grandad, Kit, and I'll be back in a tick.'

He checked the house quickly, securing the French doors in the sitting room, then the kitchen door, and turning out most of the lights. Then he grabbed Kit's bag from the hall and went out, locking the front door behind him.

They waited for him in the drive, their breath forming clouds of mist in the still, cold air. Kincaid pressed the key into Vic's father's hand, said, 'All right, then. You'd best be on your way.'

'I'll see you, mate,' he said to Kit, and

211

thumped him on the shoulder.

They walked away across the drive. When Kit reached the car he turned round and looked at Kincaid once more, then opened the back door and disappeared into the dark interior.

Kincaid watched the car pull out into the street, watched its tail lamps flash at the Coton Road junction before it vanished from his sight.

His inadequacy rose up to engulf him, and he protested aloud, 'What else could I have bloody done?'

There was no answer except the echo of his voice, and it was only then, standing alone before the dark and empty house, that he let himself believe she was gone.

Ralph was the first to break the stunned silence in Margery Lester's dining room. 'But how ... where ... an accident?'

Iris shook her head. 'Apparently not. They seem to think it was heart failure, but that's all I know.'

'Iris, are you all right?' asked Darcy, with sharp concern.

Galvanized into action by Darcy's words, Adam leapt to his feet and helped Iris into her chair.

She smiled up at him gratefully before she went on. 'The police rang Laura trying to get in touch with me, and she rang Enid. They're very anxious to notify Ian, of course.'

'Who's Ian?' asked Adam.

'Her husband,' explained Darcy. 'We should

all be so lucky. Beginning of Michaelmas term, he packed himself off to the south of France with a delectable graduate student. No forwarding address.'

'Darcy—' began Margery, but she really hadn't the heart to continue her reprimand, and for once his tone had held no malice. She felt surprised at her own sense of loss, for she had only met Victoria McClellan a few times at Faculty gatherings, but something about the younger woman had reminded Margery of herself at that age. Vic had been raising a son—more or less on her own, Margery had guessed, even before her husband's disappearance—and she'd had a sense of purpose about her own work that Margery recognized.

'Sorry, Mother,' said Darcy. 'Habit, I'm afraid. This is all rather dreadful.'

Iris looked near tears. 'I know it's selfish of me even to think it, but it's a dreadful blow to the department as well. How will we possibly replace her?' She shook her head. 'It makes me wonder if the department really is unlucky. First there was poor Henry's awful business—'

'Let's not talk about it tonight, Iris, please,' said Margery as a wave of exhaustion washed over her.

'I met her—Doctor McClellan, that is,' said Ralph. 'Did I tell you that, Margery? I liked her very much. I wonder what will happen now to her biography of Lydia Brooke?' He met his wife's eyes across the table and read some reproof in them. 'Oh, sorry. That was rather inappropriate, I suppose, but it wasn't meant avariciously. I was just curious.'

'We ought to be going, Ralph,' said Christine affectionately, 'before you put your foot in any further. Why don't you let us take you home, Iris? You've had a shock and there's no need for you to drive.'

Iris made a half-hearted protest. 'But Enid will need the car tomorrow. It's her shopping day.'

'Ride with me, then, and Ralph can drive your car,' Christine said firmly. 'There, it's settled.' She rose, the others followed suit, and they all made their way into the hall with murmured apologies and thanks.

'You'll come again, won't you, Adam?' said Margery as he bid her goodbye, for he seemed a bit lost. 'Under better circumstances?'

Adam smiled at her, and his genuine pleasure warmed her. 'Yes, I will, if you'll have me.'

Then the door closed behind them, and Margery and Darcy moved to the sitting room in unspoken accord.

'Pour me a drink, please, Darcy,' said Margery as she sank into the chair nearest the fire. 'A generous one.'

'Don't you think I should help you into bed?' he asked solicitously. 'It's been a very trying evening.'

'Don't cosset me,' she said crossly. 'Grace is bad enough without you starting in too.' She glared at him until he sighed and went to the drinks trolley.

'You're impossible,' he said, but he brought her a whisky, and he hadn't stinted too much.

214

Margery relented. 'If I need any help getting into bed, you can be sure Grace will provide it. And to tell you the truth, I'm too unsettled by all this to think about sleep.' She looked with concern at her son, who had poured himself a drink and sunk onto the sofa. 'The question is, Darcy, will you be all right? It's you who will have to deal with the repercussions of this ... awful business.'

'I know,' he answered, sounding suddenly weary. 'Why is it, Mother, darling, that we always leave our good intentions too late?' He met her eyes over the rim of his glass. 'I kept meaning to put things right with her, and somehow I never managed. It was the same with Father.'

'I don't know,' Margery said slowly. 'But one always seems to leave things unsaid. It's as inevitable as dying.'

Adam shivered in his heaterless car and wrapped the scarf more tightly round his throat. Why had he not spoken up at Dame Margery's table and said that he had known Vic? And that he, too, had liked her? He felt a stabbing of guilt, as if he had personally betrayed her by his silence.

'Don't be a silly bugger,' he said aloud. 'You hardly knew the woman.' But it didn't help, and tears smarted behind his eyelids. She had been so lovely, sitting on the moth-eaten chair in his parlour, drinking the sherry he'd poured her. In his mind's eye he saw the smooth swing of her fair hair as she turned her head and laughed at something he'd said.

There had been a delicacy about her, a waifish quality, that had reminded him somehow of Lydia. But she'd had Lydia's determination as well, he had sensed that, sensed that she wouldn't be satisfied with easy answers, and yet he hadn't been capable of giving her more.

He'd failed Lydia, too, in the end, as he'd failed everyone who mattered to him.

Suddenly the thought of going home alone to the vicarage seemed unbearable, and at the Queens' Road roundabout he kept to the right, along the Backs towards Grantchester. He would go to see Nathan—Nathan had known her, too. They could talk about her, and perhaps that would ease the dreadful emptiness inside him.

4 July 1963

Dear Mummy

I understand your distress at my news, but it simply can't be helped. I have too much work over the Long Vac to come home even for a few days. And as much as I would love to see you, it's probably not a good idea for you to visit me.

Please, please, don't worry about me. I'm quite all right, it's just that the pressures of work are a bit much right now, and I can't see anything for it but to keep my nose to the grindstone.

And there's the writing, too. Having gained some momentum, I feel I must keep it up, degree or no degree, because after all, that's the object of all this, isn't it?

216

Everything has been to further my success as a poet, and if I lose sight of that now it's all for nought.

Love,
Lydia

Adam pounded on the door of the darkened cottage, more out of reluctance to go home than in hopes that Nathan would answer. But just as he gave one last rap and turned away, he heard footsteps, and the door swung back.

He knew at first glance that his friend was very drunk, for Nathan held on to the doorknob like a man drowning, and his eyes absorbed the light like bottomless wells.

'Nathan?'

Nathan blinked, then opened his mouth and closed it again, as if his brain couldn't quite make the connection with his tongue. He tried once more. 'Adam, it's you,' he said, enunciating with care. Owlishly, he blinked again. 'Of course, it's you. You know it's you. Silly of me. I s'ppose you'd better come in.' Turning away, he walked off down the dim corridor, leaving Adam to shut the door and follow.

Adam fumbled after him, unsure of his footing in the dark and unfamiliar passage. He reached the door at the far end, and once through it he stopped to let his eyes adjust to the room's illumination. A faint light came from the decorative tubes installed under the kitchen cabinets, and from a few embers glowing in the hearth. Nathan sat in the chair nearest the fire, and on the table beside him a bottle glinted in the firelight.

Adam picked his way across the rug and lowered himself into the chair opposite. He had only seen Nathan drink like this a few times since they'd left University, and then only under great stress, and he feared he knew what had prompted it.

'Nathan, you've heard, haven't you? About Vic McClellan.'

'In College,' said Nathan, reaching an unsteady hand for the whisky bottle. 'Dinner ... High Table. Round like wildfire. Had to ... 'pologize to the Provost.' His enunciation was failing.

'You left in the middle of dinner?' asked Adam, picking the sense out of what he'd said.

Nodding, Nathan said, 'Had to. Didn't b'lieve it, you see. Went there. House all dark, locked, no one at home.' He raised his right hand and Adam saw a makeshift bandage wrapped round it, stained with dark blotches. 'Canna play piano now.' The hand fell to his lap again, as if a puppeteer had dropped the strings. 'Neighbours came, said it's true, all true.'

'Nathan, are you saying you tried to break down her door? And the neighbours came?'

Nathan smiled at him as if he'd made a brilliant deduction. 'That's it. Must've been shouting. Can't 'member.'

'Did someone look at your hand? You should see a doctor.'

218

'Doesn' matter,' Nathan mumbled, then he pulled himself up in his chair a little and seemed to try to focus on Adam's face. 'It doesn't matter,' he said carefully. 'Nothing matters now.'

Oh, dear Lord, thought Adam, he'd been a fool, a blind fool, not to have seen it. Nathan's veiled hints about someone in his life, his air of nervous excitement. And Vic McClellan's voice when she'd said Nathan's name.

'I'm so sorry, Nathan. I didn't know.'

Nathan sat forward suddenly in his chair, knocking his glass from the side table. It hit the rug and rolled against the edge of the hearth with a soft clink. 'I need to see her,' he said clearly, as if his anguish had burned momentarily through the haze of alcohol. 'Do you see? I need to hold her, touch her, so I'll know it's true. I held Jean until she wasn't Jean any more. That's how I knew.' He frowned at Adam and reached for his tumbler again, then stared in puzzlement at the vacant spot on the table.

Adam got up and retrieved the glass, and as he returned it to the table he saw that the bottle was almost empty. How full had it been in the beginning, he wondered, and need he worry about alcohol poisoning?

'Let me help you to bed, Nathan,' he said gently.

Nathan poured the last bit of whisky into his glass and swallowed it. 'Don' wanna sleep. Hafta wake up then, see?' He leaned his head

219

against the back of the chair and closed his eyes. 'Go home, Adam. Nothing to do.' After a moment he repeated, as if to himself, 'Nothing to do.'

Adam sat on, watching him until his breathing changed. Whether Nathan had fallen asleep or passed out, he couldn't tell, but his breaths were deep and regular, and he didn't respond when Adam said his name softly.

Carefully, Adam knelt by the hearth and banked the fire up, then fixed the screen in front of it. He took the lap rug that had been folded over the back of his chair and spread it over Nathan's still form, and then, not knowing what else he could do, he let himself out.

It was only when he woke in the cold hour before dawn, in his bed in the vicarage, that he realized what he'd seen in the sudden blaze as he'd made up the fire. Nathan's father's old shotgun, propped in the shadows by the back door.

As he turned the corner into Carlingford Road, Kincaid saw Gemma in the halo of light cast by the street lamp. She wore jeans and the old navy peacoat she used for knocking about in at weekends, and she sat on the steps of his building with her arms wrapped round her knees as if she were cold.

First he felt a flooding of relief, just knowing that she was alive and well, not snatched away from him, too—and then, mixed with the relief, the sort of senseless anger one feels towards a child who has narrowly escaped mishap.

He pulled the Rover into an empty spot at the right-hand kerb, got out and walked across to her. 'Why didn't you let yourself into the flat?' he said. 'Look at you—you're freezing.'

'I tried,' she said, looking up at him. 'I couldn't settle.' She pushed herself up from the steps and stood, her face on a level with his. 'The Chief told me about Vic, Duncan. I'm so sorry.'

It was then he discovered that her sympathy was the one thing he couldn't bear, and that any response he might make would threaten his precarious control. Looking away from her, he said, 'Let's go upstairs, why don't we, and have a drink.'

When they reached the flat, he discovered that Gemma had switched on the lamps and turned up the heating, and when he'd poured them both a small Scotch he joined her on the sofa. Sid jumped into his lap, purring as if he'd been gone a week. 'Hello, mate,' he said, stroking the cat's sleek, black fur. 'It's been a bloody long day, hasn't it?'

'Tell me what happened,' said Gemma. 'I only know what you told Denis.' She'd curled up in the corner of the sofa, feet beneath her, so that she could face him.

He took a sip of his drink, and while his throat still burned from it, he said harshly, 'Kit found her in the kitchen when he came home from school. The medics said there was nothing they

221

could do, probable heart attack.'

'Oh, no,' breathed Gemma, shaking her head. 'It's so hard to believe. She seemed so well on Sunday.'

'I *don't* believe it, Gemma.' Sid put his ears back, affronted, and Kincaid made an effort to lower his voice. 'It's just too much bloody coincidence.'

Warily, Gemma said, 'What are you talking about?'

'If you discount all the suicidal trappings, Lydia Brooke died suddenly and unexpectedly of heart failure, too.'

'But Lydia had a heart condition,' protested Gemma. 'Her heart failure was brought on by an overdose of her own medication.'

'And what if the suicide was manufactured? What if someone gave Lydia an overdose of her medication? That's what Vic suspected, even though she tiptoed around the obvious.'

'But why? Why would someone kill Lydia?'

'That's what Vic was trying to discover. And I didn't take her seriously.' Kincaid finally looked at Gemma, and saw the truth of it reflected in her eyes.

'You couldn't have known,' Gemma said softly, but they both knew it didn't absolve him. 'This is all speculation. And Vic didn't have a heart condition, did she?'

'Now you're arguing against yourself. That makes it all the less likely that she would die of heart failure, and it wouldn't keep an overdose of heart medication from doing the damage.'

222

'No, I suppose you're right,' Gemma admitted. 'But you can't be sure of anything until the toxicology scans come back.'

'Bloody Alec isn't even treating it as a crime scene.' Kincaid moved restlessly, causing Sid to stir in his lap.

'You can't very well blame him, under the circumstan—'

'I can and I will, if the p.m. results come back positive. It's sloppy police work, and you know it.' He glared at her, then seeing her expression, said, 'I'm sorry, Gemma. I don't mean to be churlish. It's just that ...'

'Do you want me to go?'

He stood up, dumping Sid unceremoniously to the floor, and went to the french windows. He looked out onto the darkened balcony, and after a moment said, 'No. Stay. Please.' Turning to face her again, he asked, 'What about Toby?'

'Hazel offered to keep him for the night,' she said, then frowned. 'Duncan, what about Kit?'

'That's another thing.' He came back to the sofa long enough to retrieve his glass, then began to pace. 'No one seems to know how to contact his father, so he's gone to his grandparents.'

'So?' said Gemma, sounding puzzled. 'I'd think that would be the best thing.'

'You don't know them,' he said vehemently, and felt surprised at the bitterness in his voice. 'Oh, I suppose you're right, and I'm letting my dislike of them colour my judgement. But Kit was so ... desolate.' He cleared his throat. 'I

223

shouldn't have let them take him away.'

'Duncan, don't be absurd. What else could you have done?'

'We keep coming back to that, don't we? Nothing, nothing, and nothing! But I feel so bloody useless!'

They stared at each other for a long moment, then Gemma sighed. 'I think I'll go to bed. Leave you on your own for a bit. All right?'

He nodded. 'Sorry, love. I'll be along soon.'

She came and laid her hand lightly against his cheek, then turned and went into the bedroom.

Kincaid listened to the click of the door closing, and in the silence that followed he heard the cat begin to purr. Sid had jumped into Gemma's spot on the sofa, and stood kneading his paws against the warm cushion, his eyes slitted in pleasure.

'You're easy enough to comfort, aren't you, mate?' Kincaid asked softly. 'Maybe I should take lessons.'

Tipping Gemma's untouched whisky into his own glass, he went to stand at the window again. He saw his own reflection, distorted by the lights in the house opposite, alien and unfamiliar.

Chapter Ten

In the sweet gloom above the brown and white
Night benedictions hover; and the winds of
night
Move gently round the room, and watch you
there,
And through the dreadful hours
The trees and waters and the hills have kept
The sacred vigil while you slept,
And lay a way of dews and flowers
Where your feet, your morning feet, shall tread.

Rupert Brooke, from
The Charm

Gemma woke suddenly, her heart thumping in the darkened room. It took her a moment to realize that she was in Duncan's bed, rather than her own, and that she was alone. He had come to bed, though, for she had a faint memory of the warmth of his body, and she didn't remember putting out the light.

She'd dreamt she was falling; not floating, but plummeting into some dark abyss, and even recalling the sensation brought a resurgence of panic. Sitting up, she focused on the clock's glowing red numerals. Half-past one. She slipped out of bed and groped for something to put on. Her fingers found his dressing gown, and when she'd fastened it round her and pushed her hair

225

from her face, she went out to look for him.

Kincaid sat in the middle of the sitting-room floor, amidst a sea of books and papers. He'd changed from his work clothes into jeans and pullover, and his uncombed hair flopped down onto his forehead.

'What are you doing?' asked Gemma.

He looked up at the sound of her voice. 'Couldn't sleep. I didn't want to disturb you.' His eyes were shadowed with exhaustion.

'But what's all this?' Coming to sit on the edge of the coffee table, she leaned down to stroke Sid, who had made himself comfortable on the largest stack of paper.

Kincaid made a vague gesture at the things surrounding him. 'Vic's manuscript. And anything else I could find that seemed to be related to Lydia Brooke.'

'You took Vic's papers?' said Gemma, shocked into full wakefulness. 'But that's—'

'Interfering with the evidence? Well, I suppose that's true enough, and I'll answer to Alec for it if I have to. But in the meantime, I don't know where to start.' He rubbed his hands over his face. 'I can separate Vic's handwriting from Lydia's in the loose papers, but that's about as far as I've managed. And it will take me days just to read the manuscript,' he added, his frustration evident in his voice.

'Then come to bed, please,' said Gemma. 'There's no point in any of this until you hear the results of the post mortem. You know that. And being exhausted won't help you deal with whatever comes tomorrow.'

'You're too sensible by half, Gemma, darling,' he said, sighing. 'I'll be along in a minute. I promise.'

He was as good as his word, for Gemma was still awake when he came quietly into the room and undressed in the dark. His skin felt chill where it brushed hers as he slipped into bed beside her.

'You're cold,' she said. She turned to him, pressing her body to his, and felt him stiffen against her embrace. Wondering if a sense of disloyalty lay behind his resistance, she said carefully, 'I don't imagine Vic would want you to be alone, love. Why don't you let me hold you?'

He was silent for so long she thought he might not respond, but finally he said, 'I'm afraid. I'm afraid to let go. I keep telling myself that I hadn't seen her for years—that she had no place in my life now—but it doesn't help this terrible sense of loss.' He paused, then added quietly, 'I hope I'm wrong about this, Gemma, about what happened to her. Because if someone killed her, and left her dead, or dying, for Kit to find, I swear I won't rest until I find them.'

The certainty of his words frightened her. Ranting she could discount as hysteria, and offer soothing platitudes, but for this chill resolution she had no answer. And if she, who had only known Vic for a few hours, grieved for her, how could she hope to take away any of *his* pain?

Helplessly, she said, 'Don't think of it now, love. It will be all right,' knowing the words to be meaningless, knowing that things would never really be all right. She stroked his face, and blindly he turned his head until his mouth rested against her palm.

The warmth of his breath and the touch of his lips against her skin sent an unexpected shiver of desire through her, and she gasped a soft, 'Oh.'

He took her hand in both of his and kissed it gently, and then again with a growing fierceness. When she moaned, he gathered her roughly into his arms and began to make love to her with passion of such intensity that it might have been anger, and she couldn't be sure if he thought of her at all.

But Gemma let herself be carried away, and in the end it washed them both into the comfort of a deep and dreamless sleep.

All through Wednesday morning he tried to concentrate on preparing for the Crown Prosecution Service the evidence he and Gemma had gathered on their latest case. But whenever he blinked, images of Vic flickered on his closed lids like the silent home movies of his childhood, and whenever his phone rang he lunged for it in sickening anticipation.

At lunch in the canteen, Gemma glared at him across the table until he forced himself to eat for the first time in twenty-four hours. Like Kit the night before, he found himself ravenous once he'd started, and he made short work of steak and kidney pie and chips.

He went back to his office feeling less hollow, but as the hours passed, he had an increasingly urgent sense that he should clear his desk of everything pending. Gemma had stepped out to the photocopier and he was alone in his office when the call finally came, at half-past four.

'Duncan, it's Alec here.' Byrne's voice came clearly this time, and Kincaid had an image of him sitting at his massive desk in Cambridge headquarters. 'Do you, by any chance, know the name of your ... of Doctor McClellan's personal physician?'

Kincaid knew the truth of it then, and he felt the inexorable weight of his guilt. 'What is it, Alec? What did you find?'

'Well, the post mortem is complete, and we put a rush on the tox scans. They showed rather large amounts of digitalis in her blood and tissue samples.' Byrne sounded uncomfortable, as if he found the results personally distasteful. 'Was she on some sort of heart medication?' he added hopefully.

This time, thought Kincaid, it was not going to be so easy. 'Not to my knowledge. She was a healthy, active woman, Alec, and I imagine her doctor will confirm it, although I don't know who she used.'

'Damn. I was hoping you might save us a bit of time there. We've asked her departmental secretary, who didn't know, so I suppose we'll have to start through her personal records.'

'Alec, I have some of Vic's papers,' said Kincaid, for he knew it was now or never. 'Things relating to her biography of Lydia Brooke.'

'She gave them to you when you were looking

229

into the case history for her?' said Alec, giving him an easy out.

'No, I took them last night, because it seemed possible to me that her office had been searched, and I didn't think it a good idea to leave them unattended.' This was at least a partial truth, and had the advantage of putting Byrne on the spot. If he came down too hard on Kincaid, he'd have to defend his own negligence in what he could now have little doubt was a murder inquiry.

The silence at the other end of the line indicated Byrne's awareness of his quandary. At last he cleared his throat and said, 'Um, that's rather irregular, but under the circumstances ... I suppose it's just as well. I'll need you to return them, though, as soon as possible.'

Kincaid's office door opened and Gemma came in, balancing a stack of files in one arm. She stopped when she saw that he was on the phone, then quietly placed the files on his desk and sat down in the chair opposite.

'Tomorrow,' Kincaid said to Byrne. 'But I'm not sure yet what time. Alec, about the digitalis—did the toxicologist hazard a guess as to origin? Natural or synthetic?'

'She said she couldn't differentiate, as they break down the same way. It might have come from one of several different medications.' Byrne cleared his throat. 'Listen, Duncan, I understand that this all must be very difficult for you, but you're going to have to keep in mind that you have no jurisdiction, and no official standing in this case. And I'm afraid that your personal involvement may cause you to—'

'Over-react?' Kincaid felt his barely maintained control on his temper slipping. 'Alec, surely you can't think that now? You bloody well have proof that I'm not imagining things, and that Vic wasn't imagining things about Lydia Brooke, either. Did your lads find anything at the bottom of the garden?'

Again, Byrne hesitated. 'I've just now got a team on the way—'

'Bloody hell, Alec,' Kincaid exploded. 'Everybody and their dog will have messed about round that gate by this time. What did you think you were playing at?'

'Don't tell me how to do my job, Duncan. And don't bully me. I'll conduct this investigation as I see fit, and you are just going to have to live with it.' Byrne's words were dangerously clipped.

Kincaid hadn't meant to push him so far—he had nothing to gain by antagonizing the man, and much to lose. He took a breath and back-pedalled. 'I'm sorry, Alec. You're quite right, and I'm out of line,' he said with genuine contrition. Then he added, 'I'll see you tomorrow, as soon as I can get to Cambridge,' and disconnected before Byrne could admonish him further. He realized suddenly that he was sweating, and in Gemma's white and strained face he saw the mirror of his own tension.

They looked at each other in silence, and then she said slowly, 'So. You were right. And now it begins.'

Nodding, he said, 'I'm afraid so.' He

considered the idea that had come to him last night. He'd pushed it aside, but now he found that in the interim the decision had made itself. 'Gemma, I'm going to take a leave of absence.'

'What? Now?'

'I'll talk to Denis as soon as he comes back from his meeting.'

'But you can't just take off without notice, without going through the proper chan—'

'And why bloody not? You know how much holiday time I have accrued. I'll put in for that and I'll take compassionate leave or sick leave in the meantime. I'll do whatever it takes, Gemma.'

'And damn the consequences?'

'It's too late to be talking about consequences,' he said, almost shouting at her. 'It doesn't matter now.'

She stared back at him, her mouth set in a stubborn line, but when she spoke her voice was quiet and level. 'What happens to you matters to me. Very much. I know what you're doing, Duncan, and it scares the hell out me. You don't have any intention of leaving this case to the Cambridgeshire force, do you? You know they won't give you any official sanction to investigate, but you think you can do a better job, and you're willing to risk damaging your career to prove it.'

Slowly, he said, 'What is my career as set against Vic's life?'

Gemma's eyes filled with tears. 'What you're doing won't bring Vic back. You're only going

232

to hurt yourself, love, and I don't think I can bear that.'

'I'm sorry, Gemma.' He had no desire to hurt her as well, but he knew he could not let his resolution waver. 'You're wrong. This is the only thing I can do that will help me. I have no choice. And I *can* do a better job, because I know more, and because I'm not looking for the easy out.'

'But this isn't your responsibility,' she said, leaning towards him, pleading with him. 'It's not your fault that Vic died. You couldn't have done anything more, even if you'd known what was going to happen.'

He stretched his lips into a smile. 'You could be right. But I'll never be sure, will I?'

Gemma left the Yard at half-past five. She'd hoped for another chance to talk to Kincaid, to persuade him not to act so hastily, but he'd still been in a meeting when she'd last looked in on him. He'd looked up and said merely, 'I'll be tied up for a while, I'm afraid, Gemma. I'll see you in the morning.'

Even though she knew he couldn't have said more, or excused himself from the meeting, without compromising her, it had made her feel shut out, dismissed. It was sadly ironic, she thought as she walked slowly home from the Angel tube stop, that her fear of Vic coming between them had come true only with her death. And what weapons had she against his guilt?

She was simply too tired to shop for

233

supper tonight, she thought as she neared the Sainsbury's on Liverpool Road. She'd have to hope Hazel had made enough for her, or rely on the meagre contents of her own pantry.

The busker stood in his usual spot near Sainsbury's doors, but for the first time in all the months Gemma had seen him there, he was without his dog. A few passers-by had stopped to listen to him play his clarinet, and Gemma felt, as she always did, a thrill of pleasure at the sound. She stopped, too, closing her eyes in concentration. Was it Mozart? Or was it just that she'd thought of him when Hazel had put a Mozart clarinet concerto on the CD player the other day?

When he'd finished, the busker nodded at his audience as they tossed a few coins in his instrument case, but he didn't speak or smile. It occurred to Gemma that she'd never heard him speak, and she was suddenly curious to see if he would.

As the other listeners moved off, she stepped closer and asked, 'What's happened to your dog? Is he all right?' What an arresting face he had, she thought as she watched him, with its prominent cheek bones, strong chin and long, straight nose. The close cropping of his fair hair served to emphasize the planes of his face, and his very deep-set eyes were blue.

He studied her with his usual wariness, then he shrugged and said, 'A little mishap with a car. He's in hospital.' His voice was surprisingly deep, and his accent well-educated.

'Oh. Is he going to be all right? Can you

manage ...' Her spontaneous offer of help faltered under his stare. 'I mean ...'

But he said politely enough, 'A few cracked ribs. And yes, I can manage, thank you.'

'Oh, good. It's good that he's not hurt too badly, I mean,' said Gemma, feeling more of an idiot by the minute, but she couldn't resist one last curious question. 'What's your name?'

She thought he wouldn't answer, but after a moment he said reluctantly, 'Gordon.'

'I'm Gemma.' When there seemed to be nothing else to say, she added awkwardly, 'Well, cheerio then,' and turned away.

She glanced back, once, and saw him lift the clarinet to his lips. The music followed her as she turned west into Richmond Avenue, fading until the last faint notes might have been her imagination.

The damp and dreary weather of the last few days had cleared during the afternoon, and as she neared Thornhill Gardens, pale pink, as uniform as a bed sheet, spread itself across the sky, then darkened slowly to rose. Against this backdrop the Georgian houses took on a dark and calming geometry, and by the time Gemma reached her flat she felt a bit more able to adjust herself to what she thought of as the other side of her schizophrenic life.

She found Hazel on the patio, watching the last of the sunset while the children played in the garden. When she'd hugged Toby, she sank into the chair beside Hazel and sighed.

The small table between them held a bottle of sherry and two glasses, and Hazel filled the empty glass and handed it to Gemma. 'Cheers,' she said, raising her glass. 'It sounds as though you've had a long day.' She pulled her bulky cardigan a little closer around her throat and took a sip of her drink. 'I couldn't bear to go inside quite yet. The children have had their tea, but not their baths.'

'Wouldn't have done much good, would it?' said Gemma, as the children were digging happily in the muddy spot beneath the rose bush. 'I'll bathe them in a bit.' She leaned back into the cold curve of the wrought iron chair and closed her eyes. It would do her good to watch the children play in the tub, and to hold their warm and slippery bodies as she towelled them dry.

The thought of hugging Toby brought with it the image she'd been resisting all day—Vic standing on her porch, laughing, with her arm around her son's shoulders—and with it the fear that Gemma hated to acknowledge even to herself. What would happen to Toby if she died? His father, like Kit's, was out of the picture, and just as well, for he'd certainly shown no aptitude for parenting, nor any interest in his son. She supposed her parents would take Toby, and that he would be loved and cared for, but it would not be the same. Or did she just want to think she was irreplaceable?

Hazel reached over and patted her arm. 'Tell me about it.'

'Oh, sorry,' Gemma said, startled. 'I was just thinking.'

236

'Obviously. Your eyebrows were about to meet.'

Gemma smiled at that, but then asked slowly, 'Are we really indispensable to our children, Hazel? Or do they go on quite happily without us, once the initial grief has passed?'

Hazel gave her a swift glance before answering. 'Child psychology experts will tell you all sorts of complicated things about bereaved children suffering from an inability to trust or form relationships, but to tell you the truth, I just don't know. Some do perfectly well, and some don't. It depends on the mother, and the child, and the caretakers, and those are just too many variables to allow one to make accurate predictions.' She took a sip of her drink and added, 'You're worrying about Vic's son, aren't you?'

'What's happened to him is so dreadful it just doesn't bear thinking of, but I keep thinking of it.'

'And I take it today's news is not good?' said Hazel.

Gemma shook her head. 'No. It looks as though she was poisoned.' She went on to tell Hazel about Kincaid's decision to take a leave of absence, and of her fears for him. 'He won't listen to me, Hazel. He's so stubborn, and so angry. He's even angry with me, and I don't know what I've done, or how I can reach him.'

'If I were you, I'd give him a day or two, let him start sorting it out on his own. And I suspect that his anger is due to more than the circumstances of Vic's death. Men often substitute anger for grief, because anger is the only emotion they're taught it's acceptable to feel. I don't know what else you can do, love, because I doubt very much you're going to change his mind about this.'

'The awful thing is that I understand how he feels, because I feel responsible, too,' said Gemma. 'I thought Vic had legitimate cause to be uneasy about Lydia Brooke's death, but I didn't encourage him to look into it any further.' She made a grimace of disgust, adding, 'I didn't want it to take his time away from me.'

'And you think that Vic's death must be connected to her suspicions about Lydia's death?' asked Hazel.

Shrugging, Gemma said, 'It's certainly possible. Unless someone knew enough about what Vic was doing to take advantage of it as camouflage.' She shivered. It was now almost fully dark, and the temperature in the garden had dropped. 'But Lydia is as good a place to start as any. I wish I'd had a look at those things of Vic's ...'

'Didn't you tell me that Lydia was fascinated with Rupert Brooke?'

'Yes, but I'm afraid I don't know much about him, other than the golden young Edwardian poet stuff, and, *"If I should die, think only this of me* ..." We had to memorize it at school, and I remember thinking it was bloody stupid.' Gemma looked at the children, who had moved to the edge of the flagstones and were giggling while doing something unspeakable to one of

Holly's dolls. 'I hope Toby will have more sense.'

'Men,' said Hazel, and they smiled at each other in tacit understanding. 'Well, if you're interested in Rupert Brooke, I've some things you might like to see. Because you're not going to let Duncan do this on his own, are you, love?'

Gemma hadn't made a conscious decision, but as soon as Hazel spoke she knew it to be true, and inevitable. 'No,' she said. 'I suppose I'm not.'

After the children had been bathed, and Gemma had sat down to a vegetable lasagna with Tim and Hazel, Hazel left Tim with the dishes and led Gemma into the sitting room. Glass-fronted bookcases lined the walls either side of the fireplace, and Hazel studied them for a minute, her finger against her nose, before going to the right-hand case.

'I think I put them all together, but it's been ages since I've looked at them, and the children *will* get into the books.' Hazel opened the case and bent down to survey the spines. 'Ah, here they are.' Removing a few volumes, she carried them to the sofa, and Gemma sat down beside her. 'I had rather a thing for Rupert myself at one time, so I can sympathize with Lydia's infatuation. Rupert Chawner Brooke, born 1887, son of a Rugby master,' Hazel recited from memory, grinning.

She handed the first book to Gemma. 'I've only a paperback of Marsh's *Memoir*, I'm afraid, picked up at an Oxfam bookshop, but the contemporary introduction is worth reading, and it does contain all the poems.' Frowning, she added, 'But these others Lydia wouldn't have known when she was at college. The Hassall biography was published in 1964, the Letters in '68. And the collection of his love letters to Noel Olivier was only released a few years ago. Vic would have been familiar with all of these, though, I'm sure.'

'Who was Noel Olivier?' asked Gemma. 'Any relation to Laurence?'

'The youngest of the four Olivier sisters, and I think they were cousins to Laurence,' explained Hazel. 'Rupert met her when she was fifteen and he was twenty, and he was smitten with her for years. They remained friends and correspondents until he died.'

Accepting each volume as Hazel handed it across, Gemma wondered what she had got herself into. She studied the black and white photo of Brooke on the cover of the *Memoir*, with his tumbled hair and penetrating gaze. 'He was quite stunningly beautiful, wasn't he? I wondered why everyone was so besotted with him.'

'Yes, his looks were rather spectacular,' Hazel admitted. 'But I doubt his looks alone would have generated such interest decades after his death. To me, he represents a slaughtered generation, a loss of innocence of a magnitude unimaginable before the Great War.'

'He was killed in the War, wasn't he?'

'That's the ironic thing,' said Hazel. 'He

never saw battle at all. He died in 1915, on the Greek island of Skyros, after contracting blood poisoning on a Divisional Field Day. But Churchill and the others in the Cabinet found his death, and his sonnets romanticizing the War, expedient—he made a lovely martyr to the cause. It was probably just as well for them that Brooke died when he did,' she added. 'I've always thought that his views on the War would have changed dramatically if he'd lived to see action, and that change would have been reflected in his poems.'

'Was he a good poet, then?' asked Gemma.

'I think he showed flashes of brilliance, but who knows what he might have achieved? Virginia Woolf thought he was destined to become a politician.'

'He knew Virginia Woolf?'

'It seems he knew everyone, and that an astonishing number of those connected with him became notable in their own fields. Virginia Woolf, James and Lytton Strachey, Geoffrey and Maynard Keynes, the Darwin sisters. The list goes on and on.'

'So he fascinated those who knew him, not just those who came after.' Gemma touched the photograph as if she might bring it to life.

'From the accounts I've read, he had remarkable charisma, and I suppose, in a way, it survived him.'

'It all looks so innocent,' said Gemma, who had found the photograph section in Geoffrey Keyne's *Collected Letters*.

Hazel laughed. 'There is something enchantingly nostalgic about that pre-war idyll, but I dare say it was not as innocent as we'd like to think. There was probably a good deal of naughtiness going on beneath those blazers and boaters and garden party dresses. And Rupert, certainly, was more than a bit sexually ... complicated.' She yawned and stretched. 'Stay for a last cup of tea. We'll light the fire and put some music on, and we can recite dear Rupert aloud.'

As much as she would have enjoyed spending an hour or two in the warmth of Hazel's sitting room, Gemma felt a strong desire to be home alone with Toby, to reinforce her sense of their identity as a family. 'Thanks, Hazel, but I'd better not. Toby will forget how to go to sleep in his own bed, and besides'—she patted the books in her lap—'I've got a lot of reading to do.'

30 September 1963
Llangollen, Wales

Dear Mummy,
Please forgive me for giving you my news this way. It seems unfair at best, and cowardly at worst, especially when I know you wish only the best for me. But it all happened so suddenly, and we felt such a sense of urgency, that it seemed best to take the plunge and the conventions be damned.

Morgan and I were married, yesterday, in the Cambridge registry office.

I know what you're thinking, darling, Mummy, that we hardly know each other, that we've taken leave of our senses. But we've known each other more than a year, even though it's only in the last few months that we've discovered that we see life with the same passion and intensity; and that we have the same goal, to record this life honestly, and to live it as well as we can.

And as for our senses, we've only just discovered them. Being with him makes me see things in ways I never imagined, and yet smell and taste and touch are magnified as if I were suddenly blind, and the beauty of the world around us is almost exquisitely painful. Oh, Mummy, his photographs will make your heart ache. He's so brilliant, so talented, and I'm going to be his support and encouragement, as he will be mine.

I'm writing poems that are searingly good, and Morgan's shown me that the rest—all the academic pretensions and stultifying traditions of university life—are only impediments to doing our best work. We are neither of us going back next week for the beginning of term. We're going to live instead, and practise our chosen vocations.

We've found a tiny flat in Cambridge —little more than a bedsit, really, but it's ours—and we have already moved in our few bits and pieces. Morgan has an offer of a job as assistant at a photography studio in town, and while it's the most boring of work (weddings, baby portraits, etc.), he will do it well, and it will give him the facilities to process his own photographs.

Miss Barrett has been most understanding, and has kindly offered to send some tutoring my way, and when I'm not working I am going to write and write and write.

Don't worry, Morgan's very practical, and while we won't be living in luxury we will make ends meet. And as long as we have food in our mouths and clothes on our backs, what else matters?

I promise you'll love him, too, Mummy. His brooding dark looks conceal a wonderful sense of humour and the sort of kindness I've never met in anyone but you. He makes me feel adored, and safe.

Be happy for me—
Lydia

Chapter Eleven

Would God, would God, you could be comforted.
Rupert Brooke,
from a fragment

Adam found Nathan sitting in the sun in the garden, with a rug over his knees like an old man.

He walked across the lawn, his shoes leaving a dark trail in the silver-dewed grass, and hunkered down beside Nathan's chair so that he could study his friend's face. Pale, though not so pasty as yesterday, but his eyes were still dull as river pebbles left out to dry.

'How are you?' he asked gently.

'If you mean *am I sober,* the answer is *yes,'* said Nathan, then he sighed and looked away. 'I'm sorry, Adam. Sit down.' He gestured at the other lawn chair. 'If you want to know the truth, I feel as though an enormous wave had washed through me and left me weak and empty on the beach. It's dull, and restful, and I wish it would last. But I don't think it will.'

'No,' said Adam as he lowered himself into the canvas curve of the lawn chair, 'I don't suppose so. But the worst is over.'

'Is it? I rather think not.' Nathan shivered and pulled up the rug a bit. 'Because now the bloody instinct for self-preservation has reared its ugly head, and oblivion would have been far preferable to going on. It's too bad you had your friend Father Denny come and confiscate my shotgun.'

Adam had called the Grantchester vicar in a panic the previous morning, asking him to go round and not only remove the gun, but stay with Nathan until he could get there himself. Unfortunately, Adam had two terminally ill parishioners who depended on his daily visits, but otherwise he had delegated his church duties so that he could be with Nathan as much as possible.

'Let me ring your daughters, Nathan,' pleaded Adam, as he had the day before. 'It would do you good to have them here.'

'No.' Nathan shook his head. 'I couldn't bear to have them fussing over me. And they'd be

245

a bit condescending with it, because they can't imagine anyone over thirty feeling ... what Vic and I ...'

'Passion,' said Adam. 'The young think they have a monopoly, and nothing but experience will disabuse them of it. We were the same.'

'Were we?' Glancing at Adam, Nathan said, 'You felt that way about Lydia, didn't you?'

'Yes. But age did temper it. You teach yourself to focus on other things, even to take pleasure in them. But still, I wished it had been me she'd called that last day. It took me a long time to forgive you for that.' Adam saw Nathan's eyes widen in a surprise that mirrored his own. He hadn't meant to tell Nathan that, not ever, and especially not now.

'I didn't know.'

'It doesn't matter now. But I always thought I might have changed her mind, or at least given her some comfort—'

'You think she'd have told you what she meant to do? Or that you'd somehow have divined it, when I didn't?' said Nathan, with a spark of anger.

'Can't you see her intention now, looking back?' asked Adam reasonably.

'No, I bloody well can't.' Nathan pushed the tartan rug from his legs. 'Vic asked me the same thing, but Lydia sounded perfectly ordinary that day, only perhaps a little excited about something, a bit urgent. And to think I was always glad you were spared—' Nathan broke off, and Adam thought that even now he found it difficult to talk about how he had found her.

In the silence, Adam became suddenly aware of the sparrows chirping in the hedge, and of the warmth of the sun on his face. After a moment he said, 'But it would have given me some sort of ... closure. You see, I understand how you felt ... when you couldn't see Vic.'

'Vic and Lydia,' said Nathan under his breath. 'Lydia and Vic. They're so intertwined now that sometimes I can't separate what happened to one from the other ...'

'I hadn't thought of it that way,' said Adam. 'But it is odd that Vic should have a weak heart as well ...' He thought again of his visit with Vic, and of what they'd talked about. 'All those questions Vic asked about Lydia's suicide—she didn't believe in it, did she?'

'Don't think I don't know what you're up to,' said Chief Superintendent Denis Childs. 'Or that I won't yank you back here faster than you can blink if I get the least complaint of interference from the Cambridge force.' His chair creaked as he sat back and sighed. 'Don't be a bloody fool, man. I know Alec Byrne. He's a good man, even if his predecessor may have been a bit of a slacker. Let him do his job.'

'I have no intention of keeping him from it,' Kincaid had said, and thanking his chief, had let himself out of Childs's office. And it was true, he thought, as he picked up the M11 towards Cambridge. But it was also true that he had prior knowledge that Alec Byrne was not inclined to take seriously, and that he was bound by both duty and need to make use of it.

247

The box containing Vic's papers and manuscript sat beside him, wedged into the Midget's passenger seat, for it had proved too big to fit in the boot. He was happy enough now to turn them over to Byrne, for before he'd left the Yard last night he'd photocopied every single scrap of paper. Then he'd stayed up reading until he had some sense of what Vic had been doing.

The biography, though incomplete, was as seamless and as compelling as a novel. He'd followed Lydia, the solitary child, as she grew into an ambitious young woman, seen her give up scholarship, and before his body had forced him to sleep, seen her marry. Vic's intense and compassionate account of Lydia's devotion to Morgan Ashby had made him wonder if Vic had once felt that way, too.

He intended to find out why Morgan Ashby had refused to see Vic. And he intended to see Vic's friend and neighbour, Nathan Winter, but first he had better tackle Alec Byrne.

'I'd like to see the pathologist's report, Alec,' he said, sitting once more in Byrne's office. 'I've been a good boy—surely you can have no objection.'

'And surely you've pushed the bounds of friendship and obligation far enough. You've interfered with my crime scene, for which I could have made official complaint, and on top of that you've been bloody rude and overbearing.'

This time Kincaid controlled his impulse to anger. Calling Byrne's bluff would not get him what he wanted, but grovelling very well might. 'You're right, Alec,' he said. 'I'm sorry, but I'd think you'd have done the same in my position. Vic is dead, and I don't have the luxury of good taste. What possible harm can it do to let me see the pathologist's report? I might even be able to offer some helpful suggestions.'

Byrne hesitated, his long fingers steepled together under his chin. Finally, he said, 'I'll tell you what she said, and you'll have to be satisfied with that. Doctor McClellan's heart failed due to an overdose of some form of digitalis, as you know. The pathologist couldn't hazard a guess as to when the poison was administered, because the different forms of digitalis have varied reaction times. Digitoxin is very quick-acting, while Digoxin, on the other hand, takes several hours. Most cases of digitalis poisoning result from therapeutic overdose, rather than homicidal intent, but we've tracked down Doctor McClellan's physician, and he confirms that she had no history of heart disease and was not currently taking any medication.'

'What medication did Lydia take?' Kincaid asked, wishing he could remember more of the detail from the file he'd read.

Byrne pulled another folder from his desk drawer, and Kincaid was glad to see that he had at least kept Lydia's file at hand. 'Let's see,' Byrne muttered as he opened the folder and skimmed the pages, using his finger to mark his place. 'Lydia took Digoxin for a minor heart arrhythmia, although there's a note here from the pathologist that Digoxin is

249

not usually the first choice for that condition, because the therapeutic dose is so near the toxic dose. If Lydia had not had a previous history of attempted suicide, he would have been inclined to rule it an accidental death.'

'But they can't tell if Vic was given the same thing?'

Byrne steepled his fingers again. 'No. Nor can we even be certain that Lydia Brooke actually died from an overdose of her own medication, even though digoxin was present in her body, because—as I understand it, and I'm no chemist—digoxin is one of the metabolic by-products of digitoxin.' He glanced at the report. 'The 12 hydroxy analog, to be exact, if that's any help.'

'So basically what you're telling me is that it all comes down to the same thing in the end,' said Kincaid. 'Was there anything else?'

Switching folders, Byrne said, 'Doctor Mc-Clellan had a trace of alcohol in her blood, but nothing else of interest that I can see.'

'So she might have had wine or beer with her lunch?' asked Kincaid. He didn't remember that Vic had been fond of drinking during the day, but perhaps she'd changed her habits.

'Her stomach was empty, but that doesn't necessarily tell us anything, as she'd have digested her lunch by that time anyway. We have yet to confirm where or with whom she had a meal.'

Kincaid refrained from saying that they'd had almost forty-eight hours, and just what exactly had they been doing? Instead he made an effort

250

to say mildly, 'And did you turn up anything in the garden?'

Byrne grimaced in disgust. 'You'd think a herd of cows had been milling about on the river side of that sodding gate. We've taken a few casts, but I don't expect much from them.'

More likely every busybody in the village, thought Kincaid, and any passer-by curious enough to wonder what the villagers were gawking at. But he said non-committally, 'Mmmm. And the house?'

'Nothing of interest so far, although it looks as though Doctor McClellan might have meant to make herself a cup of tea when she ... um, lost consciousness. According to the doc, she might have felt a headache coming on, or some nausea. If she hadn't been alone, it's quite possible she could have been saved.'

Kincaid closed his eyes for a moment. *Dear God,* he thought, *don't let Kit ever hear that.* The child would carry enough guilt as it was. 'What about time of death?' he asked. 'Could the pathologist narrow it down at all?'

Smiling, Byrne said, 'That's about as likely as squeezing blood out of a turnip. Her son said he thought she was still breathing when he found her at five o'clock, and I think we'll have to take that as fact, at least for now.' He shuffled the papers back into their respective files. 'The coroner held the inquest this morning, and I believe the family intend to hold a small memorial service, as the release of the body may be delayed indefinitely. They

251

feel the boy needs some sort of closure.'

For once, Kincaid had to agree with his former in-laws, but he felt certain that any real consideration for Kit's feelings came from Bob rather than Eugenia. 'Do you know when they've scheduled the service?'

'I believe it's Friday at one o'clock, in the church at Grantchester.'

'Tomorrow? They have pushed things a bit, haven't they?' The formal arrangements made Kincaid realize he hadn't rung his own parents, and that he must do so, as painful as it would be. His mother, especially, had been fond of Vic and had been very distressed at the break-up of their marriage, though she'd never criticized either of them.

'So, what's next then, Alec?' he asked as neutrally as he could manage.

'The usual routine. We've started the house-to-house in the village, in case anyone saw anything unusual that afternoon. And we'll interview her colleagues at work, of course.'

In other words, sod all, thought Kincaid, and said, 'Of course.'

Byrne sat forward suddenly, palms flat on the desk. 'I don't need your help with this investigation, Duncan, and I'll thank you not to interfere any further.'

'Oh, come on, Alec, be reasonable,' said Kincaid at his most persuasive. 'You can't stop me talking to people. After all, I can't make them answer, and I can't threaten to throw them in the nick, so why should you mind? And if I should just happen to find out

252

something, you can be sure I'll let you know. As far as I can see, it's all in your favour. Have you any leads on the husband, by the way?'

The question effectively took the wind out of Byrne's sails, and he answered grudgingly, 'He's no longer at the forwarding address he left with his college. We're checking to see if the Home Office has any record of his re-entering the country.'

'Didn't he take one of his graduate students with him? Maybe her people would know where they are.' Kincaid could tell from Byrne's expression that he hadn't been privy to this bit of information. 'I'm sure someone in his department can turn up the girl's name and particulars for you, with a little *official* prodding,' he added, grinning. 'Don't worry, Alec. I won't expect you to tell me I've been helpful, even off the record.'

Byrne sat back with an air of weary resignation. 'Just don't let me hear anyone complain you've been harassing them, or misrepresenting yourself as having any authority in this investigation,' he said, and on that friendly basis they parted.

Kincaid had a hurried and mediocre lunch at one of the pubs in Grantchester. When he'd finished, he waited until the barman had a free moment and made his way to the bar. 'Do you happen to know where Nathan Winter lives?' he asked.

The man's round, friendly face creased with instant concern. 'It's just two cottages up the

253

way,' he said, pointing back towards Cambridge. 'The white one with the black trim and the thatched roof. Lots of flowers in the front.' Studying Kincaid with undisguised curiosity, he added, 'Do you know about our Doctor McClellan, then?' He shook his head. 'Who'd have thought it? A beautiful young woman like her dying like that. And who'd have thought Nathan would go absolutely berserk when he heard she was dead. Tried to break her door down, he did, until the neighbours pulled him off and got old Doctor Warren to come and dress his hand.'

'You don't say?' Kincaid looked suitably impressed. 'Have you known Mr Winter long?'

'Since we were kids at school. That's his parents' cottage he has now. They died a few years ago, and Nathan came back from Cambridge and fixed it up. His wife had died and I suppose it gave him something new to think about.'

It was the mark of the truly insular villager, thought Kincaid, that the man would refer to a city less than two miles away as somewhere from which to come back.

'Poor man,' added the barman with easy sympathy. 'You'd think he'd had more than his share of grief as it was. And we thought he and Doctor McClellan were no more than nodding acquaintances. Just goes to show you never really know about people, doesn't it?' he said with great satisfaction.

Kincaid thanked him and took his leave before the man's curiosity could turn in his direction. Nosy neighbours were one of the world's greatest blessings, he thought as he went out into the sunshine, and that little conversation had been well worth the processed chicken and chips.

Leaving his car in the pub car park, he walked up the road, thinking about what he'd learned. Had Vic been in love with Nathan Winter? And if so, why should he be surprised she hadn't told *him*? He'd had no claim on her personal life, and he'd certainly no cause to feel this sudden stab of jealousy. Whatever the truth of the matter, it meant that Vic's relationship with Winter had been much more complicated than he realized.

He found the cottage easily. Its sleek well-kept air was unmistakable, as was the hand of a master gardener. Tulips filled the beds on either side of the front door—tall, elegant and pale pink in the background against the whitewashed cottage walls, then a shorter peony-headed tulip in rose, and beneath those, the deep-blue of forget-me-nots. Kincaid bent and picked one of the small blue flowers and slipped it in his pocket, then rang the bell.

The man who answered the door wore a dog collar, and held a bunch of herbs in his hand. Tall and thin, with curly greying hair and spectacles that slipped down his nose, he gave Kincaid a friendly smile. 'Hello. Can I help you?'

Covering his surprise, Kincaid said, 'Um, I was looking for Nathan Winter, actually.'

'I'm not sure Nathan's up to having visitors just now. If I could just tell him—'

'Who the hell is it, Adam?' called a deeper voice from the back of the house.

'My name is Duncan Kincaid. I'm Vic McClellan's ex-husband.'

The man's eyes widened. 'Oh. You'd better come in, then.' He stepped back so that Kincaid could enter. 'I'm Adam Lamb, by the way.'

So this was Adam, Kincaid thought, glad now he'd read at least part of Vic's manuscript.

As Adam led him down the passageway, he said quietly, 'Nathan's been very upset. You won't—' he broke off with a glance at Kincaid. 'But I suppose this has been very difficult for you as well.'

They reached a door, and Adam led him through it into a large room at the back of the house. 'We've been in the garden this morning,' he said, 'and we'd just come in for some lunch.'

Kincaid took in a living area to his right, done in comfortable, masculine-looking reds, and beyond it french windows overlooking a garden. Then he saw the man sitting at a table to his left, in a sort of kitchen/dining area. His white hair made a startling contrast to his smooth tanned skin and dark eyes, and as he rose Kincaid saw that he was stockily built. He looked strong and fit, and when not ill and exhausted, would probably radiate an immense vitality. No wonder Vic had been smitten.

'Nathan,' Adam was saying, 'this is Duncan Kincaid. He says he's Vic's ex-husband.'

Kincaid saw the flash of recognition in Nathan's eyes at his name, before Adam's elaboration. So Vic had spoken of him. The thought gave him a small twinge of satisfaction.

They stared at each other for a moment before Nathan came forward with his hand outstretched. He seemed to realize at the last moment that his right hand was bandaged, and quickly substituted his left for Kincaid to shake. 'Come and join us,' he said, gesturing towards a place at the small square table.

'We were just having egg and tomato sandwiches,' said Adam, dropping the herbs he'd been carrying on the kitchen work top. 'They may not be up to Nathan's culinary standards, but they're perfectly acceptable.'

'I've just had lunch, thank you,' said Kincaid as he took the indicated seat. A tantalizing odour came from something simmering on the cooker in the kitchen, and he felt his greasy meal sitting heavily in his stomach.

'Tea, then.' Adam began clearing the plates from the table, including Nathan's half-eaten sandwich. 'I'll make us all some.'

Kincaid looked on with interest as Nathan started to rise in protest, then sank back into his chair. Nathan sat watching Adam with an expression of mild consternation, as if he were unaccustomed to being looked after, but Adam moved about his friend's kitchen with competent familiarity, chopping the herbs and scraping them into the simmering casserole. 'I've got a vegetable hot-pot put together for Nathan's dinner,' Adam called out. 'It smells lovely, doesn't it? I'm afraid I only know how to do

257

vegetarian things, so poor Nathan will have to suffer it.'

Against the clatter of crockery coming from the kitchen, Nathan said, 'Vic spoke of you often. She was very fond of you, I think.'

'Did she?' Kincaid answered inadequately. Searching for something else to say, he added, 'We hadn't seen one another in years, until just recently. It seemed to me that she had changed a great deal, but now I'm not sure that I ever really knew her in the first place.'

Nathan rubbed absently at the bandage on his hand. 'Nor am I,' he said, meeting Kincaid's eyes. 'There's no way I can ever know, now.'

Adam returned with the tea things, and as he set them out, Nathan said, 'I understand the police rang you.'

'The officer in charge knew of my ... connection with Vic,' Kincaid said as he accepted a cup of tea from Adam. 'A good thing, too, as Kit had no one with him other than the police constable.'

'Do you know what's happened to Kit? I've been worried sick about him.' Nathan's hand was unsteady as he reached for his tea cup, and Kincaid noticed that Adam didn't relinquish his grip on it until the cup sat firmly on the table.

'He's gone to his grandparents'—Vic's parents, that is. And I know they've been in touch with the vicar here in Grantchester, so he might have an idea how Kit is doing.'

'The vicar?' Nathan said, as if he didn't quite follow.

'Funeral arrangements?' said Adam, with a questioning look at Kincaid.

'A memorial service. It's tomorrow at one o'clock.'

'So soon? But they've not let anyone know—'

'I'm sure Father Denny meant to come round this afternoon, Nathan,' interrupted Adam, attempting to soothe him.

'But it's not just the neighbours who will have to be notified. There's everyone at College, and in her department. I'll have to ring them—' He started to rise.

Adam put a restraining hand on his arm. 'It's all right, Nathan. I'll do it. You can make me a list in a bit.'

'What about her husband?' asked Kincaid. 'Have you any idea how to contact him?'

'Ian?' said Nathan. 'I haven't a clue. Hasn't anyone been in touch with him?'

'Not as far as I know. He seems to have flown the coop rather successfully,' said Kincaid, and saw Nathan make an automatic grimace of distaste. 'What's he like, anyway, the remarkable Ian McClellan?'

'Academically sound, as far as I know,' Nathan answered neutrally.

'But?' Kincaid prompted. 'Don't bother being tactful.'

Nathan smiled. 'All right. Ian McClellan is one of those tiresome chaps who think they know everything and everyone. And smooth with it. "Let me put you in touch with just the person ..." You know the drill.'

'An ambitious man, then? Why would

259

someone like that be willing to throw it all up to run off with a girl?'

'Ambitious only in a small sphere, I think,' said Nathan. He thought for a moment before adding, 'I didn't know the man well. But my guess would be that he'd reached the age where he was finding his own line of goods hard to believe, and he had to either find a less critical audience or reevaluate himself. The former would certainly be easiest.'

Perceptive, thought Kincaid, and from the little bit that Vic had told him, likely to be true. He sipped at his tea and looked up to find Nathan watching him.

'Why are you here?' asked Nathan. 'If you don't mind my asking. Did Vic talk to you about me?'

'Vic merely said that you were friends. But she also told me a good bit about her biography of Lydia Brooke, and I've seen the police report on Lydia's death, so I know it was you who found Lydia's body.'

'Ah,' said Nathan. 'I wondered how Vic had managed access to the details of the police report, but she didn't tell me.'

'Did she tell you she had doubts that Lydia's death was suicide?' Kincaid asked.

'No ... no, but I'd begun to guess,' Nathan said slowly, frowning.

'And do you think she had cause to be dissatisfied with the verdict? You were the one who found Lydia's body, after all.'

'I ... I don't know,' said Nathan, and Kincaid read the uncertainty in his dark eyes. 'At the

260

time I simply took it for granted that the police had investigated all the possibilities.'

'But what if they didn't?' Kincaid asked, almost to himself. Then he said abruptly, 'Why did Lydia leave everything to her former husband?'

Adam had listened to their conversation with his full attention, but without the body language that indicated he was just waiting a chance to get his oar in. A rare good listener, then, but by nature or training? 'What do you think, Adam?' Kincaid said, turning to him. 'You were closer to Lydia than anyone.'

'I'm afraid you're mistaken, Mr Kincaid,' said Adam with a small smile. 'Although I wish I could say otherwise, those days were long past by the time of Lydia's death.'

'And it never occurred to you that there was anything suspect about Lydia's death?'

Adam seemed to consider this before answering. 'No,' he said finally. 'I can't honestly say that it did.'

'Did you know Vic as well?' Kincaid asked. Vic had written so convincingly about Adam Lamb that he felt he knew the man, at least as he had been in those early days with Lydia, and he found it difficult to believe that he would tell a deliberate lie. But would he hedge the truth?

'I only met her once,' said Adam, with what sounded like genuine regret. 'When she came to see me about her book.'

'And were you able to help her?'

Adam shrugged. 'How can I tell you that?

She wanted to know what Lydia was really like, and I did my best. But that is surely a matter of perception as well—perception squared, as it were. Not only might Lydia have behaved differently towards every person with whom she came in contact, but I would then have the option of interpreting her behaviour in a multitude of ways.'

'Nicely put,' said Kincaid, grinning. 'Were you a student of philosophy, by any chance?'

'Philosophy and Comparative religion,' admitted Adam.

'Ah, so I was right,' Kincaid said with satisfaction. 'I thought I recognized that particular brand of logic.' He returned to the thread of the conversation. 'But isn't that a biographer's job, to take all those different perceptions of a person and make a cohesive whole of them?'

'But surely that's an impossible task,' argued Adam. 'Because the biographer brings his or her perceptions to it as well, so that it's never possible to create a true representation of the subject.'

'Vic knew that,' said Nathan. 'But the truth is relative, and even a portrait coloured by the biographer has its uses. It can enhance our understanding of the artist's work, as well as our understanding of ourselves.'

Vic. He could hear her speaking in Nathan's words, hear her intensity, her dedication, and he was caught unawares by the spasm of loss which seized him.

'Truth is not always relative,' he said slowly. 'I'll give you an irrefutable truth, if you like.'

262

Both Nathan and Adam stared at him, as if compelled by something in his voice. 'Vic died of heart failure, but not from an unexpectedly weak heart. She was poisoned.'

He watched their eyes, searching for that unmistakable flicker of knowledge, but all he saw was wide and uncomprehending shock.

'You're not bloody serious,' said Nathan, finally. 'That's not poss—'

'I think Nathan's been through enough already without this—whatever game this is you're playing at,' interrupted Adam. His hand had moved to Nathan's arm in a protective gesture.

'I'm sorry,' Kincaid said. 'I wish it weren't true. But I've just come from the police station. The post mortem revealed a lethal amount of digitalis in her body.'

Nathan stood up, knocking the table so that their teacups rattled precariously. He walked unsteadily to the french windows and stood looking out. Beyond him Kincaid could see the garden, designed in a palette of soft greys and greens rather than the bright colour Nathan had used in the front. Near the house, a low bed had been formed into the old-fashioned shape of an intricate knot.

When Nathan turned back to them after a moment, his face was ashen. 'Could she have taken it accidentally?'

Kincaid shook his head. 'That hardly seems likely. She'd never been prescribed any sort of digitalis, nor did she live with someone who might have substituted medications by mistake.'

'But why? Why would anyone do such a thing?'

'I don't know,' Kincaid said. 'All I can tell you is that I intend to find out. And it seemed to me that the logical place to start is with Morgan Ashby.'

'Morgan?' Adam frowned. 'Why Morgan?'

'We never got back to the question I asked earlier, did we? Why did Lydia leave her estate to a man she'd been divorced from for more than twenty years?'

'How should I know?' Nathan asked. He shoved his hands in the pockets of his corduroys and started to pace. 'Maybe she felt she owed him. They bought the house together, after all. Maybe there was no one else.'

'Or maybe she still loved him,' said Adam quietly. 'Their divorce so devastated her that she tried to take her own life.'

'What does it matter?' Nathan said, almost shouting. 'And what the bloody hell has it to do with Vic?'

Kincaid pushed his chair back, so that he could watch Nathan's agitated roaming of the room. 'Vic told me that when she tried to interview Morgan about Lydia, he was abusive. He physically threatened her.'

'So?' said Adam. 'Morgan was always a bit of a lout. And he hated us, especially.'

'Why?' Kincaid asked.

'He was jealous, of course.'

'Jealous of all of you?' Kincaid asked, surprised. 'Not just you, Adam?'

Adam glanced at Nathan before he answered.

'Well, it was mostly me, I suppose. But he didn't like any of Lydia's friends from before ... Look, Mr Kincaid, this has all been a bit much to take in,' He made a slight gesture towards Nathan, who had turned to stare out into the garden again. 'Would you mind ...?'

'I'm sorry.' Kincaid rose. 'Before I go, could you tell me how to find Morgan Ashby?'

'He and his wife have an arts studio, out west of Cambridge,' said Nathan, without turning around. 'On the Barton Road. You can't miss it. There's a farmhouse, and next to it a sort of barn painted blazing yellow.'

'You're well-informed, for someone not on friendly terms with him.'

'I didn't say I'd been in the place.' Nathan swung round to face him. 'I only know it by reputation, and I've passed by visiting friends out that way.'

'Oh, the stew,' Adam said suddenly, and rose. 'I forgot all about it.'

'I won't keep you any longer,' said Kincaid. 'Thank you both for seeing me.'

'I'll show you out.' Adam moved towards the door.

'It's all right, Adam, I'm perfectly capable,' said Nathan. 'Go see to the home fires.'

Adam shook Kincaid's hand again. 'If you need me for anything, Mr Kincaid, it's St Michael's Church, Cambridge.'

As Nathan led Kincaid towards the front of the house, he said, 'Who'd have thought old Adam had such a domestic streak? Vegetable hot-pots, of all the bloody things.' Then he stopped with his hand on the door and met Kincaid's eyes. 'You're talking about cold-blooded murder when you say someone deliberately poisoned Vic, you know, and that's just not possible. I don't believe it.'

'I know,' Kincaid said. 'But you will.'

Nathan opened the door, but said before Kincaid could turn away, 'Tomorrow ... you'll be there?'

'Yes.' Kincaid grasped Nathan's hand, then walked away. When he looked back, the door had closed and the cottage looked picture-book perfect, impervious to pain or misfortune.

He trusted his instincts, he thought as he walked back along the road towards the pub car park, and he was inclined to think that both men were genuinely grieved, as well as shocked by the news that Vic had been poisoned. Then why, he asked himself, did he have the feeling that they knew more than they were telling him?

He reached in his pocket for his keys, and felt the wilted petals of the forget-me-not.

21 April 1964
Cambridge

Dear Mummy,
I know it sounds perfectly dreadful of me to crow over someone's death, but Morgan's grandfather passed away last night and I'm so excited I can hardly sit still this morning.

There, now that I've admitted how vulgar I am, perhaps I can go part way towards excusing myself. It's his paternal grandfather, you see, who lived in Cardiff and was some sort of wealthy industrialist. He'd been ill for a long time with cancer, so it seems it's somewhat of a relief to the family, and Morgan hardly knew him anyway. The rumour flying about is that he's left an equal legacy directly to all his grandchildren, but of course the will won't be read for a few days yet.

If it's true, it certainly won't be a fortune by any means, but it would be enough for Morgan to start his own studio, and for us to put something towards a house. You can imagine what a relief this would be to me. Our little flat did well enough for just the two of us, but with the baby on the way I've been fretting a good deal about the arrangements. If we're going to be a real family we need a proper house, with a room for the baby when he's old enough.

I say he with great conviction, don't I? This is actually a bit of reverse psychology, although I'd never admit it to anyone but you. Of course I give lip service to the 'I just want a healthy baby' refrain, and I suppose I mean it up to a point. But the truth is, I desperately want a little girl, so I tell myself it's a boy so that I won't be disappointed if that should turn out to be the case. Silly and convoluted, I know.

Did you want me to be a girl, Mummy, darling? Or did you have dreams of a sturdy little boy in short trousers and braces, who would remind you of his father? Did you want children by the houseful, noisy and raucous as a flock of blackbirds, instead of one solitary little girl who was better at books than games?

Not that you've ever made me feel a disappointment, and I admire you for always making the best of whatever circumstance fate chose to send your way. But you've never passed on the secret, you've never told me how you did it. Is one born with an accepting nature, and if not, how does one go about acquiring one?

Pregnancy seems to be making me wax philosophical, as you can see. I'm not managing to write much, though, as every time I sit down and try to think, I go to sleep, just like a contented cow. I've been told that in a few months this lethargy will pass, and I'll feel a tremendous burst of energy, so I suppose I can make it up a bit then. Thanks for the advice about the morning sickness, but nothing seems to help much. I've lost some weight as I still can't keep anything down, but the doctor says not to worry.

I met Daphne for lunch at Brown's yesterday. She's exhausted, poor thing, from swotting away for her third-year examinations. I have to admit there are days when I miss the university life, though how one could miss working oneself to a miserable nub, I don't know. But those days are rare, and I find I love being able to set my own schedule. I've had two poems accepted by the *New Spectator*, by the way. That was meant to be my big news, and I got so carried away by bourgeois greed that I almost forgot.

You'll have to pop up on the train for the day, Mummy, darling. We can shop for baby things—can you believe I've taken up knitting?

I'm currently entangled in a maze of pastel wool, and see no way out.

Cambridge is so beautiful just now, as it always is at this time of year. The crocuses bloom like jewels in the green meadows of the Backs, and beyond them the still-bare trees frame the honeyed stone of Kings, and beyond that the clear blue Cambridgeshire sky. It is, I think, for that fleeting moment, the loveliest spot in the world.

Lydia

Chapter Twelve

Those that I could have loved went by me;
Cool gardened homes slept in the sun;
I heard the whisper of water nigh me,
Saw hands that beckoned, shone, were gone
In the green and gold. And I went on.

Rupert Brooke,
from Flight

The room shimmered with the aqueous green light filtering through the blinds, and when Gemma opened her eyes she thought for a moment she was still dreaming. The sharp jab to her chin from the corner of the book which lay open across her chest convinced her otherwise. She had fallen asleep reading about Rupert Brooke, and dreamed of him, golden-haired in a dim and tangled garden, surrounded by white-clothed figures. When she reached out to them, the faceless wraiths glided away into the trees.

'Ugh,' she said aloud and sat up, closing the book with a snap. Getting up, she slipped into a dressing gown and made herself coffee, then sat at the table looking out into the garden and thought about the day ahead.

She decided that she was suffering from an instant and severe case of flu, and would have to call in sick. Her record was exemplary; whether the chief believed her or not, he couldn't very well refuse her leave for illness. She'd be at a loose end without Kincaid, anyway, and she could put her detective skills to more productive use than being assigned other DCI's make-work.

Gemma wanted to know more about Lydia Brooke, and there was no better place to start than public record.

Her visit to Somerset House yielded the particulars of Lydia Brooke's birth (in Brighton, to Mary Brooke and William John Brooke, on 16 November 1942,) and her marriage (to Morgan Gabriel Ashby in Cambridge, on the 29 September 1963).

A phone call to the Yard netted her Morgan Ashby's present address, and armed with Hazel's Cambridge guidebook and one of Hazel's homemade sandwiches, Gemma set off for Cambridge at lunchtime.

All the detail available for Morgan Ashby's address had been Wood Dene Farm, Comberton

Road, and on consulting her map Gemma discovered that the Comberton Road lay west of Cambridge, not too far from Grantchester. She hoped that the farm was easily identifiable, because she didn't want to call ahead and risk immediate rejection.

She crept carefully along, examining every gate and farmhouse, but when she finally reached the place she had no doubt of it. Sculptures of brightly coloured metal hoops occupied the space between the road and the old brick-and-beam farmhouse. To the right of the house, a series of long, low barns were painted a deep sunflower yellow with blue trim, and a sign on the side of the barn nearest the road proclaimed that this was the 'Wood Dene Farm Arts Centre'.

Gemma pulled the car up in the drive beside the farmhouse and got out. Studying the layout for a moment, she decided to try the house first, but there was no answer when she knocked. She started back towards the barns, hoping for better luck there.

As she came round the house, she saw a woman in the back garden hanging out washing on a line. Brilliant white sheets flapped in the breeze, and the woman, clothes-pegs in her mouth, struggled against the wayward fabric.

'Hello,' Gemma called out, going to help, and when they had the sheet secured, the woman turned to her and smiled.

'Thanks for rescuing me. I know I should be glad of the wind on wash day, but it does make it a bit difficult to manage sometimes.' She was, Gemma judged, in her late forties, slightly built, with an open, friendly face bare of make-up and light brown hair drawn back in an intricate plait. 'I'm Francesca, by the way,' she said. 'Have you come about the studio space?'

'No, I'm afraid not. My name's Gemma James, and I was looking for Morgan Ashby, actually.'

Francesca's face clouded and she said warily, 'He's not here. Can I help you?'

'Are you his wife?' Gemma asked, wishing for the easy authority of her warrant card.

'That's right.' Francesca waited, still without a hint of a smile in her grey-blue eyes.

'I was a friend of Victoria McClellan's, you see,' said Gemma, and was surprised to find she didn't feel it was stretching the truth. 'And I wanted to ask Mr Ashby a few questions about his conversations with her.'

'Morgan didn't have any conversations with Doctor McClellan,' Francesca said flatly. 'And he wouldn't be pleased to see you. He just ran her ex-husband off with his shotgun a few minutes ago. All this business has upset him dreadfully, just when I'd hoped—'

'Duncan was here?' asked Gemma. 'Was he all right?'

'Of course he was all right,' said Francesca, sounding surprised. 'Morgan didn't *shoot* at him. He hasn't even any shells for the gun.' She studied Gemma, frowning. 'I take it you know Doctor McClellan's ex-husband well enough to be concerned for his welfare.' After looking at Gemma a moment longer, she picked up her clothes basket decisively. 'I think you'd better

272

come in and tell me what this is all about.'

'But what if ... Mr Ashby comes back?' asked Gemma, feeling a bit wary of the shotgun in spite of Francesca's disclaimer.

'If I know Morgan, he's taken the footpath up towards Madingley, and it usually takes him a couple of hours walking to simmer down enough to come home.' Francesca looked to the north, where clouds white as the blowing sheets were piling up against the horizon. 'And I think the weather will hold that long, at the least,' she added, turning away towards the house, and Gemma followed with attempted nonchalance.

Francesca took her through the back door, into the kitchen, where the aroma of freshly brewed coffee met them like a wave.

'Oh, it smells lovely,' said Gemma, closing her eyes and breathing it in.

'I'd just put the coffee on before I took the washing out.' Francesca deposited the laundry basket beside the door. 'Would you like some? It's a new blend I picked up in Cambridge the other day.'

'Please.' Gemma looked appreciatively about as Francesca filled pottery mugs and set them on a tray. It was a welcoming room, with walls the colour of tomato soup and a cheerful clutter which reminded her of Hazel's kitchen. There were even the familiar baskets of knitting wools overflowing onto the work tops and table. She'd noticed Francesca's jumper, handknit chenille in shades of heather. 'Did you knit your jumper?' she asked as Francesca peeled the top from a new bottle of milk.

'I'm a weaver by trade,' answered Francesca. 'The knitting I do for relaxation. It's mindless work.' Glancing at Gemma, as if afraid she might have offended her, she added, 'I don't mean that the patterns aren't sometimes complicated, it's just that once you know where you're going with it, you can put your hands on auto-pilot. It's a great comfort, sometimes, and a help if you're trying to work out a problem.' She added sugar and a milk jug to the tray, and started down a passageway towards the front of the house. 'Let's go through to the sitting room.'

Gemma followed her, but paused on the threshold when they reached their destination. The room first struck her as a battleground, physical evidence of personalities in conflict. The walls were pale grey, the better to showcase the framed black-and-white photographs which covered them, but before she could look closer, her eyes were drawn to the threaded loom which stood in the centre of the room. She walked over to it, unable to resist touching the cloud-soft fabric forming from the intersecting yarns—a loosely woven piece in the autumnal hues she loved.

'What is it?' she asked Francesca.

'A throw rug. They're bread and butter pieces, really—there's a big market for them—but I love them nonetheless.'

'I can tell.' There were textiles rich in colour and pattern everywhere, folded on a work table, thrown so thickly over the furniture that Francesca had to push one aside in order to

274

sit on the sofa—like a nesting mouse, thought Gemma.

She looked again at the photographs— stark, some of them intense as a slap across the face, some desolately severe, all beautiful and uncompromising, all made more palatable by the buffer of Francesca's fabrics. Perhaps it was a matter of balance rather than conflict, after all. 'Are the photos Morgan's?' she asked. 'They're rather stunning.'

'Of course they're Morgan's,' Francesca said, looking quizzically at Gemma as she positioned the tray on the coffee table. 'Did you not know Morgan's reputation as a photographer?'

'I'm afraid I don't know much of anything,' said Gemma as she perched gingerly in the rocker which sat at a right angle to Francesca. She reached for her cup and added a little milk to the coffee. 'Except that Morgan was married to Lydia Brooke, and Vic was writing a book about Lydia's life.'

'I was sorry to hear about Doctor McClellan,' Francesca said, staring at the mug in her hands. She glanced up at Gemma. 'She seemed such a nice woman—it's hard to imagine someone so young dying just like that—'

'She didn't die of heart failure, Mrs Ashby. She was murdered. Poisoned.'

Francesca stared at her. 'But surely ... that's not possible ... why would anyone want to kill her?'

'We don't know,' said Gemma. 'That's why it's important for us to know who she spoke with recently. She might have said something—'

'She did come here, but Morgan was abominably rude to her, I'm afraid, and she went away empty-handed.' Francesca's pleasant face creased in a frown. 'But I don't understand what that has to do with you—or with her ex-husband. Surely you don't mean to continue with her book?'

Gemma took a fortifying sip of coffee and plunged in. 'We're police officers, but we have no official standing on this case, only a special interest.' Watching Francesca's eyes widen, she added, 'Look, Mrs Ashby, I couldn't misrepresent myself, and I can't force you to talk to me. But I'm convinced that Vic died because of something she found out about Lydia Brooke. I want to know about Lydia—anything you or Morgan can tell me. Why wouldn't Morgan talk to Vic or Duncan about her? It's been five years since she died.'

Setting her mug on the table, Francesca stood up and went to the loom. She touched its frame for a moment, then turned to Gemma, arms folded across her chest. 'You think time makes a difference?' She shook her head. 'You don't understand, do you? Have you ever seen two people turn love into an excuse for mutual destruction? Their obsession poisoned them both. Even now, he can't let her go. She eats away at him in the dark, like a cancer.'

Appalled by the bleakness in Francesca Ashby's voice, Gemma said, 'How can you live with a man who felt—feels—that way about someone else?'

Francesca stared at her for a moment, lips

276

parted as if she were about to tell Gemma to mind her own bloody business. Then the corners of her mouth turned up in what might have been a smile. 'It's not that simple. It never is, is it?' She came back to the sofa and sat down facing Gemma. 'And, of course, I imagined things would be different. One does in the beginning. He'd left her for me, after all, hadn't he? I thought that meant he loved me more.' Shaking her head, she said, 'What I didn't understand was that I was simply the rock available in the tempest, and he was a man clinging desperately for survival. He saw the way things were going—he knew if he didn't leave, something terrible would happen.'

'What do you mean?' asked Gemma. 'What sort of terrible thing? Was he afraid she'd kill herself?'

'I don't know.' Francesca turned her palms up. 'All I can tell you is that he was frightened for them both, and for that he became the villain in everyone's eyes. They said his selfish desertion of her caused her breakdown, and her attempt at suicide.'

'Vic might not have told it that way,' said Gemma. 'If she'd had a chance to hear his side of it.'

'I tried to tell him that, but he wouldn't listen,' Francesca said, twisting her hands in her lap. 'I was even tempted to go to her myself, after she came here, but I couldn't bear for him to think I'd betrayed him.'

'What would you have said?' Gemma asked gently.

'That Lydia was unstable from the beginning. She had violent mood swings, she was unpredictable—she put him off for more than a year, did you know that? She'd hardly spoken to him for all that time, then within a couple of months she was all over him, wanting desperately to marry him.'

'You knew her then?'

'Not then,' Francesca said, and looked away.

'But you knew Morgan, and he told you about her?' pressed Gemma.

'Not then.' Francesca still didn't meet Gemma's eyes. 'Not until much later. I came to work in his studio as an assistant, helping with the props and the children, scheduling the sittings, that sort of thing. Fine arts photography was Morgan's dream, but the baby portraits paid the bills in those days.

'He was so unhappy, and he would talk to me about it, because there was no one else. We became friends.' She shrugged. 'I suppose it sounds trite.'

'You were sympathetic, and he was misunderstood?' Gemma said. 'Just because it's an old story doesn't make it any less true.' She'd even tried to cast Kincaid as the sinned-against husband, years after he and Vic had gone their respective ways. Remembering her own reaction when she'd finally met Vic, she asked, 'And what did you think when you met Lydia?'

'It's hard to separate those first impressions from what I'd heard before and what I knew after,' said Francesca, frowning. 'I'd worked there several months before she came into the studio, and by that time I'd made her into some screaming, hysterical Medusa.'

'And *was* she?' asked Gemma.

'Of course not. She was small and dark, with a husky voice and an exotic sort of prettiness, but other than that she seemed perfectly ordinary. And she was kind to me.'

'She didn't seem unbalanced?'

'Just unhappy,' said Francesca with a sigh. 'The more difficult things became with Morgan, the more time she spent with her old University friends, and that only made things worse. Morgan blamed them for everything, including her emotional problems. He said they encouraged her fantasy about being related to Rupert Brooke—'

'Related to him?' Gemma said in surprise. 'I knew she was a little obsessive about him, but—'

'By some coincidence her parents had the same names as Rupert's parents, Mary and William. Lydia's father was an orphan, and he himself was killed in the war, just days before Lydia was born. So she grew up knowing very little about her father's people, and she concocted this great fantasy that her father had been Brooke's illegitimate child, and she his granddaughter.' Francesca made a face. 'It all seems a bit pathetic, looking back on it, and I wish now that I'd had more compassion.'

'Could there possibly have been any truth to it?' Gemma asked. She was aware, after even the briefest of introductions to Brooke, what allure the idea might have had to a lonely and literary teenager.

'I don't suppose it's likely,' said Francesca. 'Brooke's life is fairly well-documented, although it's true that little of the material would have been available to Lydia at that time. If she'd known about his relationship with Noel Olivier, I imagine little Noel would have done quite well for the part of fantasy grandmother.'

'It is odd,' said Gemma, thinking of the photos of Noel Olivier she'd seen in the book Hazel had given her last night, and of the snapshots of Lydia that had been among Vic's papers. 'You could find a resemblance between them, if you were looking for it.'

'Then it's just as well Lydia didn't know to look. She'd carried things too far as it was. She saw herself as the chosen successor to carry on Rupert's Neo-Pagan revival—you know, all the *dancing naked in the woods at midnight* stuff—the cult of perpetual youth.' Francesca smiled. 'Of course, if he'd lived he'd have out-grown all that, seen it for the nonsense it was, but he hadn't the chance.'

'But Lydia outgrew it, eventually?'

'I don't know.' Francesca reached for her mug, the coffee surely now grown cold, and sank back against the cushions. 'Perhaps she considered forty-seven the beginning of middle-age. One's idea of it does tend to recede as one gets older.'

Gemma remembered the strength of Vic's certainty that Lydia had not committed suicide. 'Vic—Doctor McClellan— thought it possible that Lydia may have come to happiness later in life, or at least contentment of a sort.'

'Happy when she wasn't mad, like Virginia Woolf?' Francesca said. 'I'd like to think so. I never wished her ill.'

'You said she was kind to you, in the beginning. What about later, when she knew about you and Morgan?'

'He kept it from her as long as he could. For her sake, not his. But Cambridge is a small place, and a few months after they'd separated we ran into her in the market one day.' Francesca rubbed her palms against the knees of her jeans. 'She was civil, but you could tell she couldn't bear it. That was one of the worst days of my life.'

'Worse than the day you heard she'd slit her wrists?' said Gemma, remembering what Kincaid had told her about Lydia's first suicide attempt.

'Yes,' Francesca said without hesitation. Then she added musingly, 'It's very odd, but that axe had been poised over our heads for so long that it was almost a relief when it fell. It seemed the worst had happened, and not been as bad as we'd feared.'

'And when she died, five years ago?'

Francesca stared at the window overlooking the front garden and absently pinched a fold of fabric between her fingers. 'I don't know. We were shocked at first, I suppose, and after that we felt a sort of release. I thought he could heal then, let it go.' She seemed to bring her gaze back to Gemma with an effort, and in

281

the strong north light the lines of weariness in her pleasant face were deeply etched. 'Then we learned she'd left him the house.'

'Why did she leave Morgan the house?' asked Gemma. 'It seems a bit odd, if she hadn't seen him for years, and they'd parted so bitterly ...'

'I think she meant it as an act of reconciliation,' said Francesca slowly. 'A closing of the books.'

'And Morgan?'

Francesca met her eyes reluctantly. 'Morgan saw it as a deliberate attempt at torture. To reach out for him from beyond the grave. It's got all twisted inside him over the years—his guilt and his love for her. Morgan thought he could anchor her, but he wasn't strong enough, and he's never forgiven himself.'

'And now you try to anchor Morgan?' guessed Gemma.

'Oh.' Francesca's eyes widened with surprise. 'I suppose it might seem that way. But it's more of a balancing act, most of the time.'

'Surely an uneven one, because of Lydia?'

'Not really,' said Francesca with a certainty Gemma hadn't expected. 'Morgan loves me, probably more than he ever imagined he would. He says the peace and security I provide make life bearable for him. And he gives me such—'

A door slammed in the back of the house. A man's voice called, 'Fran! Whose car's in the drive?'

Francesca frowned at Gemma and gave a sharp shake of her head. 'Let me handle this,' she mouthed as the footsteps came down the hall.

Tensing instinctively, Gemma sat forward and gathered her handbag a bit closer to her body.

'Hello, darling.' Francesca smiled at her husband as he entered the room. 'This is Gemma. She's come about the studio.'

Gemma stopped gaping at Morgan Ashby long enough to stammer a greeting and shake the hand he held out to her. She didn't remember seeing a photo of him among Vic's papers, and certainly nothing else had prepared her. Even scowling suspiciously at her, the man was a stunner, drop-dead good-looking with a presence Heathcliff might have envied. Tall and well-built, he had a head of dark, wavy, unkempt hair, a long straight nose and dark grey eyes that made Gemma's bones feel hollow.

Francesca was speaking and the words suddenly clicked into focus in Gemma's mind. '... having a look round to see if it would do for her. She's a—' Francesca cast a quick look of appeal at Gemma.

'Potter.' Gemma said the first thing that flew into her mind, then gulped. She could barely tell a vase from a chamber pot. At least she was wearing the long skirt and jumper she'd worn to Vic's on Sunday, and thought she must look suitably artistic.

'A potter,' Francesca repeated. 'And she's a bit concerned about the kiln space. She does production work, you see.'

'Really?' asked Morgan as he sat on the arm of the sofa and rested a casual hand on his wife's shoulder. He'd relaxed as soon as Francesca had mentioned the studio. 'Of course, if you're really keen, the foundation might be persuaded to fund a new kiln for the compound.' When he smiled at Gemma, the creases round his eyes gave an indication of his age, but made him no less attractive.

Gemma struggled to collect herself, but before she could blurt out something inane, Morgan misinterpreted her blankness. 'Has Fran not explained how we operate? We have a group of benefactors who are committed to providing low-cost studio space for talented artists. This is strictly work space, though—you do understand that?' When Gemma nodded, he went on, 'We don't sell anyone's work here at the centre. The individual artists are responsible for setting up shows elsewhere.'

'You don't sell even your own things?' Gemma asked, her curiosity at least providing her with a sensible comment.

'Oh, Morgan and I don't actually use the studios,' explained Francesca. 'We're basically just caretakers for the foundation, and we have our own work spaces here in the house. Morgan's studio and darkroom are upstairs, and I prefer it in here by the fire,' she added, smiling. 'Would you like to see the available studio again?'

'Oh, no, I'd better not,' said Gemma, taking her cue. She glanced at her watch. 'I've an appointment, in fact, and I'm late as it is.' Placing her coffee mug carefully on the table, she stood up. 'You've been too kind, giving me so much of your time. Is it all right if I let you know when I've had a chance to think it over?'

'Of course.' Francesca gave her husband's hand a squeeze as she rose.

'Don't leave it too long, now,' said Morgan as he came with them to the door, and Gemma noticed for the first time the faintest Welsh lilt in his accent. 'You'd hate to miss out on an opportunity like this.'

Husband and wife stood shoulder to shoulder on the step, the picture of harmony. But as Gemma turned away, some trick of the afternoon light threw a faint shadow between them, and she wondered if Francesca Ashby were truly prepared to live *without* Lydia's ghost.

Kincaid angled the Midget into one of the pay-and-display spaces across the street from the University English Faculty and jerked up the lever on the parking brake. He hadn't realized how much his lack of official status would handicap him, and he'd driven back to Cambridge still seething with frustration over his aborted visit to Morgan Ashby. The man must be a certifiable lunatic, shouting and waving a bloody shotgun about like a toy. And if Vic had received the same sort of reception, it didn't surprise him that she'd made no further effort to contact Lydia Brooke's ex-husband.

He'd have to suggest that Alec Byrne pay the man a visit—suitably accompanied by brawny constables—but in the meantime he

285

hoped to find more accommodating sources of information here, where his non-official status might prove more help than hindrance.

After a glance at the clouds massing in the northern sky, he pulled up the Midget's top and snapped it closed, then crossed the street to the building where he assumed Vic had spent her last day.

Laura Miller, the departmental secretary, sat at her desk in the reception area, pressing the phone to her ear with one hand and scribbling with the other. She glanced up at the sound of the door, and her lips parted in soundless distress as she recognized him.

'Oh, sorry,' she said, dragging her attention back to the phone. 'Listen, could I ring you back? Ta.'

She replaced the phone in its cradle, still staring at Kincaid, and he was dismayed to see her eyes fill with tears. 'I'm so sorry,' she said. 'You have no idea ... We all are. I don't know what to say.'

He slid into the chair opposite her desk without being asked, smiling to ease the sudden tightness in his throat. 'You don't have to say anything. It must be pretty dreadful for you.'

'I've just been ringing everyone I can think of about the memorial service, but it's still such a shock. I'll ring off, thinking, *"I'll have to tell Vic the absurd thing so-and-so said,"* and then it hits me.'

'I know.' He cleared his throat, searching for a less painful topic. 'I only learned about the service this morning, from the police.'

286

At the last word, Laura's normally rosy face paled even further, and he cursed himself for an idiot. That was one he'd meant to ease into.

'They were here again before lunch, and now they say they're treating it as a murder inquiry!' Her dark eyes looked enormous behind her thick spectacles. 'I simply can't believe it. Why would anyone want to kill Vic? There must be some mistake.'

'I'm afraid there's no doubt,' he said, wishing he had some comfort to offer her. 'I'm sorry.'

'But—' Laura seemed to realize the futility of arguing, and made an effort to smile. 'I'm sorry for being difficult about it all,' she said, pushing her glasses up on the bridge of her nose and swiping at a tear that had trickled onto her cheek. 'It's just that I can't seem to stop crying. Vic and I didn't just work together—we were friends. My son Colin goes to the same school as Kit, they're even in the same form. The poor bloody kid.'

Kincaid didn't want to talk about Kit—just thinking of the boy threatened to breach the wall he'd built around his own emotions—but Laura ploughed on without waiting for a response.

'You'd think he'd been through enough, wouldn't you?' She jabbed at her glasses again as a pink flush of anger crept into her cheeks. 'And that anybody with an ounce of feeling would know he needs to go on with his life as normally as possible—anyone but his grandmother. I rang them and suggested that Kit come and stay with us after the service

287

tomorrow. He could go back to school, keep up with his sport and his friends, and he'd at least have something to think about until things are sorted out with his dad.'

'No go, I take it?'

'You'd have thought we meant to sell him into slavery. *And* cause Eugenia Potts a personal injury.' Laura closed her eyes for a moment, shaking her head in disgust, then she blinked and gave a startled exclamation. 'But you know them, of course,' she said, staring at Kincaid in consternation. 'Vic's parents. Well, I'm sorry if I was out of line, but I'm that furious.'

'You're not out of line. And I don't mind at all.' He added, smiling, 'Eugenia can be a bit ... there's no diplomatic way to put it, is there?'

Laura smiled back. 'How did Vic come from such a family?'

'I used to tell her they must have found her under a cabbage plant,' he said. He'd forgotten that.

'Have you any influence with them?' asked Laura. 'The father doesn't seem unreasonable. I'm sure he'd see that it would be better for Kit to be in a familiar environment with children his own age.'

Kincaid shook his head. 'I agree with you, but I'm afraid any intervention on my part would only prejudice them against your idea. Eugenia doesn't care for me, to put it mildly.'

'I'd call that a sterling recommendation of your character,' said Laura, and this time the smile reached her eyes.

'Good,' he said, taking advantage of the opening. 'Because I want to ask a favour of you.' He hesitated, not sure how far he should commit himself. In the end he compromised, telling her what he wanted, but not why. 'It would help me to know how Vic spent her day on Tuesday. I'd like to talk to anyone in the department who saw her.'

'Those are the same questions the police asked.' Laura looked steadily at him.

'Yes.'

'You're a detective, too. Vic told me. Are you helping the local police?'

'Not exactly.' He met her eyes. 'This is personal.'

Laura held his gaze a moment longer, then nodded once, a signal of understanding. 'I've got to run some things to the printer—' She glanced at her watch. 'Now, as a matter of fact. But I'll be back in a tic, and in the meantime you could have a word with Iris—that's Professor Winslow, if you remember, our Head of Department. And I think Doctor Eliot has a supervision finishing in about a quarter of an hour. You might catch him after that. The others are out for afternoon lectures, but then they had heavy schedules on Tuesday afternoon as well, and probably wouldn't be much use to you.' A model of efficiency now that he'd given her a direction, Laura pushed her chair back and stood up, then she paused and plucked at the fabric of her plain, grey, long-sleeved dress. 'I bought this yesterday,' she said. 'I know mourning went out of fashion with the Victorians, but it felt right, somehow.'

'They understood the use of symbols,' said Kincaid. 'We could do worse than to remember it.'

Iris Winslow didn't question Kincaid about his motives. She rose from her chair behind the scarred oak desk in her office and held out her hand to him as he sat down. 'I can't tell you how sorry I am,' she said. Her sympathy, like Laura's, seemed genuine, and he found it surprisingly hard to bear.

But Iris Winslow was both tactful and perceptive, and without waiting for him to respond, she talked of how much she had liked Vic, and of what it had been like to work with her, so that he began to feel more comfortable—and even, after a few moments, to feel as if he'd been given an unexpected gift.

'Thank you,' he said simply, when she'd come to an end. 'You've helped me fill in some of the blanks. You know I hadn't seen Vic for a long time until recently?'

'She spoke of you, though—oh, not at first, of course, but as we came to know one another better. She thought well of you.'

And he had let her down.

Dr Winslow meant it as a comfort, he knew, and misunderstood his silence. 'This has been too much for all of us,' she said, looking away from him, out the window which overlooked the gravelled car park. 'Vic's death was shock enough, but then the police, this morning, saying she'd been murdered.' She shook her head slightly.

'I know it's difficult—'

'No, it's not just that. No one finds such news easy to accept under any circumstances. But for me, it's tipped the scale. I'm tired, and I suddenly find I can't cope with things in the way I always took for granted. I've decided to take early retirement.' She turned back to him and added, with a hint of amusement in her voice, 'I don't know why I'm telling you this. I haven't said a word to anyone else.'

'I'm outside the loop,' he offered. 'I can't pass judgement, or demand an accounting of the consequences.'

Dr Winslow smiled. 'Or perhaps I only think you're too polite to do so.' She touched her forehead briefly, as if brushing at a gnat, and her brow creased. 'Or perhaps it's because you were close to Vic, and because of that I think you might understand. I saw something of myself in her, you see, and I suppose I had some unacknowledged wish that she might follow in my footsteps. And now it all seems rather pointless.'

'I can understand that,' he said, wondering if in Iris Winslow Vic had found a woman capable of giving her the sort of support and encouragement she'd never had from her own mother. He sensed that Iris's loss was real and deep, not manufactured for the sake of drawing attention to herself.

'But your confidence does give me the right to express concern, Professor,' he continued. 'And it seems to me that you've not even begun to get over the shock of Vic's death, much less deal with the aftermath. Are you sure this isn't a hasty decision?'

She adjusted one of the silver frames on her desk, but it faced away from him and he couldn't see the photo it contained. 'I've been thinking of it for quite some time,' she said. 'And it's ironic that Vic's death has removed one of the reasons for my hesitation.' Giving the edge of the frame a final touch, almost a pat, Doctor Winslow looked up at him. 'There's no doubt that Darcy Eliot will be asked to take over my position—it's well-deserved and none too soon. But Vic and Darcy were always squabbling like naughty children, and I have to admit I feared for her position without my intervention. Now there's no need.'

'Why didn't they get along?' Kincaid remembered Vic's veiled comments about problems with her colleagues.

'Oh, it's quite silly, really.' Doctor Winslow made a dismissive gesture with her hand. 'But university faculties are like any closed microcosm—the least little conflict or difference of opinion gets blown all out of proportion. Darcy didn't approve of Vic writing a biography intended for popular consumption. He thought it didn't reflect well on the department, which is more than a bit hypocritical of him, considering the success of his popular criticism.'

'That's why his name sounded familiar,'

said Kincaid. 'I'd been trying to place it. My mother's quite fond of his books, but I've never read one myself.'

'They're very enjoyable—witty and well-informed, if not always kind. And I personally have never been able to see why anything which encourages people to read, be it biography or criticism couched in terms a layman can understand, should be considered an embarrassment to the study of English Literature.' For a moment, as Iris Winslow spoke, he had seen the truth of the resemblance between this large, plain woman and his former wife.

Then Doctor Winslow rubbed at her forehead with blunt fingers and added wearily, 'But the battle against elitism is a losing proposition, and I'm hanging up my sword. I'm going to sit in my garden and learn to enjoy books again—that was, after all, what brought me here in the first place.'

'Are you feeling all right, Professor?' asked Kincaid, as she grimaced and continued to apply pressure to her forehead.

'It's just this damnable headache.' She lowered her hand and gave him a strained smile. 'Since Tuesday. Hasn't let up.'

'You've been too kind to let me take so much of your time, especially when you weren't well,' he said, preparing to rise. 'But if you don't mind I have one more question.'

She gave a nod of permission and waited, watching him intently.

'Did you notice anything unusual about Vic on Tuesday?'

Her lips tightened in an expression of regret. 'I only saw her in the morning, I'm afraid. We had a brief talk about some faculty business, then I had an appointment for lunch, and afterwards a meeting at Newnham. But she seemed perfectly all right then.' Moving restlessly, she clasped her hands together on her desk top. 'Of course, now I wish I'd come back here after lunch, as illogical as such a desire is. It wouldn't have changed anything, and I'd not have had the foreknowledge to say goodbye.'

As Kincaid stood up he looked around her office. Every available inch of wall space held bookshelves. The volumes overflowed onto desk and table, had even crept onto the extra chairs placed against the far wall, and the room had the faint musty smell of old paper and bindings. He waved a hand in a vague gesture towards the books. 'If we humans were ever as logical as we'd like to believe, I doubt literature would have got very far, don't you, Professor?'

What he didn't say was that he was just as guilty of human frailty as she—he wished the same futile wish, that he'd seen Vic just once more.

Alone in the reception area, Kincaid realized he'd forgotten to ask which office belonged to Darcy Eliot. He checked the other ground-floor doors, looking for Eliot's nameplate, then started up the stairs.

He found it on the second floor, across the corridor from Vic's.

A knock on the door brought a grumbled,

'You're bloody early, Matthews.' Kincaid opened the door and looked round it. Darcy Eliot sat half-turned away from the door, a sheaf of papers in his hand. Without looking up, he said, 'Why do you suppose God invented the watch, Matthews? Do you suppose he meant that man should be punctual, which by definition means arriving at a designated place neither early nor late?'

'I'll be sure to ask him next time we meet,' said Kincaid, amused.

Eliot swivelled round with a start and frowned at Kincaid. 'You're not Matthews. For which you should probably be grateful. He's a pimply little brute, and not likely to impress the world with his intellectual prowess. But I'm sure I know you—' His face lit in recognition. 'You're Victoria McClellan's former policeman. Or was it former husband, still a policeman?'

'The latter, I'm afraid.' Kincaid indicated a chair. 'May I?'

'Please do,' said Eliot. 'And forgive my flippancy. Old habits, and all that, but it is rather inappropriate under the circumstances.'

'Doctor Winslow's just been telling me that you had a habit of disagreeing with Vic,' Kincaid said, deciding on the direct approach.

Eliot laced his fingers over his canary-yellow waistcoat and leaned back in his chair. 'And took great pleasure in it. In fact, my days seem quite surprisingly empty without the anticipation of our little sparring matches.' He frowned, drawing together his heavy, springing brows. 'That may seem odd to you, Mr—'

295

'Kincaid.'

'—Mr Kincaid, but I assure you it meant a great deal to me. Victoria and I were the lone occupants of the eyrie, as we liked to call this floor. I could have moved into one of the larger ground-floor offices years ago, by right of seniority, but I found I'd settled in here, and the very idea of a change became almost as daunting as moving house. But I am not solitary by nature, and the coming of fair Victoria did much to relieve my sense of being incarcerated in the proverbial ivory tower.'

Kincaid thought that if Iris Winslow remained set on retiring, Darcy Eliot might be contemplating a move after all, but he could see why he'd become attached to the space. It was a pleasant room, graced with a dormer window looking north, lined with glass-fronted bookcases, and above the shelves a series of framed satirical prints was arranged on the pale-gold walls. A pipe rack filled with several expensive-looking pipes sat atop one of the cases, but Kincaid had noticed no odour of tobacco.

Following his glance, Eliot said, 'Had to give it up a few years back—the first intimations of mortality—but I couldn't quite bring myself to dispose of the pipes. They add quite the professorial touch, don't you think?'

'Undoubtedly. And your students probably appreciate your not smoking them.'

Eliot smiled. 'As did Victoria. I still indulged when she first came, and we had no end of rows about it.'

Kincaid wondered how Vic, whom he had always thought of as disliking confrontation, had adapted to daily contact with a man who so obviously enjoyed stirring things up. 'What did you find to argue about after that?' he asked. 'Doctor Winslow said you were opposed to the biography Vic was writing.'

'I wasn't opposed to Victoria's biography in particular—although I can't say I find poor Lydia an absorbing subject—just to the general idea of delving into the lives of poets and novelists. Are you a student of literature, Mr Kincaid?'

He thought of his running joke with Vic—*policemen don't read*—and decided this was one instance in which he needn't defend himself. 'Um, not particularly,' he said, putting on a rather hesitant expression.

Eliot hooked his thumbs a bit more firmly together over his middle and spoke in the rich tones Kincaid associated with the lecture hall. 'It's my belief that there's not a single example of a literary text which cannot be shown to contradict itself, therefore rendering itself meaningless. And if the text itself is meaningless, of what use is it to examine the life of its author? And, I might add, since most authors' lives differ little from that of the common man in being merely pitiable attempts to disguise crippling inadequacies, they cannot be of interest to anyone.' He rocked back in his chair and beamed at Kincaid.

'Then why bother to teach something you see as inherently useless?' Kincaid asked, wondering if he'd missed something in Eliot's argument.

'Well, one must do something, mustn't one?' Eliot said, still looking pleased with himself. 'And I find it more amusing than any other occupation which springs to mind.'

'Do I take it that Vic didn't subscribe to your theory?'

Eliot shook his head, pursing his lips in an expression of regret. 'Victoria insisted on cobbling together feminist criticism with some sort of updated version of liberal humanism— producing a hideous hybrid which was illogical at best, and smacked of metaphysics at worst.' He closed his eyes in mock dismay.

Thinking of Vic's assertion that the fact of Lydia's suicide would alter the moral implications of her work, Kincaid said, 'What you're telling me is that Vic had the temerity to assign value to literature?'

Eliot clapped his hands together. 'Bravo, Mr Kincaid. Very well put. Although you've given yourself away in the process. I did think the *vague copper* bit was a bit over done, especially in light of your accent and your bearing—you're obviously well-educated.'

And you're a condescending bastard, thought Kincaid, and smiled. He did not feel inclined to share the particulars of his background with Darcy Eliot. The man must've given Vic a chronic case of the pip. 'Now that I understand the theoretical repercussions of Vic's biography, Doctor Eliot, do you know of anyone who might have had a personal objection to Vic's researching Lydia Brooke's life?'

'Lydia was a minor poet whose early work was pleasantly facile, if derivative,' Eliot said tartly. 'She flirted with mental illness all her life, and her later poems combined a "confessional" exploration of her illness with the most trite elements of feminism. I can think of any number of people she might have offended with her poems, but I doubt her life provided the requisite drama.'

'But you knew her personally,' said Kincaid. 'You were friends at Cambridge.'

'Do you still find yourself in sympathy with everyone with whom you were at school, Mr Kincaid?' Eliot raised one massive eyebrow. 'I find that one often outgrows such relationships. Although in Lydia's case ...' He paused and gave Kincaid a considering look.

'Don't hesitate to express your opinion, Doctor Eliot,' said Kincaid.

Eliot smiled at the thinly veiled sarcasm. 'I dare say such tact would be out of character, wouldn't it? It occurred to me that there might be one person who would prefer that not all the details of Lydia's private life be made public. Lydia flirted with more than mental illness, and at a time when lesbianism was not considered quite as politically correct as it is these days.'

'Lydia had a homosexual relationship?' Kincaid asked, surprised. If Vic had been aware of it, she hadn't mentioned it to him.

'One can never be sure of the details unless one is personally involved, but that was the operative rumour. And as the lady in question is now headmistress of a prestigious girls' school—'

299

Eliot made a tut-tut sound with his tongue. 'I doubt the school governors would find the story too amusing.'

'Who was the other woman, Doctor Eliot?'

Darcy Eliot looked uncomfortable. It seemed that repeating unsubstantiated titillating rumours was all in a day's work, but naming names might press the limits of his public school code of honour. 'Why should I tell you, Mr Kincaid?'

Kincaid had expected the challenge. He leaned forward and met Eliot's gaze. 'Because Victoria McClellan is dead, and I want to know who had reason to kill her.'

Eliot looked away first. 'Well, I suppose that's reason enough, if you put it that way. Though I can't imagine Daphne killing anyone—'

'Daphne Morris? Lydia's friend from Newnham?' Kincaid had a clear image of the girl as Vic had written of her, but that was years ago. 'Headmistress of a girls' school?'

'Here in Cambridge. Just on the Hills Road, in—'

There was a tentative tap at the door, and an acne-scarred boy put his head round.

'Give me a minute more, will you, Matthews?' Eliot said testily, and the boy scuttled apologetically backwards, closing the door with a snap.

'Just one more thing, Doctor Eliot,' said Kincaid as he rose. 'Did you see Vic at all on Tuesday?'

'It was an ordinary day,' Eliot said slowly. 'One doesn't think about it at the time, and that makes it difficult to piece things together again. We passed on the stairs, we passed in the corridor, but I'd be hard-put to tell you what time.'

'Do you remember anything in particular she said?'

Eliot gave a frustrated shake of his head. 'Only the most mundane of things. "Morning, Darcy." "Do let me use the photocopier first this morning, Darcy." ' He frowned. 'I believe she said something about having a sandwich at her desk while she prepared for a supervision at half-past one—but I can't tell you if she actually did, as I was out to lunch, then had supervisions myself the rest of the afternoon.' Looking up at Kincaid, he added, without his usual air of supercilious amusement, 'I'm sorry. I suppose that's in the way of a condolence. Sometimes one finds it difficult to say these things.'

'Old habits?' asked Kincaid.

'Indeed.'

The door to Vic's office was shut, but not, Kincaid discovered, locked. He opened it slowly and went in, feeling a sense of trespass that he had not felt in her office at the cottage. He wished suddenly that he'd seen her here, in her element, doing what she loved—that he'd shared this part of her life in however small a way.

The fine hand of the local police was in evidence. The desk had been stripped bare, and its emptied drawers hung open like gaping mouths. They had left the books, and the personal photographs atop the book shelves. Those of Kit he had expected—baby pictures, a first bicycle, awkward school photos with his hair slicked into submission, a fairly recent print of him handling a punt pole with great concentration.

There was no trace of Ian. It was as if Vic had not hesitated to erase him from her life here, where his absence would not further distress Kit.

Something familiar caught his eye as he turned away—a snapshot propped behind one of the frames. It was his parents' garden, in full summer bloom. He and Vic sat sprawled in the grass, laughing, his mother's spaniel half in Vic's lap. They had been married just a few months, and he had taken her to Cheshire for a visit.

He looked away, out of the window. Vic's office lay across the corridor from Darcy Eliot's, and her window faced south, towards Newnham. Lydia's college. Vic, he thought, would have liked that.

Kincaid found Laura Miller waiting for him at her desk.

'You look a bit battered,' she said. 'I put the kettle on when I saw Darcy's supervision go up. I thought you might need a cuppa.'

He sank into the now familiar visitor's chair and loosened the knot on his tie. 'Thanks.'

Laura disappeared into a small pantry and returned a moment later with two mismatched mugs. 'Milk and sugar all right?'

'Lovely.' Wrapping his hands round the mug's warmth, he said quietly, 'Are you sure Doctor

Winslow's all right? She seems to be feeling a bit off-colour.'

Laura made a face as she scorched her tongue on the hot tea. 'I've been nagging at her the last two days to see someone about her headache, but she's that stubborn.' She glanced at Doctor Winslow's door and lowered her voice further. 'To tell you the truth, I've been worried about her since Doctor Whitecliff's death last June. It seemed to take the starch out of her, if you know what I mean, and she hasn't been the same since. We were always teasing her about trying one of Vic's teas—' She broke off, looking stricken, and her eyes filled with tears. 'Oh, damn and blast,' she muttered, scrabbling in her desk drawer for a tissue.

'Tell me about Vic's teas,' Kincaid said when she'd blown her nose.

Laura smiled and dabbed at the corners of her eyes. 'She drank this awful stuff—some sort of herbal diuretic, because she had trouble with ... you know ... water retention.'

Kincaid thought her hesitation rather quaintly old-fashioned. 'I think I get the picture,' he said, grinning.

'Well, we teased her mercilessly because we could always tell what time of the month it was by what kind of tea she was drinking. I suppose it all sounds a bit silly now.'

'Did she drink any of the special tea on Tuesday?'

'I don't know,' said Laura, her eyes widening. 'You don't think—'

'I don't think anything at this point,' said

303

Kincaid reassuringly. 'I'm just curious.'

'Vic left early, so we didn't have tea together that day. We usually do—did—around the middle of the afternoon.'

'Could she have had some on her own?'

'She kept an electric kettle in her office. She might have had a cup with her lunch, if not earlier.'

'She didn't go out for her lunch?' Kincaid asked.

Laura shook her head. 'We'd planned to go out that day, but that morning she said she'd changed her mind. She needed to work through lunch because she meant to leave early.'

Kincaid felt a pulse of excitement, and an irrational urge to free his hands. He found a bare spot on Laura's desk for his cup. 'Where did she go? When did you last see her?'

'I'm sure it wasn't anything,' said Laura, distressed. 'I got the impression she was a bit miffed about something that had happened at Kit's school, that's all.'

'She didn't say what?'

'Vic didn't like to talk about things until she'd worked them out herself. You know, like with Ian. She never said a word about having problems, then one day she walked in and said, "Oh, by the way, Ian's moved out." You could have knocked me over with a feather.'

Kincaid remembered that trait of Vic's all too well, except in his case it had been she who had moved out. 'Well, maybe we can come at this from the other end,' he said. 'What time did she leave here?'

304

Laura frowned and stared into her cup for a moment, then looked up. 'Half-past two. I remember because Darcy's supervision was late.'

'Matthews?'

She smiled. 'Matthews. Poor boy.'

'Did Vic actually say she was going to Kit's school?' Kincaid asked.

'No, not in so many words. But I could call the Head and find out if she did.' Laura brightened at the prospect of doing something. When Kincaid nodded, she picked up the phone and dialled a number from memory.

He listened to the one-sided conversation with increasing disappointment, then Laura said an apologetic goodbye and rang off.

She stared at him blankly. 'I don't understand. I could've sworn that's what she meant to do, but the Head says he not only didn't see her, but he has absolutely no idea what she might have been upset about.'

'Perhaps something happened to change her mind?' Kincaid offered. 'Did she say anything else when she left?'

Laura closed her eyes, remembering, and when she opened them again a flush stained her cheeks. 'She came downstairs all in a rush, getting into her coat and trying to balance her briefcase at the same time, and she said, "Men. They're all bloody great infants, aren't they? Too bad we can't do away with them all together." Then she waved and said, "Cheerio, ducks. See you in the morning." '

He smiled at the vivid picture. 'Sounds like

vintage Vic, in good form. Had she heard something from Ian, do you suppose? Anything odd in her mail?'

'Not that I noticed when I took the post up to her. And her phone is a direct line, so I wouldn't know about calls.'

A task for the local boys, thought Kincaid, a list of incoming and outgoing phone calls. 'So nothing unusual happened that day, and she felt well when she left here,' he said.

'Yet less than three hours later she was dead,' said Laura, staring soberly at him.

Kincaid gazed back, only half aware of her, and thought aloud. 'So where did she go, and how did someone poison her between half-past two and five o'clock?'

Chapter Thirteen

Helpless I lie.
And around me the feet of thy watchers tread.
There is a rumour and a radiance of wings
    above my head,
An intolerable radiance of wings ...

Rupert Brooke, from
Sleeping Out: Full Moon

The day of Victoria McClellan's memorial service dawned clear and cold. Gemma dressed with care, in a black skirt and matching short jacket, and taking time to plait her hair.

306

She'd spent the remainder of the previous afternoon walking around Cambridge, familiarizing herself with the city and its colleges, and returning home late had found a message from Kincaid on her answer phone. He'd given her the details of the service and asked her to ring back, but she hadn't done so.

What she had to say needed to be said face-to-face, not on the telephone, and so she had arrived early in Grantchester, intending to wait for him at the church. She found a parking spot on the High Street, below Vic's cottage, and as she climbed out she took a deep breath to clear her head of the sun-induced stuffiness of the drive. The day had warmed enough that she was able to leave her coat in the car, and the air held the unmistakable softness of spring.

From where she stood she could see the church tower rising above the trees, and much to her disappointment, its clock did not stand at ten to three as in Rupert Brooke's poem. It read a correct quarter to twelve, which ought to give her time to pay a visit to the Old Vicarage itself, the house where Brooke had lived and worked, and which he had immortalized in *The Old Vicarage, Grantchester*. Perhaps it would live up to expectations.

A short walk downhill on the curving High Street brought her to its wrought iron gates. Gemma wrapped her hands around two of the cold spikes and peered into the garden. She felt a bit like a spying schoolgirl, but then she imagined the owners must be used to the public's curiosity.

The house, which had ceased to be a vicarage even before Brooke's time, had been bought several years back by a well-known writer and his wife, a distinguished scientist. They had restored the comfortable-looking house with much respect for the Brooke legend, but the beautifully landscaped grounds bore little resemblance to the tangled and arbitrary garden of the photos Gemma had seen in Hazel's books. Rupert, she thought, would have been disappointed in its taming, for he had loved it in its wild and secretive state.

Last night she'd looked at a photo of him sitting in the sun in the garden, with his head bent over his papers as he wrote. Now, she recalled it as she gazed through the fence, and the pictures coalesced for an instant, the past superimposing itself upon the present.

She blinked and took a breath, banishing Rupert's image from the quiet and ordinary garden. A large woman with a shockingly blonde mop of permed hair moved into view—the gardener, Gemma realized when the woman knelt beside a bed, trowel in hand. It must have been the peripheral sight of the light-clothed figure that had given her such a start.

Gemma moved away from the gate, and from her less conspicuous position she could glimpse the tennis court where Rupert had played, and beyond that the garden of the Orchard Tea Room next door.

Retracing her steps to the Orchard's drive, she walked towards the river until she could see the orchard itself, with its tea-tables and canvas chairs grouped under the gnarled apple trees. They had sat under these same white-blossomed trees, Rupert Brooke and his friends, in those distant Edwardian Aprils, laughing and talking and planning futures that for many of them would never come to pass.

Someone had placed a bowl of yellow daffodils and white crocuses at the base of the war memorial in the churchyard. Gemma traced the words chiselled into the granite obelisk with a forefinger. TO THE GLORY OF GOD IN LOVING AND GRATEFUL MEMORY ** 1914–1918 ** MEN WITH SPLENDID HEARTS.

She walked round to the other side and read carved there the names of the young men of the village who had given their lives in The War to End All Wars. Rupert Brooke's was among them.

She stood with her hand on the warm stone until Kincaid's voice roused her. 'Gemma. I thought you weren't coming.'

Turning, she watched him walk towards her across the grass. She seldom saw him in a suit—he preferred the more casual sports jacket—but today he wore severe charcoal grey with a starched white shirt and muted tie. He looked tired.

'I wanted to talk to you,' she said. 'Before the funeral. That's why I didn't ring.'

He raised an eyebrow at that, but glanced accommodatingly at his watch. 'It's early yet. Let's walk a bit.'

They went through the lych-gate into the churchyard proper, and picked their way around the lichen-covered headstones. *No point in beating about the bush,* she thought, glancing up at him. 'I owe you an apology for the other day,' she said. 'I had no right telling you how to handle this.'

His lips curved in a smile. 'And when has that ever been a deterrent?'

Gemma ignored the quip. 'Especially since I know how you feel.' There was nothing he could say to that, and she knew it. A friend of hers had been killed a few months before, and though Gemma hadn't been directly responsible for her death, she would carry the weight of it with her always, just as he would carry Vic's.

She turned and looked back towards the church. An ornamental peach tree grew near the churchyard wall, and its puffy round blossoms looked impossibly pink against the emerald grass. Beyond the wall the square church tower rose, a massive counterpoint to the tree's delicacy. 'I understand why you have to find out who killed Vic, and I'm going to help you.'

Kincaid turned her towards him with a touch on her shoulder. 'Gemma, no. I appreciate what you're trying to do, but I can't let you risk your job for me.'

'It's not just for you—it's for Vic, too. And I'm already involved—you can't change that now. Besides'—she grinned at him and held the back of her hand to her forehead—'I've got a dreadful case of flu. I'm sure I'll be off work for at least a few more days.'

310

'Gemma—'

'There's nothing to stop us talking to people, is there? Yesterday I saw Morgan Ashby and his wife—'

'You did what? The man's a bloody lunatic. Are you out of your—' His face froze as he glimpsed something over her shoulder, and she wondered what had rescued her from an imminent bollicking.

'Oh, Lord,' he breathed. 'It's my mother.'

Gemma stared blankly at him. 'What?'

'I meant to tell you—I rang her yesterday. She said she'd come if she could get away.'

'From Cheshire?' Gemma squeaked. 'But it's a half day's drive.' Turning, she looked out through the gate, searching for a hint of the familiar among the people gathering before the church.

'She cared about Vic,' Kincaid said, simply. 'She wanted to be here. Come on, I'll introduce you. And we'll talk about this other business later.'

When she'd finished embracing her son, Kincaid's mother smiled and held out a hand to Gemma. 'Do call me Rosemary, won't you.'

The resemblance was there, thought Gemma, in the hair that had faded from Kincaid's rich chestnut but still sprang from the brow in the same way, and in the eyes and the shape of the mouth. 'Your dad wanted to come,' Rosemary continued to Kincaid, 'but it was Liza's day off and one of us had to mind the shop.' She looked up at him and touched the backs of her fingers briefly against his cheek. 'I *am* sorry, darling.'

'I know.' He smiled and clasped her hand in his. 'The church is starting to fill. I suppose we'd better go in.'

Gemma lagged behind intentionally, wanting to give them a few moments together, but Kincaid waited and took her arm. 'Let's sit near the back,' he said softly as he guided them into one of the last pews. He took the aisle himself, and Gemma saw him watching the mourners as they straggled in, searching each face.

The church still held the night's chill, and Gemma felt the warmth of his body when he leaned across her and whispered to his mother, 'It looks as though Father Denny has High Church inclinations.' He waved the Order of Service he'd taken from the hymnal stand. 'We may be here for a bit.'

Gemma, having been brought up strictly chapel, had never learned to feel comfortable in an Anglican service, but with Kincaid's helpful cues she managed to keep up, and discovered that she found the impersonal ritual surprisingly comforting. She let the words and the music wash over her as she gazed at the faces round her, wondering who these people were, and what they had meant to Vic. *And what Vic had meant to them,* she thought as she cast a covert glance at Kincaid's shuttered face. No public display of emotion would reveal his grief to the casual onlooker.

The service ended, and the congregation rose as the processional passed, then filed slowly out into the sun.

Gemma, Kincaid, and his mother were among the first to reach the porch. Kincaid thanked the vicar, then guided them a little ways away, where they stood watching the uncertain milling of the mourners. 'They don't quite know what to do with themselves,' Kincaid said. 'There's no reception organized, but they don't feel they should just walk away.'

'It's all very odd. I'm surprised her parents didn't lay on something,' Rosemary commented in a tone of mild censure. 'I'd not have expected Eugenia to give up an opportunity to do the right thing, or the chance of an audience.' She made a rueful face. 'Oh, dear, I suppose I shouldn't have said that.'

Kincaid smiled. 'You are a darling. And you're quite right—I thought exactly the same thing.'

'Well, I must speak to them,' said Rosemary, but without much enthusiasm.

'I'd like a word with Kit—' began Kincaid, then smiled at the woman coming towards them from the shadow of the porch. About Vic's age, thought Gemma, with chin-length brown hair and a pleasant face, the woman beamed at Kincaid as if she'd spotted a long-lost brother.

'Such a relief to have got through it,' she said as she joined them, and on closer inspection Gemma saw the smudged mascara and the slight trembling of her lips.

Much to Gemma's surprise, Kincaid took the woman's hand in his and patted it as he introduced her. 'This is Laura Miller, the secretary of Vic's department. My mother,

313

Rosemary Kincaid, and this is Gemma James.'

He'd introduced Gemma to Rosemary just as simply, without reference to rank or their professional association, and Gemma felt a bit exposed without the usual camouflage.

'I'm sorry if I'm a bit wobbly,' said Laura when Kincaid had released her hand. She pulled a tissue from her pocket and dabbed at her face. 'But I've just been cut absolutely dead by Eugenia Potts, of all the absurd things. She wouldn't even let me speak to Kit—I only meant to tell him that all his friends at school were asking after him. Whatever is the matter with the woman?'

Kincaid exchanged a glance with his mother. 'I don't know. She is behaving rather strangely, even for Eugenia. Where are they?'

'Still inside. Iris was determined to pay her condolences. I wish her luck.' Laura frowned. 'Iris doesn't need anything else to upset her just now, as badly as ...' She paused, gazing past Gemma's shoulder. '—Oh, look, here they come now.'

Turning, Gemma saw a heavy-set, older woman ploughing determinedly towards them, with a smaller, fluffier woman fluttering along in her wake.

'Who's the friend?' Kincaid asked softly.

'That's Enid, Iris's ... um, companion,' Laura said under her breath, then the two women were upon them and introductions were performed all round again.

Iris Winslow, like Laura, expressed great pleasure upon seeing Kincaid. 'I am glad you could come,' she said, and added with a dark glance at Enid, 'I thought it a perfectly suitable service, whatever anyone else might say. And I think Vic would have approved, which is the main thing, isn't it? She was never one for a fuss.'

Enid pursed her lips and made clicking sounds of agreement.

Kincaid gave a groan of exasperation. 'Don't tell me her mother's finding fault with poor Father Denny.'

'I'm afraid so,' said the tall, thin man in clerical garb who had stepped quietly up to join them. 'But I think he's quite capable of dealing with it.' He smiled, and Gemma was immediately charmed. This, she learned a moment later, was Adam Lamb, and Iris seemed almost as pleased at his appearance as she had at Kincaid's.

As Gemma listened to the snippets of conversation, she began to place these people in relation to Vic. Iris Winslow, it seemed, had been her boss, and Darcy Eliot, the large man in the mauve waistcoat who had joined them, one of her colleagues. She was not quite sure about Adam, except that he seemed to know Iris and Darcy. Then she heard Kincaid say quietly to him, 'How is Nathan holding up?' and at last she recognized a name. It was Nathan who'd given Vic the book in which she'd discovered Lydia's missing poems, and he was, she remembered Kincaid saying, Lydia's literary executor.

Adam gave a small shake of his head. 'It's been a difficult day, I'm afraid. He's just having

315

a word with Austin—Father Denny—and then I'm determined to whisk him off home.'

Was Nathan some sort of an invalid, and Adam his caretaker, wondered Gemma? But then he, too, joined the widening circle, and she saw that Nathan Winter was a striking man in his early fifties, whose white hair contrasted sharply with his tanned skin and dark eyes.

'Adam seems determined to fuss over me, but I'm quite all right,' said Nathan, as though he'd overheard. Protest he might, thought Gemma, but he did look unwell. There was a tinge of grey beneath the tan, and the dullness of shock in his eyes.

'And I have no intention of leaving until I've had a word with Kit,' he added. 'Is there any news about Ian McClellan?' he asked Kincaid.

'Not a trace,' said Kincaid. 'I've just been to see the local police this morning, and they're no further along. The man looks to have simply vanished.'

'Bastard,' said Nathan quite clearly, and there was a momentary pause in conversational buzz.

Turning to Darcy Eliot, Rosemary said brightly into the rather strained silence, 'I enjoy your books, Mr Eliot. And I adore your mother's—I've been a fan of hers for longer than I care to admit.'

'You're too kind,' Eliot replied. 'But I'm afraid my administrative duties these days don't leave me much time for such pleasant pursuits. My mother, on the other hand, seems to grow more prolific with every passing year.'

'Would that we could all possess a fraction

of Margery's stamina,' said Iris. 'I don't know how she does it.'

'She claims the occasional medicinal sherry helps a great deal,' Darcy said with a wink. 'And I dare say the same would have done all of us good this afternoon. I can't imagine what—' He stopped, drawing together his bristling eyebrows as he frowned at Iris. 'I say, Iris, are you all right?'

Iris had paled and grasped Enid's arm, but she smiled gamely at them. 'It's nothing that a small measure from your bottom drawer wouldn't put right, Darcy. Just this headache has been plaguing me these last few days.'

'Are you feeling ill, Doctor Winslow?' asked Adam, instantly concerned. 'Nathan's cottage is just up the street—do come and let me fix you some tea. Nathan does marvellous things with herbs, and I believe there's a particular blend for headache.' Taking her elbow, he turned to Nathan for confirmation, but Nathan was staring at the trio that had stepped out of the church into the porch. The faded blonde in the dark, printed suit and black straw hat must be Vic's mother, thought Gemma, and the thin, balding man her father. And between them, Kit, looking white and fiercely miserable. The sleeves of his navy blazer were too short, and somehow the sight of his bony wrists protruding beneath the cuffs made her throat tighten as nothing in the service had done.

Rosemary put a quick hand on Kincaid's arm. 'Duncan, is that Vic's son?' she asked, her voice rising on an incredulous note.

317

'Yes,' said Laura before Kincaid could answer. 'But the poor bloody kid wasn't so fortunate in the allotment of grandparents.' Her face was tight with anger.

They all stood as if mesmerized as the Potts's moved on towards the drive. 'She means to pass us by without a word,' said Rosemary, with blank surprise. 'I don't believe it.'

Her words seemed to galvanize Nathan, for he suddenly started forward, calling, 'Kit, wait!' and they all followed after him, lemming-like.

It was Vic's father who stopped and turned, and Gemma could see the displeasure in the mother's stiff posture as she was forced to wait.

'Hello, Kit,' said Nathan as he reached them. The others piled up awkwardly behind him, like witnesses to an accident. 'I only wanted to see how you were.'

Beneath the little veil on the black straw hat, Eugenia Potts's face was blotched with weeping. She held a handkerchief to her lips with one trembling hand and made no attempt to speak.

Into the silence, Kit said with the certainty of desperation, 'I wish I were dead.'

'Christopher!' Eugenia wailed. 'Have you no respect—'

'Eugenia,' said Rosemary quietly as she stepped forward. 'I was so sorry to hear about Victoria. This must be very difficult for you.'

'You don't know the meaning of difficult, Rosemary Kincaid. If you'd lost your only child—'

318

'I'd like to meet your grandson,' continued Rosemary, cutting her off in mid-sentence. She held out a hand to Kit. 'Hello, Kit. I'm Rosemary, Duncan's mother. Let's see—' She tilted her head and examined him. 'You must be ... what? Twelve? Thirteen?'

'Eleven,' Kit answered with a spark of interest, and pulled himself up a bit.

'And what do you play at school? Rugger? Football?'

'Football,' he admitted, with an anxious glance at his grandmother.

'I thought so.' Rosemary smiled. 'You look a bit like'—she turned to the men in appeal, and Gemma knew she hadn't a clue—'What's the chap's name who plays for Manchester United?'

'I feel ill, Robert,' interrupted Eugenia. 'Please take us home this instant.' She sagged a bit, and Kit winced as she gripped his arm for support.

'Of course, dear,' said Bob Potts. 'Perhaps you should wait while I fetch the car—'

'I'd like a word with Kit before you go, if you don't mind,' said Kincaid. 'It's rather impor—'

'I feel ill,' said Eugenia again, fanning herself with the Order of Service she held in her hand. 'Robert!' She started unsteadily down the drive, her hand still gripping Kit's arm.

'I'm so sorry,' said Bob Potts, shrugging apologetically. 'But I'm afraid we must go. She really is not at all well.' He started after his wife, then turned back once more. 'So sorry,' he repeated. 'It was good to see you, Rosemary.

319

Give my regards to Hugh. And ... thank you.'

The little group in the churchyard watched as he caught up to Eugenia and Kit and helped them into the car, and still no one spoke as the car pulled out into the High Street and disappeared round the bend.

Then Kincaid said quietly, 'His name really is Bob, you know. He told me once. Just plain Bob, but she insists on calling him Robert.'

'God, what a farce,' said Rosemary Kincaid, glancing at her son's composed face as she lowered herself into the sling of the canvas deck chair. 'That sort of thing is distressing enough without any added pyrotechnics.' She had insisted on taking Duncan and Gemma to tea at the Orchard, on the grounds that they all needed fortification after their ordeal, and that she had no intention of setting off for her sister's in Bedford without a much-anticipated visit with Duncan.

After a quick glance at the menu, she said, 'Let's go the whole hog, why don't we? Pots of tea and sandwiches and scones and cake.'

'Comfort food?' said Duncan with a smile. 'Or has Dad been nagging you to eat again?'

'I'd say a good dose of comfort with a dollop of nostalgia would fit the bill nicely. *"Yet stands the Church clock at ten to three? And is there honey still for tea?"* ' she quoted.

'There is,' said Gemma. 'Honestly. I saw it on the menu.'

'Then I'll go and put the order in at the window, honey included,' said Duncan, and

320

scrambled up out of the chair.

Rosemary watched his long-limbed stride as he walked away, then focused on the young woman across from her with frank curiosity. *Beautiful?* Well, perhaps not in the strictly classical sense, she thought, but certainly very attractive, with the sun glinting from her burnished copper hair and her open, friendly face alight with intelligence.

They worked together, Rosemary knew, but Duncan had mentioned her more and more frequently in the last year, and when he'd come home at Christmas she'd sensed a definite change in the status of the relationship. 'You've been good for him, you know,' she said, and saw Gemma colour slightly. 'These last few months he's seemed more relaxed than I've seen him in—well, I suppose since he was a child.'

'You were going to say, "Since he was married to Vic," weren't you?' asked Gemma.

'Yes. But I realized it's not true.' Rosemary glanced at Duncan, standing in the tea queue, hands in trouser pockets. 'He was very intense about work then—he'd just made Inspector, and there was a lot of pressure to perform. I think the marriage pulled him apart—he could never give enough of himself to either. And in the end the job won out.'

Frowning, Gemma said slowly, 'Do you blame him for what happened with Vic?'

Rosemary shrugged. 'Not really. It was a difficult situation. Vic responded to living with her mother by learning not to express her emotions. Duncan grew up in a family that

321

voiced their grievances, and so he equated her lack of complaint with contentment. By the time either of them worked out the truth, the damage was irreparable.' She smiled at Gemma's intense expression. 'So the moral is, my dear, if something he does gets on your wick, you'd better bloody well tell him.'

'Oh.' Looking surprised by the off-colour expression, Gemma laughed, as Rosemary had intended.

'Men aren't very good at working things out for themselves, you know,' Rosemary added affectionately. 'Sometimes you have to give them a prod. I understand you have a son.'

'Toby. He's three, and a devil with it,' said Gemma, with obvious pride in his precocity. 'Would you like to see a photo?'

Rosemary took the snapshot and gazed at the small blond boy with the impish grin. And as if he weren't enough to contend with, she thought, their lives were about to become infinitely more complicated. Would Gemma be willing to stick with Duncan if it meant compromising the security of her own child? 'He's lovely,' she said. 'Absolutely lovely. And I'm sure he runs you ragged.'

'Who, me?' asked Duncan, returning at last with the tea tray. 'I know I'm lovely, but I do try not to take advantage. Sorry about the delay, by the way, but it was choc-a-bloc with people wanting tea in the garden. Can you imagine?'

'The wasps seem enthusiastic about the idea, as well,' said Rosemary as she swatted at the one exploring her sandwich. 'So you'd best prepare for battle.'

They all tucked in with newly discovered appetites, and as they ate Duncan gave them encapsulated sketches of the cast of characters at the funeral.

'You mean Vic was having an affair ... or a relationship—whatever you want to call it—with Nathan?' said Gemma, scattering a few scone crumbs in the process. 'That rather puts things in new light.'

'Why? Did you fancy him yourself?' asked Duncan, lightly, but Rosemary wondered if he'd felt a prick of jealousy over the engagement of Vic's affections.

'I thought he looked rather ill, today,' said Gemma as she spread strawberry jam on the last half of scone. 'Under other circumstances, though ...' She smiled mischievously. 'But I'm temporarily unavailable. I've lost my heart to a young man named Rupert, and they've some lovely postcards and things up at the front. So if you don't mind ...?'

'Of course not,' said Rosemary as Gemma popped the last bit of scone in her mouth and finished her tea. 'Would you choose the best one for me? I'll add it to my collection.'

'You're going to say motherly things, aren't you?' said Duncan when Gemma had disappeared round the kiosk. 'And tell me she's a nice girl.'

'She is a nice girl, though she'd probably resent both of the epithets. I would say that she's an attractive and sensible woman, and I

323

hope that you appreciate her.' Rosemary's tone was half-teasing, but she watched him with concern. He was too bright and brittle—she feared what would happen when the coping mechanism failed. And as much as she hated to add to his burdens, she saw no choice. Quietly, she added, 'And I did want to talk to you, darling.'

Still determinedly playful, Duncan answered, 'That's the second time someone's said that to me today, and I fear it bodes no good.'

'I don't know that good or ill have much bearing here. It's more a matter of dealing with the truth.'

'Truth?' Duncan frowned with evident unease. 'What are you talking about, Mother?'

'Tell me what you see when you look at Kit, love.'

'I see a nice kid who's been dealt a bloody awful hand of it, and it's bloody unfair,' he said with vehemence, but she saw no flicker of comprehension.

Rosemary took a last sip of her tea, then said slowly, 'Let me tell you what I see, darling. When Kit came out of the church today, between his grandparents, I thought for a moment I was hallucinating.' She reached out and laid her fingers briefly on his hand. 'I saw you. Duncan at twelve years old. Not in his colouring, of course—that came from his mother—but in the shape of his head, the way his hair grows, the way he moves, even his smile.'

'What?' His face drained of colour.

'What I'm trying to tell you is that Kit is your child. The genetic stamp is as unmistakable as a brand.'

He closed his mouth, made an effort to swallow. 'But that's impossible ...'

'The consequences of sex are usually all too possible, darling,' said Rosemary with a smile. 'Don't I remember giving you the birds and the bees lecture—'

'But what about Ian? Surely he's—'

'Duncan, do some simple arithmetic, for heaven's sake. The boy is eleven—you and Vic split up almost twelve years ago. I'm sure you'll find his birthday falls within six to eight months of the time you separated.' Rosemary looked at his glazed expression and sighed. 'I'd guess Vic didn't know she was pregnant when she moved out—I don't suppose you know when she started seeing what's his name?'

'Ian. I'd like to think it was after she left, but I don't know.'

Rosemary smiled. 'Let's say very shortly after, then, for argument's sake. But I'm sure the truth of the matter became evident over time, at least to her.'

'I don't believe it. Surely you don't think Vic knew all along ... when she rang and invited me ...' He trailed off, still working out the implications.

'And I'll wager that's what has got Eugenia Potts in such a state, as well. She may not be admitting the resemblance to herself, but I imagine seeing you and Kit together gave her a bloody great shock.'

'Kit ... oh, Christ. She did go right round the twist when she saw me with him the other night.'

'She certainly never cared for you. To your credit,'—she smiled at him—'because you wouldn't dance attendance on to her.'

He was silent for a long moment, absently pushing cake crumbs about on his plate with his finger. Then he looked up at her. 'Why couldn't I see it, then, if it's so bloody obvious?'

'I suppose it's because our images of ourselves are so static. We literally don't see ourselves the way others see us—we base our self-concept on the one view we see every morning in the mirror. But if you were to place a photo of yourself at that age next to one of Kit, you'd see it.'

'But what if you're wrong? This is all based on pure speculation and ... and intuition,' he finished a bit lamely. He was, thought Rosemary, grasping at straws in a last-ditch effort at denial.

'Who was it at Christmas telling me how important intuition was to a detective?' When he didn't smile, she sighed and said, 'Darling, I could very well be wrong. And I don't like to meddle. Under other circumstances—if Vic were alive, and she and Kit and Ian were all living happily as a family—I might not have said anything. But as things are now ... how can you afford not to be sure?'

21 June 1964
Cambridge

Dear Mrs Brooke,

Please forgive my writing, but I couldn't bear to tell you our news over the telephone. Lydia is in Addenbrook's, quite ill after suffering a miscarriage last night. The baby was a boy, and I have called him Gabriel after my father. There will be a service here in the hospital chapel tomorrow.

Lydia is weak and feverish from the haemorrhaging, and I am unable to calm her. She seems to think this is somehow her fault, a punishment, and no amount of reasoning will change her mind.

Could you perhaps come straight away? It may be that you can comfort her where I cannot.

Morgan

Kincaid rang the bell of Gemma's flat well after dark, hoping she was home, hoping she would consent to see him, for he'd left her abruptly on her own in Grantchester with only a muttered assurance that he'd ring her later.

Afterwards he'd walked blindly through the village until he'd reached the footpath along the Cam, and after that he couldn't say how long he had walked, or even in which direction. But the temperature had eventually begun to drop, his feet in their slick-soled shoes to hurt, and he found himself back at his car on the High Street as the sun dropped below the rooftops.

He'd driven back to London with his desire for company growing as urgent as his earlier need for solitude, and now he breathed a sigh of relief when he heard the click of the latch on Gemma's door and a sliver of yellow light spilled out onto his face and hands.

'Gemma? May I come in?'

She pulled the door back further and he saw she'd changed into old jeans and a jumper. As he stepped into the tiny flat he saw the picture books spread over the bed, and a boy-shaped lump under the duvet. 'Is it too late?'

'We were just reading,' said Gemma, giving an exaggerated nod towards the bed. 'But Toby seems to have disappeared. I think he ate the magic pebble that makes little boys invisible, and I can't find him anywhere.'

Kincaid cleared his throat and put on his best Sherlock Holmes voice. 'Let me put my detective skills to use. Where's my magnifying glass? All right, Watson, the game's afoot!'

There followed the elaborate ritual of hide-and-seek, as they ignored the occasional suppressed giggle from under the bedclothes, until finally the missing boy was brought to light with much squealing and tickling.

'More, more! Hide me more!' wailed Toby as Gemma carried him off to bed, but she tucked him in with a promise of another story in the morning.

I missed all this, thought Kincaid with an unexpected stab of loss.

'Are you all right?' asked Gemma as she carefully shut Toby's door. 'What on earth happened to you this afternoon?'

He sat at the half-moon table, and she pulled out a chair so that she could face him.

'I don't know where to start,' he said, absently rearranging the candles Gemma kept on the table.

'Start at the beginning. What did your mother say to you? You were white as chalk when I came back from the kiosk.' She leaned forward and traced the line of his jaw with her fingertips, the gentleness of her touch belying the impatience of her words.

'You're too observant by half,' he said, stalling, but she refused the bait and merely watched him in silence. He took a breath. 'My mother says Kit is the spitting image of me at the same age. She says she thinks Kit is *my* son.'

Gemma's eyes widened, the pupils dilating with surprise until he saw his own reflection in them. 'Dear God,' she breathed. 'How could I have been so blind?'

'You don't doubt it?' He found he'd hoped for at least a token protest, and yet he felt some small kernel of satisfaction in her immediate recognition.

Shaking her head slowly, she said, 'I saw it myself—the resemblance. He seemed so familiar, as if I saw him every day.' She touched his face again, with a look of wonder. 'And I do. But you—how could you not have known Vic was pregnant?'

He pushed his chair back and stood, feeling suddenly confined in the flat. 'We could go for a walk,' he suggested.

329

'I don't like to leave Toby.'

'No, of course not. Silly of me.' *Bloody hell.* He hadn't got used to the responsibility of one child, much less two. He wouldn't know where to begin.

The odd sense of claustrophobia grew heavier, and searching for an excuse for movement, he fumbled in the breast pocket of his suit until he felt the book of matches he'd picked up yesterday in the pub. *You never knew when things might come in handy.* Bloody Boy Scouts had drummed that one into him, and he supposed it had come in useful. Had Kit been a Boy Scout? Could he tie knots? Whistle through his teeth? *He wouldn't know where to begin.*

Leaning forward, he lit the candles, and when he'd blown out the match, he said, 'Things were strained between Vic and me. We hadn't been ... sleeping together much—'

'It only takes once,' Gemma interrupted with a grin.

'Well, yes.' *Christ, this was awkward.* There had been an argument, and a passionate reconciliation, some weeks before Vic left. He had forgotten.

'Was she unusually emotional, those last few weeks? The hormonal changes at the onset of pregnancy are powerful enough to—'

'What you're saying is that Vic might have walked out—which was irrational and unlike her—*because* she was pregnant?' There was no room to pace. He forced himself to sit on the foot of the reclining leather and chrome chair he called the torture cradle. 'I should have seen it. You're quite right.'

'That's not the way I meant. And she might not have known herself—'

'But I failed her then, as well.'

Gemma slid from her chair to kneel at his feet, so that she could look up into his face. 'Bollocks. You can't change what happened. There's no point indulging in that sort of thing. What you have to decide is what you're going to do now.'

'What can I do?' he protested. 'Kit's life has been disrupted enough as it is. He thinks Ian is his father—'

'Do you really think Ian is going to be much use to him, even if he should come back? And Kit's prospects with his grandparents are worse than dismal.' Removing her hands from his knees, she sat back on her heels, but kept her eyes fixed on his face. 'I think, love, that it's your life you're afraid to disrupt.'

Chapter Fourteen

And because I,
For all my thinking, never could recover
One moment of the good hours that were over.
And I was sorry and sick, and wished to die.

Rupert Brooke, from
Pine-Trees and the Sky: Evening

331

3 September 1965
Cambridge

Darling Mummy,
You are so sweet to be concerned for me, but
as much as I'd love to have you here, I'm
fine, really. (Though I must admit it's rather
amusing to have you and Morgan conspiring
treats behind my back, and I feel rather like the
heroine in a Victorian novel, propped up in bed
having my boiled egg and toast on the tray you
sent.) You have enough to deal with just now,
with Nan ill, and Morgan makes a gloweringly
tender and surprisingly competent nurse-maid.

But although this most recent miscarriage
has been relatively easy, I've decided not to
try again. I've schooled myself not to want it
so desperately, but still the cycle of hope and
disappointment is wearing, and it keeps me from
getting on with my work. It's been difficult for
Morgan, too, and he says no child is worth my
health and well-being. So I'll soldier on, and try
to count my blessings.

I find I can't bear all the radiantly fecund
young wives of our married friends, but
Daphne's been a comfort, and visits often.
Morgan seems to be prepared to tolerate her
for my sake.

There is wheat among the chaff, darling,
Mummy. I've had an offer from a small
press here in Cambridge to publish my latest
collection of poems. They mean to specialize
in the avant-garde, and I'm quite set-up to be
considered so. It will mean some work, to revise

and finish the collection, but I look forward to it. Just think, a book, at last! It will be a child of sorts, I suppose.

We were right, you know, Morgan and I, in deciding that our art must come from experience. It's the daily stuff of living, bloody as it sometimes is, that gives the photos and poems the sting of truth.

Morgan's been approached by a London gallery to do a solo exhibition! They want all of the Welsh miner series, and anything else he can get ready. You'll have to come up to London for the opening, and we'll make an evening of it.

So try not to worry—I promise I'll have shocking roses in my cheeks by the time you see me next.

Love,
Lydia

The smell of coffee teased Kincaid up through the layers of consciousness like a hooked fish. Finally, he could no longer deny wakefulness, but lay with his eyes still closed, trying to figure out who could possibly be making coffee in his flat.

Then it dawned on him that he was not in his flat at all, nor in his bed, but Gemma's.

Ordinarily it made her uncomfortable for him to stay, because of Toby, but last night she had insisted, and they'd made love with the silent urgency of two teenagers fearing discovery. Just the memory of it stirred him to arousal, and he opened his eyes, hoping to find her still sleep-tousled and willing to come back to bed.

She sat, fully dressed, at the half-moon table, drinking coffee and shuffling pages of typescript.

'You were just using me last night,' he said, injured.

Gemma looked up and smiled. 'Your powers of deduction are astounding, sir.' She stretched, showing an inch of bare skin at the waist as her jumper rose above her jeans. 'Sorry about the coffee. I was afraid the smell would wake you, but I couldn't wait any longer—'

'That's what you said last night,' he teased, then added, *'how* long have you been up?'

'You don't want to know.' She turned another page of the manuscript.

He'd told her last night that he had a copy of Vic's book locked in the boot of his car, so she must have lifted his keys while he slept with the skill of a pickpocket. 'Sneak.'

'I've brought in your emergency kit from the boot as well,' she said, referring to the shaving things and change of clothes he kept packed for unexpected overnights.

'Then I suppose I've no excuse for staying in bed,' he answered regretfully, but the light filtering in from the garden through the half-opened blinds was turning from the green of early morning to gold, and Toby would doubtless be up soon.

'I think we should see Daphne Morris this morning,' said Gemma a few minutes later, watching him as he tucked in his shirt-tail.

'Gemma—'

'No more argument,' she interrupted firmly.

'We've done all that.'

'You're impossible,' he said, knowing it was a capitulation, yet feeling an unexpected sense of relief.

'You said last night that Darcy Eliot implied Lydia had a lesbian relationship with Daphne Morris.' She tapped the manuscript. 'If Vic suspected that, there's no hint of it here, but what if she'd just recently come across it? The headmistress of a girls' school would certainly have a lot to lose if something like that got out.'

He looked up from tying his shoe. 'Vic interviewed Daphne Morris, it's in her notes. She said Daphne gave the impression she hardly knew Lydia.'

Gemma raised a sceptical eyebrow at that. 'That's obviously not true, on the basis of Lydia's letters alone. Do you know what school it is?'

'No, but I know roughly where it is, and it shouldn't be hard to ferret out the rest. What do you suppose headmistresses do on a Saturday?'

Headmistresses, it turned out, went away to their country cottages, but Daphne Morris had been delayed and was still packing. They had been shown into the sitting room of her private apartments by a thin woman with pockmarked skin and a protective attitude. 'You won't keep her, will you?' she said as she turned to go. 'She needs every bit of her weekend—'

'It's all right, Jeanette.' The woman who came into the room sounded affectionately amused. In jodhpurs and boots, with her fresh skin and her glossy russet hair tied back with a scarf, she looked like an advertisement from *Country Life.* 'I promise I'll be out of your hair in a quarter of an hour.

'She thinks I'm going to murder someone if I don't get away for the weekend,' continued Daphne Morris, giving an exasperated roll of her eyes as Jeanette went out. She started towards them with her hand out-stretched, but must have seen their faces freeze, because she hesitated and dropped her hand. 'What is it? Have I said something wrong?'

'You really don't know?' asked Gemma, surprised.

'I'm sorry,' said Daphne, sounding a bit wary now, 'but perhaps Jeanette got it a bit muddled. Who did you say you were?'

Kincaid introduced himself and Gemma, adding, 'We're from Scotland Yard, Miss Morris.' After all, he thought as he showed her his warrant card, that was the truth, strictly speaking, and he'd come to the conclusion that they weren't likely to get anywhere without calling on their official standing. 'We'd like to talk to you about Victoria McClellan. We understand she came to see you about Lydia Brooke.'

Daphne frowned. 'Yes, she did, but I don't understand what it has to do with you.'

He glanced at Gemma, who widened her eyes and gave a minute shrug of her shoulders in response. Either Daphne Morris didn't know about Vic's death, or she was an astonishing

336

actress. This was a development he hadn't expected. 'Miss Morris, perhaps it would be better if we all sat down.'

'Oh,' she said with a start. 'Do forgive me. My manners seem to have flown out of the window.' Daphne gestured to the sofa which faced the marble fireplace, and took a small gilded chair for herself. The flat had a serene and formal atmosphere which suited her classical looks, but also gave it an impersonal quality. There were no photographs, no open books, no magazines or newspapers, knitting or needlework. 'Now, please tell me what this is all about.' She had a natural authority as well as graciousness, thought Kincaid, and she'd just shown a hint of the headmistress.

'Victoria McClellan,' he began, and cleared his throat. Bloody hell. 'Doctor McClellan—'

'Doctor McClellan died on Tuesday,' said Gemma quietly, coming to his rescue.

'But how dreadful ...' Daphne looked from Gemma to Kincaid in concerned surprise. 'I hadn't heard. One never expects one so young—'

'She was murdered, Miss Morris. Poisoned, in fact,' Kincaid said baldly, watching her. 'We believe there may be some connection to her research on Lydia Brooke.' He would have sworn the paling of her already creamy skin, the widening of her dark eyes, were reflections of a genuine emotion, but was it shock or fear? Before she could recover, he said, 'When Doctor McClellan interviewed you, you gave her the impression that you and Lydia were merely acquaintances, old school chums whose paths occasionally crossed.'

'But I—'

'When, in fact, you and Lydia Brooke had a long and close friendship. Why would you have wished to mislead her?'

'I didn't deliberately mislead her,' Daphne protested. 'But why should I have felt compelled to discuss my personal affairs with a complete stranger? I have a right to my life, and my memories—'

'But what about Lydia?' interrupted Gemma. 'Surely if you cared about Lydia you'd have wanted her portrayed accurately. And Lydia's letters certainly suggest that you might give the most unbiased picture—'

'Letters?' whispered Daphne, her face ashen. 'What letters?'

'Oh, Doctor McClellan had access to Lydia's letters, of course,' said Gemma brightly. 'Did she not mention that? Including Lydia's extensive correspondence with her mother over the years, in which she mentioned you repeatedly. It appears that you weren't on the best of terms with Morgan Ashby. Was there some particular reason why Morgan disliked you?'

For a moment Daphne seemed too stunned to answer, then she rallied. 'It's none of your business. And I didn't give a damn how Lydia appeared in Doctor McClellan's book. Biography is a useless exercise, a picking over of bones when the meat is gone.' She took a breath and clasped her trembling hands together. 'Look, I'm not saying that Victoria McClellan didn't have good

338

intentions, but no amount of letters or interviews could ever have conveyed—'

'Well, that's rather a moot point, now, isn't it?' Kincaid drawled. 'Because there won't be a biography. And if someone preferred that the details of Lydia's life remain buried, then they'd be feeling quite comfortable with it all, wouldn't they? Enjoying weekends in the country and all that.' He smiled. 'It has come to our attention, by the way, that you might have had very good reason to safeguard the details of your relationship with Lydia Brooke, Miss Morris. Say if your relationship was of an ... unorthodox ... sexual nature, for instance? I doubt that would go over smashingly well with the school governors.' He looked round with evident admiration. 'It is rather a prestigious institution, as far as girls' boarding schools go, I understand?'

Daphne jerked to her feet, knocking the delicate gilded chair over backwards, where it bounced soundlessly on the soft carpet. Ignoring the chair, she shouted, 'You've been talking to Morgan, haven't you? He'd say anything to hurt me, the jealous, paranoid bastard. Did he tell you that he was arrested for assaulting Lydia?' Their surprise must have shown in their faces, because she went on with great satisfaction, 'Oh, yes. Did he tell you he broke her ribs? And her jaw? Did you think Morgan's famous artistic temper was all bark and no bite?'

'When exactly did this happen?' asked Gemma.

The calmness of Gemma's tone seemed to

339

communicate itself to Daphne, for she wiped a shaking hand across her mouth, then touched the hair that had escaped its binding. She had large hands, Kincaid noticed, more suitable to a milk maid than a goddess.

'I shouldn't have said that. I promised Lydia I'd never tell anyone.' She shook her head. 'And I've never in all these years broken a promise to Lydia.' Her eyes filled with tears.

'There will be records, you know, hospital admissions and so on, if we're forced to trace them,' Gemma continued. 'But it would be better coming from you. Was this shortly before Lydia died?'

Daphne gave her a look of blank incomprehension. 'I'm sorry?'

'You told us Morgan attacked Lydia,' Kincaid said carefully. 'Did this happen near the time of her death?'

'Lydia hadn't seen Morgan for years when she died, as far as I know. This was just weeks before they separated. She came to me.' Daphne groped backwards for her chair, and Kincaid moved quickly to right it for her. 'Why do you keep talking about Lydia's death?' she asked. 'What has that to do with anything?' Daphne's hands gripped the seat of the gilded chair beneath her thighs as if it were a frail craft on a storm-tossed sea.

'Vic—Doctor McClellan—thought that Lydia's death might have been ... engineered,' said Kincaid. 'She was, in fact, *convinced* that Lydia Brooke was murdered. And don't you find it rather odd, Miss Morris, that Victoria McClellan should have been murdered, too?'

Somehow I never thought it would come to this. Fragmented. Observed and observer. The first Lydia dispassionate, rational, knowing there were only two inevitable conclusions— death or division.

The other Lydia knows death would have been the better alternative.

Lydia watches Lydia lying foetus-curled in the sweat-soaked bed. Lydia knows it for sabotage, knows the other one couldn't bear the fine, clean strength of what they had between them. So the other poisoned it, a word here, an expression there, provoked when she should have comforted, drew blood with savage appetite.

And Lydia watched, Electra tongueless, mute, the poet silenced.

There will be no more.

'She never denied it,' said Gemma, glancing at Kincaid as he drove.

'Who never denied what?' he asked, frowning, distracted by the traffic at the Newnham roundabout as he signalled for the Barton Road.

'Daphne never actually denied her relationship with Lydia.'

'Maybe she didn't think the allegation worth denying,' Kincaid suggested, looking away from the road long enough to grin at her. 'Maybe she thinks we're as round the twist as Morgan Ashby. Maybe by this time she's called the Yard to complain about our irrational behaviour—we have, after all, just accused a respected professional woman of having a homosexual relationship, not to mention murder, on the basis of nothing whatsoever.'

Stung by his reckless sarcasm, Gemma said hotly, 'She's not telling the whole truth. She was relieved when I said the letters were to Lydia's mother. I'm sure of it.'

'She also seems to have a cast-iron alibi for the afternoon of Vic's death.'

They had spoken again to Jeanette, and had a look at Daphne's daily calendar, both of which confirmed that Daphne had had a full schedule of meetings and appointments on Tuesday, but Gemma was not ready to capitulate. 'There are always holes in alibis. And we don't know where Vic went when she left the English Faculty that afternoon. What if she went to Daphne's flat? Daphne could have slipped out of her office and met her with no one the wiser.'

She knew from the look on his face that he'd considered the possibility, but rather than agreeing with her, he said, 'Now that we've already done six impossible things before lunch, as well as buggering any claim to reputable behaviour, how do you suggest we persuade Morgan Ashby to sit down and have a nice pleasant conversation about all this?'

Gemma felt the knot of dread in her stomach expand at the thought. She had lied to Morgan Ashby, and that was something even a calm and stable man might not take too kindly. But she smiled at Kincaid, and said carelessly, 'Well, if your pretty face won't do the trick, I suppose we'll have to rely on my charm.'

They went by farmhouse rules this time, and knocked at the back door first. They hadn't seen the car, but their hopes that it was Morgan who was out, and that Francesca would be able to pave the way for them, were soon dashed.

Morgan opened the door scowling, as if he'd been expecting someone else, but it soon became obvious that they were not more welcome. 'You,' he said to Kincaid. 'I thought I told you to bugger off.' Then he glimpsed Gemma, half-hidden behind Kincaid's shoulder, and for an instant his face started to relax into a smile. 'What are you doing here, Miss Ja—' Breaking off, he looked from Kincaid to Gemma again, and the scowl came back in full force. 'You weren't here about the studio at all, were you? You were bloody snooping. I should have bloody known.' He shook his head in disgust. 'All right, I've had enough. I've said it before, and this is the last time I'm going to tell you—either of you. Fuck off.'

'Mr Ashby,' called Gemma, as Kincaid put out a hand to stop the door shutting. 'We're police officers. Both of us. From Scotland Yard. We need to talk to you.'

Morgan gave Kincaid a disdainful look, but at least her sally had kept him from shutting Kincaid's hand in the door, thought Gemma.

'Scotland Yard? So that was a load of bollocks

you fed me, too,' Morgan said to Kincaid. 'All that sob story about Victoria McClellan being your ex—'

'It was true,' said Kincaid. 'Vic came to me because I'm a policeman, when she began to feel uneasy about Lydia's death.'

'Lydia's death?' repeated Morgan, hesitating for the first time. 'What are you talking about?'

Gemma stepped forward into the opening Kincaid had created with his arm. She had felt a sense of rapport with Morgan Ashby, and now she gambled on it. 'Look, Mr Ashby, please let us come in. We won't take up more than a few minutes of your time.'

Morgan stared at her for a moment, brows drawn together as though he meant to refuse, then he suddenly shrugged and stepped back. 'Say what you have to say, then, and get it over with.'

As an invitation, it was less than gracious, but Gemma moved quickly into the kitchen, and Kincaid followed, closing the door. Socks and underthings hung drying on a rack suspended above the Rayburn, and Gemma smelled potatoes boiling on the cooker's top. Her stomach rumbled, but she couldn't tell whether it was from hunger or nerves.

Morgan stood with his backside against the cooker, and didn't invite them to sit down. 'What do you mean uneasy?' he said, glancing from one to the other. 'Why would McClellan have needed to go poking about into Lydia's death. Isn't the simple fact of it enough?'

'There were several things that worried Vic about Lydia's suicide. But first let's go back a bit.' Kincaid stepped forward, physically crowding Morgan, and Gemma bit her lip on an admonition. She knew his aggression was an instinctive reaction to Morgan's belligerence, but her gut feeling told her it wasn't the way to handle him.

'We've just come from a visit with Daphne Morris,' Kincaid said. She saw Morgan tense at the name, his pupils dilating until the grey in his eyes disappeared into black, but Kincaid smiled and continued, 'It seems you were all quite well-acquainted. She told us some fascinating things about your relationship with Lydia. There was a little matter of a reported assault, for instance, and some fractures—'

Gemma heard the crack of Morgan's fist against Kincaid's jaw almost before she saw it—then came a flurry of punches too quick for her to follow and they were straining together, panting, their faces fierce with intent, and blood welled crimson-bright from Kincaid's split lip.

It seemed to take her aeons to cross the mere two paces of kitchen floor, then she was shoving and shouting at them. 'Stop it! Both of you! Morgan, listen to me. Lydia didn't commit suicide. Someone *killed* her. Do you hear me? It couldn't have been you—you'd never have poisoned her. But someone did, and you have to help us. Morgan—'

Then suddenly Kincaid had Morgan's arm pinned back in a hammer lock, and Morgan was grimacing with pain.

'Let me go, goddamn it!' he shouted, kicking at Kincaid's shin, but Gemma sensed the fight had gone out of him.

Kincaid eased up, but said furiously. 'You bloody well keep your hands to yourself, okay?'

Morgan jerked his arm out of Kincaid's grasp and stepped away, touching the blood trickling from his nose. He gave a perplexed look at the smear on his fingers, then frowned at Gemma. 'Why should they bother to kill her?' he said. 'Didn't they do enough damage as it was?' To Gemma's horror, his face contorted in a sob.

She guided his now unresisting body into one of the chairs at the kitchen table, then dampened a dishcloth and handed it to him. Slipping into the chair opposite, she said gently, 'Who hurt Lydia, Morgan?'

'Bloody perverts.' Morgan dabbed at his nose. Even though he seemed to have got his face under control, unshed tears glistened on his lower lashes.

'Are you talking about Daph—' Kincaid began, but Gemma made an abrupt shushing gesture with her hand, and after a moment's hesitation, he sat down at the far end of the table and held his handkerchief to his lip.

'She's a cunning bitch,' said Morgan. 'She bided her time, all those years—faithful, dependable Daphne, waiting for an opening.'

'Was Lydia sleeping with Daphne?' asked Gemma, in a carefully neutral tone.

'Sleeping.' Morgan gave a bark of laughter. 'Bloody euphemism for what they did. All of them, not just Daphne, and Lydia held it up to me, taunted me with it when we had rows. They made her ill, twisted her so that she could never have a normal relationship.

'She had night terrors, did you know that? She'd wake up screaming and sweating from dreams she never remembered. And the worst of it was that she couldn't bear to be happy. We'd get along well for a bit and then she'd start picking at things, starting rows. Sometimes I think now that she wanted me to hurt her, but I was too close to it then. I couldn't see it.'

'Did she want you to hurt her so she'd have an excuse to leave you?' asked Gemma. 'That's what happened, isn't it?'

'Oh, no. You've got it all wrong.' Morgan shook his head. 'She ran to Daphne, but she came back in a few days, and things were all right for awhile.'

'Then she started in at you again,' said Gemma, now beginning to see the pattern of it.

Morgan nodded, closing his eyes for a moment. Then he said slowly, 'It was when I found myself shaking her with my hands round her throat that I knew I had to be the one to do it.'

Sensing Kincaid stir at that, Gemma gave a quick shake of her head. She waited, resisting the impulse to hurry Morgan, or to speak for him.

'I pried my hands away, and I felt as though they'd never be clean again. How had I let her bring me to that? Later that night, when she had cried herself to sleep, I packed my things and

347

walked out. The next day I filed for divorce. I gave her the house, and everything in it.' He looked up at Gemma beseechingly. 'Was it such a terrible thing to do, abandoning her that way?'

'You couldn't have done anything else.' Gemma allowed herself to touch his hand. 'Morgan, who was it that made Lydia ill? Besides Daphne?'

The skin beneath his eyes crinkled as he frowned at her. 'Adam, of course. The spoiler of her virginity, she liked to call him, or the Lamb of God. She thought it funny.'

'Just Adam?' she asked.

'Adam, and Darcy Eliot, and that bloody hypocrite Nathan Winter, who went on afterwards to become the perfect morally upright husband and father,' Morgan sneered.

'You're saying that Lydia slept with *all* of them?' Gemma refrained from making eye contact with Kincaid. 'Including Daphne?'

'She told me I was unreasonable because I didn't want them coming round, after we were married.'

'But you gave in about Daphne, didn't you? After Lydia lost the babies, because Daphne was the only woman she could bear to be around. What about afterwards, when you'd separated? Did they continue to see one another?'

Morgan shook his head. 'I don't know. I didn't see Lydia again, except for the few occasions when we couldn't avoid running into one another.' He sounded suddenly very tired.

'There was Francesca.'

'Francesca kept me sane. Still does, though it's a job I don't envy her.' Morgan attempted a smile. 'We'd both have been better off if I'd—' He paused and tilted his head, listening. 'She's home now. Back from the shops. I can recognize the sound of the bloody old Volvo's engine a mile away.'

A car door slammed nearby. They waited, and after a moment the back door swung open. Francesca Ashby stepped in, her pleasant face creased with anxiety. She took in Morgan's face, with the traces of blood drying black beneath his nose, and dropped her parcels where she stood. 'Morgan! Are you—'

'I'm fine, love, don't worry,' he reassured her.

'But—' She glanced at Kincaid, whose cheekbone was beginning to darken in a bruise, then at Gemma. 'What happened?' she asked as she went to stand beside her husband.

'Something that should have happened a long time ago,' he said, putting his arm around her waist. 'But I'm not sure I can explain it. It's over, Fran. Finally. They say that someone killed Lydia. She didn't commit suicide.' He looked at Kincaid for the first time since their scuffle. 'Are you sure of it?'

'There's no physical proof at this point, but I think it's fairly certain,' said Kincaid.

'And you think this same person may have killed your Doctor McClellan?'

Kincaid nodded. 'Do you have any idea who might have done such a thing?'

'No,' said Morgan slowly. 'And it's an odd thing, but I find I don't really care.'

'Morgan, you can't mean that.' Francesca stepped away from him, sounding shocked.

He looked up at her. 'I don't mean I think it right, or that I don't care about justice for her, in a detached sort of way. But don't you see what this means for me, Frannie?'

'It was never your fault, Morgan, no matter how she died.' She stroked his hair. 'You didn't need that sort of absolution.'

'But I did,' he said softly. 'I'm going to sell the house, Fran. Will you help me?' He turned to her, and when she gave him a nod of confirmation, he gave a long shuddering sigh and rested his head against her breast.

Gemma and Kincaid sat for a moment, watching Francesca's still face, then got quietly up from the table and let themselves out.

Chapter Fifteen

And I recall, lose, grasp, forget again,
And still remember, a tale I have heard, or known,
An empty tale, of idleness and pain,
Of two that loved—or did not love—and one
Whose perplexed heart did evil, foolishly,
A long while since, and by some other sea.

Rupert Brooke,
from *Waikiki*

'So where does this leave us?' Kincaid asked as he picked up his cheese and tomato sandwich, then winced as his first bite caught his swollen lip. Gemma had already started on hers, and he watched the egg mayonnaise squish generously over the edges of the brown bread as she bit into it.

They'd chosen a basement tea room off St John's Street, partly on Hazel's recommendation, and partly because he had made an appointment with Ralph Peregrine, and the offices of the Peregrine Press were nearby. Kincaid had to admit the tea room was a charming enough place, a warm retreat with heavy oak furniture and bright Blue Calico tea services, but the drawing of Alice in Wonderland on the restaurant's paper menus made him think of Vic.

'You shouldn't have pushed Morgan, you know,' said Gemma a bit reproachfully, but her expression was concerned as she watched him explore his lip with a careful fingertip. 'You're going to have a lovely bruise on that cheekbone as well,' she added in a tone of dispassionate interest.

'The man is a wife beater—by his own admission, he nearly killed Lydia—how can you possibly make excuses for him?' Kincaid countered defensively.

'You don't usually let your personal prejudices get in the way of your judgement.' Gemma looked at him over the rim of her blue and white teacup. 'And besides, I'm not sure it's true—that Morgan's an abuser, I mean. I think he has a rotten temper, and that Lydia pushed him—'

'You're not saying that Lydia deserved what she got?' he sputtered through a mouthful of sandwich. 'That's preposterous. I can't believe you'd—'

'Of course I don't mean that,' she said, just as hotly. 'I'm not saying that what Morgan did was right, only that I think this was something strictly between Morgan and Lydia, a combination of personalities that drove them both beyond their limits. Besides, for most men who abuse women, it's a chronic pattern, but I'd be willing to bet you a month's wages that Morgan's never laid a finger on Francesca in all the years they've been married.'

'So? That doesn't mean he didn't murder Lydia twenty years later.'

'No, but not that way.' Gemma shook her head emphatically. 'Morgan acts out of temper. Poisoning requires deliberate forethought, intent to harm, and I don't think he's capable of it.' More thoughtfully, she added, 'What I'd like to know is whether Lydia really deliberately triggered these episodes, or if that's just his perception of it—a way of excusing himself.'

'Well, there's no way we can know that, is there? And I can't see any point arguing with you unless we turn up something else that incriminates Morgan Ashby,' said Kincaid with a sigh. 'Once you make up your mind you're as immovable as Mohammed.'

Gemma's smile held the satisfaction of victory.

'Then don't you think we need to follow up what Morgan told us? We can't see Daphne again until Monday, but we could have a go at Darcy Eliot and Nathan Winter.' She finished her tea and patted her mouth demurely with her serviette.

'All right,' he conceded. 'But I still want to see Ralph Peregrine first. I'm not happy about those missing poems.'

When they had paid their bill, they climbed the steep staircase back to street level, passing through the ground floor shop with its selection of linens and laces. Kincaid saw Gemma reach out towards a particularly elaborate tablecloth displayed near the door, but she dropped her hand without touching it and followed him out onto the pavement.

The weather had changed in the half-hour they'd been inside. Dark clouds had scudded in, and the air held a damp chill. 'It must be this way,' said Gemma, as they came to a halt at the intersection of St John's and a tiny lane. Remembering that she'd told him she'd done a recce the day before yesterday, he followed her without question. They passed a shop selling English cheeses, and olives in an array of colours ranging from pale green to deep aubergine. Beyond that, a shop displayed handmade chocolates, and then, just before they reached Sidney Street, they saw an unobtrusive door bearing a brass nameplate with the Peregrine Press logo.

There was no bell, but when Kincaid tried

the latch the door swung open. They stepped into the foyer, and saw that a flight of stairs led directly up to the first floor and another door of frosted glass. 'Are you sure someone's here?' asked Gemma. 'It's quiet as the proverbial tomb, and it is Saturday, after all.'

'Peregrine said he'd be working,' Kincaid reassured her as they climbed the stairs. He opened the glass door on the upper landing and allowed Gemma to enter first.

They found themselves in an ante-room of sorts, in that it contained a shabby sofa and a coffee table much marred by drink rings, but the rest of the available space was taken up by haphazardly shelved books and assorted piles of paper. Most of the books seemed to bear the familiar Peregrine imprint, and there were multiple copies of many of them. The door to an inner office was closed, and Kincaid heard a man's voice speaking intermittently—Ralph Peregrine must be on the phone.

'I see the elegance associated with the Peregrine Press doesn't extend to the working quarters,' he said, rifling one dusty pile of paper with his thumb. 'Are these manuscripts, do you suppose?'

'It doesn't seem very organized, does it?' Gemma wrinkled her nose. 'It's a wonder they manage to publish any—'

'Hello. Thought I heard voices.' The inner door had swung open soundlessly, and a thin, dark man in cords and a cherry-red pullover stood on the threshold, smiling at them enquiringly. 'You must be Mr Kincaid.

I'm Ralph Peregrine.'

After Kincaid had introduced Gemma, who was blushing slightly, Peregrine escorted them both into his office. 'We'll be more comfortable in here,' he said, seating them in two Queen Anne chairs that looked as if they'd been pilfered from someone's dining room. The room's ambiance was definitely a notch above that of the ante-room, however. The desk, although piled dangerously high with books and papers, looked expensive, and the carpet under their feet had the cushiony feel of good quality. To the left of the desk a new-model computer sat on a specially designed table, and below it a printer. Kincaid rather liked the idea that the end product of the latest technology remained printed words on bound paper.

Peregrine propped one hip on the front edge of his desk and faced them, his back to the light pouring in from the large window behind his desk. Folding his arms across his chest in a relaxed posture, he asked, 'Now, how can I help you?'

It's a case, thought Kincaid. *Just state the facts and don't let thinking of Vic get in the way.* He cleared his throat. 'As I said over the phone, it's about Lydia Brooke's last book, the one published posthumously. Vic McClellan discovered some poems among Lydia's effects that she felt sure should have been included in that manuscript. I wondered if perhaps you had made an editorial decision not to include certain poems in the finished book?'

'I should think not,' answered Ralph, sounding

amused. 'Lydia and I had a good working relationship, meaning that I didn't fiddle about with her words.' More soberly, he added, 'And I would have been even less inclined to do so after her death, when it was no longer possible to consult her. I published Lydia's book as it was given to me, with every effort to make it something that would have pleased her.' He took off his spectacles and rubbed the bridge of his nose, frowning. 'I do remember thinking at the time that there was a certain lack of continuity in the placement of the poems, but in the light of Lydia's death, I blamed her depression.'

'Were the pages of the manuscript numbered?' asked Gemma.

Ralph shook his head. 'No. Lydia would play with the order of the poems until the very last, and because she used a typewriter, renumbering a manuscript every time she made a change would have been a real headache.'

'So someone could easily have slipped a page here and there out of the manuscript?' Kincaid suggested.

'Well, I suppose so,' said Ralph, looking nonplussed. 'But why on earth would anyone want to do that?'

'We don't know. We only have Vic's assertion that something was wrong.' Kincaid blinked, as if that would erase the image of Vic's animated face as she waved the sheaf of poems at them.

'Doctor McClellan was certainly the expert on Lydia's work, but if she suspected that the manuscript had been tampered with, why didn't she discuss it with me?' asked Ralph. The man had an intelligent face, Kincaid thought as he watched him, accentuated by alert, dark eyes and the high forehead exposed by his receding hairline. It wouldn't do to underestimate him.

'She only discovered this a few days before she died,' said Gemma. 'I doubt she had the chance to consult you.'

'Have you any idea who might have had access to Lydia's manuscript before you yourself read it?' Kincaid asked.

Ralph glanced round at a profusion of books and papers equalling that of the front room, and shrugged eloquently. 'You can see how things are. I feel like Sisyphus trying to keep up with all the projects, and my assistant only keeps the stone from backsliding a bit. There are always a fair amount of people tramping through here, as well, but we've never seen any need to be security-conscious.' He tilted his wrist and glanced furtively at his watch. 'Surely it's just as possible that Lydia herself decided to remove the poems for some reason? And I can't imagine what bearing this has on Doctor McClellan's death. This all seems a bit far-fetched, if you don't mind my saying so.'

'Not only might it have something to do with Doctor McClellan's death, it may be connected with Lydia's death as well.' Kincaid, watching Ralph carefully, saw the speed with which he drew a conclusion from the vague statement.

'Lydia? What do you mean?' Ralph sounded genuinely surprised, and he glanced from Kincaid to Gemma as if seeking confirmation.

'We think it quite possible Lydia Brooke may

have been murdered,' Kincaid said.

Ralph stared at him. 'Murdered? But ... that's just not possible. Lydia was a middle-aged poet of moderate success, with a history of depression. Why would anyone want to murder her?'

'That's what we were hoping you might tell us, actually,' said Gemma, with a smile. 'We thought you might have a more objective view of her, since yours was primarily a working relationship. And you had been together a long time.'

'Yes,' Ralph said slowly. 'We had. Lydia was one of the first authors I took on, and we grew up together, so to speak. We were incredibly naive about the publishing business in the beginning, both of us, but Lydia was forgiving of my mistakes. I was very fond of her.' He removed his glasses and pinched the bridge of his nose again, and when he dropped his hand Kincaid could see the red marks left by the spectacles' nose pads.

Looking quizzically at the wire frames dangling from his thumb and index finger, Ralph said, 'I've a habit of sitting on them, I'm afraid.' Again, he gave a barely perceptible glance at his watch, and added, 'Look, I'm sorry, but I really don't know what else I can tell you. Lydia was opinionated, more so as she got older, and sometimes inclined to get on a bit of a soapbox about things. But since when are those reasons to kill someone? She was also generous with her time and advice—she often helped younger poets—and must have had people in her debt.'

'And in her personal life?' prompted Kincaid.

'Lydia didn't share details of her personal life with me, other than the usual chit-chat about creeping damp and leaks in the roof.'

'What about Morgan Ashby?'

'I met him, of course, when Lydia and I first began working together. But I don't think he particularly cared for me, and we never made it a social relationship. I invited them for dinner once, I remember, near the end of their marriage, but it wasn't a success.' This time the glance at his watch was overt. 'Look, if you don't mind, I've an appointment—'

They heard the sound of the ante-room's outer door opening and closing, then a woman's voice called, 'Sorry, I'm early, Ralph, darling.' The inner door swung open. 'Oh. Do forgive me, Ralph,' said the voice, silvery and breathless. 'I didn't realize you had guests. I'll just—'

'No, come in, Margery, please.' Ralph crossed quickly to the door, and Kincaid and Gemma turned awkwardly in their chairs, trying to see behind them. 'I do wish you wouldn't run up the stairs,' said Ralph, in a tone of affectionate exasperation.

'Don't fuss, darling. You know it makes me feel old,' she answered, laughing.

Kincaid stood quickly as the woman came into the room on Ralph's arm. She was in her seventies, thought Kincaid, dressed all in grey, and matched her voice more perfectly than anyone he had ever met.

'Margery, this is Superintendent Kincaid, and Sergeant James, from Scotland Yard.' Ralph nodded at them. 'Dame Margery Lester.'

She looked the picture of the famous novelist, Kincaid thought, this woman whom his mother so admired. And if she still possessed a great talent, she had once been blessed with great beauty as well. Margery Lester was still beautiful, patrician, blue-blooded even to the faint blue cast to her porcelain skin. It surprised him that his mother, with her Labour leanings, should be so enamoured of a woman who embodied generations of wealth and breeding, but perhaps he was underestimating his mother. Perhaps, he thought, as he met Margery Lester's bright and intelligent eyes, he was underestimating them both.

'Dame Margery,' he said, and took her hand. When she'd greeted Gemma, he insisted she take his chair. 'My mother's a great admirer of yours,' he added as he moved to stand beside Gemma. 'I'm beginning to wonder if I might have missed out on something.'

'They're not "women's" books,' said Margery, smoothing the skirt of her pale grey suit over her knees. 'I quite despise this tendency to put flowery covers on them, but the marketing people will have their way. I can only hope husbands pick them up when their wives aren't looking and discover there's a good story inside.' She smiled as if anything might be forgiven a person who read.

'Would anyone like something to drink?' asked Ralph, slipping gracefully into the role of host. 'The sun must be over the yardarm somewhere, and it is Saturday, after all. I can do G & Ts quite adequately, except for the limes, I'm afraid.'

'Never touch the stuff,' said Margery briskly. 'Doctor's orders. I wouldn't say no to a small sherry, though.'

Ralph glanced enquiringly at Kincaid, who found himself suddenly of a mind to become a little better acquainted with Margery Lester. 'I wouldn't mind following Dame Margery's example,' he said, and sensed Gemma's startled glance before she murmured an acceptance.

While Ralph busied himself with retrieving a bottle and a set of fragile-looking rose-coloured crystal from a cabinet, Kincaid leaned over and, raising his eyebrow, whispered in Gemma's ear, 'We're not exactly on duty, after all.'

'What brings you here, Mr Kincaid, if you don't mind my nosiness?' asked Dame Margery, and he wondered if her hearing was as acute as her wit.

Ralph looked up from pouring the sherry. 'They'd some questions about Victoria McClellan.'

'Oh, that was too dreadful.' Margery shook her head. 'I met her several times, you know, at faculty functions, and thought her absolutely charming. One just doesn't expect things like that to happen to someone one knows.' She glanced at Ralph as he handed her a sherry. 'It makes our little project seem quite frivolous, doesn't it?'

'It wouldn't have seemed frivolous to Henry,' said Ralph as he offered a glass to Gemma, then Kincaid.

'What project is that, Dame Margery?' asked Gemma.

'I've been helping Ralph put Henry White-cliff's notes into some sort of publishable form. Poor Henry died last summer before he could finish his manuscript.' Margery lifted her glass to Ralph, who had poured his own sherry. 'Cheers,' she said, and took a small sip.

'That name rings a bell,' said Kincaid, frowning. 'Wasn't he the Head of Department before Doctor Winslow? Why does everyone refer to him as "poor" Henry?'

'It's unconscious, I suppose,' said Margery with a sigh. 'But it does seem as though poor Henry—see, I've done it again.' She smiled and deliberately corrected herself. 'It seems as though Henry Whitecliff had to bear more than his share of tragedy, and he was such a lovely, kind man that he seemed even less deserving of it than most.'

Ralph returned to his position at the edge of his desk. 'Henry's only daughter disappeared just before her sixteenth birthday. I remember her vaguely—we were near the same age, though not at the same school.'

'She was a beautiful girl, Verity, very bright and loving, but a bit headstrong— just the sort to be tempted by the idea of running away to Swinging London when she'd had a row with her parents. Henry and Betty were devastated, of course, and for years they followed every possible lead, hoping against hope that she would come home. Then Betty developed cancer.' Margery came to a halt, clasping the stem of the sherry glass with both hands. Her hands were still beautiful, Kincaid noticed, with slender, tapering fingers, but the blue veins stood close to the surface and her knuckles were slightly enlarged, as if she suffered with arthritis.

After casting a concerned glance at Margery, Ralph took up the story. 'After Betty died, Henry retired from the English Faculty and began his book, a thorough and detailed literary history of Cambridge. He meant to dedicate it to Verity, and I think that thought kept him going for years. Then one night last summer he went to bed and didn't wake up the next morning.' He shrugged. 'A blessing, people always say when that happens, but it seems a bit unfair to me. No chance to tie up loose ends, or to say goodbye.'

Would it be any better, Kincaid thought, *if he'd had a chance to tell Vic goodbye? To say all the things he might have said?* He dragged his attention back to Margery.

'... so Ralph and I thought we should see the book finished, and published,' said Margery. 'A labour of love, if you will.'

Ralph patted a thick stack of manuscript pages near the centre of his desk. 'We'll have galleys by June, in time for the anniversary of Henry's death. Sounds a bit morbid, but I think he would have appreciated it.' He stared at the manuscript a moment, then looked up at Kincaid and frowned. 'Those poems you were asking me about—I'd like to see them. I'm not as well-versed—excuse the pun—in Lydia's work as Doctor McClellan, but I might be able to tell if the poems belonged in the manuscript. I don't like the idea that anyone's manuscript pages might have gone walkabout from my office.' Turning to Margery, he added in explanation, 'They say that Doctor McClellan found some poems she thought should have been included in Lydia's book.'

'I'd be glad to let you see them if I had them,' said Kincaid. 'But we didn't find them among Doctor McClellan's papers. They've disappeared.'

'How very odd,' said Margery, musing, her gaze still resting on Henry Whitecliff's manuscript. 'There's another unfinished book now—Victoria McClellan's. I know how dedicated she was to this project—it would be a shame to let it all go to waste.'

'Margery, don't even think it,' said Ralph, sounding horrified. 'You've too much to do as it is, and the doctor's cautioned—'

'As if he knows anything about it, the desiccated old stick,' said Margery in disgust. 'He'd have me mummified in no time, if I listened to him.' She smiled at Ralph, forgiving him. 'I appreciate your concern, darling, but you know it's work that keeps me going, and if I should end the same way as Henry, then so be it.'

'Dame Margery,' said Kincaid, 'I'd suggest you leave this particular project on the shelf for awhile. I'm concerned for your health in a more concrete way—working on Vic McClellan's manuscript might prove very dangerous indeed.'

27 March 1969
Cambridge

Dearest Mummy,
You know ginger biscuits cheer me like nothing
else, and I will nibble at them when I can't bear
the thought of real food. I've put the tin in the
middle of the kitchen table, so that I can have
them with my tea while I watch the chaffinches
in the garden.

It's a comfort to know you're thinking of
me. It has been a long winter, but I think I'm
reconciled to things now. Morgan has a lover, I
saw them in the marketplace. He looked white
with misery, and I'm sure he thinks I wish him
ill, but I don't. I feel too empty for that, light
and unanchored as an abandoned husk, and I
think only when the divorce decree becomes
final will I gain substance again. Writing comes
slowly, if at all, and that I miss more than
anything.

Old friends have rallied round—Adam with
pots of nourishing soup and ministerial good
cheer, and I'm grateful enough for his company
to ignore the hopeful undercurrents. No one is
worth what I've been through these last few
months, years, really.

Every so often Darcy pops round for cocktails
and shares all the academic gossip, and I dare
say his acerbity is easier to take than outright
sympathy. Nathan Winter and his wife, Jean,
have just had their first baby, a girl called
Alison, and I'm to be godmother. I managed

my shopping for her christening gift (a silver cup with her name and birth date engraved) with some fortitude, and treated myself to dinner at Brown's afterwards.

Daphne's been a rock, of course, but she had finally to make a decision about the teaching position in Bedford, and I could only encourage her to take it. It's a well-known public school, and will do her career prospects good. Bedford is only an hour's drive, and we'll still manage to see one another at weekends, so I'm consoling myself with that thought.

I heard a rumour yesterday at the greengrocer's that the Beatles are breaking up, and I found myself crying quite ridiculously among the cabbages and the carrots. It was utterly nonsensical—I thought to myself that they each had their own separate lives and families, that it was time for them to move on—but I felt an overwhelming sense of loss. It's as if they symbolized our hopes and our innocence, and I felt suddenly that I'd lived through the passing of a generation.

I can see your lips curve in that knowing smile even as I write these words. When you were my age you had lived through the war, been widowed, borne a child, and for you the loss of a generation was counted in hundreds of thousands of lives.

If only we could absorb one another's experiences, altering our emotional as well as our intellectual perceptions, then we might prevent so much suffering, such sorrow. But then I realize that we can do this, at least in a small way, through fiction, and poetry, so perhaps my battlefield has some merit, after all.

Love,
Lydia

Kincaid had Gemma ring Laura Miller at home, asking where they might find Darcy Eliot on a Saturday afternoon, and she'd sent them to All Saints' College. 'He's had the same rooms for donkey's years,' said Laura. 'I've always envied the male dons living in college—drinking college wine, eating at High Table, being waited on hand and foot. I think that's why Darcy's never married—he couldn't bear to give it up,' she added, laughing, and rang off.

They stopped at the Porter's Lodge, and were directed towards the back of the college. Gemma walked slowly, conscious of Kincaid's impatience, but ignoring it. She glanced down at the folded brochure she'd taken from the porter, then up again at the buildings forming the four sides of the quad they'd entered from the Porter's Lodge. 'This is the Front Court,' she said. 'And that must be the entrance to the chapel on the left. We go through here'—she pointed to the building straight ahead—'and come out the other side.'

When that passage had been safely negotiated, she stopped and consulted her map again. 'This must be the Elizabethan Library, on the right. Isn't it lovely? Look at all the tiny panes in the windows.'

'Gemma—'

'And these are the perennial beds,' she

367

continued, pointing at the freshly turned black earth bordering the library. 'It says here that they're one of the college's best features.'

'It looks like clumps of dead stems to me.' Kincaid gave her a withering glance. 'You've been spending too much time with Hazel. You're beginning to sound like a gardener.'

'They'll be lovely in another month or two,' she said a little wistfully, with a sudden wish that she might see them then, but she knew it to be unlikely.

'Gemma—'

'All right.' She started walking again across the lawn, following the line of buildings that curved along the right-hand side of the park-like garden, ending at the wall overlooking the Cam. With the mutability Gemma was coming to expect from Cambridge weather, the clouds had again released the sun, and within the precincts of the daffodil-studded garden it felt quite like spring.

Darcy Eliot's staircase proved to be the last in the building nearest the river. Following the porter's instructions, they climbed to the first floor and easily found the door with *Eliot* inscribed on its brass plate, but before they could knock it swung open.

'Bill rang to say you were on your way,' said Darcy Eliot, with every evidence of pleasure. 'But I'd begun to think you'd fallen in the Cam.' He stepped back and gestured them inside.

'I'm afraid I was sight-seeing,' said Gemma, with an apologetic wave of her map.

'And I can't blame you. All Saints' is rather

a jewel—small enough to be accessible, don't you think?' Eliot considered them curiously. 'It's rather refreshing to find anyone interested in architecture these days. The world is full of Philistines.' He wore a large cashmere pullover in a robin's egg shade of blue, and looked considerably more rumpled, and more human, than when Gemma had seen him at the memorial service. 'Do sit down,' he added, indicating a sofa upholstered in a velvet almost the same shade of blue as his sweater.

But Gemma was already crossing the room as he spoke, drawn by the windows in their deep, stone embrasures. The men followed, and stood either side of her as she gazed out.

'That's St John's you can see across the bend in the river,' said Darcy, pointing. 'It's quite lovely, isn't it? I never tire of my view.'

One of the casements was cranked open a few inches, and Gemma felt the air move against her face, cool and fresh. 'Yes, I can see that,' she said, with a concerned glance at Kincaid beside her, still silent.

She was accustomed to a consistency on his part which allowed her to function as the volatile half of the partnership, but his behaviour over the last few days had been unpredictable. He seemed to ricochet from a forced, feverish pleasantness, to a sharp-tongued sarcasm, to the withdrawn silence he exhibited now.

In that moment she realized how much she had come to depend on him, even when she argued with him and questioned his decisions. The sense that she might no longer be able to count on his strength frightened her.

Well, I'll carry us both, she resolved, but she had the feeling it was going to take all her wits. She turned to Darcy Eliot and smiled.

'You must feel king of the castle up here,' she said, looking about her as she let him lead her back to the sofa. The room was comfortably opulent, with much gilt in evidence on picture frames and mirrors, and a coordination of colour and fabric that spoke of a professional hand in the designing. In the centre of the wall opposite the windows, an ornate, mahogany bookcase displayed multiple copies of Darcy Eliot's books—some with the now-familiar Peregrine logo—and Gemma found the little vanity rather endearing.

Darcy seated himself at the other end of the sofa, carefully crossed one ankle over the other knee to reveal a colourful argyle sock, and said, 'To what do I owe this visit, other than the attractions of my college?'

This had been Vic's college, too, Gemma remembered with a quick glance at Kincaid.

He turned, but didn't come to join them. 'We've just had a very pleasant visit with your mother,' he said. 'I hadn't met her before.'

'Please don't tell me my mother inflicted the damage to your face.' Darcy stared with frank curiosity at Kincaid's swollen lip and purpling cheekbone. 'Her manners are usually exemplary.'

'Her manners *were* exemplary.' Kincaid smiled and ignored the probe. 'We seem to have interrupted her meeting at the Peregrine Press, but she was quite gracious.' He crossed to the sitting area and sat in the armchair opposite Darcy.

'Ah, my mother's other child,' said Darcy, sounding faintly amused. When Kincaid raised a questioning eyebrow, he went on. 'Did she not mention she was on the Board of Directors?'

'She only said she'd been helping Peregrine with Henry Whitecliff's manuscript.'

'Henry was on the Board, as well,' said Darcy. 'Both of them from the beginning. But Peregrine Press would never have seen the light of day without my mother's considerable assistance, financial and otherwise. She and Ralph have had a long and productive relationship.' He smiled, and Gemma felt a bit shocked, wondering if he could possibly mean what she thought he meant. Dame Margery must be at least twenty-five years older than Ralph Peregrine, if not more. Surely ...

'... Vic tell you that she thought some poems might have been removed from Lydia's last manuscript?' Kincaid was saying as she picked up the conversation again.

'You're not serious.' Darcy looked from Kincaid to Gemma, his smile fading. 'You *are* serious. Surely you don't think Ralph had anything to do with it? He's as honest a chap as you could ever come across.'

'We don't know anything at this point, except that Vic was worried about this manuscript,' said Kincaid. 'I thought she might have mentioned it to you.'

Darcy smoothed the sock on his crossed ankle

before lowering his foot to the floor. 'No, she didn't. And I doubt I'd have been Vic's first choice as a confidant, I'm sorry to say. We didn't always see eye to eye as far as Lydia's work was concerned.'

'I remember that you weren't an admirer of Lydia's, Doctor Eliot. I find that interesting, in the light of the close ... nature of your relationship.' Kincaid settled back in his chair, his posture more relaxed as Darcy appeared less comfortable.

'Lydia and I were friends for many years, but I've never considered friendship grounds for wholesale professional admiration. That sort of thing does not tend to increase one's standing in academic circles.' Darcy sounded as though he'd expected a bit more sophistication from Kincaid.

Kincaid raised an eyebrow. 'Does that mean that one is required *not* to praise good work by friends, for fear of being thought weak and undiscriminating? That seems a sort of reverse hypocrisy.'

Darcy gave a bark of laughter. 'I should have learned not to underestimate you the first time we spoke, Mr Kincaid. And you're right, of course, but since I genuinely did not approve of the direction of much of Lydia's later work, I don't think I'm guilty of hypocrisy on that count. I find the idea of the *confessional* voice quite revolting, regardless of the owner.'

'But perhaps I can accuse you of being less than truthful about Lydia herself, Doctor Eliot. You hinted to me about Lydia's relationship with Daphne Morris, but you didn't mention the fact that it was all a bit more complicated than that. According to Morgan Ashby—'

'So that's what happened to your face,' said Darcy, grinning. 'Had a little run-in with Morgan's famous temper, did we? You should—'

'According to Morgan Ashby,' interrupted Kincaid, 'you and Lydia were lovers. In fact, Morgan seems to think that Lydia slept with everyone—you, Adam, Nathan, *and* Daphne.'

'Morgan Ashby is a certifiable paranoid,' said Darcy, unfazed. 'And insanely jealous. The man should have been locked up years ago.'

'Are you saying that what he told me isn't true?' asked Kincaid mildly.

Gemma, watching the two men from her corner of the sofa, was content to observe for the moment. She felt relieved, after what had happened with Morgan, that Kincaid seemed his unruffled self again.

'I'm saying "so what if it is true?" ' said Darcy. 'This was the sixties—remember the Profumo Affair? We were riding the crest of the great sexual revolution, imitating in our rather tame and provincial way what we thought they must be doing in London. We were young, we were away from home, and we were drunk with the idea of our own daring.' He grinned. 'God, just thinking of it makes me realize how middle-aged and conventional I've become.'

'If these ... things ... happened before Lydia married Morgan, then why did he feel so threatened?' Gemma asked. 'She seems to have been quite devoted to him.'

Darcy made a face. 'Besotted might be more accurate. Of course, Lydia always did have a bit of an obsessional streak, but I thought she had better sense than to focus it on a man of Ashby's background.'

'Background?' said Gemma, her hackles rising. 'What does Morgan Ashby's background have to do with it?'

'Oh, you know, Welsh mining family, salt of the earth and all that—and the bloody great load of puritanism that came with it. He couldn't bear the idea that Lydia had enjoyed anyone else, no matter how much she loved him.' Darcy paused, knitting his thick brows together, then added, 'I don't think Ashby much liked the idea of anyone enjoying anything, for that matter, including himself.'

'I doubt that could be said of you, Doctor Eliot,' said Gemma with a smile. She glanced towards the sideboard, where a drinks tray held glasses ready beside an ice bucket and a dish of cut limes.

'Certainly not,' he said in mock offence. 'Though I have to admit that a meeting of my graduate students seems quite dull after being reminded of the good old days.' He smiled at her in a way that made her suddenly aware that he was still a very attractive man, then he gave an exaggerated sigh. 'But even *I* cannot escape duty entirely, especially as it looks as though I may need to take on some of Iris's workload.'

'Is Doctor Winslow all right?' Kincaid asked with quick concern.

374

'She has an appointment to see a specialist about her headaches on Monday,' said Darcy. For the first time his voice held no hint of the teasing tone Gemma had come to expect. 'This has been going on for some time, and I must admit I feel rather uneasy about it,' he continued, shaking his head. 'Iris is one of my mother's oldest friends. If anything should happen to her—' Looking up, he met Gemma's eyes. 'Well, there's no point borrowing trouble, is there? I hate having come to the age where one has these constant intimations of mortality. It's most unsettling.'

'But I understand that you're first in line for Doctor Winslow's position if she retires,' said Kincaid. 'You must find that rather gratifying.'

'*I understand* being synonymous with *rumour has it?*' Darcy flicked a speck of dust from his trouser leg. 'I learned a long time ago not to put too much credence on the academic grapevine. As in all small and incestuous communities, things tend to get blown out of proportion.'

Kincaid tilted his head to one side, as if the remark had reminded him of something. 'Vic was aware of that, too, and she said she thought it curious there was so little speculation at the time of Lydia's death. It was assumed a suicide, and dropped at that.'

Darcy gave Kincaid a puzzled look. 'Everyone who knew Lydia knew her emotional history. We were distressed at the news, but not surprised. What else was there to say?'

'One might have said that it was all a bit too convenient, Lydia living up to everyone's expectations like that. Vic began to think so. She became convinced, in fact, that Lydia did not commit suicide at all.' Slowly, Kincaid added, 'She was quite sure that Lydia was murdered.'

For a moment Darcy sat without protesting, his face expressionless, then he shook his head. 'I'm afraid, Mr Kincaid, that this is a case of the biographer taking on the characteristics of her subject. When Victoria McClellan first came to the department she displayed every evidence of a sound and practical personality. It only illustrates the development of a rather unhealthy identification with Lydia that she should have come to embrace such nonsense.'

Kincaid smiled. 'And I might have agreed with your argument, Dr Eliot, were it not for the indisputable fact that Vic herself was murdered. Had you forgotten that?'

'I'm having a bit of a hard time with this,' said Gemma with a glance at Kincaid's profile as he once again negotiated the Newnham roundabout. This time their destination was the Grantchester Road, and Nathan Winter's cottage. 'I had boyfriends before Rob, of course, but only one at a time.'

'And no girlfriends?' Kincaid said with a sideways smile.

'Not in that sense,' Gemma said a little primly. 'Does that make me conventional?'

'Very.' The smile became a grin.

'I suppose it must be my background, then,' she said, joking, but she heard the hint of injury in her own voice.

Kincaid glanced at her. 'You're just fine the way you are, Gemma. Don't ever think otherwise.' He touched the backs of his fingers to her cheek for a moment. 'If anyone's background was conventional, it was Lydia's,' he added as he reached for the gear lever. 'A schoolmistress's daughter from a small village.'

'What would she say to a baker's daughter from North London?' Gemma mused. 'I'm beginning to feel what Vic must have felt—I wish Lydia would suddenly appear and talk to me, tell me what she thought, what she was really like.'

'We can try asking Nathan,' Kincaid suggested as he slowed. They'd come to the scattered houses marking the beginning of the village, and across the fields to their left they could see the line of trees following the course of the Cam.

'And Adam Lamb,' added Gemma. Of all of them, he's the one seems most unlikely, doing ... you know ... what they did. There's such a gentleness about him.'

There was no sign of Adam's battered Mini in front of Nathan's cottage, however, nor was there any immediate answer when they rang the bell. They rang again and waited, listening for any sound from within the house, but Gemma heard only the faint chirping of birds and the occasional swish of tyres on the tarmac.

'We could try the garden,' Kincaid suggested, stepping back from the porch and looking to either side. 'There seems to be a path round to the right.'

He started in that direction and Gemma followed. As she stepped carefully on the spaced flagstones, a sweet smell rose from beneath her feet. She stopped and knelt, picking some of the tiny green stems growing in the crevices of the walk. She rubbed the leaves between her fingers, then held them close to her nose. The heartiness of the scent made her close her eyes for a moment. 'Thyme, isn't it?' she said to Kincaid, who had stopped to watch her. 'Look, there's all different varieties.'

'Like Prince Charles's Thyme Walk at Highgrove? That's a bit grand for a village cottage, don't you think?'

'I think it's lovely.' Gemma stood and brushed at the knee of her trousers. 'Makes me want to roll in it, like a cat in catnip.'

'Feel free,' he said, with an amused lift of his eyebrow.

They had come to a stone wall with a white gate set in it. He reached over its curved top to unfasten the latch, and once through the gate they found themselves in a tunnel-like passage formed by arching yews. Gemma felt the drop in temperature and shivered a little at the cool, dank smell, then they came out the far end into the back garden. Patches of sunlight skittered across the grass, dappling Nathan Winter as he knelt beside a knot-shaped bed.

He was digging furiously in the earth with a hand trowel, and they watched him for a moment before he looked up and saw them. The wind ruffled his fine white hair, but he wore only an old jumper that looked as though it had been in intimate contact with the compost heap, and dirty canvas trousers. Bright dots of colour flamed in each cheek, and Gemma thought that in spite of the physical activity he looked less well than he had the day before. As they walked across the lawn towards him, he sat back on his heels. A half-dozen small green plants littered the ground beside him, their roots exposed.

'Did you like the tunnel?' he asked as they reached him. 'Kit liked to play in it. He was still young enough for imaginary games of soldier or explorer—another couple of years he'd have been smoking cigarettes and kissing girls under the yews.'

Gemma felt a little chill, for Nathan spoke as if Kit were dead, too, or at least as lost to him as Vic. She glanced at Kincaid, but his face was closed, unreadable. He hadn't spoken of Kit since the night before, and she had no idea what he must be feeling.

Since Nathan showed no sign of getting up, Gemma lowered herself to the grass. Hoping to turn the conversation, she touched one of the wilting plants and asked, 'What are you digging up?'

'Bloody lovage.' He jabbed savagely at the earth with the trowel. 'I planted them for Vic, but there's not much point, now, is there?'

'Vic's teas, of course,' Kincaid said suddenly, shaking his head. 'How stupid of me.' Sinking to one knee, he looked Nathan in the eye. 'You made Vic's teas, didn't you, Nathan? I remember Laura saying it was lovage she drank.'

Nathan stared at him. 'Who else do you think would've mixed them? But lovage makes a broth, really, not a tea. It tastes a bit like celery.'

'Do you grow foxglove in your garden?'

'Of course there's foxglove, just back of the lavender, along the walk.' He started to point in the direction of the flagged path that led from the tunnel's exit to the patio, then looked back at Kincaid.

His face paled, so that the spots of colour on his cheekbones stood out as if they'd been painted on. 'You don't think I put foxglove in Vic's tea? What kind of an idiot do you think I am?' He lurched to his feet and staggered slightly.

For a moment Gemma wondered if he were drunk, but thought she would have smelled the alcohol on his breath.

Kincaid, who'd stood as well, reached out a hand to steady him. 'Could someone *else* have put it in Vic's teas?'

'I picked the leaves myself, and hand-dried them in the kitchen. Then I put them in little zip-top bags for her.'

The pain in her neck made Gemma realize she was still kneeling. Pushing herself to her feet, she said, 'What about after she took the bags to school, Nathan? Could someone have added foxglove then? Would she have tasted it?'

'I don't know. Foxglove's very toxic—it wouldn't take much. And the taste of the lovage might be strong enough to disguise any bitterness.'

380

Gemma heard the tremble in Nathan's voice. Shock, she thought, and illness? Reaching out, she touched his neck. He flinched away from her hand, but not before her fingers had registered the heat.

'Nathan, you're burning up with fever. What were you thinking of, out here in this wind?' To Kincaid she whispered, 'Let's get him in the house.'

Kincaid took his elbow and urged him towards the patio. 'Let's all have a cuppa, Nathan. Where's Adam?'

Nathan let himself be led without protest. 'Finally got him to bugger off,' he said. 'Told him his cardie and false teeth set needed him a damn sight more than I did.' Suddenly he twisted his arm from Kincaid's grasp and looked back. 'My trowel. Have to wash ... Always wash it.'

'I'll get it,' said Gemma, and ran back for it.

'... funny thing is, now he's gone I actually miss him,' Nathan was saying when she returned, his voice slurring a bit. 'Old sod. Least he lets me talk about her, doesn't change the bloody subject.' He swung round suddenly and looked at Gemma, his eyes fever-bright. 'They think they're being kind. But they're not.'

They manoeuvred Nathan in through the French doors on the patio and settled him in the nearest armchair. By this time, his shivering had developed into hard chills, and as Kincaid found a rug to cover him, Gemma went into the kitchen to make tea.

381

When Kincaid joined her she said softly, 'A hot drink may help, but I think he's really ill. I'm surprised he's not delirious.'

'Near enough, and getting worse by the minute,' said Kincaid. 'I've Adam Lamb's number in my wallet. I'm going to give him a ring.' He slipped out the French doors again, and Gemma saw him pull the cell phone from his pocket as she filled the kettle at the sink.

It took her a few minutes to find her way round the strange kitchen, and by the time she had everything assembled, Kincaid had returned from the patio. As he took the tray from her, he said in her ear, 'Adam's on his way, and he's called the doctor to meet him.'

Then they tiptoed into the sitting room to find that all their whispering had been in vain. Nathan was fast asleep.

They sat at the kitchen table, drinking their tea and listening to Nathan's slightly raspy breathing. 'It won't work,' said Kincaid.

Gemma had been looking round the room, thinking how pleasant it was, and wondering if Vic had come here. 'What?'

'It's too quick. If someone put foxglove in Vic's tea at school, she'd have been ill by the time she left.'

'Did she drink the stuff at home, too?' Gemma wondered. 'She might have had a cup once she arrived.'

Kincaid shook his head. 'Forensics didn't find a trace.'

'Could someone have removed it afterwards?'

'Kit's dark shape in the garden?' He stared at her. 'No one's explained that.' His mouth tightened. 'But if she were still alive, how could they have been so thorough?'

Gemma jumped as a sound like a gunshot came from the street, followed by a mechanical cough and splutter. 'Adam?' she said, and downed the last of her tea.

He let himself in before they could get up, and greeted them quietly as he came through into the sitting room. He looked harried, his hair tangled from the wind, his collar askew, but Gemma felt the same immediate comfort in his presence she'd felt at the memorial service.

A close look at Nathan seemed to confirm an opinion, for he was shaking his head as he returned to them. 'I've been afraid of this. He was ill like this after Jean died. It seems to be his way of dealing with shock.'

'Will he be all right?' asked Gemma.

'This seems to have hit him very hard. And the last time he developed pneumonia,' said Adam, then he smiled and seemed to make an effort to sound more cheerful. 'But he's stubborn as an ox—this may be simply his body's means of making him rest. And I'm sure the doctor will pump him full of all sorts of things he'll despise when he's coherent enough to know it.' He grinned and added, 'Thanks for ringing me. I'll wait for the doctor, and stay with him afterwards.'

Gemma took a last look at Nathan as Adam escorted them towards the front of the house. With his pale hair and his flushed face relaxed in sleep, he looked surprisingly child-like.

'Adam,' said Kincaid when they reached the door. 'We heard some odd things today, about Lydia and Nathan, and Darcy, and even Daphne Morris. Morgan Ashby told us—'

'It's quite true,' Adam interrupted flatly.

Kincaid stared at him. 'But I thought you and Lydia—'

'Oh, I had that honour, all right, although if I'd known what would come after I'd never have done it. Youth is no excuse for irresponsible behaviour, and ours caused Lydia no end of grief.'

Gemma saw weariness in his eyes. 'You loved Lydia, didn't you? How could you let her—'

'How could I stop her?' he said with a quick, impatient gesture of his hands. 'What you don't understand is that Lydia always got her way, no matter the consequences to her or to anyone else.'

Chapter Sixteen

... I stand here for sense,
Invincible, inviolable, eternal,
For safety, regulations, paving-stones,
Street lamps, police, and bijou residences
Semi-detached. I stand for Sanity,
Comfort, Content, Prosperity, top-hats,
Alcohol, collars, meat ...

Rupert Brooke, from
the satire *John Rump*

Kit trudged into the wind, his hands in his pockets, his head tucked, turtle-like, into the collar of his jacket. The air smelled sharply of rain, and although it was only a few minutes past four o'clock, the lowering clouds had caused the street lamps to flicker on.

But Kit didn't mind the damp cold or the early dusk. He'd been glad of any excuse to get out of the house—had offered, in fact, to fetch his grandmother's favourite biscuits from the supermarket at the edge of the housing estate.

Eugenia had frowned at him from her bed, and in desperation he'd resorted to guile. Smiling falsely, he said, 'Please, Grandmama, it will only take me a few minutes, and then you can have Orange Cremes with your tea. I'm sure it would make you feel ever so much better.'

He waited, holding his breath, smile pasted in place, until the crease between her brows relaxed and she pulled the mauve bed-jacket closer to her throat with a little sigh.

'Mind you don't tarry, Christopher. You can make your grandfather's tea when he comes in. I'm sure I can't be expected to look after everyone,' she added, and Kit almost snorted in disgust. His grandfather had been waiting on her hand and foot since Kit had been there, even though nothing seemed to please her, or to distract her for long from the box she kept close to her side. It held things from his mother's childhood; school reports and photos, crayon drawings, medals from spelling competitions, a bit of lace from a party dress.

'Of course not, Grandmama,' he said, as convincingly as he could manage. 'I'll take care of everything.'

'Fetch my bag from the sitting room, then, and I'll give you a pound. You'll not need more than that, and I'll expect to see the change.'

Leaning back against the cushions, Eugenia closed her eyes, as if her little speech had exhausted her, and Kit did as she asked before she could change her mind. She wasn't ill enough to loosen control of her purse strings. Did she think he couldn't be trusted to take a pound without pilfering?

She'd confined herself to bed after the funeral yesterday, much to Kit's relief, and he suspected to his grandfather's as well. He and Grandad had played endless games of cards in the kitchen, and for a time his grandfather's quiet undemanding company had eased the weight in his chest. But today an urgent phone call had sent Grandad to his insurance office after lunch, and in her husband's absence Eugenia had become more and more fretful, fussing at Kit over trivial things until he felt he'd scream.

Now his steps slowed as the rows of brown-brick semi-detached houses came to an end. He knew if he looked up he'd see the Tesco at the end of the road, but he stared determinedly at the toes of his trainers, shuffling them against the pavement. His right shoe had come undone, and as he squatted to tie it he thought of his mum's nagging about his laces.

Suddenly he saw her vividly before him,

386

pushing her hair from her face with an exasperated smile. He froze, one knee up, hands stilled on his wayward laces, afraid the tiniest movement might dissolve the vision.

'You'll break your neck one of these days, Kit, mark my words,' she said, laughing. As she reached out to ruffle his hair, her image faded, and he felt nothing but the wind.

Pain stabbed through his chest and he sobbed, his careful control shattering. Why her? Why couldn't it have been him instead? Then he wouldn't be here, now, with this ache inside him that was more than he could bear. Kit pressed his face hard against his knee and wept.

At first the rushing sound seemed a part of the buzzing in his head, but slowly he recognized it as separate from himself. His sobs subsided as he listened. It wasn't the wind—the wind had been constant, a moan just below consciousness. He looked up, scrubbing at his face, and then the rain was upon him in a cold wave, stinging, pelting, soaking him to the skin within seconds.

Kit pushed himself up from the ground like a sprinter and ran in a blind, instinctive dash for shelter. He heard the change in the timbre of his pounding feet as he reached the tarmac of the supermarket car park, then the Tesco loomed before him. Realizing the back was nearer, he swerved towards the rubbish bins and slid into a stack of cardboard boxes. Here the overhang of the loading bay blocked the worst of the rain, and he collapsed against the boxes, gasping.

After a moment he pushed his sodden hair

from his forehead and looked down at his dripping clothes. Grandmama would kill him. He could hear her already.

'Christopher, how much sense does it require to get out of the rain? And now look what you've done—I'm sure you've ruined my carpet.'

'Bitch,' he said, under his breath. Liking the sound of it, he filled his lungs and shouted into the rain. 'Bitch! Stupid cow!' But the wind sucked the sound away, and beneath it he heard something else. Was that a scrabbling beneath the boxes? A whimper? He listened, then knelt and lifted up the nearest overturned box. Two boot-button black eyes stared back at him, then the dog whimpered again and cringed away.

'It's okay,' Kit said softly. 'I'm not going to hurt you. You're wet and cold, too, aren't you, doggie?' He went on in the same sing-song voice, saying any sort of rubbish that came into his head and holding his hand out, palm up. The dog had a shaggy grey-brown coat—some sort of a terrier mix, Kit guessed—and he suspected that the matted, wiry hair hid prominent ribs.

After a few moments the dog inched forward on its belly and licked his outstretched fingers. 'Good dog, that's a good dog,' Kit whispered, turning his hand until he could stroke the dog's ear, then gently touching its back. It flinched but didn't move away, and beneath his hand he felt it shivering. 'What am I going to do with you?' he said gravely, as if he expected an answer. 'You can't stay here like this, with no shelter and nothing to eat.' He stopped stroking the dog's back as he thought, and it turned to nuzzle his hand, prompting him to begin again.

At the touch of the dog's cold nose against his palm, resolution filled him. He dug in his jacket pocket for the twine his grandfather had been using that morning to teach him Snakes and Ladders. It was a makeshift excuse for a collar and lead, but it would have to do.

21 March 1970
Cambridge

Dearest Mummy,
Isn't it odd how one gets attached to places? During the months with you and Nan, I dreaded coming back to Cambridge and trying to pick up the pieces of my life. It seemed only our cottage would ever feel like home to me again, and I wanted nothing more than the comfort of our domestic routine. What to make for tea ... a bit of digging in the garden ... a new novel from the library ... these small things made up a manageable universe.

But all the while I could feel the urge to write growing in me, as inexorable as the rising of sap in the spring. I must write, blessed or cursed, it's what makes me who I am, and to do so I must stand on my own, however wobbly.

But you knew this all along, didn't you, Mummy, darling? You pushed me ever so gently, until I saw it for myself. And the funny thing is that, once here again, in this house which I'd thought would be filled with ghosts, I feel at home. By some odd process it is no longer Morgan's house, or even Morgan and Lydia's house, but mine, and it is reassuringly familiar.

I try to keep things simple. A schedule helps keep the black thoughts at bay, so I spend an hour or two a day pottering about the house, putting things to rights, then a couple of hours reading, then no more than two hours writing. Any longer and I find I begin to fray, but I'm learning to recognize the danger signals now.

I haven't ventured out much yet—too many people at once make me feel a bit fragile still, and well-meaning acquaintances tend to ask questions I'm not ready to answer. Nathan and Jean have had me to dinner, though, and treated me as though I'd never been away. We had the most ordinary and domestic of conversations, all about Alison's nappies and the best ingredients for lentil soup. Jean is expecting again.

You asked about Adam. He's been his usual solicitous and generous self, but I can sense his need, and I'm afraid he wants more than I can give. I can't afford to lose myself in any man, not ever again, and I fear I lack the necessary bit of ballast which allows other people to conduct a romance without going overboard. I dare not risk it.

Your loving,
Lydia

Chapter Seventeen

The unheard invisible lovely dead
Lie with us in this place ...

Rupert Brooke,
from *Mummia*

He slept the deep and dreamless sleep of exhaustion, not stirring when the oblong of uncurtained window paled to grey, then to rose, then to the clear washed blue of an April morning. When the phone rang, he fumbled for it with a vague awareness of the sound's meaning.

Managing to get the receiver to his ear, he mumbled, 'Kincaid,' as he opened one eye and squinted at the clock. Eight o'clock on a Sunday morning. Bloody hell. This had better be good.

'Duncan?' The voice was strained, apologetic. 'This is Bob Potts. I'm sorry to disturb you, but I'm afraid we have a problem and I didn't know who else to ring.'

Kincaid heard the panic beneath the carefully chosen words, and came fully awake. 'Problem? What sort of problem?'

Potts cleared his throat. 'It's Kit. He seems to have ... um ... that is, he seems to have gone missing.'

'What do you mean, missing? Surely he's

just gone out for a bit,' Kincaid sat up, and in spite of his calming words, he was aware of the sudden pounding of his heart.

'His bed's not been slept in. I went to wake him ...' Potts paused and cleared his throat again. 'I've looked everywhere. There's no trace of him, and the dog's gone, too.'

'What dog?' Kincaid remembered Vic telling him that one of the great regrets of her childhood was that she'd never been allowed a pet. Her mother had disliked animals, and Kincaid thought it unlikely that Eugenia's feelings on the matter had mellowed. He reached for the pad and pencil he kept by the telephone. 'I think you'd better tell me exactly what happened.'

'Kit brought a dog home from the supermarket, a stray mongrel,' said Potts. 'But I really don't see what—'

'Just start from the beginning. I won't have a clear picture to work with unless you tell me everything.' Kincaid tried to keep the impatience from his voice.

'All right,' Potts agreed, still sounding reluctant. 'It seems Kit found this dog behind Tesco's yesterday afternoon, while he was sheltering from a rainstorm. He made up his mind to keep it, and, of course, Eugenia ... um ... that is, we didn't think it appropriate.' Potts hesitated a moment before adding, 'Kit was rather upset, although we did reach a compromise.'

'And what was that?' Kincaid asked, with some scepticism.

'I convinced Eugenia to let him keep the dog

in the garage overnight, until I could take it to the shelter this morning. I assured him that they would do their best to find it a home.'

Some comfort that would have been, when Kit must have known that the dog's chances of adoption and survival were slim at best. 'I take it Kit wasn't happy with your solution?'

'Uh, no,' said Potts, and from his tone Kincaid could imagine Kit, white-faced and silent with fury. 'He went to bed without his tea, so this morning I thought I'd take him his breakfast first thing—'

'Were any of his things missing?'

'I ... I don't know. I didn't think of that,' Potts answered, sounding more distressed. 'I looked for him outside at first—I thought he must have taken the dog for a walk, but surely he'd be back by now. It's been more than two hours ...'

'Did he leave a note?'

'Not that I've seen.'

That could be good news or bad, thought Kincaid. 'Did he take any money?'

'I ... I'm afraid I don't know that, either. If you'll hang on a moment I'll have a look.' There was a clatter as Potts put the phone down. Kincaid heard voices, muted at first, then Eugenia's strident tones came more clearly. Potts came back on the line.

'Eugenia had a twenty-pound note in her purse yesterday, and now it's missing,' he said, his voice rising in competition with his wife's.

'How could he?' Kincaid heard Eugenia wail.

'After all we've done. We've suffered enough as it is—'

'I think it's Kit who's suffered quite enough,' Kincaid snapped. 'You should be glad he took the money. It makes it less likely he meant to harm himself.'

'Eugenia, for God's sake, be quiet,' shouted Potts. Into the stunned silence that followed, he said, hesitantly, 'You don't think ...'

Regretting his outburst, Kincaid said, 'I didn't mean to frighten you. I'm sure he's all right. But he's shocked and grieving, and we have to consider that his behaviour may not be predictable just now.'

'What should we do?' asked Potts, making an obvious effort at control.

Kincaid thought. The local force were not going to show much enthusiasm in looking for a boy missing only two hours, but he'd give them a ring and ask them to at least check hospital admissions. In the meantime he'd better think of something useful for Bob Potts to do—anything at all being better than waiting. 'Do you have a recent photograph of Kit?' he asked.

'He gave us a framed copy of his school photo for Christmas,' said Potts, sounding puzzled. 'But what—'

'Take it to the bus and train stations. Kit had enough money for a fare. Ask the ticket vendors, and anyone else who looks like they've been hanging about for a bit. A boy with a dog should be easy to remember. I'll give the local police a ring and ask them to keep an eye out, but at this stage we're better off looking ourselves.'

394

'You mean you'll help?' Potts sounded surprised and grateful, making Kincaid wonder what he'd expected.

'Of course, I'll help.' And God forgive him if he failed Kit the same way he'd failed Vic. He should have seen this coming.

Under a flat grey sky the road to Cambridge stretched in a now familiar ribbon across the plains. Kincaid stayed in the fast lane, and the speedometer needle quivered as he pushed the Midget to its limit.

As he drove he tried to ignore the images that flashed unbidden into his mind—Kit injured, Kit tattered and as lost as the homeless runaways he saw begging outside the Hampstead tube station. He wondered if the gut-wrenching panic he fought was part of what it meant to be a parent, and with that thought he realized he'd come to accept the idea that Kit was his son.

But beyond that realization he could not go—not yet, not until Kit was safely found. Now he needed to concentrate on the present, making sure he'd covered every contingency. He'd left Bob Potts sounding a bit stronger, then he'd gulped a cup of tea while pulling on jeans and pullover and making phone calls.

The Reading police responded as expected, but agreed to make a few inquiries. Laura Miller said she'd not heard from Kit, but would ring round and let him know immediately if Kit had contacted any other friends, and Gemma promised to wait at the flat until he called.

Rubbing his hand across the stubble on his

chin as he neared the Grantchester junction, he thought out his options. He knew from experience that the first few hours in the search for a missing child were critical. If his instincts proved him wrong, he'd have to call out the big guns and order a full-scale search, working outwards from the Reading neighbourhood where the Potts lived.

Kincaid left the motorway and soon reached the outskirts of Grantchester. The streets seemed eerily empty, with only the curls of smoke rising from the occasional chimney giving evidence that the village hadn't succumbed to some Brigadoon-like enchantment. He slowed almost to a crawl as doubt assailed him. Why had he wasted precious time on such a half-baked idea? Kit couldn't have made it here, had probably never intended to come here. He was probably in London by now, being approached by one of the pimps always on the look-out for runaways to recruit as rent-boys.

But even so, he stopped the Midget in the street, not on the gravel drive where the noise would warn anyone inside. Climbing out of the car, he closed the door softly and stood surveying the house. It seemed to him that it had already acquired a deserted look, although it had been empty only a few days, and the pink stucco looked garish against the dull sky.

He began a careful circuit of the house, checking the doors and windows in the front, then letting himself into the back garden through the gate. The French doors onto the patio were locked, as he'd left them, but when he reached

396

the kitchen window he noticed a slight gap in the bottom seal. His pulse quickening, he squeezed in amongst the shrubs and pushed up on the casement. It slid up easily, and after a moment's consideration, Kincaid levered himself through the gap as quietly as possible.

Dusting himself off as he looked round the kitchen, he saw no evidence of occupancy. Had he left the window unfastened, after all? Although at the time he'd thought he was fully capable, he found now that his memory of the night of Vic's death was patchy at best.

He checked the sitting room, finding it as he'd left it, then Vic's office, which now showed the same evidence of police thoroughness as had her office at the English Faculty.

Quietly mounting the stairs, he methodically eliminated first the spare bedroom, then Vic's room. He stood in the hall, aware of the beating of his heart, aware he was postponing the obvious choice till last, so afraid was he of failure. Taking a steadying breath, he eased open the door to Kit's room.

After the dimness of the corridor, he was blinded by the light from the uncurtained window. He stood for a moment, blinking, and as his eyes adjusted, he saw the bed was empty, the duvet unwrinkled. His heart sank. He'd been wrong, and the time spent coming here could not be recovered.

Then just as he turned away, he heard a sound—a rustle, and a very faint thumping. He stopped, listening, and as it came again he was able to pinpoint it. Slowly, he crossed the room and edged round the end of Kit's bed, until he could see into the space between the bed and the wall. A small, shaggy dog lay on a crumpled quilt, head on its paws as it looked alertly at him, while its tail gently thumped the floor.

And beneath the quilt lay Kit, eyes closed, one arm thrown over his head as if he'd been dreaming. He was still wearing his anorak, and his chest rose and fell in a deep and regular rhythm as he breathed through his open mouth.

The wave of giddiness that swept through Kincaid made his knees suddenly weak. He sat down on the bed and reached out to pat the dog, which thumped its tail a bit harder. 'Some watchdog you are,' he said with a laugh that sounded suspiciously shaky, and at the sound of his voice Kit stirred and opened his eyes. Kincaid saw the beginning of a smile as Kit recognized him, then alarm as he realized he'd been discovered.

Kit pushed himself up, trying to escape the entangling folds of the quilt and the dog's weight on his legs. 'I'm not going back,' he said as he managed to free himself.

'Hello, Kit.' Kincaid smiled at him. 'What on earth are you doing down there?'

Squatting now, Kit leaned back against the wall and regarded him with a puzzled expression. After a moment, he said, 'Hiding. I thought if they came for me, they might not think to look behind the bed. I told Tess to be quiet.'

'She's a very well-behaved dog. It was only

her tail wagging that gave you away. Why did you call her Tess?'

Kit reached out to stroke the dog. 'Because I found her behind Tesco's.'

'Oh, of course,' said Kincaid. 'Silly of me not to twig. Have either of you had anything to eat?'

'Beef burgers. The second lorry driver bought us both beef burgers. But that was a long time ago.'

'I take it you hitch-hiked your way here, then?' asked Kincaid. Thank God Kit had come through his journey unharmed, but this was not the time to lecture him on the danger of riding with strangers.

'Four lorries,' said Kit with a touch of pride. 'We walked from the motorway, though. I was afraid someone I knew might stop if I tried to thumb it.'

'I'll bet you're hungry again,' Kincaid said easily. 'There's a café not far from here on the motorway. What do you say I buy you a real lorry-driver's fry up? We'll get something for Tess, too.'

Kit tensed and gathered the dog to him. 'I told you, I'm not going back to Reading. If you try to make me, I'll just run away again.'

Watching the stubborn set of Kit's mouth, Kincaid wondered if he looked like that when he dug his heels in over something. *Like father, like son.* And if that were the case, the best way to win the boy's cooperation was to treat him as honestly as he would like to be treated himself. After a moment's thought, he said, 'I

399

understand how you feel, Kit, but you've got to be reasonable about this. You know you can't stay here on your own—'

'My dad will come back. I know he will, and then I can stay—'

'That may be true, but in the meantime, you can't stay here for more than a few hours before someone else comes looking for you—either the police or your grandparents. And you know your grandfather's frantic. You don't want him worrying about you.'

'She won't care what's happened to me. All she cares about is her bloody carpets.'

Kincaid sighed. 'Does that make your grandfather's feelings any less important?'

Kit stared at him, then his mouth relaxed and he gave a little shrug. 'I suppose not. But I can't go back. They won't let me keep Tess.'

'I promise you we'll try to work something out. And I promise I won't do anything without discussing it with you first. But we have to start somewhere, and it seems to me that breakfast is a pretty good beginning. What do you say?'

For a long moment Kit didn't respond, then he gave an infinitesimal nod and said, 'What happened to your eye?'

Once seated in the clean anonymity of the Little Chef, Kincaid and Kit ordered eggs, bacon, sausage, mushrooms, tomatoes and fried bread, to be washed down with a pot of tea. They'd left Tess in the car with the small blanket Kit had found for her, and she settled down to wait with the resignation of a dog accustomed to it.

At the cottage, Kit had washed his hands and brushed his hair, then gathered his things up without further complaint. When he was ready, he'd produced a spare key from the drawer in the kitchen.

'Did I not latch the window?' Kincaid had asked, still a bit concerned over his lapse.

'The lock doesn't quite catch,' said Kit. 'You wouldn't have noticed. But I always get in that way when I forget my key. It makes Mum fur—' He'd stopped, stricken, and Kincaid had hustled him out of the cottage with an arm round his shoulders.

This time Kincaid kept the key, and they had driven to the Little Chef in silence.

Their tea arrived, hot and strong, and as they stirred their cups, Kincaid glanced at his watch and pulled his phone from his jacket pocket. 'I'm going to ring Gemma and ask her to let your grandad know you're all right. No, wait,' he added as Kit started to protest, 'That's all for now. We're going to take this one step at a time. Fair enough?'

Kit gave him a nod, and Kincaid wished he were really as confident as he was attempting to sound. What he hadn't told Kit was that he didn't know what to do next. The only thing of which he felt sure was that returning Kit to his grandparents right now might mean losing him for good.

Dialling Gemma's number, he filled her in briefly, then said, 'Ring Kit's grandfather and tell him he's all right, that he's safe with me. Nothing more. Then give Laura Miller a ring,

401

too, would you, love?'

'What are you going to do?' asked Gemma. 'You have no legal right to keep him with you without their permission.'

'I know,' he answered guardedly, 'but I don't see any alternative at the moment.'

There was a pause, then Gemma said, 'Bring him here, then, until we figure something out. At least there's a garden for the dog.'

'Will Hazel and Tim mind?'

'I'll just go and have a word. See you in an hour or two,' she added and rang off.

Kincaid eyed Kit, who had been listening intently in spite of the arrival of his breakfast. 'We're going to visit Gemma for a bit,' he said as he picked up his fork and tucked into his eggs. 'Okay with you?'

Instead of answering, Kit frowned and said, 'I didn't know you knew the Millers.'

'They were worried about you. Gemma and I were worried about you. And I imagine all the friends that Laura Miller rang were worried about you, too.'

Kit looked a bit sheepish. 'I didn't think of that. Honestly. I only thought—'

'I know. Sometimes we lose our perspective.' Kincaid waved his fork at Kit and grinned. 'Eat up. All those hours without food probably stunted your growth.'

'You sound just like my mum,' Kit said, concentrating on cutting his sausage. He ate in silence for a few minutes, then looked up at Kincaid. 'It wasn't any good, you know. Going home, I mean. It didn't bring her back.'

Gemma stood at Hazel and Tim's kitchen sink, up to her elbows in suds, washing up the remains of Sunday lunch. Kit had eaten two huge helpings of Hazel's spaghetti, in spite of his late breakfast.

His initial reserve had quickly melted, the thawing process helped along by the immediate and limpet-like adoration of Toby and Holly. Hazel and Tim had welcomed him kindly but without fuss, and after lunch Hazel had tactfully suggested that he might bathe Tess in the big clawfooted tub upstairs. Now he and Kincaid were giving the dog a blow-dry in front of the sitting-room fire, helped—or more likely hindered, Gemma thought with a smile—by the small children, and Hazel and Tim had taken the opportunity to go for a walk.

Gemma had been glad of a few moments alone. The sight of Duncan and Kit together had made her feel quite unexpectedly queer. It seemed that her knowledge of their possible relationship had altered her perceptions, for she now found the resemblance between them so unmistakable that she was amazed she hadn't seen it instantly. That, she might have expected, but she had not been prepared for the aching tenderness she felt for them both. And the tenderness was mixed with unease, for she was not only worried about Kit, but concerned about how their involvement with Kit would affect all their lives.

The door opened and Kincaid came in, brushing dog hair from his pullover. 'I'm sure

I smell like wet dog,' he said, grinning. 'But Tess is definitely improved. The next thing will be to get Kit into the tub.'

Wiping her hands on a tea towel, Gemma went to him and put her arms round his waist. She looked up into his face. 'You don't have any doubt now, do you?'

He pulled her closer to him and stroked her hair. 'No,' he said softly. 'And that frightens me. It's funny—I've even begun to be afraid I'll find out it's not true. What if Ian McClellan comes back and takes him off to France?'

Gemma pulled back so that she could look at him again. 'We can't think that far ahead. Let me make us a cuppa and I'll fill you in on this end.'

He released her, and in a moment she brought two steaming mugs to the table. 'What did his grandfather say when you rang him?' he asked as they sat down.

'He seemed relieved, and said he'd wait to hear from you. But I could hear Eugenia in the background. She's determined to punish Kit for running away.' Gemma shook her head. 'What I don't understand is how Vic turned out as well as she did, coming from that sort of home.'

Kincaid frowned as he thought about it. After a moment, he said, 'I think Eugenia was difficult when Vic was a child, and self-centred, but not to the extreme we're seeing now. It's possible that the deterioration in her personality has been progressive.' He looked up and met Gemma's eyes. 'And I think at some level she is suffering

404

genuine grief, and lashing out at others is her way of dealing with it. Or not dealing with it.'

'You're being too kind,' said Gemma.

He shrugged. 'All right, then. The woman's just a bloody bitch. But what matters is that she's no fit guardian for Kit in her present state, and it's likely she never will be.'

'Hazel says Kit can stay in the spare room here as long as necessary, and when I talked to Laura Miller this morning, she said she'd offered to have Kit with them, at least until the end of term.' Gemma put her elbows on the table and leaned forward. 'That's what he needs—school and friends and some sort of normal family life.'

'You don't have to convince me, love.'

'You just have to convince his grandparents, and Laura said Eugenia turned her down flat.'

'I know,' he said as he took out his cell phone. 'But I have no intention of approaching Eugenia about anything. And I intend to play things my way.'

He punched in a set of numbers, then hit *send*. 'Hello, Bob? It's Duncan here.' After a moment, he said, 'No, no, he's fine. But he's going to stay the night with friends here in London. They're psychologists—they know the best way of dealing with these things. There was another pause while he listened, then he continued, 'I think you can convince Eugenia that she needs a respite. You have my phone number—you can reach me anytime. We'll talk tomorrow.'

As he rang off, Gemma became aware of another presence in the room. Turning, she saw that Kit had slipped in from the hall. Before Kincaid could speak, she touched his arm and gestured towards the door.

'Was that my grandfather?' said Kit, his face expressionless.

Kincaid nodded. 'Hazel and Tim have asked you to stay here for tonight, if that's okay with you.'

'Why can't I stay with you?'

'Come sit down and have some tea, Kit,' said Gemma, giving Kincaid time to formulate an answer.

As Kit came slowly to the table, Kincaid said, 'I'm sure you'd be fine on my sitting-room sofa, but there's no access to the garden for Tess. I live in a top floor flat.' He paused a moment. 'If it would make you feel more comfortable about staying here, I could stay next door at Gemma's—that is, if it's all right with her.'

Gemma made a face at him as she handed Kit his mug. 'I think that could be arranged.'

'What about tomorrow?' asked Kit, still wary.

'We're working on that.' Kincaid studied him as he sipped his tea. 'Would you like to stay with the Millers for a bit, if we could arrange it? They want you to come, and you could go back to school, see your mates.'

'What about Tess?'

'Laura said they'd be glad to have Tess,' volunteered Gemma. Laura had, in fact, been

406

sputteringly furious at the idea of Eugenia refusing to let him keep the dog.

Kit looked down at his untasted tea and frowned. 'I'm not sure I want to go back to school.'

'It'll be awkward for a day or so,' said Gemma, 'because they won't know what to say to you, but after that it'll be okay.'

Shaking his head, Kit said, 'It's not that. It's Miss Pope.'

Gemma glanced at Kincaid, who raised his brows in surprise.

'Who's Miss Pope?' he asked. 'One of your teachers?'

'English.' Kit grimaced. 'I hate English. I'm going to be a biologist like Nathan. And I hate Miss Pope.'

Gemma sensed that there was more here than a subject preference. 'Did Miss Pope do something that made you particularly angry?' she asked gently.

Kit nodded. 'She ... she said bad things about my mum. About my mum and my dad. She said that if my mum had been a proper wife, Dad would never have left.'

'Oh, Christ,' Kincaid whispered. Then he said, carefully, 'Kit, did you tell your mum about this?'

Kit's eyes filled with tears, and he wiped angrily at them as he nodded again. 'The day before she ... At first I thought maybe that was why she died—because she was upset. They said it was her heart ... and then last night ...' He stopped and sniffed.

'Go on,' said Kincaid. 'What happened last night?'

'Tess wasn't the only reason I ran away. I heard them talking. Grandmama said Mummy ... she said Mummy was murdered. But I don't understand. Why would someone want to kill my mum?'

Kincaid closed his eyes for a moment, and Gemma guessed he was marshalling all his patience not to curse Eugenia in front of Kit. 'We don't know,' he said. 'The police are trying to find out. But in the meantime, you need to understand that whatever happened, it's not your fault. It had nothing to do with you.'

A muffled squeal came from the sitting room, followed by giggles and excited barking.

'Oh, dear,' said Gemma. 'We've left the little demons alone too long.' She pushed back her chair.

'I'll go,' offered Kit, jumping up. 'I left them watching *101 Dalmatians*. Maybe they've decided to make a fur coat out of Tess.' He left the room and Gemma sank back into her seat.

'I know two things now,' said Kincaid. 'One, we can be pretty sure where Vic went when she left the English Faculty that afternoon. And two,' he paused and met her eyes across the table, 'I'm not letting him go back to Reading, no matter what it takes.'

Chapter Eighteen

I said I splendidly loved you; it's not true.
Such long swift tides stir not a land-locked
sea.
On gods or fools the high risk falls—on you—
The clean clear bitter-sweet that's not for me.

Rupert Brooke, from
Sonnet (January 1910)

The Park Lane Hotel, Piccadilly
5 June 1974

Dear Mummy,

Sorry I haven't written lately, but there's been so much going on it's hard to squeeze in a moment to think, much less keep up with correspondence.

I came up yesterday for my launch party and decided to stay a few extra days. Sometimes it does one good to get away from provincial life and provincial company for a bit. Tonight I'm making up a party with several (rather glamorous) London friends for the theatre and dinner at the Savoy after.

The launch party yesterday was lovely. It will make next week's punch-and-biscuit affair at Heffer's seem even drearier than usual. Daphne will be lurking about hoping not to be noticed, while Darcy bores everyone within earshot with a lecture on the intricacies of deconstructionism. You know what they always say, *if you can't write* ...

At least we won't have Adam mooning about like a forlorn crow, since he's off do-gooding somewhere in Africa.

Did you see the piece in *The Times?* If not, I'll send you a copy. It seems my work is finally getting the critical attention it deserves, though I think the reviewer could have been a bit better informed.

Must dash, people waiting.

Love,
Lydia

This time Gemma and Kincaid were left to cool their heels in the plushly upholstered anteroom of Daphne Morris's office. They'd left London early in Gemma's battered Ford Escort, Kincaid having expressed concern over the Midget's acquisition of a new noise, and they'd made good time to Cambridge considering the Monday morning traffic. Kit had agreed to stay behind with Hazel and the children without too much protest.

Daphne's assistant, Jeanette, still wearing the baggy cardigan Gemma remembered from Friday, informed them that the headmistress's schedule didn't allow time for unexpected visitors, and if they wanted to see her, they'd have to wait until she finished her history lecture.

But before the appointed hour was up, Daphne herself appeared, looking every inch the headmistress in navy suit and upswept hair. She ushered them into her office and took a seat behind the massive barrier of her desk. 'What can I do for you this morning?' she asked with the smooth smile and the touch of impatience Gemma imagined she used when dealing with annoying parents.

'Did you have a nice weekend?' Kincaid countered as he made himself comfortable in one of the rather feminine visitor's chairs. 'Relaxing and all that?'

Daphne merely watched him, but Gemma saw her make an aborted reach for the pen on her desk, then clasp her hands together on the desktop.

'I hope so, because we had a very interesting weekend, didn't we, Gemma?'

Daphne glanced from Gemma to the darkening bruise under Kincaid's eye, her unease more evident. 'If this is a social call, Mr Kincaid, I really must—'

'We had a very productive visit with Morgan Ashby, as you may have noticed'—Kincaid smiled—'once he had calmed down a bit. It seems Morgan felt he had a good reason for disapproving of your relationship with Lydia—beyond the fact that Lydia had been intimate with you.'

'Of course we were intimate,' said Daphne with a touch of exasperation. 'Lydia was my closest friend.'

'Don't prevaricate, Miss Morris. You know perfectly well that's not what I meant, but if you want me to spell it out for you, I will. You

411

had an ongoing sexual relationship with Lydia Brooke. According to her husband, she bragged about it when they had rows. She must have enjoyed making him feel inadequate.' Kincaid shook his head as if disappointed. 'She didn't tell you that, did she?'

'I don't know what you mean. I—' Daphne swallowed and clenched her hands together. 'It's not true. She'd never have told Morgan. She said he tried to bully her into admitting it, but she wouldn't.'

'Do you mean you didn't have sex with Lydia, or simply that Lydia wouldn't have shared your secret with her husband?' Kincaid paused, frowning, then added with an air of discovery, 'And if she told him, she might have told others, too—she might even have gone so far as to tell someone who could use it to damage your career.'

'No!' Daphne stood up, gripping the edge of her desk. 'You don't understand. Morgan was a raging paranoid. He imagined things, and if Lydia told him anything it was because he frightened her. They were poison for each other, and he drove her—'

'Why did she marry him, then?' asked Kincaid, and Gemma thought of Morgan thirty years ago, dark and dangerously handsome. The intensity of his need for her must have seemed flattering at first, and she doubted Lydia would have had the judgement to see what might lie behind it.

'I don't know,' said Daphne. 'I never knew. All I can tell you is that something happened that summer. Lydia was never the same after that.'

'Morgan says it was you who changed Lydia—drove her over the edge—you and the others.' Kincaid leaned forward and jabbed his finger at her for emphasis. 'She slept with all of you—you and Adam and Nathan and Darcy—and the strain of it made her ill.'

'We've seen Darcy, too, and he confirms the story,' said Gemma, gently. 'You may be right about Morgan's paranoia, but we have no reason not to believe Darcy when he says you and Lydia were lovers. Why should he lie about it?'

Daphne stared down at her white-knuckled hands, and after a moment she let go her grip on the desk and walked slowly to the window. With her back to them, she said, 'Darcy is a right bastard. What would he know about lovers—or love—when he never understood anything but his own gratification? And it was so much more complicated than that.' She fell silent and stood looking out into the manicured school grounds.

'More complicated than what?' Gemma prompted.

'Lydia ...' Daphne shook her head. 'I loved Lydia from the very first moment I saw her, running up the staircase at Newnham with her arms full of books, laughing. She seemed so much more alive, more intense, than other people. You thought if you could just get close enough to her, some of that specialness would rub off on you, like fairy dust.

413

'But there was a vulnerability about her, too, and I suppose that's what made her a good victim for Morgan.' Turning to face them, Daphne continued, 'I'll tell you what you want to know, because I'm tired of hiding things. It's gone on far too long ...' She closed her eyes for a moment, then began on the exhalation of a breath. 'We'd experimented a bit at college, but it was just that for Lydia—experimenting. It wasn't until she came back to Cambridge after her suicide attempt that we began to have a serious affair, but even then she had a different agenda. She was only seeking comfort, emotional support. She'd decided she couldn't risk another relationship with a man, and with me she felt safe.' Daphne's smile held little humour. 'Even at college she'd only really enjoyed it when the boys were watching, and so she was more or less doing me a favour in return for stability and companionship.'

'And you knew it,' said Gemma.

'Oh, I tried to fool myself at first, but you can't keep that up for very long. And as Lydia found her footing again she began to find me ... tiresome. Her work was becoming quite successful and she was moving in much more sophisticated circles than her old friends could offer.' Daphne paused, staring past them with an unfocused gaze.

'So she broke off your relationship, and you started planning your revenge,' said Kincaid.

Daphne gave him a startled look, then tilted her head back and laughed aloud. 'Don't be absurd, Mr Kincaid. It was I who broke things

414

off between us. I didn't care for feeling like a burden to anyone, so I left Lydia.' More soberly, she added, 'But I didn't foresee the consequences.'

'What happened?' asked Gemma, with a quelling look at Kincaid.

'Lydia was utterly and absolutely devastated.' Daphne paused, but there was no tension in it. She leaned back against the window sill, her arms folded loosely across her chest, as if the telling of her story had released her. 'She wrote to me, saying she drove away everyone who mattered to her, because she hated herself. The letter came in the post after she'd crashed her car into a tree outside Grantchester.'

This had been the second suicide attempt, thought Gemma, the one for which Vic had found no explanation. 'And after that?'

'She recovered slowly, and I supported her. I stopped asking for more than she could give me, and we became friends in a different way. Those were the best years of my life, from that time until Lydia died.' The certainty and the complete lack of self-pity in Daphne's words made Gemma feel chilled.

'And nothing else happened before she died?' asked Kincaid. 'No rows, no odd behaviour?'

Daphne shook her head. 'I'm sorry to disappoint you, Mr Kincaid, but there was nothing out of the ordinary. And I certainly didn't kill Lydia to protect my reputation, if that's what you're getting at. Nor your Doctor McClellan. I'd been considering early retirement even before Lydia's death. That's why I bought the weekend cottage, you see, so that Lydia and I could work together, her on her poetry, I on my novel.'

Pausing, Daphne seemed to come to some decision. 'All weekend I thought about what you said, that Lydia may have been murdered. I don't know who would have done such a thing, and I hate the idea of someone taking her life before she was ready to let it go. But it's also a sort of release, because it lets me believe that I wasn't wrong about her happiness, about what we had together those last years. And if that's the case, I owe it to her to finish what we began. I'm going to write that novel, and I had better get started. I think I've finally come to terms with the fact that Lydia won't be there to listen to it.'

'Who besides Daphne really grieved for Lydia?' asked Gemma as they walked down the school's curving drive towards the car park. 'I mean the Lydia of the present, as she was when she died, rather than the Lydia of the past.' It was a bright, blowy day, and the wind whipped her skirt, wrapping it round her legs. She had to stop and brush a wayward strand of hair from her face before she could see to unlock the car.

'Vic,' Kincaid said when they had sealed themselves in the car's calm interior. 'I think Vic grieved for her.'

Gemma glanced at him as she fastened her seat belt. He'd been unusually silent all morning and she didn't know if worry over Kit or the case occupied him the most. 'You don't really think Daphne Morris had anything to do with Lydia's death, do you? Or Vic's?'

After a moment he shook his head. 'What motive could she have had, other than concealment? And then why reveal anything to us? We had no proof. They must have been very careful to leave no written evidence of their relationship. I don't think Vic even guessed.'

Gemma turned the key in the ignition and listened to the Escort's engine cough and sputter its way to life. 'What now?' she asked. 'We seem to have come to a bit of a dead end.'

'I think we need to have a word with the very tactless Miss Pope,' said Kincaid, his face grim. 'I rang Laura last night. She said the boys' school is in Comberton, just the other side of the motorway from Grantchester.'

After a brief consultation of the map, they were once again circling the Newnham roundabout. But this time they stayed on the Barton Road, bypassing the Grantchester cut-off, and had soon run through Barton and into Comberton. The village had none of the charm of Grantchester, but seemed rather a suburban enclave with its quiet clusters of semi-detached houses. It looked, thought Gemma, a nice place for children.

They found the secondary school without difficulty, a large, sprawling building just off the main road. An enquiry at the office sent them to the staff room, where they were told they might be lucky enough to catch Miss Pope between classes.

The corridors were filled with uniformed children changing classes. They parted round

Gemma and Kincaid as if the adults were of no more interest than stones, and their voices echoed from the walls and ceilings like cannon-fire. Gemma thought of Kit here a week ago, as silly and raucous as the boys she saw now, an ordinary child thinking of exam papers and football.

The break room contained half-a-dozen teachers in various stages of correcting papers and drinking coffee. When Kincaid asked for Miss Pope, the woman sitting alone and unoccupied except for a coffee raised her head. A dishwater-blonde with prominent roots, she was a little plump and a little over made-up. Her eyes were red, as if she'd been weeping.

She looked up at them uncertainly. 'Yes, I'm Miss Pope. Can I help you?'

Kincaid introduced them and asked if there were somewhere they might talk alone.

'You're from Scotland Yard? But what—I mean ... Why me? What is this about?' She twisted her hands together, shredding the tissue she held.

'It won't take long, Miss Pope,' Gemma reassured her. 'We just have a few routine questions we'd like to ask you.'

'Well ... I suppose it's all right,' she said, frowning. 'There's an empty classroom just down the hall that we could use, but I've a class in five minutes.'

The man at the next table had been making little pretence of ignoring their conversation, and after glancing again from Kincaid to Gemma, Miss Pope said, 'Shelley, would you take the

418

register for me if I'm a bit late?' She then led them down the corridor to an empty classroom.

Kincaid closed the door, shutting out the sound of the children's last scramble for their rooms before the bell. 'Miss Pope, did Vic McClellan come to see you last Tuesday afternoon?'

Elizabeth Pope's mouth began to tremble and her eyes filled with tears. 'I never meant any harm, honestly I didn't. I told her I never meant to hurt poor Kit ...' She pulled another bedraggled tissue from the sleeve of her ruffled blue dress and dabbed at her eyes.

'Do you mean the conversation Kit over-heard?' asked Gemma, pulling a fresh tissue from her handbag and offering it.

Miss Pope gave her a grateful smile and blew her nose. 'It's just that I've an awful habit of running my mouth without thinking, and he's such a lovely man ... Doctor McClellan, that is, so good-looking, and always so charming when he came to the school. I didn't see how she could let him go like that ...'

'What exactly did Vic say to you?' asked Kincaid a little more gently, with an obvious effort to control his impatience.

'She was angry, of course. I couldn't blame her. She said Kit was very distressed, and would I please ...' Miss Pope winced and hesitated, but after a glance at Kincaid she went on. 'She said the separation had been difficult enough for Kit as it was, and would I please not gossip about things that were none of my business. Then

419

she said that no one ever knew the truth of a relationship except the people in it.' She'd began wringing her hands again, and the tissue joined the remains of the others. 'When I think that a few hours later she was dead, and that I should have upset her when she wasn't feeling well ... And, oh, poor Kit. What's to become of him now?'

'What do you mean, she wasn't feeling well?' Kincaid asked quietly, but at his tone Miss Pope looked up and stilled her hands.

'She was pale. At first I thought it was because she was angry, but then after we'd talked she said she felt a bit under the weather. A headache, she said. And she was sweating, I remember that. I offered her some paracetamol, but she said she'd go home and have a cuppa.'

Kincaid looked at Gemma. 'If we'd known she was already ill—'

His beeper went off, shrill in the empty classroom. Removing it from his belt, he glanced at the message. 'Nathan Winter wants us to ring him right away.'

'It couldn't have been Nathan Winter, do you see?' Kincaid pulled his cell phone from his pocket as they pushed through the school's swinging front doors. 'She must have been poisoned before she left work, not after she got home. And it can't have been digitalis—digitalis acts too quickly.' He'd been transferring the number from his pager to his phone as he talked, and as they reached the car he pushed *send*.

'Nathan, it's Duncan Kin—' He stopped,

listening, then said, 'Bloody hell. Can you stall him until we get there? Good man. Ten minutes.'

He disconnected and looked at Gemma. 'Ian McClellan's at the cottage, loading things into his car.'

Chapter Nineteen

Love wakens love! I felt your hot wrist shiver,
And suddenly the mad victory I planned
Flashed real, in your burning bending head...
My conqueror's blood was cool as a deep river
In shadow; and my heart beneath your hand
Quieter than a dead man on a bed.

Rupert Brooke,
from *Lust*

'It still doesn't make sense,' said Kincaid as Gemma reversed the car from the school car park. 'If it wasn't digitalis, it must have been digoxin. But the expected reaction time for digoxin is five to six hours. According to Laura, Vic showed no symptoms of illness when she left the English Faculty at half-past two—and yet she died just after five o'clock. So it was too slow for digitalis, and too quick for digoxin.' With part of his mind he heard himself speaking, as if Vic's death had been something removed from him, a statistic, a simple problem to be solved—yet he knew his detachment was

421

essential if he were going to find her killer. He would have to hold on to it ... for now.

Glancing at Gemma, he found her scowling at the rear end of the farm tractor creeping along ahead of them. They were not going to make record time to Grantchester. He thought a moment, then opened his notebook and checked a number. Dr Winstead, the pathologist at High Wycombe General Hospital, had proved helpful to Kincaid on several occasions since they'd met during an earlier investigation, and if Kincaid remembered correctly, he was something of an expert on poisons.

'Hello, Winnie?' he said when the direct number rang through. 'Duncan Kincaid here.'

After responding to Winstead's cheerful greeting, Kincaid gave him a rough outline of the case, adding, 'Do you know of anything that might potentiate digoxin, making it act more quickly than expected?' He rolled his eyes as Winstead began a lecture on the metabolic breakdown of poisons derived from digitalis. 'Wait, Winnie, I don't have much time. Just give me a list, okay? Resperine ... Quinidine ... succinylcholine ...' he repeated as he wrote in his notebook. 'Laxative abuse ... calcium or potassium loss due to diuretics—' Giving Gemma a startled look, he said, 'Winnie, what kind of diuretic? Does it matter if it was natural or pharmaceutical? She drank diuretic herbal teas.' He listened a moment. 'Could someone have put the tablets in her tea? How many would it have taken? She had no history of heart trouble, but Lydia did. Right. Right.

Okay, thanks, Winnie. I'll let you know.'

'What?' Gemma asked as he rang off. Just then the road widened and she zipped round the tractor. 'Bloody nuisance,' she muttered.

'Winnie said the tea might have potentiated the digoxin, although he doesn't know if it would have disguised the taste of the tablets. The tablets are small, though, and very soluble. Lydia would have needed very few, as she was already sensitized to the medication—Vic maybe twice that.'

'So it probably would've tasted bitter,' said Gemma, but Kincaid didn't answer. They'd crossed the motorway and would be in Grantchester within minutes. He supposed he hadn't really expected Ian McClellan to come back ... and he supposed he'd expected to feel relieved if McClellan did ... surely that would be best for Kit, after all, to stay where he'd been happy and secure ...

And it was all absolute bollocks, Kincaid thought as they reached the High Street junction. What he really felt at the prospect of confronting Ian McClellan was a deep and simmering anger, and the thought of McClellan taking Kit out of his life brought with it a frightening sense of loss.

Gemma pulled into the cottage's drive with a spray of gravel, blocking the new-model Renault parked near the back door. Nathan Winter stood near the Renault's bonnet, talking to a slender, bearded man in a brown corduroy sports jacket, and from their gestures, Kincaid surmised that the discussion was not friendly.

As he and Gemma got out of the car, he heard McClellan say, 'As far as I know this is still my bloody house, and neither you nor anyone else is going to stop me taking my things from it.'

'Good morning,' Kincaid said as they came up to the two men, 'you must be Ian McClellan.'

McClellan turned, glaring at them. 'Who the hell are—' He stopped, his eyes widening as he focused on Kincaid. 'My God,' he said slowly. 'I don't believe it. The ex-husband himself, riding to the rescue. You've a lot of nerve coming here.'

Kincaid's anger rose in a dizzying, sickening rush. Before he quite knew what he was doing, he'd grabbed the front of McClellan's jacket with one hand and jerked him close. 'That would be offensive if Vic were alive,' he said. 'And now—'

'Duncan.' Gemma took his arm, pulling at him. 'Duncan, let him go.'

Taking a breath, he released McClellan's jacket and stepped back. 'You're the one who left her,' he said, jabbing his finger at McClellan. 'And Kit.'

'So you want to talk about Kit, do you?' McClellan smiled and leaned back against his car, folding his arms, but a pulse beat in his neck. 'I'd say you left it a bit late.'

Kincaid stared at him. 'What—what are you saying?'

'I'd have known you if I'd bumped into you in an alley. She kept photos of you, did you know that? Tucked away in her favourite books, in her office, in her desk. I used to wonder whether

424

she took them out and compared him to you, checking his progress.'

'Bloody hell,' Kincaid breathed, shaking his head. 'You knew all along.'

'What?' asked Nathan, stepping between them. 'What are you talking about?' He still looked ill, but his face no longer had the flush of fever.

Until that moment Kincaid had completely forgotten Nathan's presence. 'Nathan, why don't you and Gemma—'

'I didn't mind so much at first,' McClellan continued as if he hadn't been interrupted. 'She swore she didn't know for certain, and I felt generous then. She'd chosen me, hadn't she? And a child was a child, after all, and I was a civilized, enlightened man.' He laughed.

Nathan touched Kincaid's arm. 'Is he saying Kit's your son?'

'I didn't know,' Kincaid said quietly. 'Not until a few days ago.' He turned back to McClellan. 'What changed, then?'

McClellan shrugged and looked away. 'I thought there would be others. A son of my own ... a daughter, even. But she was too concerned with her career. "Not this year," she'd say. There was always some excuse. And all the while she watched him.' He turned his sharp glance back to Kincaid. 'I must say it didn't take her long after I left to think of an excuse to call you.'

'It was no bloody excuse, man!' Kincaid shouted, furious again. 'She's dead, for God's sake. Don't you feel anything for her?'

'What would you know about what I feel?' McClellan shouted back. 'What I feel is none of your fucking business, so why don't you just shut the fuck up, okay?' He wiped spittle from his lip with the back of his hand, and his eyes were wet with unshed tears.

Gemma stepped in close to McClellan, separating him from Kincaid with her body. 'Look, Ian, why don't we all start over from the beginning,' she said. 'You two standing here blaming one another is not going to get us anywhere.'

'Then let me get on with things,' said McClellan with a weary gesture towards the house. 'I've a few more boxes to load before I turn the keys over to the estate agent.'

Kincaid stared at him blankly. 'Estate agent? You're not—'

'Selling up? Did you think I'd come back here, to live in this house?'

'But what about Kit?' said Kincaid, shaking his head in disbelief. 'He should go back to his school—'

'Who said anything about Kit? I'm going back to France, just as soon as your friend the Chief Inspector finishes checking my visa.'

'But you're Kit's legal guardian. You can't just—'

'Chief Inspector Byrne said he was with his grandparents. I'm sure that's what Vic would have wanted for him.'

'What Vic wanted? How do you know what Vic wanted?' Kincaid was shouting again. 'And you—you raised him as your son. How can you abandon him like this?'

Raising his hands in angry frustration, he saw that they were shaking. Oh, Christ, he was losing it. He closed eyes and took a deep breath. For Kit's sake he had got to pull himself together. Gemma said something softly, anxiously, to Nathan, but the words were snatched by the wind.

Kincaid blinked. *Use your head, man. Pretend it's a case, just another case.* He dropped his hands, lowered his voice. 'Look, Ian. We need to talk. Why don't we go inside for a bit.'

'I'll make us some tea,' offered Gemma.

McClellan seemed to look at her for the first time. He shook his head. 'Not in the kitchen. They said she ...'

'I'll bring it to you in the sitting room,' Gemma said. She led him towards the house, and Kincaid and Nathan followed.

'I didn't know about Kit.' Nathan sounded bewildered. 'She never said.'

Glancing at him, Kincaid thought he had the stunned look of someone who's been punched once too often. Was he wondering what else Vic had kept from him? 'Vic was good at keeping secrets. And so, I think, was Lydia. Perhaps that's one reason Vic was so drawn to her.'

In the sitting room, Nathan perched uneasily on the footstool, while Ian sank into the chair occupied just a week ago by Vic and Kit. The room had the cold, stale smell of disuse and long dead fires.

For a brief instant, Kincaid tried to imagine the three of them—Vic, Kit, and Ian—together

427

as a family. What arguments had Ian's jealousy and resentment fuelled? And what wounds had Vic kept to herself? 'Where were you on Tuesday, Ian?' he asked as he sat down.

'Don't you start,' said Ian, but without much aggression. 'I've been over all that with Chief Inspector Byrne. I was in the south of France, where I live with my lover. It was through her parents that the college reached me. I came as soon as I heard.'

The graduate student, thought Kincaid. Ian had found unquestioning adoration from a woman too young to know better, and he was not going to give that up in order to take responsibility for an eleven-year-old boy he didn't consider his own. 'You weren't even going to see him, were you?' he said in disgust.

'It's not what you think,' Ian protested. 'I didn't want to upset him—'

'Bollocks! How do you think he's going to feel when he finds out you couldn't be bothered—'

'Shut up!' Ian rose half out of his chair. 'Just bloody shut up. It's too close. I can't bear it. I can't see Kit without seeing her in him, and I don't think I can stand that. Don't you see? I loved her—' He broke off and covered his face with his hands.

After a moment, Kincaid said, 'Listen, Ian, Kit's not with his grandparents. He ran away.' He caught a glimpse of Nathan's startled expression and raised a restraining hand. 'I found him here. He's staying with some friends in London until we can get things sorted out.'

Ian raised his head. His eyes were bloodshot,

the lids swollen. 'But why would he do such a thing? He was always a good kid, in spite of—'

'All this—Vic's death—I don't know how bad things were with his grandmother before, but she's impossible now. She means to keep him, and she's not fit to do it. And I don't know how much power her husband has over her.'

'Oh, Christ.' Ian rubbed his forehead. 'Eugenia was always a bloody bitch. But I thought with Kit—'

Kincaid shook his head. 'Kit won't stay, and we can't take a chance on what might happen to him if he runs away again.'

'I can't have him with me, do you understand? And I can't come back.' There was a hint of apology in Ian's words.

'Let me tell you what I have in mind.' By the time Gemma came in with the tea, Kincaid had outlined a plan.

When they'd filled their mismatched mugs from the teapot, Kincaid said, 'Ian, as far as Kit's concerned you're his dad. He needs to see you. Tell him these arrangements are your idea of what's best for him. Tell him you'll have him for a visit at the end of term. Surely you can give him a half hour, after what he's been through ...'

Ian looked away, and Kincaid thought he would refuse even that. But after a moment he rubbed at his face again and sighed. 'All right. I'll come this evening. And I'll make the necessary arrangements with his grandparents. They've no right to dispute my decision.' He

429

wrote Gemma's address on a page torn from Kincaid's notebook.

Kincaid met Ian's eyes as he returned the pad. 'Don't tell him about me. He doesn't need that right now.'

Ian held his gaze, then gave a barely perceptible nod of agreement. 'I'll get the rest of my things,' he said. 'Now—if you don't mind—' He gave them a slightly sardonic smile as he stood.

'Ian,' Kincaid said before he could leave the room, 'you haven't found one of Vic's books in with your things, by any chance?' He described the Marsh *Memoir*. 'And there were some poems—'

'Lydia's poems?' said Nathan. 'The ones Vic found in the Marsh book?' He frowned at Kincaid. 'Why didn't you ask me before? Vic gave them to me.'

15 December 1975
Cambridge, Addenbrooks Hospital

Dear Mummy,
No, I can't come home. As much as my heart cries out to see your dear face, and to receive the comfort only you can give, I must get well on my own. Oh, physically, I'm all right—a few lacerations, bumps and bruises, nothing that won't heal. They shall keep me in hospital, 'under observation,' for another day or so, and after that Daphne will come and look after me as it's her Christmas break.

I honestly don't think I meant to harm

430

myself, though I'd toyed with the idea of the grand gesture. I saw myself noble and tragic as Virginia Woolf walking into the river, stilling the clamouring voices of madness, but it was only my own voice I wanted to silence, the one that kept telling me what I'd become.

What have I done to deserve Daphne's forgiveness, or yours? Why do you insist on loving me in spite of myself? I've spent years trying to run away from my life, my past, my self. I've written shallow and sensational poems which traded on others' misery. I've sold my voice for a few pretentious reviews in *The Times*. I've shunned my friends for the company of sycophants. I've tried to lose the last bit of myself that mattered, but your love held me accountable. I see now that I must try to live up to it—I can't bear it otherwise.

Lydia

They'd spent most of the afternoon at Parkside Police Station going over things with Alec Byrne, and had achieved little more than confirming that Ian McClellan's documents did indeed show him to have been out of the country at the time of Vic's death.

Byrne had received their account of Miss Pope's evidence that Vic had already been ill by half-past three with a distinct lack of enthusiasm. 'We'll go over the statements again, but I really don't see that this puts us much farther forward,' he said. 'We've no apparent motive for Doctor McClellan's death—or for Lydia Brooke's in the event she did not commit suicide—and

431

now it seems that these poems you thought the murderer had stolen were simply misplaced.' Byrne steepled his long fingers together. 'Quite frankly, Duncan, we've not had a single good lead on this case, and my manpower resources are dwindling. You know how it is. I've a missing child to deal with, and the mugging of an eighty-year-old woman in her bed.' He shrugged.

'You're telling me you're turning Vic's case over to a file clerk. Alec—'

'If anything turns up I'll put every available officer on it. But in the meantime ...' Byrne cast a look of appeal at Gemma, then turned back to Kincaid. 'What would you do if you were in my shoes?'

Kincaid had reluctantly conceded Byrne's point, his sense of frustration mounting. Would he keep on, he wondered, if he weren't personally involved?

By the time they'd driven back to London and pulled the car up on the double-yellows in front of Gemma's flat, he had arrived at an answer. Like Alec, he had learned to accept a percentage of failure in his job. But he had spent all his adult life learning the art of catching killers—and with knowledge came responsibility. Someone had deliberately set out to murder Vic, not only taking her life, but changing her son's life for ever. He would not give up until he knew the truth, no matter how long it took, or what it cost him. He would see justice done, for Vic ... and for Lydia as well.

The morning's wind had given way to an

unexpectedly warm and hazy afternoon, and they found Kit playing in the garden with the children. He was humming tunelessly as he built something with old bits of brick, and he gave an uncomplicated smile of pleasure when he looked up and saw them watching. It seemed that at least for a few moments he'd found some solace.

Kincaid had taken him aside then, telling him that Ian had come back, but only temporarily, and would take him and Tess to the Miller family that evening. Kit stared at him a moment, his face unreadable, then turned on his heel and disappeared into the house without a word.

Now, looking out the kitchen window in the growing dusk, Kincaid wondered what he had expected? Relief? Anger? Disappointment? Anything at all, he thought, would have been better than the silence in which Kit had collected his things, then gone out into the garden with Tess.

He could barely make out the outline of boy and dog huddled together on the flagstone steps. 'What's he thinking?' he said as Hazel came to stand beside him. 'Why do I feel as though I've failed him?'

'You've done the best you could under the circumstances,' said Hazel softly. 'Sometimes there just aren't any right answers. And he may not really be thinking at all. Emotional overload—too much to take in at once. Give him a while to find his balance.'

'Did I make a mistake in not telling him the truth now?' Kincaid asked. 'Is it better for him to think that the man he's seen as his father doesn't love him, or for him to learn that he's not who he always thought he was?'

Hazel didn't answer, and in the moment's silence they heard a thump and faint laughter from upstairs, where Gemma was giving Holly and Toby their baths before tea. 'Professionally, I'd say you're doing the right thing,' Hazel said slowly. 'Personally, I know how difficult it must be. For the time being, give him all the reassurance you can that you mean to stay in his life. Let him get used to the idea.' She touched his arm and looked up into his face. 'But Duncan, you must be absolutely sure of your commitment to him, or it's better not to do anything at all.'

'I realize that.' He looked out into the garden. For the first time he understood the magnitude of Gemma's responsibility to Toby. Was he capable of making the same commitment, capable of giving Kit the stability he needed? And how would he know until he tried?

The doorbell chimed. 'I'll go,' said Hazel. 'Why don't you have Kit run up and tell Gemma and the little ones goodbye. I'll show Ian into the sitting room.' She gave his elbow a squeeze and smiled. 'Trust your instincts. That's a good bit of what parenting is about.'

Gemma chewed on a pencil as she stared at the papers she'd spread out on Hazel's kitchen table. As literary executor, Nathan had asked to keep the original poems found in the Marsh *Memoir*, but he'd made them copies before they left Grantchester, and Gemma had begun going over them as soon as they'd returned to London.

She looked up as the corridor door swung open and Kincaid came in. 'Are they gone?' she asked as he sat down across from her. His tie hung loosely, and his hair stood on end where he'd absently run his hand through it.

He nodded. 'Yes. I've just rung Laura Miller to say they're on their way.'

'I thought it better not to add to the audience, so I had another go at this stuff,' she said, gesturing at the nest of books and papers she'd accumulated. 'How was Kit with Ian?'

'He barely spoke. Ian tried, I'll give him that.'

The children had thrown their soft damp arms round Kit's neck when he'd come up to say goodbye, and as she watched him cling to them, she'd sensed the precariousness of his emotional control. 'It was hard for Kit to leave. And you didn't want to let him go,' she added softly as she saw the weariness in Kincaid's face. He'd been through so much in the past week ... but how could he begin to sort out his feelings for Kit until he found some resolution over Vic's death? And how could she help him?

Looking back at the poems spread before her, Gemma said hesitantly, 'You know I'm not a poet, and I haven't been to university. But I've been reading Vic's manuscript, and as many of Lydia's poems as I could find, and I think Vic was right. These poems are different. There's a feeling of urgency, and a directness to them

435

that the earlier poems don't have.' She frowned as she touched the sheets on the table, then separated one poem from the rest. 'They seem to begin with a more general feeling, a theme. Listen to this one.' Settling back in her chair, she began to read with careful diction.

> They have taken my voice
> severed tongue at the roots
> sucked anger away like breath
> stolen from the mouths of babes
>
> In the beginning was the word
> but it was not ours
> they left us only the
> whispers of our mingled blood.
>
> And yet we participate willingly
> in the conspiracy of our loss
> passing this mute legacy
> our gift to our daughters.

Gemma looked up at him as she finished. Searching his face, she shook her head. 'It doesn't mean anything to you, does it? But I feel it—here.' She pressed her fist to the centre of her chest. 'It's about women not speaking up, not having voices, and yet we teach our daughters the same behaviour. Do you see?'

'I think so. But what has that to do—'

'Wait. As the poems go on the theme seems to become more specific, until you get to this one, the last. Listen. It's called "Awaiting Electra".'

436

Ancient laughter stirs in the deep
heart of the dimly remembered green
wood by the close and
sacrificial Pool.
The poets wait in uneasy slumber
for her coming
their feet whisper on the leaf-thick
path and the old pulse
quickens in the dappled light.
Silver slides over the
bell of her hair over
the innocent landscape of
her skin and she smiles as
they ease her down into
the dark water waiting.
She feels the wild springing freedom
then the old fear, the truth of it
sudden and piercing as a child's rape.
Lost to years, she lies forgotten
betrayed in the mallow-tangles
of the still black summer.
Who will speak for her now? Truth
unmourned, untold in the ice heart
of our memory?

Gemma's reading had grown more halting as
she progressed through the poem, and now she
stared at the page until the print blurred and the
words began to shift and scramble. It was odd,
she thought as she noticed the hair standing up
on her forearms, that the words made her feel
things which went beyond words. But there was
something more here even than that, she was
sure of it, if she could just sort it out ... She

looked up at Kincaid. 'She's telling a story, isn't she?'

'I suppose you could say all poems tell stories, they're a way of assimilating our experiences.' He tapped the page. 'This one is probably a metaphor for coming of age, the loss of virginity—'

'No, no'—Gemma shook her head—'I mean she's telling a story about something that really happened. The beginning reminds me of the things I've been reading about Rupert Brooke and his friends swimming naked in Byron's Pool—the poets' pool—do you see? There's this feeling of tingling anticipation about it—but then something happens, something dark and unexpected—'

'Gemma, don't you think that's a bit farfetched?'

'Is it? Lydia is dead. Vic is dead. And someone wanted these poems. Just because Nathan had them doesn't mean that Vic's killer wasn't searching for them.' She stared at him, and after a moment he nodded.

'Go on, then.'

Slowly, speaking aloud as she thought, Gemma said, 'Strip away the images. What does she tell us happens? Think like a policeman—find the bare bones.'

Kincaid frowned and ran a hand through his hair. 'There's a rape. A child's rape.' He slid the page across the table, turning it his way up. 'But she doesn't actually say—'

'She only suggests it. But she tells us that a girl goes to a pool in the woods where the poets

438

are waiting for her.' Gemma retrieved the page. 'She's naked—'

'Virginal—'

'They take her into the pool—'

'Rape her—'

'She's lost, betrayed. What does Lydia mean?' Gemma asked as she skimmed the poem once more. '... *lost in the mallow-tangles of the still black summer?*'

'Mallow grows round ponds,' said Kincaid. 'Might she have drowned?'

Nodding, Gemma said, 'But what has it to do with Lydia? Why is the girl waiting for Electra?'

'Who's waiting for Electra?' asked Hazel, coming into the kitchen. She'd been settling the children in the sitting room with a video, so the adults could have their dinner in peace. 'It sounds like a play.'

'It's the title of a poem,' said Gemma. 'Who exactly was she, anyway? What we learned at school has gone a bit fuzzy.'

Hazel lifted the lid from a pot of chicken soup and gave it a stir. 'Electra was the daughter of Agamemnon and Clytemnestra, who urged her brother Orestes to kill their mother in revenge for the murder of their father.' Tasting the soup, she said, 'Just about ready,' then added, 'I guess you could say that Electra was the voice of vengeance, although she herself was powerless to act.'

'The voice of vengeance,' Gemma repeated, rotating the page once more. 'You see? It's about women's silence again, about the need

439

to speak up ... Does Lydia see herself as Electra here, telling the truth?' She closed her eyes for a moment and pinched her forehead. 'What if the poets in the poem aren't Rupert Brooke and his friends, but Lydia's poets? Adam, Nathan, Darcy and Daphne? Do you remember what Daphne said this morning? About Lydia and Morgan ... *something happened that summer and she was never the same afterwards*—it's all here, the references to the long ago summer. And if Lydia is Electra, who is the girl?'

'How can you be sure Lydia's not talking about herself?' asked Kincaid, still sounding sceptical as he spun the page back towards him. 'What if it was Lydia who was raped? Surely that's trauma enough to make one change one's patterns.'

But Gemma felt like a terrier with a rat in its teeth—she knew she'd caught hold of the truth, and she meant to shake it until it gave itself up to her. 'No ... if the poets are Lydia's poets it couldn't have been that—she'd slept with them all already ... But what else didn't they want anyone to know? Something Alec Byrne said today made me think ...' Frowning, she searched her memory. 'A missing child ... he was looking for a missing child. But there was a girl who disappeared a long time ago ...' She blinked as the scrap of conversation in Ralph Peregrine's office came back to her. 'The daughter of Margery Lester's friend. What was her name? Hope? Charity?'

'Verity,' said Kincaid, and she heard the sudden spike of excitement in his voice. 'Verity

Whitecliff. The daughter of Henry Whitecliff, the former head of the English Faculty.'

Spoon still in hand, Hazel had come to sit with them, and now she reached out and rotated the page with the tip of her finger. 'The poem talks about *Truth unmourned, untold* ... What if *Truth* is a person here, as well as an abstract quality? Verity is an old word for truth.'

Kincaid said slowly, 'What if Verity Whitecliff didn't run away, after all? What if she was murdered?' He took his notebook from his pocket and entered a number into his cell phone.

'Hello, Laura? It's Duncan again. I've a question for you. Can you tell me exactly when Verity Whitecliff disappeared?' He listened for a moment, then said, 'Right. I'll tell you what it's all about when I know more, and in the meantime I'd rather you didn't mention this to anyone. Right. Thanks.' Disconnecting, he looked from Hazel to Gemma. 'Verity Whitecliff slipped out of her house on Midsummer's Eve, 1963, and was never seen again. She was wearing a summer dress, and she took nothing with her. She was fifteen years old.'

'Dear God.' breathed Hazel. 'The poor child. And her parents ...'

'Lydia married Morgan in September of 1963.' Gemma felt a sense of the inevitable, as if she were powerless to stop the unfolding of the past. 'Within weeks of Verity's disappearance, she not only got herself dangerously involved with a man she'd refused to have anything to do with during the previous year—she gave up what had mattered to her above all else. She left University.' She met Kincaid's eyes. 'What could have been so terrible that it caused her to alter her life for ever?' she asked, but even as she spoke the truth felt cold and heavy inside her.

The gentle trill of Kincaid's phone made them all jump. He fumbled for it, then barked, 'Kincaid.' His mouth tightened as he listened. 'We'll be there as soon as we can,' he said, and rang off.

Gemma felt a jerk of fear. 'What's happened?'

'That was Adam Lamb. He says Father Denny rang him and said Nathan's shotgun has disappeared from the vicarage. Then Adam tried to ring Nathan. There was no reply.'

Chapter Twenty

Oh, is the water sweet and cool,
Gentle and brown, above the pool?
And laughs the immortal river still
Under the mill, under the mill?

Rupert Brooke, from
The Old Vicarage, Grantchester

'What if we're wrong?' Gemma felt a stab of doubt as she buckled herself into the passenger seat of her Escort. 'What if Verity Whitecliff really did run away? We haven't a smidgen of proof that she didn't.'

Kincaid manoeuvred out into the Liverpool

442

Road traffic, heading north towards the Ring Road. Gemma had handed him the keys without protest, knowing he'd push the car harder than she dared. 'It's a bloody great assumption, all right,' he said. 'But it's the only thing we've come up with that makes sense out of what we do know. It wasn't only Lydia's life that changed after that summer. Nathan married Jean and apparently severed all but the occasional connection with the rest of the group. And Adam decided to go into the church.'

'What about Daphne and Darcy?' said Gemma. 'They seem to have kept on pretty much as before.'

'Maybe they weren't involved. I doubt Daphne would have mentioned that summer to us if she'd anything to hide.' He glanced at Gemma. 'What's wrong?'

'What if ...' she began slowly, 'you don't suppose ... what if it was Lydia who killed Verity? And she kept attempting suicide until she finally succeeded.'

'And Vic just happened to die from an overdose of a heart medication she didn't take?' Kincaid raised an eyebrow. 'That won't wash. I think Lydia was silenced, and Vic as well when she got too close to the truth.'

'Then what really happened the night Verity disappeared?' Gemma thought of the time a boy had convinced her to climb out the window of her bedroom in the flat over the bakery. She'd been afraid to go further than the corner, and her father had caught her sneaking back in the bakery door. All in all, it had hardly been worth

443

a few furtive kisses. 'Which of them enticed her out?' she wondered aloud.

'She might have known any of them,' said Kincaid. 'Lydia and Darcy were reading English, but they were all interested in poetry and would surely have been acquainted with Henry Whitecliff.'

'They must have seemed glamorous to Verity—reciting poetry, all that sort of thing. She'd have felt flattered to be included. They were older, the boys were all goodlooking—'

'And Lydia had the allure of sexual experience,' Kincaid finished for her. 'I can understand why Verity might have found them irresistible, but what did they see in her?'

'Sophistication is never so much fun as when you're impressing somebody with it. Verity would have provided an audience. Perhaps they planned a harmless prank that night to impress her ... an initiation.' Gemma closed her eyes and thought of the lines of the poem. 'They waited for her in the woods,' she said softly. 'Maybe they even wore Edwardian costumes. When she came, they told her they were going to pretend to be Rupert Brooke and his friends. They undressed her, and took her into the water ... then somehow it all went wrong.'

Shivering a little, Gemma imagined them running through the woods in the darkness, laughing at their own daring like children playing hide and seek. Wood nymphs, possessed by Pan ... Had their calling on pagan gods unleashed more than they'd bargained for?

She focused her mind on the practical. 'If it

wasn't Lydia who killed Verity, it must have been one of the boys,' she said, knowing she couldn't refute it. She thought of the sweetness of Adam's smile, of his competent concern for Nathan—and she thought of Nathan's ravaging grief over Vic's death. Surely that was no act. 'But could it be grief *and* guilt?' she wondered aloud.

'What?' Kincaid glanced at her, then focused again on the road.

'Nathan. What if he killed Vic, and it's guilt he's feeling now?'

Kincaid thought for a moment, then shook his head. 'I don't believe it. I don't think that someone who'd committed two murders as calculated and cold-blooded as these would suddenly be overcome with remorse. It's not emotionally consistent. And why would Nathan have shown us the poems?'

'Adam, then?' she suggested reluctantly. 'Vic was killed after she saw Adam. She might have told him what she'd discovered—'

'Vic told us herself that she only found the poems in the book later that night,' argued Kincaid. 'So he couldn't have known about them.'

'But what if Lydia rejected Adam all those years because she knew he'd murdered Verity? He'd have built up a lot of anger and resentment towards her, and when he saw the poems she'd written, it all boiled over.'

'And what about Vic?' asked Kincaid, sounding sceptical. 'Why would he kill her?'

'We can't know what Vic said to him that

445

day. Something might have triggered memories, or made him feel threatened.'

Kincaid shrugged. 'I suppose that's possible. But let's go back to the poems. If we assume that the murderer was frightened by what Lydia revealed in them, we have to assume that the murderer had read them. Right?' He glanced at her. 'Then why wait until Lydia had turned in the manuscript to kill her?'

'Unless ... they only had access to the poems after Lydia gave them to Ralph Peregrine to publish,' Gemma said slowly. 'That would rule out Daphne on another count, wouldn't it? She must have read the poems as Lydia was writing them—'

He thought for a moment, then asked. 'So who would have seen the poems after Lydia delivered them to the publisher?'

Gemma chewed on her fingertip. 'Ralph, of course. Probably Margery Lester.'

The light blinked amber, then green. 'Margery Lester gallivanting naked in the woods with her son Darcy and his friends? And Ralph was still at school then. There's no evidence that he even knew the others at this point.' Kincaid shook his head as he shifted into first gear. After a moment, he said, 'It's too complicated. Let's try another tack. If Lydia was killed with her own heart medication—an opportunity taken—then when the murderer began to feel nervous about Vic, he went back to the tested method. But where did he get the digoxin this time?'

Gemma gazed out at the North London suburbs passing by. The halogen street lamps glowed yellow, haloed by the moisture in the air. *Margery and Ralph ... What did that make her think of?* The scene in Ralph's office came back to her again. Margery, breathless from her climb up the stairs, her skin and lips faintly tinged with blue. 'I'll bet Margery Lester has a heart condition,' she said, suddenly breathless herself. 'Probably congestive heart failure, from her colour. I'm sure of it. And isn't digoxin the usual—'

'Quinine!' Kincaid thumped his hand on the steering wheel. 'Remember the list of potentiators Winnie gave us? Quinidine was one of them, and tonic contains quinine. Margery refused the gin and tonic Ralph offered her—something about it being against doctor's orders—so she knew that certain substances strengthened the effect of the digoxin. She could easily have known about Vic's teas, and next to Ralph, she's the most likely person to have seen the manuscript.' Frowning, he shook his head. 'But we've said it's not likely Margery killed Verity—and it doesn't fit the poem.'

'What if ...' Gemma tried to collect the featherwisps of ideas floating in her mind into something cohesive. She thought of Margery, elegant, gracious, successful—what could possibly drive a woman like that to commit murder? Slowly, she said, 'What if Margery killed Lydia and Vic to protect Verity's killer?' *And who would Margery protect but her own son?* She saw it then, in its blinding simplicity, as the pieces came together in her mind.

'You're saying Margery killed them to protect

Darcy?' Kincaid glanced at her, his brow creased in concentration.

She shook her head. 'No. It's easier than that. Everything we've said about Margery holds true for Darcy as well. Access to his mother's medication would have been easy—all he had to do was offer to pick it up at the chemist for her.'

They'd reached the motorway. As Gemma stared out the window, the damp surface of the tarmac glistened like oil, reflecting light back into her eyes. 'Margery doesn't drink gin and tonic, but Darcy does,' she said, remembering his easy hospitality, and the dish of cut limes in his flat. 'And he would have known about the quinine—'

'And keeps a bottle of gin in his desk,' said Kincaid. 'We were wrong about the tea. He dissolved the tablets in a gin and tonic, counting on the tonic's bitterness to disguise the taste, and the quinine to increase the poison's effectiveness.'

'But how did he get Vic to drink it? She wasn't in the habit of drinking at lunch.'

'She can't have learned the truth about him, or she'd never have accepted the drink. But he must have feared she was close. I think he made her an unprecedented apology for his behaviour. Vic would have felt she couldn't refuse a peace offering. And once he'd got her to drink the poison, he waited, then cycled to the cottage when he thought he'd given it enough time.'

'Kit's shadow at the bottom of the garden,' said Gemma. 'Darcy took a terrible risk.'

448

'Oh, he's quite capable of risk. Vic must have still been alive when he searched the cottage, then afterwards he went straight to his mother's dinner party as if nothing had happened.' Kincaid's voice was flat, and a look at his profile in the intermittent light from passing headlamps made Gemma feel uneasy. 'Darcy's objections to Vic's biography of Lydia had nothing to do with his aesthetic principles, and everything to do with keeping the past buried,' he continued. 'When he couldn't do that, he tried misdirection. It was he who put us on to Lydia's relationship with Daphne, remember?'

'But what about Lydia's manuscript?' asked Gemma. 'How would he have known about the poems?'

'Perhaps Lydia had said enough to make him suspicious. Writing the poems may have been Lydia's way of working herself up to a public denouncement. Remember she'd rung Nathan that day, saying she wanted to talk to him about something?'

'Or maybe Darcy ran across it lying about in Ralph's office, quite by chance, and couldn't resist having a look,' said Gemma. 'The poems would have screamed betrayal to him, so he removed the most damaging ones.'

'And once he'd done that, he'd have realized that Lydia had to be silenced. Either way, access to the manuscript would have been easy enough,' Kincaid said. 'I'd guess Darcy's always had carte blanche at the Peregrine Press, considering his mother's position, and it's not as if the manuscripts were kept in a vault.'

'Easier than that, even,' said Gemma, remembering the Peregrine logo she'd seen on the spine of one of Darcy's books in his flat. 'If Ralph published his books as well. He might have been in and out of the office working on one of his own manuscripts.'

'He removed the poems after assuring himself that Ralph hadn't read them, then paid an unexpected visit to Lydia,' Kincaid said with certainty. 'It must have seemed foolproof to him, and it very nearly was. He unscrewed the porch light so that he wouldn't be seen leaving, then offered Lydia a gin and tonic. What could be more welcome after a warm day of working in the garden? Perhaps he left for awhile, then came back to set the stage for her apparent suicide. Music, and candles, and the poem in the typewriter.'

'Why Rupert Brooke, though?' asked Gemma. 'Why not fake a suicide note?'

'My guess is he got carried away with his own sense of drama. It was misdirection again, making it look as though she still grieved over Morgan Ashby.'

'What I don't understand,' said Gemma, frowning, 'is why the others protected him after Verity's death.'

'They must have felt culpable, guilt by association. And they had a strong sense of group identity. No one could tell what Darcy had done without betraying the others.' Kincaid paused as he overtook a slow-moving lorry. 'But I think that's come to an end. Only Nathan and

Adam are left, and Nathan has nothing to lose. You'd better ring Alec Byrne. Ask him if quinine showed up in Vic's routine toxicology scan, then tell him he'd better meet us in Grant—'

'The poems,' Gemma said, smacking her palm against her forehead. 'Nathan only read the poems for the first time this afternoon, just as we did. And if we figured out what happened to Lydia and Vic, how much easier will it have been for him?'

Then in some garden hushed from wind ... How had it gone? *Warm in a sunset's afterglow* ... After that had come something about lovers, but Nathan couldn't quite bring it back. Rupert had been big on gardens and sunsets and moonlight, he remembered, and Lydia had loved the dream-like quality of those poems.

He might be dreaming now, he thought as he watched the deep green shadows moving under the stillness of the trees. The air had a shimmering translucence to it, almost as if it were under water, and it smelled of springs long past.

But he felt the cold steel weight of his father's old shotgun across his knees, and he knew himself to be awake, sitting in the dusk at the bottom of his garden. When it was full dark he would go.

His feet would remember the path ... *the leaf-thick path* ... the way they had gone more than thirty years ago ... He had tried for so long to forget what happened that night, buried it in his love for Jean and for his daughters, his work, his gardens. And yet he had come back here, to this house by the river, and his reckoning.

How had he not seen what monster they'd created with their silence? First Lydia, then Vic ... dear God, his blindness had condemned her as surely as if his own hand had slipped the poison into her drink.

Nathan rose and stood by the gate a moment, one hand on the latch, the other clasped loosely round the worn grip of the gun. *The poets wait ... for her coming* ... Lydia had not allowed herself to forget, she'd kept it sharp and clear, then distilled it into words. The poem had been intended for him, for Adam, for Darcy. When he'd read it that afternoon, after Kincaid and his sergeant left, he'd known that as surely as if Lydia had spoken to him. Was that why she'd rung him the day she died? Had she waited until the girls were grown and gone, and Jean dead, so that he would be free of his need to protect them?

Unlatching the gate, he began to pick his way across the pasture in the light of the rising moon ... *the old pulse quickens in the dappled light* ... There had been moonlight that night, and *the girls wore white, floating dresses, they always wore white* ... no, that was another time, another memory. On this night Daphne had not come, she'd been called away unexpectedly, and her absence had spared her.

The river path felt smooth and familiar beneath his feet. He needed the familiarity now, even welcomed the memories as tinder to his purpose. They'd bicycled from Cambridge, he and Lydia and Adam. *Lydia wore a gypsy dress, and dangling earrings. She'd pinched a rose from the college garden and fastened it in her dark hair. She'd bought shirts for him and Adam at a jumble sale, white with flowing sleeves, and when they put them on she kissed them and called them her lords.* It was Darcy who waited for Verity and brought her in his mother's car. He'd fancied her, and they'd laughed about it.

To his right as he passed he saw the gleam of the Orchard's gate, and behind it the gnarled silhouettes of the apple trees. *White blossom falling, the air heavy with wasps ... they sat in the low canvas chairs, eating tea and cake and discussing the merits of free verse ... tawny-haired Rupert, stuffing cake in his mouth, laughing as the crumbs spilled ...* No, that was only an old photo, it was just the four of them, Nathan, Adam, Daphne, Lydia ... *it was May Week and the blossom was long gone ... they were punchy tired from swotting for exams, silly and sentimental with it, and as he looked round the table at each of their faces he thought how much he loved them, wished he could stop time ... Lydia knew, she always knew. 'Let's celebrate,' she said. 'We don't have to grow old. We'll swim naked in Byron's Pool tonight.' Rupert hadn't wanted to grow old, and Rupert had the last laugh ...*

He'd reached the Old Vicarage now ... *Rupert sat in a chair in the tangled garden, dressed in tennis whites, books spread before him on a table. They hovered over him like ghosts, did he sense them there? He'd known how fragile was the boundary between the living and the dead ... Rupert stands*

453

on the bank and sheds his clothes, body golden, awkward hands and feet ... Is the water sweet and cool, gentle and brown, above the pool?

Byron's Pool ... Still in the dawnlit waters cool his ghostly lordship swims ... The night is warm and close, heavy with moisture, Nathan and Adam and Lydia wait for her in a bower among the pink-petalled mallow, they pass round a bottle of wine, a joint Lydia's begged from a musician friend ... sight, sound, and touch so sharp and intense, time stretches ... Verity comes, so lovely and unfinished, the thick straight honey of her hair smells of roses ... they undress her among the soft leaves, moonlight slides over her skin and she laughs at the lightness of their fingers as they caress her ... Adam sings a snatch of 'Till There was You', they collapse into hysterical giggles while Darcy watches in impatient arousal, his breath rasping in Nathan's ear ... 'Come,' Darcy coaxes her, 'I'll be Rupert, you be Virginia, well have a midnight swim,' and he eases her down into the dark water ...

Nathan takes the rose from Lydia's hair while Adam unfastens her sandals ... her body emerges from the dress like a butterfly from a chrysalis ... Nathan brushes the petals of the rose over her skin ... at that moment Lydia is the most beautiful thing he has ever seen, the delicate curve of her neck, the slope of her shoulder, the perfect fulness of her dark-nippled breasts ... she laughs up at him as Adam kisses her toes ...

A cry from the far side of the pool, faint as a night bird, a stirring of the water ... Nathan lifts his head to listen, but Lydia pulls him down to meet her mouth as she begins to unbutton his shirt, he falls helplessly into the warm rushing darkness of her lips and her tongue ... then with some scrap of awareness he feels Adam stand, hears him say, 'Darcy?' and again, 'Darcy?'

A muffled sound again, a splash, then Darcy's voice, a high scream of panic, 'I can't find her! I can't bloody find her!' Adam is into the water by the time Nathan stumbles to his feet and follows. The cool water fills his clothes, his strokes are heavy, the few yards an impossible distance.

Adam reaches Darcy first, disappears beneath the surface, rises gasping. 'It's like pitch!' He shakes Darcy by the shoulders. 'Where did she go under? You bloody fool! Tell me!'

'There!' Darcy points. 'Just there. I didn't mean—'

Nathan dives, opening his eyes in the velvet blackness. Tendrils brush against him, then something more solid, a hand. He follows it, pulls her easily, unresisting, into his arms. A push to the surface, 'I've got her!' A kickstroke, cradling her head above the water, then Lydia helps him pull her weight up the slippery bank. 'She's not breathing. Oh Christ, she's not breathing.'

Adam kneels beside him, holding his fingers to her throat. 'No pulse, I can't find a pulse—'

Darcy wails, 'I only meant to stop her crying out! She didn't want—I never meant to hurt her—'

'Shut up!' Lydia screams, and Nathan hears a slap. She tugs on Nathan's arm. 'Get help, we've got to get help.'

'No time.' He tries to remember a sixth-form first-aid course. Clear the airway. Compress. Breath. Compress. Breathe. Her lips are cold, her skin

flaccid beneath his fingers. No breath resists the invasion of his own. Breath blurs into compression, compression into breath. Sweat pours from his body, drips onto her still breast, until he feels Adam pulling him away.

'It's no use, Nathan. You can't help her.' Adam holds him in his arms. Lydia is crying, little frightened hiccupping sobs.

Darcy drops to his knees beside them. 'It wasn't my fault. I never meant to hurt her. She shouldn't have—'

'Shut up! You bastard!' Lydia is on him in a fury of kicks and pummelling fists. 'You stupid fuck. You drowned her, you bastard. We've got to ring the police, tell someone—'

Panting, Darcy managed to twist her arms behind her back. 'You won't. You won't tell anyone. Because you're responsible, too.'

Nathan pulled away from Adam's restraint. 'That's crap, Darcy. You know we didn't—'

'But no one else will, will they?' Darcy is cold and urgent now. 'Tell them just what happened, why don't you? You brought her here, undressed her, gave her wine and drugs, but you didn't touch her after that, oh, no. And even if they believe you, you'll be sent down, you know that, don't you? Your parents will have to know, of course, and yours are ill, isn't that right, Adam? It might even kill them, but I don't suppose that matters as long as you're doing the right thing.'

'Fuck you, you son of a bitch,' said Adam, but Nathan heard the uncertainty in his voice. He thought of his own parents' pride in him, the first child in his family to go to university, and of

456

Lydia's mother ... A look at Lydia's stricken face told him the shaft had hit home.

'Whatever happens now won't make any difference to her, you see that, don't you?' said Darcy. 'I'm sorry she's dead'—his voice quavered and he cleared his throat—'but it was an accident, and I don't see how ruining our careers and our parents' lives will help her.'

'You're crazy.' Nathan licked his lips. 'We'd never get away with it.'

'No one would ever know. Not unless one of us tells.' Darcy looked at them each in turn. 'And if one of us tells, we'll all suffer for it.'

In the silence Nathan saw his hoped for First in Natural Sciences turn to dust, saw his parents shamed beyond bearing by the scandal. And he had tried to save her, he'd done all he could ...

'What ...' began Lydia so softly that he might not have heard. She rubbed a dirty hand across her tear-streaked face. 'What would we ...'

Darcy sat back on his heels and closed his eyes for a moment, then took a shuddering breath. 'I know a place, in the Fens ...

Nathan crossed the road below the mill and took the path to Byron's Pool. It was treacherous where it ran along the river, humped and barred by twisting tree roots, and he went carefully in the dark. When he reached the edge of the clearing by the pool, he stopped. After a moment he made out a darker darkness between the trees a few yards away, then he heard the snap of twigs beneath shifted weight.

'Darcy.'

457

'You were always punctual, Nathan. It's one of your more endearing traits.' Darcy stepped forward, brushing at his waistcoat. 'But I didn't know you had a penchant for the cloak and dagger. This is a bit much, insisting on a clandestine meeting in the woods—'

The air felt warm and moist against Nathan's skin, as it had that long ago night. He knew now what he should have done then, he had always known, just as he'd somehow known it would come to this. He felt his rage settle into icy calm. 'You're a bastard, Darcy,' he said. 'You were always a bastard, but until today I thought you had some scrap of human decency. I didn't know until today that you'd killed them—Lydia ... and Vic.'

He heard Darcy's quick inhalation, sensed him regrouping. 'Don't be absurd, Nathan.' Darcy's voice held the concerned condescension one used to a child.

'You're talking absolute nonsense. You've been ill, and I'm afraid your policeman's been giving you very upsetting ideas. Why don't we go back to your place and have a drink, talk it over.'

'Do you think I'd be fool enough to drink with you? Lydia should have known better—she knew what you are—but even she must have believed you wouldn't sink to premeditated murder.'

'You've no proof of anything,' Darcy said, still unruffled, but Nathan saw him lean forward a bit, shifting his weight onto the balls of his feet. The moonlight washed the colour from his

458

clothes, making a monochrome of the affectation of his waistcoat.

'I don't need proof.' Nathan swung up the barrel of the gun and racked in a shell, the sound ominous and unmistakable in the silence. The gun rested easily in his hands now, angled slightly across his body. His father had taught him to shoot, years ago, the old pump action shotgun had been his pride and joy ... *Never point a gun at someone, son, unless you intend to shoot them.* 'It's long past that,' he said, and he wasn't sure if he answered Darcy or his dad.

'Nathan, you can't let some stranger's suspicions destroy a lifetime of friendship,' said Darcy, changing tacks. 'We have a history together, a past to protect. You can't just throw that away.'

'Oh, but I can, you see. One can't be friends with a hollow man, Darcy.' Nathan caught the glint of a watch chain with the rise and fall of Darcy's chest. When had Darcy started wearing a watch chain? He hadn't needed the silly waistcoats or watch chains, once. His charm and facile wit had been enough—enough to make Lydia see Rupert in his ruddy good looks, enough to fool them all. 'You manipulated us. All these years, you counted on our loyalty to each other binding our silence, and when you saw that failing, you resorted to murder. Did it get easier each time, Darcy? Vic wasn't as much of a threat as Lydia—she might never have put all the pieces together.'

'Not without your help. And I couldn't chance that collaboration, could I? If you came

459

to doubt Lydia's suicide, I couldn't be sure you wouldn't succumb to the same self-righteousness that was Lydia's undoing. Though I have to give the fair Victoria credit for dogged persistence,' Darcy added.

Nathan felt his self-control cracking, his fury seeping through like acid. 'You bastard. I loved her—did you know that? And her life meant nothing more to you than an inconvenience. But she outwitted you in the end. They both did. Lydia kept copies of the poems you took from the manuscript, hidden in a book she left to me, and Vic returned them to me after she'd read them. That's why you didn't find them when you searched her cottage. The police have them now.'

Darcy laughed aloud. 'And a fat lot of good that will do them. Give it up, Nathan. It's hopeless. And even if you were foolish enough to tell them where to look for Verity's bones, it's only your word and Adam's that I was even there that night.'

Nathan saw his error in the split-second it took him to bring the gun to bear on Darcy's chest. *His word and Adam's.* He had underestimated his opponent, he should have realized that when Darcy made his first admission. Darcy would kill him, if he could, then Adam. It didn't matter what they could prove—even the suggestion of Darcy's involvement in any of the deaths would lose him his coveted position in the Faculty, Dame Margery would see to that if no one else did.

But even as he felt the pressure of the stock

against his shoulder, the pinch of the trigger as he squeezed it, Darcy lunged for him. The gun went off as Darcy hit the barrel a hard upward blow, wrenching it from Nathan's fingers.

The gun jerked in recoil, then Darcy's weight carried them to the ground. Pain seared through Nathan's shoulder as the gun flew out of his hand. Blackness ... he couldn't see and his ears rang from the sound of the gun. A warm saltiness on his lips—his blood or Darcy's? Wetness at the back of his head ... more blood? No, water, his head was half in the pool, and the pressure against his throat came from Darcy's encircling hands.

Chapter Twenty-One

Say, is there Beauty yet to find?
And Certainty? And Quiet kind?
Deep meadows yet, for to forget
The lies, and truths, and pain? ... oh! yet
Stands the Church clock at ten to three?
And is there honey still for tea?

Rupert Brooke,
from *The Old Vicarage, Grantchester*

Kincaid swung left at the High Street Junction and pulled the Escort up behind Adam Lamb's Mini. Light spilled out from the open door of Nathan's cottage.

'I don't like the look of this,' he muttered as

461

he pulled up the handbrake and vaulted out of the car. He heard Gemma close behind him as he started up the walk.

Adam hurried out to meet them before they reached the door, scarecrow tall and thin in full clerical black. He shook his head at the sight of their questioning faces. 'No joy, I'm afraid. No one's seen him. Father Denny and some of the church wardens are searching along the river bank with torches.' His face was creased with worry and exhaustion. 'I said I'd wait here for you.'

Kincaid took Adam's arm and pulled him into the hall. 'Adam, tell us about Darcy and Verity Whitecliff.'

'Oh, dear God.' Adam sagged against the wall as his face drained of colour. 'What ... what has that to do with this?'

'Did he kill her?' Kincaid pressed him, a hand on his shoulder. 'Did he kill Verity?'

Adam rubbed a trembling hand across his face, then he seemed to gather strength. Straightening up, he said, 'It's more complicated than that. We all felt responsible. We should never have allowed it to happen.'

'Did he kill her? Yes or no?' Kincaid squeezed his shoulder, urgency driving him.

Adam winced as Kincaid's fingers bit into the nerve, but he held Kincaid's gaze. 'Yes,' he said on a sigh. 'Yes, he did.'

Kincaid released Adam's shoulder and, glancing at Gemma, read the brief flare of triumph in her eyes. They had been right, after all. 'Adam, we think Lydia meant to tell what happened.

462

She wrote a poem about Verity's death which we believe Darcy removed from the manuscript of her last book. Vic found a copy in a book Nathan had given her, but Nathan didn't know it was there. He may have read it for the first time this afternoon.'

Looking from Kincaid to Gemma, Adam said slowly, 'You're saying that Darcy killed Lydia and Victoria McClellan, aren't you? And that Nathan has just discovered it?'

'Yes.' Gemma laid a gentle hand on his arm. 'What would he do, Adam?'

Adam shook his head. 'I should have seen this. Perhaps not when Lydia died, but at the very least when Doctor McClellan began to question the manner of her death. I've been willfully and sinfully blind.' He closed his eyes for a moment, and when he opened them they were luminous with tears. 'We all thought we could make reparation for what we'd done, each in our own way. But it wasn't enough. Nathan will know that now. I fear the worst.'

Kincaid felt the sharp jab of foreboding. 'Where would he go? To Darcy's college?'

'I don't—'

'Shhh.' Kincaid held up his hand, listening. He could have sworn he'd heard a faint crack of sound in the still air. 'Did you hear it?'

'A gunshot,' said Gemma. 'Could it have been a gunshot?'

'It came from that direction,' said Kincaid, pointing towards the bottom of the village. 'I'd say a good half-mile away.'

'The Pool,' said Adam. 'Byron's Pool. Past

the Mill about a quarter mile. That's where he'll have gone.'

Kincaid thought strategy for a moment. 'Can we find it?'

'There's a sign post. And the path is clearly marked,' said Adam. 'But I can show you—'

'No, you stay here and wait for Chief Inspector Byrne,' said Kincaid, already half out the door. 'Show him the way,' he called over his shoulder as he sprinted for the car, Gemma on his heels.

'Would Darcy agree to meet him?' said Gemma as they slammed their doors and the engine coughed to life.

'I don't think Nathan will have had the advantage,' Kincaid answered grimly. The lights of the houses flashed by as they sped through the village, then they were dipping down to cross the old stone bridge by the Mill. Kincaid slowed as they began the curving ascent on the other side. 'There!' He pointed at a sign post, faintly legible in the beam of the headlamps. 'Byron's Pool. And there's a car park.' The small gravelled area was empty.

'Nathan walked,' said Gemma as Kincaid stopped the car. 'But Darcy must have left his car somewhere else. He won't have meant to be seen. Torch under the seat,' she added as they scrambled out of the car. 'Look, there's the path.'

Kincaid reemerged from the car with the torch. 'We'll not use it just yet,' he said quietly. 'Our eyes will adjust in a minute or two, and there's no sense making targets of ourselves.'

Putting his hand on Gemma's shoulder, he felt her vibrating with tension. For an instant he thought of ordering her to wait for him there, but he didn't like the idea of leaving her alone, unarmed, and possibly blocking Darcy's exit from the car park. He squeezed her shoulder. 'Stay behind me, love, and at the first sign of trouble, go for back up.'

The path was uneven, but lighter in colour than the surrounding leaves and bracken, and as his eyes learned to differentiate he began to pick up speed. The car park soon disappeared, swallowed by the trees, and the night sounds rose round them.

'Wait!' Gemma's hand clamped his elbow. 'I heard something,' she breathed in his ear.

He listened, straining into the darkness. A rustle ... then a sound that might have been a faint human grunt of pain. Nodding at Gemma, he turned and went on, placing each foot more carefully than before. *Cowboys and Indians ...* he thought, conscious of every snapping twig. As a child he'd always wanted to be the Indian, and he had a sudden intense memory of the smooth rolling motion of his feet as he crept through the woods. Then he came round a twist in the path and stopped short.

They stood at the edge of a small glade faintly illuminated with moonlight. On the other side, two bodies grappled on the ground, and a few feet away he saw a gleam in the grass. The gun.

Then the body on the top heaved itself up, turning towards them with the heavy menace of a cornered beast. Darcy.

Kincaid dived without thought, a soaring lunge that brought him skidding across the grass onto the gun. He rolled with it in his hands and scrambled to his knees.

Darcy stood before him, swaying slightly. Half his face and neck looked black in the dappled light—a shadow? No, blood, Kincaid realized. He got one foot underneath him and rose slowly to his feet without shifting the stock of the gun from the hollow of his shoulder, or its aim from the centre of Darcy's chest.

He could shoot Darcy. Now. The thought came with cold clarity. *Self-defence. Justifiable homicide. Who would question it? He had broken so many rules already, why not one more?*

Darcy shifted on his feet, balancing his weight on flexed knees.

He meant to run. Let him make his break, then shoot him. No one could say it wasn't right.

The whites of Darcy's eyes flashed as he looked from side to side. His hands clenched into fists.

'Lie down on the ground,' said Kincaid, slowly. 'Put your hands behind your back. If you don't do as I say, now, I *will* shoot you.'

For a moment Darcy stood, and Kincaid tensed, preparing for the recoil of the gun.

Then Darcy dropped heavily to his knees. 'I need help, medical attention,' he said. 'He shot me. I'm injured.'

'Down!' Kincaid shouted, his anger and frustration breaking on a rush of adrenaline. 'I don't care if you bleed to death, you son of a bitch. Do you understand that?' He motioned with the gun, and Darcy lowered himself to the ground with a groan. 'Gemma—'

She'd reached Darcy. 'I've got a scarf.' Quickly, she knotted his hands together, then ran to Nathan.

Kincaid heard her whisper, 'Oh, dear God, please ...' as she knelt beside him.

'Is he breathing?'

'I think so. Yes.' She struggled to lift Nathan's head from the water. 'But he's covered with blood—'

There was a racking, retching cough, then Nathan's voice gasping, 'His. It's his. I shot him.'

Then Kincaid heard the screech of tyres and the slamming of car doors, and a moment later he saw the flicker of torches moving through the trees. Lowering the gun, he said, 'It seems the cavalry has arrived.'

'I didn't know how much I wanted to live until he had his hands round my throat,' said Nathan, his voice little more than a hoarse whisper. They sat round the table in his kitchen, he and Adam, Kincaid and Gemma, drinking herbal tea.

The medics had dressed the worst of his cuts and abrasions, but he'd refused to go to hospital. 'I thought I wanted to die,' he continued after a sip of tea. 'I thought I'd shoot him, then shoot myself. But I failed on both counts.'

Gemma touched her slender fingers to the back of his hand. 'You didn't fail, Nathan. You didn't need Darcy's death on your conscience.

467

And it wouldn't have made Vic's death, or Lydia's, any less a waste.'

'We all failed,' said Adam. 'We failed ourselves, and we failed Darcy. He wasn't always so wicked. I don't think he meant to kill Verity. But she refused him, and he couldn't control his temper.' Pausing, he eased his finger between the clerical collar and his neck. 'We'll never know what he might have become if we'd held him accountable for what happened that night.'

'You will hold him accountable now,' said Kincaid.

After a preliminary assessment, the medics had taken Darcy to Addenbrook's, accompanied by police guard. He'd suffered considerable blood loss from the shot embedded in the right side of his face, neck and shoulder, but he'd been protesting his innocence and threatening legal action even as they closed the ambulance doors.

'Your testimony will be essential to the prosecution's case.' Kincaid looked from Nathan to Adam. 'But it will mean revealing your own parts in the cover-up of Verity Whitecliff's death, regardless of the personal consequences.'

'I think we've had quite enough of secrets,' said Adam.

Nathan looked up at them, his eyes dark. 'What chance have you of getting a conviction on nothing but our word? There won't be any evidence left of how Verity died, or that he killed her.'

Kincaid glanced at Gemma. 'We can only

recommend to the Crown Prosecution Service, but my guess is that they'll charge him with Vic and Verity's deaths, and use Lydia's for evidence of system in Vic's case. We've the best chance of finding physical evidence in Vic's case, and in Verity's the court can rule based solely on the testimony of witnesses. And that means you and Adam.'

'I'll do whatever it takes,' said Nathan, then he shook his head. 'If I'd only known what Vic suspected ...'

'We're all going to have to live with our *ifs*,' Kincaid said heavily, and rose. 'I'd advise you to get some rest. You're going to need it.'

They said goodbye to Nathan and Adam at the door. When Kincaid shook Nathan's hand, he felt the kinship of those who pass through the eye of the same needle. They had loved Vic, and she was gone.

He followed Gemma slowly to the car and handed her the keys, suddenly too exhausted to drive. Climbing in beside her, he slumped in his seat, but before she could start the engine he reached for her hand and held it between his.

'I thought you were going to shoot him,' said Gemma, turning to him.

'So did I.'

'I dare say he deserved it.' She searched his face. 'Why didn't you?'

He thought for a moment, trying to formulate an answer in words. 'I'm not sure,' he said finally. 'I suppose because it would've meant accepting violence as a solution.' He traced his fingers lightly over Gemma's, then looked

469

up into her eyes. 'And then what would have separated me from Darcy?'

1 September 1986
Cambridge

Darling Mummy,
I have been in a black hell this past week, railing against fate for taking you from me, railing against you for not letting me cling to false hope. Until now I'd begun to believe I'd been tested in my life—I'd even been smug enough to think I'd endured more than my share and that I'd emerged with some sort of fire-forged honour.

But when your news came I found nothing had prepared me for this, that the courage I'd taken such pride in was a mere travesty, and I thought I could not bear it.

I woke early this morning to find frost on the window panes and the first crisp hint of autumn in the air. I dressed and went out, compelled by an urgency I didn't understand, and walked until I reached the river meadows. It was you who taught me about the healing power of walking—about the magic in the harmony of breath and stride that opens the connection between heart and mind.

Then somewhere in that clear space between field and sky, I saw my anger for what it was.

Losing you means I must grow up, at last, and I've been kicking and screaming like a child unwilling to come into the world.

I saw that I'd underestimated the strength

470

and capacity of your love for me, but that you had not done me the same disservice. You thought me equal to the task before me, and so I must be.

Why are the old truths so simple and so hard to learn? Love is a two-edged sword—it can be no other way. I will be forever blessed by your love, and forever diminished by your loss.

Lydia

The air under the yews felt cool and damp against Kit's face. It had a musty, humic odour that reminded him of the way the mud smelled when he dug in the riverbank, but his flash of pleasure at the thought quickly faded. There didn't seem much point, now, in wanting to be a naturalist.

Tess whimpered and pulled at her lead, but Kit stood fast, not yet willing to move from the dimness of the tunnel. He carried the books Nathan had lent him, and it felt to him as if returning them would sever his last connection with the village.

Mrs Miller had brought him to the cottage that morning to help him pack up the remainder of his things, then had agreed to return for him after he'd visited Nathan. Colin had offered, awkwardly, to come with him, but Kit refused. He'd wanted a few minutes alone to say goodbye to the cottage.

When they'd driven away, he stood for a long while in the front garden, gazing at the house, memorizing its lines and imperfections, then he'd kicked the estate agent's sign as hard

471

as he could. It wasn't fair. Nothing was bloody fair. How could his dad bear the idea of some other family living in their house? And how could his dad leave—

Kit stopped at that point in the well-worn groove of his thoughts. He didn't want to think about his dad any more. Giving a gentle tug to Tess's lead, he stepped out into the sunlight of Nathan's back garden.

Nathan knelt at the edge of the knot bed, digging in the earth with a trowel. He looked up, smiling, as Kit and Tess came across the grass. 'Hello, Kit. Is this your dog, then?'

'Her name's Tess,' said Kit, dropping to his knees beside him.

'She's lovely,' said Nathan, scratching her rough coat and the pink insides of her ears. 'Why don't you let her have a run in the garden?' he suggested. 'It's secure enough.'

'What are you planting?' asked Kit as he unhooked Tess's lead and watched her bound across the grass towards the robins feeding near the hedge. 'They're not very pretty.'

Nathan sat back on his heels, resting the trowel on his knee as he looked at the bedraggled row of herbs. 'No, I suppose they're not. I was ill, you see, and I dug them up. But my friend Adam came along afterwards and put them in water for me. They'd have died if he hadn't.'

Kit frowned. 'Why did you pull them up, if they weren't dead?'

Nathan reached out and smoothed the soil round the last herb with the palm of his hand,

472

then he said, slowly, 'I planted these for your mother. I thought that if I pulled them up, I wouldn't miss her so much. But I was wrong. Sometimes it helps to remember.'

Kit stared at him with a flash of adult understanding. 'You loved my mum, didn't you?'

'Yes. I did.' Nathan watched him carefully. 'Do you mind?'

'I don't know,' said Kit, for his brief spasm of jealousy had been replaced by the thought that Nathan, at least, might understand how he felt. 'No ... I suppose not.' He looked again at the neat row of plants, then held out the plastic carrier bag. 'I brought your books back.'

Nathan glanced at the bag, but didn't reach for it. After a moment, he said, 'I want you to have them. We can talk about them when you come to visit. Will you come to see me?'

Kit watched Tess happily rooting about at the bottom of the garden, felt the heat from the mid-day sun soaking into his hair like warm honey, and for an instant, in that bright place, he felt his mother's presence a little nearer.

He nodded.

Chapter Twenty-Two

He wears
The ungathered blossom of quiet; stiller he
Than a deep well at noon, or lovers met;
Than sleep, or the heart after wrath. He is
The silence following great words of peace.

Rupert Brooke, from
a fragment of an elegy found
in his notebook after his death

Kincaid and Gemma stood at the end of the bridge over the dike at Sutton Gault, the expanse of the East Anglian sky stretching grey and limitless above them. Below, the forensics team worked carefully in the soft ground at the water's edge. They'd begun yesterday, under Adam Lamb's direction, but the failing light had forced them to postpone until this morning.

'I've brought you some coffee,' said the local inspector, crossing the grass towards them with two steaming polystyrene cups. 'Why don't you go in and have some lunch while you wait?' He gestured over his shoulder at the neat pub tucked in the hollow of land below the road. 'It's early enough you might get in without a booking. Folks come all the way from London for the food here, believe it or not, it's that good.'

'Some other time, thanks,' said Kincaid. 'I think we'll just wait here for now.' Coppers became callous enough over the finding of bodies—he couldn't count the times he'd grabbed a take-away on route to a crime scene—but lingering over a posh lunch while the forensics lads dug for Verity Whitecliff's bones didn't seem right to him. It had become a personal matter.

As the inspector scrambled down the steep bank to rejoin the team, Gemma moved nearer to Kincaid. She'd wrapped her hands round the hot cup to warm them, for the wind that whipped along the top of the dike was vicious. 'I keep thinking of what it must have been like for them that night, burying her. I've even dreamt of it.'

Kincaid glanced at her. She'd replaced the blood-stained scarf she'd used to tie Darcy's hands with a new one in dull plum, and the colour made her hair blaze in contrast. 'It must have seemed a nightmare,' he said. 'But all their suffering doesn't excuse their silence.'

'No,' she answered softly, so that he had to bend his head to hear her against the wind. 'But she didn't go unmourned ... and the truth will be told.' Frowning, she added, 'I'm not sure I'd have Dame Margery's strength.'

He thought of their visit to Margery Lester the previous afternoon. She'd received them in her dove-grey drawing room, as impeccably dressed as when they'd seen her last, but she looked impossibly fragile, as though she'd aged years since that day a mere week ago in Ralph

Peregrine's office. Since then she had borne the news of her friend Iris Winslow's brain tumour, as well as her son's arrest for murder.

While the police had not found Kincaid's missing case notes, they had discovered a small enamelled box containing digoxin tablets in Darcy's possession. When questioned, he claimed he carried them in case his mother should need them.

'Was your son in the habit of keeping your medication for you, Dame Margery?' Kincaid asked, when they'd refused her offer of tea or sherry.

'I have never asked him to do so,' she said carefully, disguising a tremble in her hands by folding them in her lap.

'Have you ever known him to carry your medication?' Kincaid said, narrowing it down.

'No. No, I have not. It's not like nitroglycerin, Mr Kincaid, to be used in the event of pain. Digoxin is taken on a regular basis.' She spoke calmly, evenly, and yet Kincaid knew she must be aware of the implications.

'Dame Margery, have you noticed any discrepancies in your prescriptions lately?'

She looked away. 'Yes. I had to have my last bottle replaced several days earlier than usual.'

Gemma made a small movement of surprise.

Margery turned to her. 'Did you think I would lie, Miss James? That would be pointless—the chemist's records will tell you the same thing—and it would be wrong. I will not deliberately discredit my son, nor will I protect him.' Her hands clenched in a spasm,

476

and she looked at them in unexpected appeal. 'Did I fail as a mother? Would my son have turned out differently if I had put him before my work?'

'Dame Margery—'

She shook her head. 'You can't answer that, Mr Kincaid. No one can. It was unfair of me to ask.' Gazing through the French doors at the early roses in her garden, she said quietly, 'He was a lovely child. But even then he liked his own way.'

After a moment, Margery unclasped her hands and fixed her direct gaze on them. She sat as still and straight as when they had come in, and in her eyes he saw a formidable determination. 'I'm going to finish Victoria McClellan's book,' she said. 'I will not allow her work to be wasted ... regardless of the personal ... difficulty. She and Lydia deserve to be heard. And Verity ...' For the first time her voice wavered. 'I owe a debt to Verity I can never repay.'

Gemma's touch brought Kincaid back to the present. 'Will you tell Kit about Lydia and Verity?' she asked.

Nodding, he said, 'I suppose I must. He deserves to know why his mother died.'

'Duncan.' To his surprise, Gemma slipped her arm through his as if she didn't mind who saw. 'What are you going to do about Kit?'

He looked out into the flat distance, saw endless changing possibilities he could not predict or control. He could only feel his way, action by action, circumstance by circumstance, into new and uncharted territory. 'I'll ring him every day, if I can. See him as often as possible. Then, when he's had time to get used to me ...'

'You'll tell him the truth?'

'Yes. No secrets. And we'll go from there.'

Gemma tightened her grip on his arm. After a moment, she said, 'It frightens me, a bit. It will change things between us. For better or worse, I don't know. Maybe it will just be different.'

He grinned at her. 'It scares the hell out of me.'

A shout came from below. The inspector beckoned to them, and they began the precarious climb down the bank. When they reached the bottom, they picked their way to a dry tussock near the excavation site and squatted to see what the forensics specialist held in his gloved hands.

'You were bang on,' he said, looking pleased with himself. 'Human scapula. And there's more. But the decomposition's quite advanced. It's going to be a job getting her out.'

The fragment of bone looked too small, too delicate to be human, thought Kincaid, and the leaching soil had stained it the colour of old ivory.

Gemma reached out, her fingers hovering over the bone as if she might caress it. She looked up at him. 'It seems Lydia was the voice of vengeance, after all.'

The publishers hope that this book has given you enjoyable reading. Large Print Books are especially designed to be as easy to see and hold as possible. If you wish a complete list of our books, please ask at your local library or write directly to: Magna Large Print Books, Long Preston, North Yorkshire, BD23 4ND, England.

This Large Print Book for the Partially sighted, who cannot read normal print, is published under the auspices of

THE ULVERSCROFT FOUNDATION